**Jessy had been watching him
all through the reception...**

Dalton couldn't say why he hadn't approached her, asked her to share a piece of cake, talk with him, dance with him. Then his gut clenched hard, his chest tightening, and he remembered: because he probably would have spontaneously combusted. From the moment he'd walked into the church and seen her sitting there all beautiful and sexy and focused on him, all he could think was, *Is it time? Please, can it be time?*

It was stupid, he thought as he walked to her. He was thirty-two years old. He'd been married. He'd had sex with his share of women. Hell, he'd had sex with *this* woman. But he hadn't known then what he knew now. Now it was...

The rest of his life.

Acclaim for the Tallgrass Novels

A Man to Hold On To

"4 1/2 stars! Through her beautiful storytelling, Pappano deftly expresses the emotions that come with love and loss. The genuine love that grows between Therese and Keegan melts the heart. Pappano's latest packs a powerful punch."
—RT Book Reviews

"A powerful and welcome return to Tallgrasss...Pappano excels at depicting deep emotion...including plenty of humor."
—Publishers Weekly (starred review)

A Hero to Come Home To

"Pappano shines in this poignant tale of love, loss, and learning to love again...[She] creates achingly real characters whose struggles will bring readers to tears."
—Publishers Weekly (starred review)

"Pappano's latest is a touching story about loss, love, and acceptance. Tender to the core, her story is filled with heartwarming characters who you can't help but fall in love with, and she tells their stories candidly and poignantly. The ending will simply melt your heart."
—RT Book Reviews

"A wonderful romance with real-life, real-time issues... [Pappano] writes with substance and does an excellent job of bringing the characters to life."
—HarlequinJunkie.com

"Poignant and engaging...Authentic details of army life and battle experience will glue readers to the page."
—*Library Journal*

Also by Marilyn Pappano

A Hero to Come Home To
A Man to Hold On To

A Love to
Call Her Own

Marilyn Pappano

FOREVER

NEW YORK   BOSTON

Forever
Hachette Book Group
237 Park Avenue
New York, NY 10017

www.HachetteBookGroup.com

Printed in the United States of America

First Edition: August 2014
10 9 8 7 6 5 4 3 2 1

OPM

Forever is an imprint of Grand Central Publishing.
The Forever name and logo are trademarks of Hachette Book Group, Inc.

The Hachette Speakers Bureau provides a wide range of authors for speaking events. To find out more, go to www.hachettespeakersbureau.com or call (866) 376-6591.

The publisher is not responsible for websites (or their content) that are not owned by the publisher.

ATTENTION CORPORATIONS AND ORGANIZATIONS:

Most Hachette Book Group books are available at quantity discounts with bulk purchase for educational, business, or sales promotional use. For information, please call or write:

Special Markets Department, Hachette Book Group
237 Park Avenue, New York, NY 10017
Telephone: 1-800-222-6747 Fax: 1-800-477-5925

*As always, for my Sailor
and my hero, Robert*

If a man does his best, what else is there?

—General George S. Patton,
United States Army

I think it's important that people know what goes on after the knock at the door.

—Surana Prince,
widow of Sergeant Mycal L. Prince,
killed in action in Afghanistan,
September 15, 2011

A Love to
Call Her Own

Chapter 1

Monday mornings came too damn soon.

Jessy Lawrence rolled onto her back and opened her eyes just enough to stare at the shadows the sun cast across the bedroom ceiling. It was high in the sky. Ten o'clock, maybe eleven. In the four weeks since she'd lost her job, she'd been sleeping in late. Why not, with no more annoying alarm clock beeping at six forty-five? No more dressing up, putting on makeup, smiling for customers who annoyed her so much that she wanted to smack them. No more caring whether she was late or if she looked more ragged than she should or if anyone noticed—like that nosy hag, Mrs. Dauterive—she was having a tough day.

It should have been heaven.

If possible, she was more miserable than before.

After her eyes became accustomed to the sun's glare, or what there was of it peeping around the edges of the blinds, she turned her head carefully to the nightstand and bit back a groan. It was twelve twenty-one. Officially afternoon. She'd slept away the whole morning.

She should shower. Brush that god-awful taste from her mouth. Put some drops in her eyes so they didn't feel so puffy. Get something to eat—proteins, vegetables, carbs, fruit. She'd been subsisting on junk food and booze so long that she couldn't remember the last time she'd had a real meal.

She should get dressed, too, walk down the street, buy a copy of the Tallgrass newspaper, and check out the help-wanted section. She needed a job. A sense of purpose. A reason to get out of bed in the morning…or afternoon, as the case may be. She didn't need the money. Bless Aaron and the United States Army, his life insurance would cover her expenses for the next few decades even if she did nothing but loll on the couch.

What she did need was a reason for living. It was two years and eight months too late to crawl into Aaron's grave with him, and she didn't deserve to be there anyway. He could have done so much better than her if he'd survived his last two weeks in Afghanistan.

But he hadn't survived, and she had, and here she was, wasting her life. It was shameful.

She sat up, her head pounding, and slowly eased to her feet. The shuffle to the bathroom jarred every pain sensor in her head and made her stomach do a queasy tumble. Once inside, she peed, turned the shower to hot, then faced herself in the mirror. She wasn't a pretty sight.

Her red hair stood straight up on top, a counter to the flattened frizz that cradled the sides of her head. At some point in the last day or two, she'd put on makeup, then failed to remove it before crawling into bed. Shadow smeared and mascara smudged, giving her eyes a hollow, exaggerated look. Deep circles underneath emphasized their emptiness. Indentations from the pillow marked her cheek and forehead, and her usual healthy glow had gone gray and pasty.

It was a wonder small children didn't run away at the sight of her.

Only because small children didn't frequent the places she did.

Steam was forming on the mirror when she sighed, turned away, and stripped off her tank and shorts. She took a long shower, scrubbing herself once, twice, closing her eyes, and letting the stinging water pound into her face. By the time she was ready to get out, it had turned cold, bringing shivers and making her teeth chatter.

Four weeks since she'd been fired from the bank—all because some snotty teenage brat with a sense of entitlement could dish it out but couldn't take it—and she hadn't told anyone yet. Not that there were many people to tell, just the margarita girls, her best friends. None of them banked at Tallgrass National. Like her, they were all Army widows, and like her, they kept their accounts at the Fort Murphy Federal Credit Union.

She should have told them at the first Tuesday Night Margarita Club dinner after the dismissal happened. She liked to think she would have, except all the earthshaking going on in their lives was the good kind: weddings, babies, mad love, and lust. They didn't get fired from their jobs; they didn't keep secrets or prove themselves to be colossal losers like Jessy did. If they knew all her failings, they would lose respect for her, and she would lose the most important people in her life. Better that she stay quiet awhile longer.

God, how she wished she could talk to someone.

For the first time in years, she mourned the family relationships she'd never had. They lived in Atlanta: mother, father, two sisters with husbands and children who got regular gifts from their aunt Jessy but wouldn't recognize her if she break-danced in front of them. She couldn't recall the last time she'd gotten an affectionate hug from her mom or a word of advice from her father. She'd been such a disappointment that she was pretty sure, if asked, Prescott and Nathalie Wilkes didn't even acknowledge the existence of their middle daughter.

She got dressed, finger-combed her hair, then wandered through the empty apartment with its high ceilings and tall windows to the kitchen. A quick look in the refrigerator and freezer showed nothing but a few bottles of water, condiments, and some frozen dinners, age unknown. The pantry held staples: rice, pasta, sugar, plus a lonely can of pinto beans and some packets of instant mashed potatoes. The cabinets were empty, as well, except for a box of oatmeal and another of instant pudding. Like the childhood poem, her cupboards were bare.

Except for the one below and to the left of the sink. *Out of sight, out of mind,* the old saying went, but the bottles in that cabinet were never far from her mind. That was her problem.

She needed food, real food, healthy food. Though she wasn't much of a cook, she could learn. She could fill a few of her empty days with taking care of herself: eating properly, exercising, cleaning, detoxing herself. It was a momentous project, but she was worth the effort, right? And what else did she have to do?

She would start with shopping, she decided, grabbing

her purse and keys and heading toward the door before she could talk herself out of it. She was a champion shopper, though she preferred to look for killer heels and cute outfits and Bobbi Brown makeup. She could handle a sweep through Walmart, maybe even grab a burger at the McDonald's just inside the door, and at this time of day, she wouldn't risk running into any of her margarita sisters. They would all be working, as they believed her to be.

After locking up, she took the stairs to the street level, stepped out into the warm May afternoon, and stopped immediately to rummage in her purse for a pair of dark glasses. Cars passed on Main Street, a few steps ahead, and a few shoppers moved past, running errands on their lunch breaks or grabbing a meal at one of the nearby restaurants. Jessy loved living right in the heart of downtown Tallgrass, on the second floor of a sandstone building that dated back to Oklahoma's statehood. She loved the busy-ness of the area during the day and the quiet at night, her only neighbors few and far between in other converted spaces.

Her car was parked down the alley in a tiny lot shared by the owners of Serena's Sweets next door and a couple other businesses. She drove to First Street, then headed south to Walmart, stoically ignoring the bank at the intersection of First and Main as she passed. They'd replaced her with ease—people with the skills to be customer account reps weren't hard to come by, else Jessy couldn't have done the job—and after electronically sending her final paycheck, they were done with her. Not even Julia, the account rep she'd known best, had bothered to contact her.

Walmart was always busy, even in a military town where service members and their families had the option of the post exchange and the commissary. She parked at the far west end of the lot, figuring she could use the exercise and a little fresh air, since among the many things she couldn't remember was the last time she'd seen daylight. She felt a tad like a vampire—had looked like one, too, in the mirror before her shower.

Determination got her into the store and all the way to the back, where she started with bottled water. Municipal water in Tallgrass tasted like it came from one of those shallow ponds that cattle stood in on hot summer days. She added milk, two percent, though she wasn't sure for what. But healthy diets included dairy products, right? She tossed in a twelve-pack of Greek yogurt and added fake egg blend, turkey bacon, whole-grain bread— whatever caught her attention as she trolled the aisles.

She was standing in front of the jarred pasta sauces, remembering the spaghetti sauce Aaron had taught her to make—ground beef, tomatoes, mushrooms, onions, and just a bit of sugar—when a crash jerked her attention to a woman fifteen feet away. A jar of pizza sauce lay splattered on the floor around her, its bright red spotting her jeans like blood, and she was clenching her cell phone tightly to her ear.

Such a look on her face.

Jessy went hot inside, then a chill spread through her. She knew that look. Dear God, she'd *lived* that look. She still wore it in her nightmares, still saw it at times in her mirror. That awful, heart-stopping, can't-breathe, can't-bear-it look of shock and pain and anger and grief and pure, bitter sorrow.

The nearest shopper edged her cart away from the woman while sneaking looks. Other customers and a few stock boys barely old enough to shave stared at her outright as she sank, as if in slow motion, to the floor, a wail rising out of her, growing with anguish until it scraped Jessy's skin, uncovering her own barely scabbed-over anguish.

This shouldn't be happening here, and it damn well shouldn't be happening with Jessy. Therese—she was motherly, loving, kind. Carly, too. Ilena, Marti, Lucy, and Fia could empathize and offer comfort with the best of them. Jessy didn't comfort. She didn't reach out. She couldn't handle her own emotional messes without turning to the bottle. She certainly couldn't get involved in a stranger's emotional messes.

But no one was helping the woman. No one was trying to move her off the glass-shard-littered floor, giving her any assistance or, barring that, any privacy. Jessy knew too well what it was like to grieve alone. She'd done it for eighteen months before she'd met her margarita sisters.

She knew in her heart that this woman had just found out she could be a margarita sister, too.

Her first step was tentative, her stomach knotted, her chest struggling for air. Too soon she was beside the woman, though, sobbing amid the broken glass and splattered sauce as if she, too, were broken. She was older, probably in her fifties, gray roots just starting to show in her brown hair. Her clothes were casual but well made: faded jeans in the hundred-dollar price range, a cotton shirt whose quality shone in its very simplicity, stylish leather sandals. Dior clouded the air around her, mixing with the scent of tomatoes and basil, and the gems on the fingers that still clenched the cell phone were tastefully impressive.

Jessy noticed all those things to delay that first touch, that first word. What did you say to a person whose world had just shifted so dramatically that it might never be normal again?

Trying to channel Therese, Carly, and Ilena, Jessy crouched beside the woman, touched her, and said, "I'm so sorry." Three totally inadequate words that made her feel almost as low as the jerks gawking from both ends of the aisle.

"Patricia? Patricia, are you there?" The tinny question came from the cell phone.

Gently Jessy pried the phone free and raised it to her ear. "Hello?"

"Who is this?"

"A friend of Patricia's. What did you tell her?"

"Oh. I thought she was alone. At least, she was when she left her house." The voice belonged to a man, old, smug, with a touch of a whine. It brought back long-ago memories of visits from Nathalie's parents, a hateful old woman and a spiteful old man. "I told her there's two Army officers all dressed up in their finest lookin' for her. I bet it's about her husband, George. He's in the war, you know. Over in—"

Jessy disconnected and pocketed the phone. Despite the Army's best intentions, things sometimes went wrong with casualty notification calls: no one home but kids who called their parent in a panic, nosy neighbors who couldn't resist being the first to pass on bad news. She'd received her call at work, just about this time of day on a Wednesday, back from lunch and summoned into the bank president's office to face a weary chaplain and a solemn notification officer. *We regret to inform you...*

Army wives knew that soldiers on their doorsteps never brought good news, especially during wartime. Just the sight of that official government-tagged vehicle in the driveway, those dress uniforms, those somber expressions, was enough to break their hearts before they started beating again, slowly, dully, barely enough to sustain life, or pounding madly until it felt like it might explode.

Everyone in the margarita club had been through their own notification, and every one remembered two things about it: the unbearable grief and those five words. *We regret to inform you...*

"Come on, Patricia," she said quietly, wrapping her arm around the woman's shoulders. "Let's get you off the floor. Let's find someplace quiet."

Unexpected help came from one of the young stockers. "The manager's office," he volunteered, taking hold of Patricia's arm and lifting her to her feet. "It's up at the front of the store."

Jessy paused to take the woman's purse from her cart—her own bag hung messenger-style over her head and shoulder—then the three of them moved haltingly down the aisle. By the time they reached the end, a heavyset guy in a shirt and tie was hurrying toward them, a dark-haired woman on his heels. The manager, she presumed, and likely an assistant. Maybe she could turn Patricia over into their care and get back to her shopping. Get those awful memories back into the darkest corners of her mind.

But Patricia was holding on to her like they were best friends, turning a stricken look on her. "Please don't go... You know... don't you?"

Jessy claimed sometimes that she could recognize a drunk from a mile away. Could a newly widowed woman recognize someone who'd been through it before?

Her smile was a grimace, really, but she patted Patricia's

hand, feeling like the biggest fraud that ever lived. "I know," she admitted. "I'll stay."

* * *

Dalton Smith gave the palomino colt one last assuring rub, then headed toward the house. The animals were all cared for, including the colt who'd opened a laceration on his leg, so now it was time to feed himself before he went to work on the tractor sitting uselessly inside the shed. The hunk of machinery was as cantankerous as its owner and broke down a lot more. He ought to give in and buy a new one, or at least new to him.

But in this economy, ranchers didn't pay the bills by giving in, not without a hell of a fight first. Besides, he'd been working on old hunks since he was ten. Ranching 101, his dad had called it.

When he cleared the barn, the first thing he noticed was Oz, the stray who'd adopted him, stretched out in a patch of lush grass. He lay on his back, head tilted, tongue lolling out, all four legs in the air, letting the sunshine warm his belly. When he'd come limping down the driveway, the shepherd had been painfully scrawny and covered with fleas and ticks. Five weeks of regular meals had turned him into a new dog. His coat was thick and shiny, his ribs no longer showing through his skin. He had retired his herding instincts, suckered Dalton into giving him a cushy new home, and was making the most of it.

The second thing Dalton saw was the dusty RV parked behind his truck. He groaned, and Oz opened one eye to look at him. "Some watchdog you are," he muttered as he passed the dog. "You could've at least barked."

Not that he really minded a visit from his parents. Since they'd retired to South Texas six years ago, they'd spent more than half their time traveling the country in that RV, and any time their route wandered near Tallgrass, they dropped by. His dad helped with chores, and his mom filled his freezer with home-cooked meals. There wasn't a piece of equipment made that David couldn't fix or a house that Ramona couldn't make feel like home.

It just took a bit of effort for Dalton to make himself sociable.

Unfazed by his criticism, Oz jumped to his feet and fell into step with him, heading for the back door. As Dalton pried his boots off on the top step, he scowled at the dog. "You're gonna wish you'd warned me. Mom doesn't allow animals in the house." He might have bought the house from his folks, but that didn't make it any less Ramona's house.

The first thing he noticed when he walked inside were the smells. The house never stank; he wasn't that bad a housekeeper. It just sometimes smelled a little musty from the dust accumulated everywhere. At the moment, though, it smelled of beef, onions, jalapeño peppers, sugar, and cinnamon, and it made his mouth water. How many times had he come home to the aromas of hamburgers, Spanish fries, and cinnamon cookies in the oven? Hundreds.

Dad was sitting at the kitchen table, reading glasses balanced on the end of his nose, the Tallgrass newspaper open in front of him, and Mom stood in front of the stove, prodding the sliced potatoes, onions, and peppers in a pan filled with hot Crisco. She looked up, smiling brightly. "Sweetheart! I thought I was going to have to send your father looking for you. I hope you haven't eaten lunch yet because there's way too much food here for just your dad and me."

Before Dalton could do more than hug her, her gaze shifted lower to Oz. "Didn't I already tell you once that you couldn't come in?"

As Oz stared back, Dad spoke up. "Ramona, you're the queen of the house on wheels parked out there, not this one. If Dalton doesn't mind having him in here, then you don't get to mind, either." He folded the paper and laid it aside as he stood. Tall, lanky, his face weathered from years working in the sun and wind and cold, he looked the way Dalton expected to look in thirty years. "How are you, son?"

No handshakes for David. He was a hugger. It used to drive Dillon, Dalton's twin, crazy, being twelve, sixteen, eighteen, and getting hugged by his dad in front of everyone. Knowing that was half the reason Dad did it was enough to make it bearable for Dalton. Noah, the baby, never minded it at all. He was more touchy-feely than the rest of the family combined.

"Good," Dalton replied as Oz defiantly pushed past Ramona and went to his water dish. "I wasn't expecting you guys."

"Don't worry, we're just passing through." Mom spooned the Spanish fries onto paper towels to drain, then tossed in a second batch. "Our friend, Barb Watson—do you remember her? She and her husband, Trey, stopped by here with us a few years back. Anyway, Barb died yesterday, so we're heading home for the funeral."

"Sorry." Dalton went to the sink to scrub his hands.

"It's such a shame. She was only eighty-three, you know, and she got around as well as I do. She was too young to die—"

In an instant, everyone went still in the room, even Oz. Mom's face turned red, and her hands fluttered as if she could wave away the words. "Oh, honey...I didn't mean..."

To remind him of his wife's death. No one in the family talked about Sandra, not because they hadn't loved her or didn't miss her, but because it had always been so hard for him. It had been four years this past January—four years that his grief and anger and the secret he'd guarded had made tougher than they had to be.

She'd been a soldier, a medic, on her second combat tour when she'd died. Twenty-seven years old, way younger than his parents' friend Barb, bleeding out in the desert thousands of miles from home. Losing her had been hard enough. Knowing she'd died in war had made it worse. Finding out she'd chosen to die had damn near killed him, and keeping that knowledge from everyone who'd loved her had almost finished the job.

What had eaten at him the most? The heartbreak of losing her so young? The ache in his gut that she hadn't trusted him? The anger that she hadn't given him any say, hadn't cared a damn about what he wanted? Most days he wasn't sure, but at the moment he thought maybe it was the guilt every time he lied by omission to the family. Her parents, her sisters, his parents, and Noah—they all believed she was a hero, tragically killed doing the job she loved, saving fellow soldiers. They believed she would have done *anything* to come home to them.

They didn't know she'd lacked the courage to come home. They didn't know she'd chosen to die in that damned desert and leave them forever.

And though it hurt soul-deep, Dalton intended for them

never to find out. He wished like hell he didn't know. He would make damn sure their families didn't.

"It's all right, Mom. I know what you meant." Shutting off the faucet, he dried his hands on a dish towel. He took care to rehang it perfectly straight on the rod, then slipped his arm around his mother's shoulders. "Oz and I are starving. Are those burgers about ready?"

                    *   *   *

Benjamin Noble was dictating notes in the small workspace outside the exam rooms that made up his pod of the clinic when the office manager came around the corner. He paused, wasting a moment trying to decipher the look on her face. Luann was competent, capable, and faced crises on a regular basis without so much as a frown, but this afternoon the smallest frown narrowed the space between her eyes.

"Dr. Noble, you got a call from a Jessy Lawrence. She asked you to call your mother. Said it's urgent."

She offered him a pink message that he hesitated to take. His cell phone was on vibrate, as it always was while he saw patients, but he'd felt it go off three times in the last half hour. Jessy Lawrence's name had shown up on caller ID, but since he didn't know anyone by that name and she'd left no voice mail, he'd ignored it.

"Urgent" messages from Patricia were common enough, given their relationship, that this one didn't concern him. It could mean she wanted a diagnosis of her cough over the phone or information about hormone replacement therapy, despite his polite reminders that he was an orthopedic surgeon. It could mean she'd made the acquaintance of a friend's children or grandchildren and wondered about her own or that she was feeling a rare moment of remorse.

Remorse that had come way too late.

"Thanks, Luann. I'll take care of it when I get a chance." He pocketed the number, breathed deeply to clear his head, then picked up the dictation where he'd left off. His exam rooms were filled with patients, and they'd run out of chairs in the waiting room an hour ago. Clinic days were never good days for dealing with his mother.

Honestly, he couldn't imagine a good day for dealing with his mother.

Twenty years ago she'd walked out on the family. She hadn't just left his father for another man. She'd left all of them—Dad, him, and his sisters. Ben had been fifteen, old enough and busy enough with school to not be overly affected, but Brianne and Sara, eleven and nine, had missed her more than any of them could handle.

Not the time to think about it. He put on a smile and went into room one. "Mrs. Carter, how'd you do with that last shot?" Picking up the needle his nurse had waiting, he sat on the stool and rolled over in front of the patient on the table. She was fifty-five—Patricia's age—and had severe osteoarthritis in her right knee, bone grating on bone. The injections weren't a cure but helped delay the inevitable surgery. Though she'd recovered beautifully from the total knee replacement on her left, she was hoping to put off a repeat of the brutal rehab as long as she could. He didn't blame her. It was human nature to put off ugly things, the crinkle of paper in his pocket reminded him.

He positioned the needle, deftly pushing it in, and was depressing the plunger when his cell phone vibrated again.

His hand remained steady. Whether giving shots, inserting appliances to strengthen badly fractured bones, or sawing through the femur or tibia to remove a diseased knee, his hands were always steady.

The nurse blotted Mrs. Carter's knee and applied a Band-Aid while they exchanged the usual chatter—*Don't stress the joint for twenty-four hours, call me if you have any problems, see you in six months if you don't*—then he returned to the workspace to dictate notes again. There he pulled out the cell and looked at it a moment.

He routinely told his patients to call him if they had any problems, but that courtesy didn't extend to his mother. Granted, his patients didn't abuse the privilege—most of them, at least. There were a few for whom hand-holding was part of his job, but when Patricia was needy, she did it to extremes.

He was still looking at the phone when it began to vibrate. Jessy Lawrence again. He might ignore her, but she apparently had no intention of remaining ignored. Since he had no intention of being stalked around his office by a stranger on a smartphone, he grimly answered. "This is Benjamin Noble."

There was that instant of silence, when someone was surprised to get an answer after repeatedly being sent to voice mail, then a husky, Southern-accented voice said, "Hey, my name is Jessy Lawrence. I'm a—a friend of your mother's over here in Tallgrass."

He'd heard of the town, only an hour or so from Tulsa, but he couldn't remember ever actually having been there. "I didn't know she was back in the state."

Another moment's silence. She clearly thought it odd that he didn't know where his mother was living. When Patricia had left them, she hadn't made much effort to stay in touch except when guilt or selfishness pushed her, and he'd learned not to care.

"She is," Jessy said at last. "If you've got a pen, I'll give you her address. Ready? It's 321 West Comanche—"

"What is this about, Ms. Lawrence?"

"I'm sorry, Benjamin— Dr. Noble. There's no easy way to say this. Your stepfather was killed in Afghanistan. Your mother just found out. She needs you."

A bit of shock swept through him, momentary surprise, the instinctive reaction a person felt upon hearing of someone's death. Though he'd met George only three times— at his, Brianne's, and Sara's high school graduations—Ben could feel regret that the man had died, that Patricia now found herself a widow.

But not a lot of regret. Patricia's loss couldn't possibly equal what he and his sisters had gone through when their father died. Rick Noble had stayed when Patricia left. He'd loved them, taken care of them, been both father and mother to them, and losing him had broken their hearts.

And it was Rick's own heart, broken when the love of his life abandoned them for another man, that had led to his death at forty-six. Yet Patricia expected Ben to mourn that man's death? To drop everything and rush to her side to be with her?

That wasn't going to happen.

"Give her my condolences, Ms. Lawrence. If you'll excuse me, I've got patients waiting."

"But—"

He hung up, returned the phone to his pocket, then on second thought laid it on the counter beneath a stack of charts before heading to room three. Out of sight, out of mind, the old saying went. He hoped it held true today.

* * *

Patricia, Jessy had learned in the past hour, was Patricia Sanderson, wife—now widow—of Colonel George Sanderson. He'd been in the Army twenty-nine years and would have been promoted to general or retired by the end of thirty. Patricia had been in favor of retiring. She'd grown tired of traveling from assignment to assignment and never wanted to face a moving van and a stack of cartons again.

And she had a bastard of a son.

Immediately Jessy regretted that thought. She was proof that not all parent/adult child relationships were healthy. She hadn't spoken to her own parents in years and had had LoLo Baxter, the casualty notification officer, inform them of Aaron's death. They hadn't called, come to Tallgrass for the funeral, sent flowers or even a damn card. That didn't make her a bitch of a daughter.

It had just made her sorry.

"Is that coffee about ready?" LoLo came into the kitchen, bumping against Jessy deliberately on her way to choose a cup from the wooden tree. The major had the toughest job in the Army: telling people their loved ones had died. The first time—delivering tragic news, watching the surviving spouse collapse, getting dragged into the grief—would have destroyed Jessy, but LoLo had done it countless times with grace and great empathy.

She'd made the worst time of Jessy's life a little easier to bear, and Jessy loved her for it.

"I talked to the son," Jessy said as LoLo poured the coffee, then sipped it and sighed. "He said, and I quote, 'Give her my condolences.'"

LoLo didn't appear surprised. She'd seen families at their best and their worst. *The stories I could tell,* she'd once said. Of course, she hadn't told them. Was there someone she did share with? Someone who helped ease her burden and made it possible for her to continue doing her job?

Jessy didn't know. Though all the margarita sisters knew LoLo, none of them knew anything about her personal life. She was compassionate, kind, supportive, and a mystery.

"Any other kids?"

"Two daughters, both in Tulsa. She doesn't have their phone numbers, and I doubt the doctor's going to cough them up." Jessy fixed her own coffee, with lots of sugar and creamer, then peeled an orange from a bowl on the counter. She hadn't gotten anything to eat yet, and her stomach was grumbling. She glanced toward the doorway. Down the hall in the living room, Patricia was sitting with the chaplain, their low voices punctuated time to time by a sob. She lowered her own voice. "Her son didn't know she was living in Oklahoma."

"Any other family?"

"No one on George's side besides some nieces and nephews she doesn't really know. Her sister lives in Vermont, her brother in Florida. They're both currently on vacation in Canada and will try to come for a few days before the funeral. They've both got kids, so they're going to contact them."

LoLo leaned against the counter, cradling the coffee cup, and studied Jessy solemnly. Was she remembering that no one came to be with Jessy when Aaron died? "You know her from the bank?"

"No. Never met her before today."

"So you picked a stranger up off the floor, dusted her off, and brought her home. That's a tough thing to do, Jessy."

With someone else, Jessy could have been flippant. *Tougher than you know.* Or *Not tough at all; I am Superwoman.* But LoLo did know. She'd done way more than her share of picking people up off the floor. Instead of saying anything, Jessy focused on sectioning the orange.

"I was at the bank yesterday."

Heat flooded Jessy's face, and her gut clenched. "I thought you banked onpost."

"I do. I went there with one of my wives." Always supportive, doing anything she could to help the women whose tragedies brought her into their lives. "Someone else's nameplate was on your desk. So were his things."

"Yeah." She mumbled around a piece of orange, sweet and juicy.

"You making a career change?"

Reaching deep inside, Jessy summoned the strength to meet her gaze, to smile brashly. "Yeah. I always hated that job."

"You have any plans?"

Besides falling apart? "I'm thinking about it." She thought about a lot of things. She just never found the energy to actually do anything. Going to get groceries today had been a big deal—and look how that had bitten her on the ass. Two hours now she'd been tied up with Patricia Sanderson, and she didn't know how to extricate herself. She'd hoped the son would head this way as soon as he got the news, but she might as well have told him there were clouds in the sky for all the concern he'd shown.

As long as LoLo and the chaplain were there, she could leave. Even knowing that eventually they would both have to leave, too. Knowing that eventually Patricia would have to be alone in her house, surrounded by memories of her husband, drowning in her grief. Eventually everyone had to be alone.

But not yet. Jessy could cope awhile longer. It wasn't like anyone else in the entire world needed her.

"Maybe this time you'll find a job you like." LoLo drained the last of her coffee and squared her shoulders. "I should get back in there."

Jessy watched her go, figuring that in a few minutes the chaplain would come in for coffee and a break. Kind of a tag team comforting. With her stomach still too empty, she opened the refrigerator, located a couple packages of deli meat, mayo and mustard, some pickles and cheese. Sooner or later, Patricia's friends would start showing up with casseroles, fried and rotisserie chicken, sweets from CaraCakes, pop and doughnuts and disposable dishes, but in the meantime, a sandwich or two would stave off hunger for her, LoLo, and Lieutenant Graham. If Patricia was like Jessy, she wouldn't eat for days. If she was like Therese, she would be sensible and eat even though she had no appetite, and if she was like Lucy, bless her heart, she would stuff herself with food to numb the pain.

Sure enough, about the time she finished putting together the fourth ham and turkey sandwich, Lieutenant Graham came into the kitchen. He wasn't as experienced as LoLo; his lean solemn face showed the bleakness of his burden.

Chaplains made Jessy uncomfortable. She hadn't been raised in church and had never found a reason to start attending as an adult. Aaron's service had been held at the chapel on Fort Murphy, and the memory didn't make her eager to return. Besides, chaplains were good people. Earnest. They didn't make the mistakes Jessy couldn't seem to escape.

"We didn't get lunch. This looks good," the lieutenant said as he accepted a plate. "We called one of her neighbors who's coming over as soon as she can get away from the office. I think she's asked about as many questions as she's capable of processing at the moment."

"She'll think of more." Jessy's first questions had been simple: How had Aaron died, and why? The how had been understandable: He'd been shot by a sniper. She still struggled with the why.

There had been more questions, of course. When would he get home? What did she have to do? How did one arrange a funeral? Where could she bury him?

And more: Had he died instantly? Had they tried to save him? Did he suffer? How did they know he didn't suffer?

Would she be able to see him, touch him, kiss him once more when he got home?

Could she tell him how very, very sorry she was?

The chaplain took a seat at the breakfast table, ate a bite or two, then gazed at Jessy. "LoLo says you've been through this."

Her hands tightened around the coffee mug. She forced herself to loosen her fingers, pick up a plate, join him at the table, and to take a bite to settle her stomach. "Two and a half years ago," she said at last.

"I'm sorry."

Why did the words sound so much more sincere coming from him than they did from her? Because he'd probably never let anyone down. Never failed to live up to others' expectations. He was a man of God.

She was just a woman.

With way too many flaws and way too many regrets.

Chapter 2

The blast of a horn startled Lucy Hart from her thoughts. With a glance at the green light overhead and a glimpse of the driver behind her gesturing impatiently, she got the car moving again, just barely reaching the speed limit. Part of her was in a rush to get home; her friend needed her, and Lucy was always quick to respond to people who needed her.

The rest of her, though, was dragging her feet. She was good for all kinds of emergencies. Car trouble, pipes breaking in the middle of the night, rides to doctors' appointments, heartbreak, unexpected babysitting—she'd handled all that and more. Being there and helping out were her biggest talents, after her mouthwatering cooking and baking. Her family had called her *little mama*, an endearment she'd been happy with while waiting to become a mother for real.

But comforting a friend who'd just lost her husband hit a little too close to home. Though six years had passed since Mike's death in Iraq, though all her closest friends had lost their husbands to combat, the memories this new death raised...

Grimly, she pushed back the thought. Patricia needed her. End of discussion.

Traffic was light through town and virtually nonexistent once she turned onto her street. She pulled into the driveway, then hurried into the house. Her dog, Norton, was waiting in the kitchen, wagging his tail hard enough to sound like a bass drum. Though she wanted to get to Patricia's quickly, one thing couldn't wait; otherwise, Norton would flood the kitchen.

She gave him a scratch, then let him out the back door into the unfenced yard. He wasn't the brightest dog in the world, but he did understand that home was where the special stuff was: food, treats, doggy bed, and the yellow rubber ducky he loved dearly. He would never run away and leave the duck behind.

After changing clothes, Lucy let Norton in again, gave him a couple of home-baked treats, then grabbed the bread she'd baked the night before—banana nut and cranberry— and a tub of cream cheese. "You be good," she told him. "I don't know how long I'll be gone, but I'll come back to check on you. Don't disappoint me."

The animal gave her a look that suggested she might as well be speaking Vulcan, then slid into a boneless heap, head on his paws to watch her go. She locked the door and set off across the yard, halfway to its perimeter, when her next-door neighbor called her name.

"Hey, Luce! You're taking food to someone who isn't me?"

Joe Cadore sat on his deck, feet propped on the railing, a fitness magazine in his lap and a bottle of water in his hand.

His blond hair needed a trim—always—and his jaw looked as if he'd forgotten to shave that morning, turning his usual boy-next-door good looks into breath-catching *isn't he hot?* sex appeal. Luckily, she was immune to it. With an appetite befitting a physically active guy, no kitchen skills, and no wife or significant other, he had a great appreciation for the goodies that came from her kitchen, thus the basis of their friendship.

Reversing direction, she moved a few feet closer to him. "I'm taking it to Patricia's. Did you hear? Her husband—" Her voice wobbled, and she took a breath.

Bless his heart, Joe didn't need to hear more to understand. Concern furrowed his forehead, and he dropped his feet with a thud, rising from his chair. "Oh, man. I'm so sorry. George was a good guy." After a moment, his voice softer, he asked, "You okay?"

His concern was sweet and eased the tightness around her heart just a little. "Yeah. Just...a lot of memories."

"Do you want me to come along?"

The constriction eased a bit more. What kind of guy volunteered to wade into a situation that was sure to involve an overload of women, emotion, tears, and grief? Then she answered her own question: a good friend. She'd been blessed with so many of them. She hoped Patricia had a bunch, too, because she was going to need them in the months ahead.

"I appreciate the offer, but...let me see how she's doing first." She started across the yard again, then glanced back. "By the way, there are two more loaves of bread on my kitchen counter for you if Norton doesn't get to them first." Joe had a key to her house so he could do favors like letting the dog out if she ran late, and she had one to his house so she could...Well, just because. He didn't have any pets, not even any plants, and had never asked her to do anything for him.

"I'll share a piece with him." His broad grin was dazzling. "I knew you loved me. Thanks, Luce."

She crossed the grass into Patricia's backyard, then circled the house. Under normal circumstances, she would have gone to the back door and knocked, holding up her goodies to entice Patricia into letting her in. There wouldn't be any normal circumstances for her friend for a long while.

The only cars in the driveway were a government vehicle and a small red one she wasn't familiar with. Though there were other CNOs—casualty notification officers—Lucy hoped Patricia had gotten Loretta Baxter. LoLo was so very good at her job.

Lucy climbed the steps to the gracious porch with its wicker furniture and potted flowers that contrasted perfectly against the red and white stripes of the American flag rippling in the breeze. Thinking she should do something with her own porch, she turned back to the door when it opened and blinked in surprise. "Jessy! I didn't know you knew Patricia."

"I don't. I didn't. I do now." Jessy grabbed her arm and pulled her inside, closed the door, and swept her down the hall to the kitchen, where she put the bread and cream cheese on the counter. Of all their margarita sisters, Lucy would have thought Jessy the least likely to comfort in a tragedy. Not that Jessy wasn't sympathetic and generous. It was just that she doled those things out in her own way, which was usually brash and blunt.

In a few terse sentences, Jessy explained how she'd

wound up at the Sanderson house. "Damn, can you believe it?" she muttered.

"Of course I can. It proves what I have always suspected of you. You may be snarky and flippant on the outside, but on the inside, you're warm, soft, and gooey just like the rest of us." Knowing Jessy would resist, Lucy wrapped her arms around her and planted a messy kiss on her cheek. "You're a good woman, Jessy Lawrence."

Sputtering, Jessy wriggled away. "And you're insane. Cover for me while I make my getaway."

They approached the living room together, both stopping a few feet out of sight. Jessy eyed the front door as if gauging how quickly she could reach it and be gone, then turned her assessing gaze on Lucy, whispering, "Are you sure you can handle this?"

"It's got to be easier than the first time around."

"I don't know about that. If things get quiet for one minute, all I can think about..."

Is Aaron. Practically like it was yesterday. Lucy knew how that went. Witnessing other people's pain brought a new edge to hers.

"We all think about our husbands more at times like this. But we have years of scars over the wounds in our hearts. No matter how much we love them, no matter how much we miss them, we don't hurt the way Patricia does because her wound is so fresh." Lucy blinked away a sheen of tears. "Has anyone contacted her children?"

Jessy snorted. "I called her son. He wasn't jumping in his car to drive over here anytime soon."

"I knew there was some problem there." That had been apparent more in the things Patricia didn't say than the things she did.

"Yeah, there's a problem, like he doesn't give a shi—" Jessy shrugged. "Damn, I've got to get going. I've let my gooey side show for way too long. I need some red meat, some wild dancing, and a handsome cowboy or two to buy me a drink—" Again, she cut herself off, grimacing. Bumping against Lucy's arm, she went into the living room and to Patricia, sitting on the couch near LoLo.

Lucy smiled. Every woman could use some red meat, wild dancing, and handsome cowboys from time to time, but Jessy was no more likely to go out and indulge than Lucy was. She talked big, but the margarita club knew she hadn't looked twice at an available man since Aaron's death. Every person's grief had its own schedule. When the time was right for Jessy to consider romance again, she would, and like Carly and Therese, she would be incredibly happy the second time around.

Lucy could envision all her friends getting a second chance, but it was harder to put herself into that position. They were all smart, pretty, and talented at everything they tried. Most of them held interesting jobs or had interesting hobbies, while Lucy was a secretary whose only interest outside work was making tantalizing foods that put way too many pounds on her. She'd gone from average to fat, made worse by the fact that she was only two inches over five feet. In this shape, she wasn't exactly dating material, and that was okay. Better to stay single the rest of her life than to risk a second time with what Patricia was going through.

With a deep breath to fortify herself, Lucy walked into the living room. Upon seeing her, Patricia promptly burst into tears, sank into her arms, and sobbed as if her heart were broken. Sadly, Lucy knew, it was.

*   *   *

By the time Dalton turned off the computer and headed upstairs, the house was silent. His parents had gone out to the RV as soon as Dad saw the ten o'clock headlines, despite Dalton's offer of a bedroom, and Oz dragged up the steps soon after. Normally, Dalton would have been asleep an hour ago, but restlessness had kept him awake. He'd thought catching up on his paperwork would settle him—it usually bored him comatose—but it hadn't. His body was tired, but his mind wasn't surrendering yet.

Avoiding the creaky places on the stairs and in the second-floor hallway, he got ready for bed, shut off the light, and nudged Oz from the middle of the bed. If Mom didn't like dogs in the house, she *really* didn't like them on the beds, but she hadn't said anything. Maybe she'd finally begun to think of this house as their former home. More likely, David had warned her again not to fuss.

Moonlight came through the curtains, bright enough to cast deep shadows, to glint off the silver frame on the dresser. Every week he dusted the frame, but he never looked at the picture it held. He didn't need a photograph to remind him of that moment immediately after he and Sandra had gotten married in Las Vegas, when they'd both been happy and hopeful, with no worries other than how quickly they could get back to the hotel to celebrate. Life had had such potential that day. He'd never imagined just how damn wrong it could go.

He stared at the frame until his eyes got gritty, then he rolled onto his other side, where there were only shadows. As he resettled, he realized the tension that usually gripped him when he thought about Sandra wasn't there. It still hurt. It still made him angry, but not so much as before. Was he finally putting it behind him? Was there some potential for a normal life for him again?

He had this suspicion that of course the potential was there. He just had to be smart enough to recognize it and willing enough to accept it. He'd dug himself into such a bleak hole after Sandra died. He'd lost touch with all his friends, did his best to keep her family at arm's length and to avoid any but short, superficial visits with his own family. He'd forgotten how to live, how to be sociable or, hell, be just plain civil.

He'd felt like shit and acted like it so long that he was sick of it.

Behind him Oz began to snore, low rattling sounds. Dalton hadn't wanted a dog until the mutt showed up and showed him he did. Oz had been starved, lost, or more likely, dumped by an idiot owner who assumed all country people wanted everyone else's throwaways. He'd had an awfully tough time of life, but he hadn't dwelled on it. Once he'd made himself at home here, he'd forgotten the rough times and focused on appreciating the good life.

There wasn't one thing special or unique about the miseries in Dalton's life, and he had a lot to be thankful for. He was healthy. He was making a go of the ranch he'd loved for as long as he could remember. His parents were alive and happy, and Noah was exactly where he should be in his life, with no major mistakes hanging over him and all those possibilities ahead. Dalton was feeling the need, just kind of simmering but there all the same, to get himself to exactly where he should be in his life.

And part of it had to do with the pretty little redhead he'd met two months ago who wouldn't get out of his head.

That March Saturday hadn't been his proudest moment. Dalton, who'd never once hooked up casually, had done just that with the redhead, and in a cemetery, no less. A few words, a trip to a bar, too much to drink, crossing the parking lot to the shabbiest motel in the county, then sneaking out while she was asleep and pretending not to know her the next time he saw her.

She was the first woman—the only woman—he'd been with since Sandra. She'd given him a few hours of passion, of feeling *something* besides sorrow, and he'd thanked her by treating her exactly the way Dillon would have. For the first time in his life, he'd acted like Dillon's twin and not in a good way.

But Jessy Lawrence, like her red hair implied, was stubborn. She was always there in the back of his mind: pretty, emotionally worn like him, dealing with her own sorrows. Images of her that March day, so sharp and alive, echoes of her Southern drawl that had lured him from his bleak life for an afternoon. Every time he went into town, any flash of red hair made his gut tighten. He'd even gone to the bank where she worked just to see her, only to find some scrawny guy at her desk. Had she been promoted? Transferred? Had she moved away?

Would he ever see her again?

Maybe. There was that need, buzzing down deep in his gut, whispering to him that life could get better. That he didn't have to settle for barely surviving. That he could get to where he was supposed to be.

If he was smart enough to recognize the chance, and willing enough to take it.

* * *

With three arthroscopies behind him, Ben left the hospital for the clinic across the street, jogging the four flights of stairs to his floor. He got a quick look at the patients in reception, a fair number of their faces familiar to him, then ducked through a door into the treatment area and into his office. He so rarely spent time there that it was the last place anyone trying to find him would look.

He hadn't slept well the night before. He'd ignored a number of calls from Lucy Hart, presumably another friend of Patricia's, and he'd had to tell his sisters, Brianne and Sara, about George. Like him, they'd been bemused. *I'm sorry Colonel Sanderson died,* Brianne had said. *I'm sorry when any of our troops die. But he wasn't our father. He wasn't even our stepfather. We never knew him.*

Sara had been blunter. *Like we're supposed to care about her loss?*

Ben hadn't been able to force himself to offer their dad's usual advice: *She's your mother. Naturally you love her. She divorced me, not you kids.*

But Patricia had, in effect, divorced them. She hadn't raised them, hadn't been there for them, hadn't even bothered to let them know she was back in Oklahoma. Their love for her had fled the state not long after she had.

He opened an energy bar and ate a chunk of it before scanning his schedule for the day. It was busy, as always, and no matter how much time was allotted to each patient, he always found himself needing more. Sawing off femur heads, hammering in titanium appliances, and screwing pieces of a joint back together were the easy part of his practice. Remembering to take time to really listen was something he struggled with. The clinic was chaos from the moment the first patient walked in until the last one left, and it was seriously tempting to give in to the urge to go go *go*. Especially when something was on his mind that he didn't want there.

The ring of his cell brought that particular *something* right back to the forefront. Every time it had rung since Jessy Lawrence's first call, he'd flinched. Considering he paid for the damn phone and the damn service, the flinching had gotten really annoying really fast.

Lucy Hart. Again. Scowling, he answered curtly. "Hello."

"Oh, hi. Hey. I wasn't really expecting..." A deep exhalation. The accent wasn't Southern, like Jessy's, or the voice husky. This could be any woman from anywhere. "I'm Lucy Hart in Tallgrass. I'm a friend of your mom's. Is this—this is Ben, right?"

He could lie, but that would only get him off the hook for the moment. Apparently, Patricia's friends were persistent, so he'd still have to deal with the matter. Though he'd thought he'd done that yesterday. "Yes."

"Look, Ben, I know you're busy, and your relationship with your mom hasn't been good for a while, and you're thinking you hardly knew her husband and certainly aren't mourning him." Another long breath. "But we all make mistakes. I'm guessing your mom's were pretty significant. But she's in a really bad place right now, and it would mean the world to her to see you and your sisters. You know, when you lose someone you love, it makes you think a whole lot about the other people you love, especially the ones you're disconnected from. Please, Ben, she really needs someone here."

She should have thought about that before she ran out on us. You screw people over, you can't expect them to be there for you when you need them.

"What about her brother and sister?" He sounded cold and didn't care. None of what had gone wrong between him and Patricia had been his fault. None of what was going on now was his concern.

"They'll be here for the funeral."

"When will that be?" He wasn't interested. Just the sort of questions people asked.

"We don't know. George's body will be shipped back to the States and—and prepared, then he'll be escorted to wherever she chooses to bury him. It can take a few days or up to a week and a half. It just depends."

Lucy's voice quavered, turning thin and reedy, and damn it, he had a soft spot for quavery voices. He'd yet to see the patient or family member who didn't need reassurance before heading in to the OR. Unlike the listening, that always came easily to him: a pat on the arm, a moment's conversation, a promise that he would take care of them, the comfort of a familiar face.

Days alone, waiting for her husband's body to come home. Ben couldn't imagine Patricia holding up that long without someone to lean on. Lucky for her, she had Lucy Hart and Jessy Lawrence, and surely the Army had some sort of support system in place. But not him. He had patients and surgeries and a life of his own.

"People change, Ben." Lucy's voice was softer. "They regret things they did. They regret things they didn't do. I'm not asking you to make up with Patricia. I just think if you show her compassion now when she really needs it, it'll mean something to you later."

Forgive, his dad had often preached. *Not for the person who wronged you, but for yourself. You deserve better than to waste time and energy on resentment.*

He had a lot of resentment. Would forgiving his mother ease some of it? Could he do that for her? Or at least, like Dad advised, for himself?

Grudgingly he said, "I'll think about it." Before Lucy could do more than inhale sharply in surprise, he warned, "But don't keep calling me. I'll let you know when I've decided."

*   *   *

Jessy awoke bleary-eyed around eleven, her head aching, her mouth dry and gross, her eyes puffy. One glance at her pillowcase confirmed that (a) she'd forgotten to take off her makeup the night before, and (b) she'd cried herself to sleep.

After the long, sad, awful afternoon with Patricia Sanderson, she hadn't been able to keep memories and images out of her mind. Her own notification call, knowing what LoLo was going to say before she opened her mouth, the sorrow, the shock, the guilt. Aaron's dignified transfer by private jet from Dover Air Force Base to Tulsa, then by hearse to Tallgrass. Choosing flowers, arranging the service, clasping the flag presented graveside by the post commanding general.

The overwhelming sadness and guilt.

Other people claimed tears were cathartic, but not Jessy. They made her feel like she was drowning in sorrow long after the last one had fallen. She never felt better after crying. It was torture, one drop at a time, and required a recovery period, best accompanied by a bottle of Patrón.

Steadfastly avoiding the kitchen, she showered, dressed, and put on makeup. Her wardrobe ranged from girl-next-door to serious professional to sex-on-four-inch-heels. To-day, with a light hand on the cosmetics, orange cargo shorts, and a striped shirt, she was in girl-next-door neighborhood. She wasn't sure what she was dressing for, other than *going out*—feeling the way she did, she wasn't staying in the house with the Patrón—until she went to the closet for shoes.

Her gaze caught on the camera bag on the shelf. Now, taking pictures was cathartic. She'd learned with her first camera, when she was fourteen, that the world was safer when she looked at it through a lens. She could capture the stark, lush, harsh, kind beauty in any single instant. If ugliness managed to intrude, she could Photoshop it out and create perfection. Ilena Gomez, her preggers margarita doll, had called her photos haunting and majestic, a compliment that had lingered for weeks in Jessy's heart. Still did.

Even so, she hadn't picked up the camera in a month. There wasn't a lens long enough to distance her from the mess of her life.

After pulling on a pair of sandals with thick rubber soles, she picked up the bag, retrieved the battery that was always in the charger nearby, then her purse, and left the apartment. When she pulled out of the alley a few minutes later, she headed north. She didn't know where she was going, but out of town sounded good.

The Oklahoma countryside always seemed peaceful, except when storm clouds hurtled across the sky, and even those had incredible beauty. In her four years there, Jessy had gotten only one photo of a tornado, but she hoped for another chance someday, preferably an impressive one that formed quickly and broke apart just as quickly without doing any damage.

Not today, though. She just wanted to feel the camera in her hands, to look around her with that protective distance in place, to enjoy the sun and breathe the fresh air, and to hopefully get rid of a bit of the ugliness inside her.

Seeing a pasture with cattle ahead, she slowed and turned onto the dirt road that fronted it. A few hundred feet down, she parked at the side of the road, right wheels close to the bar ditch, took out the camera, and crunched over gravel on her way to the pasture fence. The boards, though worn gray with weather and time, held securely under her weight, so she climbed to the top, balancing carefully as she focused the lens on the nearest cow. Deep red and white, it chewed lazily, methodically, its huge eyes watching her with disinterest.

"I'm just another two-legged oddity in your world, aren't I?" Jessy murmured, snapping off pictures, close up and from a distance, cows and babies, trees and fence and sandstone boulders and sky. Something unwound in her gut, so slowly that it took her a while to realize it was tension seeping away. She'd missed this feeling of capturing a perfect moment in time, of preserving the scene, of creating something that would long outlast her. She'd needed it, needed something that wouldn't leave her feeling ashamed as so much of her life did.

Traffic passed on the highway, but she ignored it as she turned to face the opposite direction. The field across the road was overgrown, enclosed with rusty barbwire that sagged between ancient wooden posts. Though it had once been cleared, red cedars were taking over again, along with sumac seedlings that would provide gorgeous splashes of color come fall. Wildflowers grew in patches: Indian paint-brush, black-eyed Susan, purple coneflower. Clumps of iris spread in straight lines about thirty feet from the road, bearing a few blooms among the spent flowers that had already faded.

Jessy crossed the road again, racking up pictures from every angle. She was crouched next to the ditch, lens directed to the irises, when fine vibrations transmitted from the ground to the soles of her feet. A pickup truck was coming down the road, a dust cloud trailing behind it like a balloon bobbing after a toddler. She glanced at the dust, then the camera, and stood, folding her arms against her chest and over the camera to protect it.

The driver stopped well short of the stop sign, waited a beat, then eased forward until the truck was even with her. Oklahomans were friendly, she reminded herself. A quick hello-how-are-you-doing, and he would leave her in non-dusty peace.

Then she saw him, and peace was the last thing on her mind.

Memories assailed her—a sunny afternoon, the sweet fragrance of flowers filling the air. A little conversation, an ill-advised invitation, and a much-needed distraction on a tough day. She had suggested a beer and a burger at Bubba's and he'd agreed. She'd made the drive to the bar knowing she would drink too much, get too bold, wind up in bed with him, then regret it forever, but she'd gone anyway. At that moment, filling the emptiness inside her, even just for a while, had seemed worth the shame and disgust that would follow. She knew the pattern; she'd gone through it countless times before.

But Dalton Smith had disrupted the pattern. Unlike the men before him, he hadn't been anonymous. He hadn't disappeared from her life as abruptly as he'd entered it.

She'd seen him again, and again, and she'd felt . . . something.

Jessy was afraid of feeling that something.

He studied her much the way the cow across the road had—brown eyes, impassive expression, no sign of interest—except little lines crinkled the corners of his eyes, and his fingers were tightening around the steering wheel. He hadn't expected to see her out this way, and it wasn't a pleasant surprise. He didn't think much of her—only fair since she didn't think much of herself.

The dust settled as he looked at her and she looked back. Fighting the urge to move—fleeing to her car seemed a good idea—she waited for him to speak, remembered he could be very slow about that, and blurted out the first words that bypassed her brain and reached her mouth. "Why are those irises growing like that?"

His gaze shifted from her to the flowers in the field, then back again. "This is the old Jefferson place. A tornado took it out about twenty years ago, but left the irises in the front flower beds."

She looked at the flowers again, imagining a snug little house behind them, white with a broad porch, maybe a swing, and curtains fluttering in the breeze. A home destroyed in a matter of seconds, lives changed. Her own familiarity with instant disaster sent a shudder through her and led to her next inane question. "How many tornadoes have you seen?"

"None." The corner of his mouth quirked. "The Smith family knows how to take shelter."

"I don't know where I'd take shelter. I live downtown, second floor of the Berry Building." Lord, she was babbling now. This was no conversation to be having with a man who'd seen her at her worst in their first-ever encounter and hadn't been impressed in their subsequent meetings.

"That building has a basement. Underground is always good."

"And maybe wind up with the entire building collapsed on top of you?"

His mouth quirked again. A person who didn't know better could be forgiven for mistaking it for a smile trying to get free. "Better than getting blown·away at two hundred miles an hour." After a moment, he added, "In a corner or under the stairway."

"I'll keep that in mind." Her rent included a storage area in the basement, so she had access. She just had trouble picturing herself down there in the middle of an unholy storm with no lights, probably no cell phone service, and who knew what kind of little skittering, slithering creatures. Her bedroom closet, though not as safe, was clean and comfy, and if she did get blown away, at least it would be with her cameras and her shoes.

They just looked at each other for another moment. She'd never been the sort to find herself at a loss for words, especially with men, but that was exactly where she was now. They'd already discussed weather—how lame was that? If he would just go on his way...

He nodded in her direction. "What are you hiding there?"

She blinked before remembering the camera. She held it up, then lowered both arms to her sides. She'd been more comfortable, she immediately realized, with them crossed. "I didn't want it to get dusty."

"You like taking pictures of scrub and weeds?"

"No, I was photographing the wildflowers—" Realizing they probably were weeds to a rancher, she broke off. "Actually, I stopped to take pictures of the cows over there. The one in front is a pretty girl. She liked posing for the camera."

He glanced to the right, and this time it was obvious he was controlling a smile. She hadn't yet seen him smile, but she would bet it was worth preserving with a close-up glossy. "Don't tell his owners. They paid good money for the calves they're going to get from him."

She was coming off lame and dumb. Heat crept up her neck and into her face, but she managed a careless shrug. "What do I know? Once you put them in little foam containers, they all look alike."

"Supermarket beef." He gave a shake of his head. "I haven't eaten beef from a grocery store in... well, ever that I can recall."

"Yeah, well, I haven't butchered something I've raised since birth and served it up for dinner."

"That's the way of the world. Sometimes you eat. Sometimes you get eaten."

Halfheartedly she looked for another vehicle so he would have to move on, but it wasn't likely. She'd driven the country roads around Tallgrass for hours and learned that two cars constituted heavy traffic. Anyway, somewhere inside, a small traitorous part of her was sort of enjoying the conversation, though she wasn't sure how that could be. How many times had she hoped never to see him again? How many times had she thought it would be best if they could treat each other as complete strangers? How often had she desperately wished they'd never met?

Not as often as she should have. Yeah, she'd been

shameless. Yeah, he'd seen her obnoxious, drunk, and naked. Yeah, he'd had obvious regrets, and she did, too.

But there was something about Dalton Smith...

* * *

"You like Herefords?"

It wasn't the smoothest question a man could ask a woman, Dalton acknowledged, but it wasn't just his people skills that had grown rusty over the years. Hell, when the only creatures he talked to five out of seven days a week had four legs, it was easy to get out of practice with the art of conversation.

Jessy blinked those emerald green eyes once before glancing at the "pretty cow" in the pasture. "Is that what the red-and-white ones are?"

"Yeah."

"They're pretty."

Pretty tasty, too. He kept that to himself. "You ever seen a Belted Galloway?"

She shifted her weight from foot to foot. "Since I don't have a clue what it is, I'm gonna say no."

Maybe cows weren't the best topic of conversation, but it was a subject he could discuss, apparently, with anyone. Even a delicate little city girl who couldn't tell a bull from a heifer. "It's a breed of cattle. Mostly black with a white band around the middle, though I know a guy who has a few red-and-white ones. That's what I raise, them and palominos."

He'd swear her ears literally perked up. "You raise horses?"

"Yeah. The girls are very pretty. You can—" Realizing

what he'd been about to say, he clamped his jaw shut. Invite her to his house? Just because he'd had that thought last night about getting back to a normal life? Because she'd gotten under his skin in that one afternoon and made him remember what it felt like to be alive?

Because she was the only woman he'd thought twice about since Sandra. And yeah, because she'd gotten under his skin that afternoon.

She was watching him warily, her eyes shadowed, reminding him that he hadn't treated her the way he'd been taught to treat women. He'd walked out on her while she slept, pretended not to know her, been rude. It was only the last time they'd been together, sharing a table at Bubba's, that he'd behaved in a way that wouldn't have made his mother smack him.

With a growl from his stomach, he glanced at the dashboard clock. He'd intended to get a hamburger in town before making stops at the post office and the feed store. But he wasn't completely out of anything vital, and the bills he was mailing could wait another day, and Jessy was silent, watching and waiting, and...

He drew a breath, then blurted out, "My ranch is a few miles east. You want to see the animals and—" He removed his Stetson, ran his fingers through his hair, then reseated it. "And maybe have a sandwich or something?"

It was the hardest question he'd asked in a long time.

She was quiet a long time, then a shaky smile lifted the corners of her mouth. "Okay, um, sure," she said, avoiding his gaze, her fingers clasping, then loosening on the camera. She actually managed to come off as shy—a trait he never would have imagined in the smoking-hot sexy redhead he'd met two months ago. "I'll follow you."

As she pivoted to walk to her car, Dalton pulled into what was left of the Jefferson driveway, backed out again, and started slowly toward home.

In four years, he'd never invited anyone to the house, and now twice in two months he'd done just that—first with Dane Clark, a soldier from Fort Murphy who had a soft spot for palominos, and now Jessy. Not only would she still have a hold on his brain, now she would be leaving memories of herself in his house, with his animals, on his property.

Though it had worked out with Dane, the first friend Dalton had made since high school, having Jessy there could be a step forward with reclaiming his life...or two steps back.

He kept his speed down to minimize the dust, and Jessy stayed far enough back to avoid the worst of it. When he turned into his driveway, dirt so hard-packed it took a fully loaded stock truck to raise a particle of dust, she closed the distance, parking a half beat after him under the oak.

Inside the house, Oz barked, his face popping up at one window, then another, ears perked and yelps increasing with frustration that he couldn't get to their visitor. "I have to let Oz meet you before he takes out the front door. You want to eat first?"

Jessy hesitated, camera strap and purse strap over one shoulder, arms across her middle. "Yeah, sure. I skipped breakfast."

She walked to the house with him, but her head was constantly moving, gaze sliding over the structures, the fences, the pastures, the horses, the wood swing, the honeysuckle gone wild where the old well house had finally collapsed, taking note of everything as if she found it all deeply interesting. At least, more than him.

Or to be fair, maybe she was more comfortable with things than with him. He sure as hell was.

He gave Oz a firm command to sit before cautiously opening the front door. This would be his first official introduction to anyone outside the family, and its success depended more on Jessy than on the mutt. Did she like dogs, hate them, fear them, prefer cats? Was she going to shriek, maybe shove Oz away?

Oz's butt was hovering a few inches above the floor when Dalton stepped inside, and his entire body vibrated with excitement. His long pink tongue dangled from the side of his mouth, and he was sniffing the air so thoroughly and so fast that it was a wonder he didn't hyperventilate.

"Oh, you have an Australian shepherd! He's beautiful!" The words came from behind Dalton and from the area of his knees, because she was crouching on the floor, sending out let's-play vibes as strongly as the dog.

No need to worry there. With a hand gesture, he released Oz, who closed the distance with one jump, leaning his body against hers with enough force to make her wobble before she readjusted to sit on her butt. She appeared to know his next move would be to climb into her lap for some serious scratching and grateful licking, and she was prepared for it.

She likes your dog. That's always a good thing. It sounded crazy, but he'd known there was serious potential between him and Sandra when she'd fallen in love with his horses the first time she'd seen them. Animals were too big a part of ranch life to get involved with a woman who didn't like or, worse, was afraid of them.

Leaving Jessy and Oz to bond, he went into the kitchen and washed up, then foraged inside the refrigerator. He'd offered a sandwich or something, and that was one thing he knew he could provide. Mom had roasted two chickens for dinner the night before, baked a couple loaves of bread, and made a dewberry cobbler. She'd also brought four quarts of home-canned pickles and a bowl filled with vine-ripe tomatoes from one of their South Texas neighbors.

Steps sounded a moment before Jessy's voice. "He's a sweetie."

"More like a pain in the—" Dalton broke off the mumble. His mother's presence was still in the kitchen, and she'd always warned the boys to watch their language, not just around women but with everyone. It was a sign of respect.

The dog trailing behind her, Jessy went to the sink to wash her hands. A good five feet separated them, but Dalton could feel her heat, sultry and tantalizing, and smell her fragrance, something grassy, light, like a field of spring flowers after a hard winter.

"I wouldn't have taken you for a dog person," he commented, keeping his gaze tightly locked on the tomato he was slicing except for an occasional quick glance.

"I've never had a pet of any kind. My mother didn't like small, pesky creatures. She couldn't get rid of the three she had, but she could certainly keep any more from invading." A little snort sounded faintly. "She would have forbidden the squirrels and birds from setting foot in her trees if she could have."

Those few sentences said a lot. So did her manner—the way her gaze never settled on anything while she was talking, the tightening of muscles in her jaw, the tension that held her shoulders rigid. So Jessy's mother had considered her children pesky creatures to be tolerated. Must have been fun growing up in that family.

"You the oldest?"

"Middle. My parents originally intended to have only two kids so they wouldn't have to deal with a middle child, but they had sex on their schedule one too many times. My little sister came along, and they were stuck with a middle child, after all."

Dalton turned his knife to the cold chicken breast. Like his dad, he paid strict attention to his stock, breeding for one quality or another. But kids, Dad always said, were a whole other prospect. They were what they were, sometimes because of their parents, sometimes in spite of them.

He bet there was a lot of spite between Jessy and her mother.

"Where do they live?"

"The Atlanta 'burbs. Southern by birth and Georgian by the grace of God." Cynicism didn't shine through her voice, but it was there just the same. "There have been Wilkeses and Hamiltons in Georgia for a hundred years longer than Oklahoma's even been a state."

"If they leave, will the Grand Old South collapse without them?"

"They like to think so. The current residents would be grateful as hell. My parents do have opinions." She said it in a lofty way that, again, told him a lot about them. Finished drying her hands, she hung the towel on the wooden bar, spread it neatly, then looked at the food he'd laid out. "Can I help?"

"There's a loaf of bread on the stove."

She picked up the foil, unwrapped it, and set the bread

on a cutting board. "Hey, someone forgot to put this loaf through the slicer. It's all one piece."

Dalton traded knives for a serrated one, sliced the heel from the loaf, and tossed it to Oz before cutting four soft slabs for their sandwiches. "You're lucky. Mom doesn't share her fresh-baked bread with just anyone." It wasn't true. Ramona baked for family, friends, and neighbors, newcomers to their neighborhood, and fellow members of their church. When things were good, she baked to celebrate. When things were bad, she baked to commiserate.

Bending, Jessy inhaled deeply of the sweet, yeasty fragrance. "Do your parents live here?"

"Texas. They stopped by yesterday and spent the night."

"So with your brother going to school in Stillwater, it's just you around here."

He glanced out the window, listened to the quiet, felt the emptiness. It was never supposed to be this way. The plan had always been simple: Like his dad and uncle before him, all the way back to the brothers who'd started the Double D, he and Dillon were supposed to take it over when they were grown, work it together, succeed or fail together.

But Dillon had let him down when he took off thirteen years ago. It had taken Dalton a good long while to readjust his thinking. He didn't need a brother when he had a wife who loved the ranch as much as he did. Sandra was going to take Dillon's place in the plan, and their kids would have pitched in, too, and life would have been good.

And then Sandra had let him down.

God, he'd never intended to wind up this way: living alone, working alone, *being* alone.

Grimly aware that Jessy was waiting for an answer, he managed a curt one. "Yeah. Just me."

Chapter 3

Rising from her chair, Lucy gently removed the near-empty coffee cup from Patricia's limp fingers, then covered her with a throw before taking the dishes into the kitchen. The poor woman was mentally and physically exhausted and had finally fallen deeply asleep.

Colonel Hodges had been happy to give Lucy a few days off from her secretarial job at the post hospital to be with Patricia. Other than quick trips home to care for the dog and, this morning, to shower and change clothes, she'd been at the Sanderson house nearly twenty-four hours.

They had cried together, talked, prayed, and spent hours in deep, numbing silence. They'd slept on the living room couches since Patricia couldn't face a night in the bed she'd shared with George for twenty years.

Lucy had been just the opposite. She hadn't wanted to get *out* of her and Mike's bed. She'd been convinced his smell remained in the linens and especially his pillow, and she'd stayed there for the better part of three days. And

Marti Levin, her best friend whose husband had died with Mike, had been drawn to Joshua's closet for the same reason.

Lucy was tired. She wasn't built for a night on a couch or used to hearing someone else's breathing while she tried to sleep. It had been six years since Mike's death, and except for twice-a-year visits from her parents, she was always alone at night.

She inserted a mug in the coffeemaker and set a cup of extra-bold, intense dark-roast brewing. Sliding a couple of pastries from CaraCakes onto a foam plate, she took it and the coffee out onto the front porch, careful to close the front door quietly.

The wicker rocker was comfortable, the light breeze fluttering the flag and making the temperature perfect. Two gold ribbons, fashioned into elaborate bows, hung on the railings alongside the broad steps. Last night's visitors had brought them, along with food, flowers, and cards.

Like Lucy, Marti, and all their friends, Patricia was now a Gold Star wife. It was an exclusive club, but the price of admission was dear. Lucy would give anything in the universe to go back to her Blue Star status as a wife whose husband had served and come home.

A set of chimes tinkled next door, and from somewhere down the block came the sounds of children playing. In the backyard across the street, a couple of teenage girls sunned themselves beside a pool, with occasional snippets of music drifting on the air. It was a beautiful summer day; life going on as usual everywhere but here.

When a car turned onto the street, she gave it little more than a glance—small, expensive, gray—until it slowed to a stop at the front curb. The air suddenly seemed quiet when the engine shut off, but the driver simply sat there. Thanks to the tinting on the windows, all she could see was a figure, no details, but it tightened her gut.

Ben Noble had wavered at the end of their phone call this morning, saying he would consider a trip to Tallgrass, and a single, young surgeon might drive an expensive, powerful car. A son facing an errant mother might hesitate, getting his emotions under control, before approaching her house.

She was leaning forward in the rocker, half ready to rise to her feet, when finally the driver's door opened. The man who emerged looked nothing like Patricia: six foot, solid but lean, his hair jet black, his skin a rich, warm, roasty shade. Sunglasses hid his eyes, but she would bet they were dark, too. His mouth was set in a thin line, his jaw squared, as he stepped onto the sidewalk and, for a moment, just looked at the house.

Lucy could tell the moment he noticed her. A person would think at her weight, she'd be the first thing he saw, but she'd learned better. In the past six years, she'd become pretty easy to overlook. It made it kind of hard to keep thinking she would marry again and have a family someday when no guy ever looked at her. Even the nice guys like Joe, who didn't mind being friendly with a plump chick, usually didn't *really* see her.

And let's face it, child, you passed plump thirty pounds ago.

Admonishing herself in her beloved grandmother's voice didn't make her feel any better.

As the newcomer started moving, so did she, setting her coffee on one small table, nestling her pastries behind a pot of overflowing vinca on the other. With a mental reminder to reclaim the food before it lured insects or worse to the porch, she got to her feet, wrapped her fingers tightly around the coffee mug, and moved closer to the steps.

Lord, he was even better looking up close. Once on the porch, he removed the sunglasses, revealing eyes that were bitter coffee brown and intense. She would guess he was about her age—thirty-four—and obviously comfortable financially. She might never wear them, but she could recognize a hundred-dollar pair of jeans and Ray-Ban sunglasses when she saw them.

"Are you Ben?"

Looking as if he'd rather bolt for his car, he nodded curtly. "You're Lucy."

His gaze skimmed over her, and within three seconds she felt completely cataloged: short, fat, average hairstyle, average makeup, average clothing. Oddly enough, though, she didn't feel dismissed. Most hunky guys she met did just that, unless they were young enough to mistake her for surrogate mother material. With all the young troops that passed through the hospital at Fort Murphy, it had happened before.

"Your mother's asleep. I'd rather not wake her just yet. She's had a tough twenty-four hours."

He murmured something that she took to mean he'd rather not wake Patricia, either. Lucy was curious about what had happened between them, but beyond asking for her son, so far Patricia's focus had been entirely on George.

She waved toward the chairs. "Why don't you have a seat? Would you like something to eat? We've got all kinds of good stuff inside."

"No, thank you. I'm good." He seated himself in one of

the chairs, looking as if he expected an electric current to zap through it at any minute.

Returning to her own chair, Lucy hoped he couldn't see the plate of food she'd stashed. She was embarrassed about choosing both a cinnamon roll and a cheese Danish, even if it was her lunch, but she would be humiliated if she got caught hiding it.

"I guess I should ask how she's doing." Ben's voice was deep, heavy with the Oklahoma accent she'd learned to love. There was a reason the state produced so many country music stars, and in her opinion, that accent was part of it.

"It's going to take a while to accept that it's not just a bad dream, that George is really gone, that all their plans and their hopes and future are gone. It's a big adjustment."

His gaze locked on his hands. Long fingers, short nails, just as she'd expected of a surgeon. Those hands wielded instruments that made people's lives better; they helped people to heal. Could he do the same for his mother? Would he?

"Has she told you?"

The question was unexpected, his tone a shade vulnerable. "What went wrong? No."

His stiffness returned. "Just as well. Her version probably wouldn't have much in common with the truth."

"Everything in our past is colored by our perceptions," Lucy said gently. Ben had his truth; Patricia had hers; and reality might be one, the other, or somewhere in between. But the stern look he shot her didn't encourage her to pursue the subject. "Do your sisters also live in Tulsa?"

"Yes."

"Will they be…" She paused to consider her words.

Coming to the funeral seemed a little too blunt, *checking on their mother* a little too presumptive. "Visiting Patricia?"

He gave her another of those looks and changed the subject again. "You seem awfully young to be friends with her."

Lucy smiled. Mike had always told her she was pretty, *but when you smile, you're incredible.* Just the memory was enough to make her smile and, sometimes, *feel* incredible. "Don't you have friends who are younger or older?"

"Acquaintances. But most of my friends are in my age range."

"Mine, too." Fia was the youngest of her besties, but they still related. Patricia was probably the oldest of her local friends, and about the same age as her mother. "I live on the next street over. Our backyards connect. When they moved here from Louisiana, I brought a pot of gumbo, bread pudding, and pralines to welcome them to the neighborhood, and we've been friends ever since."

"I'd be friendly for gumbo, bread pudding, and pralines, too," he muttered.

Lucy smiled again. Everything else about her might be just average, but her food was exceptional. Joe would eat at her house three times a day if he could manage it.

"When was that? When you brought the gumbo."

"About a year ago. George deployed four months ago." And those four months would have been easier on Patricia if she'd had family to offer her emotional support. Had she tried her best to protect her kids from the fallout of the divorce? Had their father kept them away from her? Had she willingly given up her claim to them?

Lucy's friend Therese's stepchildren's mother had done that, and now she was nothing more than a bit player in the

kids' lives. Of course, Catherine Matheson didn't care—
yet. Someday, Lucy was sure, she would regret it, like Patricia did.

"You don't sound like you're from around here," Ben remarked.

"I grew up in El Cajon, California. My husband got orders to Fort Murphy about eight years ago and..." Arms
open to embrace the neighborhood, she finished, "I'm still
here."

The hint of a scowl wrinkled his forehead. Had Patricia's past mistake been falling in love with a soldier? Had
she already been divorced from Ben's father, or had she left
him for George?

"Is he still in the Army?"

Now it was her turn to study her hands. They weren't
pretty, her fingers weren't long and slender, and her manicure was in need of a redo. But they could cook. They
could bake. They could scratch Norton and pat shoulders
and dry tears. "No. Mike died in Iraq six years ago."

After a moment of utter silence, as if he weren't even
breathing, she looked at him again. "That's why I kept calling. Because I know what Patricia's going through. I've
been there and done that, and no one should ever have to
do it alone."

* * *

Jessy and Dalton ran out of casual conversation about halfway through lunch. Normally, silence didn't bother her.
Hell, she spent enough time by herself these days. But normally she wasn't sitting at a kitchen table across from a man
she'd had sex with and now was finally getting to know.

You like doing things ass-backwards, don't you?
Aaron's teasing voice echoed in her head.

She pushed his memory aside and looked around the room. There was a formal dining room a few feet down the hall, but the kitchen, with its oak table and four generous chairs, was clearly where most of the living went on. It was modern enough to be convenient, but retained enough of its old character to feel timeless. The wood floor had been worn by millions of steps of bare feet, socked feet, and cowboy boots. A rack near the door held two cowboy hats and three baseball caps, along with a pair of threadbare gloves that still had a few jobs' wear in them.

Unlike most kitchens she'd seen, there was no island in this one, just plenty of open space to allow a person to move about freely. Thick mats fronted the sink, the range, and the prime workspace on the counter, and a couple of good-sized windows allowed wide-ranging views of the barn, a couple of sheds, and the pasture where black-and-white-striped cattle—

"They look like Oreo cookies," she blurted out.

Dalton blinked. "I told you they were black with white bands."

"Yeah, but you didn't say they look like Oreos." She stuffed the last bite of her sandwich into her mouth. "Can we go see them?"

He answered by standing and taking their empty plates to the sink while she got her camera. They left the house by the rear door, Oz trotting alongside until they got to the big oak tree thirty feet back, where he immediately trampled a circle in the grass and settled in.

"I'm guessing he's not a working dog."

"You'd think, being a shepherd, he'd want to herd *some-*

thing, but nope. Maybe when he's more comfortable here, his instincts will kick in."

"More comfortable?" She glanced back at the dog, on his back now, feet bobbing in the air as he shifted to keep his balance. "He lives in the house. You feed him your mom's home-baked bread. I bet he sleeps on your bed, too, doesn't he?" Immediately the image of *her* in his bed popped into her mind, and her face flushed pink. So did his. He looked away, and she did, too, and she fumbled trying to make her point. "It doesn't sound like he could get any more. Comfortable, I mean."

"Oz was a stray. He's only been here about a month." His voice was steady, but he still avoided looking her way, which she knew because she was sneaking peeks his way. "I think he's still adjusting to not having to scavenge all the time for food and trying to stay out of trouble."

So Dalton hadn't brought Oz here expecting him to earn his keep. He'd fed him, likely doctored him—according to Lucy, fleas and ticks in Oklahoma were fierce—and given him a place to live simply because the dog needed it.

Compared to the time she and her sisters had found a frail, sickly kitten. *We can take her to the animal doctor,* Jessy had pleaded, *and she'll be all good.* But their mother wasn't about to bother with a filthy stray. She told them she'd found the kitten a good home, but the next morning Jessy had seen the gardener burying its tiny, stiff body.

It was a good thing she and her sisters hadn't gotten sick.

As they reached the fence surrounding the pasture, she gratefully took shelter behind her camera and focused on a calf, who lifted his head to stare at her, his mouth moving occasionally to chew the grass he was eating. "Are they nice?"

"The Belties?" Dalton stood a few feet away, his hands resting on the top wire of the fence. "They're even-tempered, though you could piss one off if you tried."

"I could piss off Saint Paul himself if I tried."

The comment surprised a laugh from him, though not much of one. He was facing the same problems everyone in the margarita club faced, though his might be even tougher. There were support groups for widows, but she didn't know of any that included men. Women were expected to need help, to ask for it, while men were supposed to somehow muscle through.

But a startled laugh was a start. Did he realize the day would come when laughter, happiness, and smiles would be a daily part of his life again? When he would feel alive and hopeful again?

She'd seen it with Carly and Therese, with Lucy and Ilena and the others. She hoped someday she would experience it for herself.

"Belties are descended from an old Scottish breed and were bred for harsh climates, so they fit in fine with Oklahoma's extremes. Their outer coat sheds rain, and the undercoat keeps them warm. They do well grazing in rough terrain and on grasses that other breeds won't eat. Plus their beef is top-ranked for flavor, tenderness, and juiciness."

Jessy had been taking pictures while he talked but stopped at that last sentence and lowered the camera to look at him. "Look at those faces. How could you..." With a shudder, she started framing shots again. "It's enough to make a woman go vegan."

"Yeah, I think that's illegal in Oklahoma."

Really, she loved a good hamburger or steak, and Lucy made a beef roast to die for, but Jessy'd never come eye to big brown cow eye before. Like she'd said earlier, when they were processed, packaged, and displayed in the refrigerator case at the commissary, they looked like dinner. Seeing them as sweet-natured big ol' pets was disconcerting.

Dalton stood quietly while she exhausted the photo ops with the cows, then she turned the camera his way. Unaware, he continued to gaze at the animals, or across the pasture to the line of distant trees, or judging by the seriousness of his expression, maybe all the way off to Afghanistan. Her finger hovered above the shutter.

Other than her best friends, she didn't like people in her pictures. They were clutter, distracting from the scene she wanted to preserve, messy and full of emotions. She had enough of that in real life. If she allowed them in her photographs, taking them would no longer be an escape.

Yet she took the shot anyway, then shifted the camera a few inches to the left and quickly snapped a few of the barn. At the first click, he looked at her, then away, obviously uncomfortable with the idea of being photographed. He didn't have to know she'd done so, did he? "Other than the margarita club, I don't take pictures of people," she said carelessly.

"Why not?"

"People are the only subjects in the world who complain about the end result. The cows, the barn, Oz"—she clicked a picture of the dog—"couldn't care less what the photo looks like. But people whine. Not *my* people, but people in general."

If she was any judge, she'd say the information eased his discomfort enough that he didn't pursue the matter. "The margarita club...They meet tonight, don't they?"

Jessy tilted her head to one side. From what she knew, Dalton was pretty much a loner, preferring his animals and land over socializing in town. She'd bet he rarely heard gossip or listened to it when he did. "How do you know about the margarita club?"

"Dane told me."

Her eyes widened. "You know Dane Clark?"

"He painted that fence over there."

She spared a glance for the white boards around the corral. "Hm. He helped Carly paint her living room. He's just a handy guy to have around, isn't he?" Before he could respond, she went on. "He hasn't even been at Fort Murphy that long. How did you meet him?"

Dalton started walking, and she fell in step beside him. "He likes palominos."

"So...what? He went looking for someone who raised palominos?" That definitely didn't fit with what she knew of Dane, especially in his first couple months in town. "No, I know: He was driving by, saw your horses, told you they were pretty, and you invited him back."

"Pretty much."

They reached the horse pasture, and she photographed the beautiful golden horses with their white manes and tails. In the right light, their coats would gleam like a new gold coin, giving them an almost knight-maiden-fantasy look. Jessy glanced at Dalton, wondering if she could invite herself back to catch that perfect light.

After a time, she lowered the camera and leaned on the board fence, keeping her gaze locked on the horses.

"We've never had any guys come to the Tuesday Night Margarita Club, but…" It was hard to say the rest of the words. The margarita dolls were her best, only friends. They didn't know that she was a drunk, or that she slept around, or that she wasn't as good and honest and honorable as they were. Dalton knew, and what one knew, the others eventually found out.

Still, she forced herself to finish. "You would be welcome there."

With anyone else, she would have said he was considering it, the way he grew thoughtful, his forehead furrowed, his gaze distant. But she had no doubt what his answer would be. He wasn't the type to ask for help, certainly not from strangers, and women, no less. Cowboys didn't show weakness.

And connecting with the club, when she was a member…Wasn't gonna happen.

"No, thanks," he said at last, and relief seeped through her even though she'd known he would refuse. As long as he didn't tell Dane, her secrets were safe.

"I appreciate lunch and the photo ops, but you've got work to do and I'd better get back to town."

They reached the house before he asked, "Did you quit the bank job?"

She stumbled over a step, and his fingers wrapped around her arm, holding her upright until she caught her balance. His hand was strong, callused, and spread heat all the way through her body. Flushed, heart racing, even a little light-headed, she attempted a laugh. "You'd think I'd do that when I'm wearing four-inch heels and have a lot less foot in contact with the ground."

He stood a step below her, but she still had to look up to

see his face, impassive as usual but with a tiny bit of something in his eyes. Attraction? Arousal? His nostrils flared slightly as he breathed in, like an animal catching scent of his prey...or his mate.

Jessy swallowed hard, willing all the little nerve endings in her body to go numb. She'd been with enough men to shame her, and she'd done so much more with *this* man than a simple touch. She was way too jaded to feel anything special in something so innocent.

At least, she should have been.

Slowly his fingers uncurled, but even after he let go, she still felt the shape of his hand in her very pores, and her lungs refused to accept more than the smallest of breaths. How long had it been since a man had left her breathless?

Holding on to the railing, she took the last few steps to the porch and politely waited for him to open the screen door. As they went inside and toward the kitchen, he asked again, "What about that job?"

Oh, yeah. The reason she'd tripped in the first place. She'd thought no one in her world besides LoLo Baxter knew she didn't work at the bank anymore. She hadn't exactly lied to LoLo, unless omission counted. She just hadn't said the words: *I got fired.*

Now LoLo and Dalton knew something about her that her girls didn't know. Discomfort crept along her spine, and with deliberation she turned the question back on Dalton. "How do you know I'm not working there?" Then: "Have you been checking up on me?"

His sun-dark skin reddened all the way to the tips of his ears. "I went in to take care of some business, and some guy was at your desk. That's all."

Oh, God, he really had checked up on her. She'd just

been teasing, but if he hadn't, there'd be no reason for his whoops-got-caught reaction. He'd gone to the bank with the expectation of seeing her. Now her own skin was reddening, and she knew from experience that blushing wasn't a good look for her. Suddenly anxious to jump in her car and drive like her hair were on fire, she fumbled with putting the camera in its bag and snatching up her purse.

"Life's too short to work at a job you hate." She flashed a smile that was as phony as she was and hastily started back the way they'd just come. "Like I said, I appreciate everything, but I've kept you long enough. If I got any fabulous pictures of your animals, I'll let you know. Thanks for everything."

He stopped at the porch—she felt the instant the distance between them widened—then waited until she was at her car to speak. "Hey, Jessy."

Startled, she looked up. Was that the first time he'd used her name? Then the realist inside her spoke up. *So what? It's a name. Even that old hag of a supervisor, Mrs. Dauterive, called you by name. Doesn't mean a damn thing.*

Dalton shifted as if he regretted stopping her, dragged his fingers through his hair, then, with an almost belligerent tone, asked, "You want to have dinner tomorrow night?"

Realist Jessy: *Oh, no no no. He* knows *you, Jessy, and you cannot handle a man who knows you. Even Aaron didn't know the real you. Besides, he was a one-night stand like all the others. You go out on a date with a one-night stand, you're looking at a relationship.*

And after Aaron, she didn't deserve a chance at another relationship.

But Dalton was awfully handsome, and she was a sucker for handsome. And he was lonely, and she related to that. And he was aware of her flaws—some, at least—and willing to see her again in spite of them.

Before she could say the right thing, she blurted out the totally wrong one. "Sure. Want to meet in town?"

"Six thirty?" He waited for her nod. "I'll pick you up."

"Okay." She gave him her address with an unsteady smile, and her hand trembled as she waved before sliding into the car. That wasn't anticipation twirling in her stomach. It wasn't a bit of a thrill over the prospect of her first date since she and Aaron had gotten married, and it certainly wasn't pleasure at the thought of seeing Dalton again.

She told herself that all the way back to the paved road, but she didn't manage to believe it.

*   *   *

Ben shifted in the wicker chair. He'd been at the house longer than he'd intended and hadn't come face to face with his mother yet. He couldn't deny sitting on the porch with Lucy was a much more pleasant way to spend the day than listening to Patricia's self-centered *me me me*. Granted, she had a reason now to lock in on herself, but she'd never needed one. In Patricia's life, she came first.

When he turned around again, he caught a glimpse of a paper plate with dessert stuck behind the plant there. Lucy's? Had she been uncomfortable about eating in front of him? With his schedule, he grabbed food whenever a few minutes opened up and ate it too quickly to properly appreciate it, whether it was chips from a vending machine or takeout from his favorite restaurant.

A phrase popped up in his memory, one Brianne had

heard a lot: *She'd be pretty if she'd lose weight.* Or: *She's got such a pretty face. Too bad about that weight problem.* Or worse: *She's really pretty, but damn, she's fat.* Brianne had gotten back at them all, though. She'd finished college, gotten a job, started eating healthy and being active, and she'd lost all that stressed-out, bad-diet weight. On top of that, the pretty girl had become damn near breathtaking as an adult. *One big win for you, kid.*

Lucy was pretty, too. She had brown hair that fell to her shoulders, natural, no additional colors streaked in. Her eyes were blue, her skin flawless, her smile even and also natural. Nothing posed about that smile. She had an unfortunate tendency to discount her own accomplishments, but people dealt with insecurity in different ways, and she was obviously very compassionate. He could see why Patricia wanted her for a friend.

"Will you be spending the night in town?" Lucy broke the quiet that had settled over them with the soft question. "I have a thing at six that I can't miss, but I can fix dinner before I go, and I can come back when I'm done."

It would be easy to say, *Yes, come back.* He'd brought a bag with everything he'd need for an overnight stay, just in case, but he'd much rather stay in a motel than at his mother's house. He didn't want to be a guest in her and George's house, in her and George's life.

But Lucy had already given up a lot of time, even taking off work, and Ben had come here to— To stop the phone calls from Lucy and Jessy? To do the right thing in his father's eyes? To take the family responsibility so neither Brianne nor Sara would have to?

One answer was sure: not to rebuild some sort of relationship with Patricia.

Maybe he'd come for karma. As Lucy had said on the phone, *If you show her compassion now, it'll mean something to you later.*

Beside him, she laughed. "I'd hate to ask you a difficult question if it takes you this long to answer a yes/no thing."

He heaved a dramatic breath. "Yes, I'll stay the night. No, you don't need to fix dinner. I'm sure there's enough food in the kitchen to feed the whole neighborhood. Just remember, though, if this goes really bad, I'm holding you responsible."

Her second smile showed she didn't take him seriously. "Trust me, no matter how it goes, you'll have the satisfaction of knowing you tried—"

Behind her, the front door swung inward, the ribbons on its wreath drifting in the air. Ben's gut tightened, his fingers gripping the chair arms as if trying to splinter them. This was a really bad idea, maybe the worst he'd ever had. He should have told Lucy no way in hell. He should have changed his name and his phone number and moved someplace where Patricia would never find him.

It took forever for her to step outside, and the first thing he noticed was her bare feet—also one of the earliest things he remembered about his mother. She'd loved kicking off her shoes, inside or out, and had even married his father in her fussy, girly white gown and bare feet.

Pointless memory.

"Oh, Lucy, I woke up and thought you were gone. I know I'm taking up way too much of your time, but you can't imagine how much comfort it gives me, having you—" Finally Patricia noticed him, her words stopping midflow, her brow trying to wrinkle but failing. Botox.

It took a moment, but she finally reacted, clapping both

hands over her mouth. "Ohh!" Another little squeak escaped her, making him wish he were anywhere but there. He'd lived twenty years with nothing but occasional calls and even rarer visits. He could easily live another twenty that way.

Lucy stood, and Ben did the same, but he didn't move closer.

"Benjamin Richard Noble. Oh, my lord, you always resembled your daddy—all you kids did—but you've grown into the spitting image of him." Patricia moved forward, bypassing Lucy, both hands reaching out. "You came. I prayed you would, but I didn't think—"

She stopped before touching him, but not in time to keep him from shrinking back. Hurt crossed her face, and tears wet her eyes when she smiled. "I didn't know if I'd ever see you again, and here you are. It's all right. You can relax. I won't grab you and give you kisses all over your face." As if to prove it, she folded her arms across her stomach.

Another unwanted memory: the happy noises three kids could make when they were getting kisses all over their faces.

"Come in, please. I'll fix you some food. You, too, Lucy. That nap made me feel so much better. I'll wait on you for a change." She loosened her arms and slid one around Lucy's shoulders, guiding her toward the door.

Lucy didn't shrink away at all, but then, she wasn't the one Patricia had abandoned. She had a great relationship with her parents, he'd learned during their conversation. With her sisters and brother, they were one big happy, if widespread, family.

He followed the two women into the house, gazing at

stuffy paintings on the walls, antiques in the living room and the study, and furniture in off-white and pale yellow. Expensive Asian rugs, delicate lamps, and knickknacks everywhere added up to a house that was definitely not child-friendly.

The kitchen was big and airy, filled with granite, stainless, and wood. Along with the food offerings spread along the counters and the island, pieces of Frankoma pottery were displayed on the walls and the wide shelves of a peeling white-painted cabinet. Patricia had always been fond of the Oklahoma-made pottery with the prairie green glaze, but he and his sisters had chipped so many pieces she had resigned herself to packing away what survived.

She'd taken it with her when she'd left them behind.

Lucy sat on a stool at the island, then swiveled the next one around and patted the seat. "Sit."

He obeyed. Ordinarily he would offer to help, but there was nothing ordinary about today, and rushing around seemed to help calm Patricia's nerves. She fixed plates of cold fried chicken, potato salad, tabouli, and baked beans reheated in the microwave and poured glasses of iced tea strong enough to make a mug of black coffee run the other way. Once she'd pulled a stool around to the opposite side, she sat, bowed her head, and murmured a prayer.

His mother was saying the blessing. He'd never experienced that firsthand until he was in high school and having dinner at a friend's house. When had Patricia found God? What did He think of her past actions?

They talked little during the meal, and most of that was Lucy. Her desire for him and Patricia to get along was obvious in her bigger smiles, her darting gaze, and her faster rate of speech. He was sorry to disappoint her, but he was only here so he could say he'd tried.

Too soon after the late lunch, Lucy checked the time, then slid to her feet. "I've got to go, Patricia."

Patricia glanced at the wall clock and smiled faintly. "Of course. It's Tuesday, and the margarita club never misses a Tues—" Her voice broke off, and a lone tear slid down each cheek. "I guess I'm eligible for membership now. I love you, Lucy, but I never, ever wanted—"

She stopped with a hiccup, and Lucy wrapped her arms around her. "Of course you didn't. No one wants to be in the margarita club, not a single one of us. But we know what you're going through, we know how tough it is, and we're always ready to listen or cry with anyone who needs it. All you have to do is give us a call."

Ben shifted uncomfortably. So Lucy's *thing* tonight was some sort of support group meeting with other Army widows. That sounded depressing.

And Patricia qualified to join them. Mother or not—bad mother or not—that was depressing, too.

Lucy calmed the last of Patricia's tears, hugged her, told her she would come back after dinner to check on her. Next she took Ben's hand in both of hers. "It was nice meeting you, Ben. I'll see what I can do about that fry bread tomorrow."

"You still like fry bread." Patricia delicately wiped her eyes with a napkin. "You ate so much of it that I always worried you kids were going to turn into giant pieces of grease-laden dough."

Lucy held Ben's hand a moment longer, gave him a covert wink, then let go and said her *good-bye/back later* on the way out the back door. When it closed behind her, the quiet in the house went from normal to tomb quality in a heartbeat. Patricia broke it too late, too soon, her voice quavery and too bright. "Would you like to have coffee in the living room?"

Of course not. But he picked up the cup and saucer she'd set in front of him and followed her down the hall. When she'd been his mother, she'd always smelled of cookies or fabric softener or the girls' powders and lotions. Now the fragrance was definitely adult and vaguely familiar, something one of the women at the clinic wore.

Patricia sat on one sofa, tucking her feet onto the cushions, covering her legs with a throw, and balancing her coffee in both hands. He chose a chair nearer to the other sofa, one with sturdy legs, a spindly back, and no illusions of comfort, and they studiously pretended they didn't feel awkward as hell.

It was his turn to break the silence, and he did with the obvious. "Lucy is nice."

Patricia's smile brightened her face but couldn't disguise the fact that she was barely holding herself together. Lines bracketing her mouth and her eyes, a weariness that came from much more than a lack of sleep, the barely perceptible tremors that never left her hands... So this was what grieving looked like for her up close. Ben hadn't known, since his father's death hadn't been more than a blip on her horizon. She'd already been well established in her new life by then.

The bitterness inside him reflected more than the bitterness of the coffee.

"Lucy's a good friend," she agreed. "She needs a family to take care of, but since she never had children, she's adopted all of us."

Ben's jaw clenched. "A family's not the answer to everyone's prayers."

Patricia drew one pink-polished nail around the rim of her coffee cup. "I guess you mean that personally."

"I guess I do."

"Oh, Ben, I love my family. I've always loved you. I just…"

Loved George more? Needed to be free from all the demands, the whining, and the dramas? Couldn't be bothered to make the effort for you and the girls?

She sighed heavily. "I know you're carrying a load of resentment, and you're entitled to every bit of it. I was a terrible mother. I was selfish. I didn't think about the long-term consequences of what I was doing. It was…It was a difficult time for all of us, and I'm so sorry."

Another forgotten memory: night after night, getting the girls to bed while their dad tried to lose himself in late hours at work. Eleven-year-old Brianne, her brown eyes huge and brimming with tears, saying, *She'll come back. She'll tell Daddy she's sorry, and she'll come home, and everything will be the way it was.*

And Sara, two years younger but ages more cynical: *She's not coming back, Bree. She's not sorry, and even if she was, that doesn't make everything okay.*

And he, going to bed after they were settled, staring into the darkness, too old to cry, gritting his teeth, clenching his fists, unable to admit even to himself that, like Brianne, he missed his mother. He'd wanted her back.

Even at nine, Sara had nailed it. *I'm sorry* were just words, too easily said, too often meaningless. In that spirit, he flatly repeated them. "I'm sorry, too."

Chapter 4

After a shower and a change into denim shorts, a wildly colored top, and a pair of flip-flops, Jessy left her car parked in the alley out back and set out for The Three Amigos. The sun warmed her back as she walked east, waving at Miss Patsy in Selena's, saying hello to the pedestrians she passed. She liked the walk in all types of weather—had even made it in snow a few times—but that wasn't her reason for doing it. The fact that it was the only exercise she got most weeks wasn't the reason, either.

There wasn't much she wouldn't do, as her actions of the past ten years proved, but the one line she never crossed: She never drank and drove. Tonight she wasn't even going to have a margarita. It wasn't as if it was required. Ilena, pregnant since they'd met her, hadn't tasted anything stronger than coffee at their dinners. Carly rarely finished the one margarita she usually ordered, and every time Lucy started a new diet, the drink was the first thing to go. She preferred her meager calorie allowance with substance, not in liquid.

Though the dolls would notice if Jessy abstained. Jessy wasn't known for her abstinence. She could drink them all under the table, and they knew it. But none of them knew how much she drank away from them. None of them knew she was a drunk. But if she gave them a reason—an excuse—they would accept it.

Tonight she didn't even want a drink, really. All the fresh air had cleared her mind, and taking photographs again had soothed her spirit. She didn't need alcohol tonight.

Though just a sip would taste good. She had a fine appreciation for the taste of good tequila.

But appreciating, wanting, and needing were totally different things.

From a block away, The Three Amigos looked like a burst of warm summer sun in the midst of a dreary winter day. Its colors were bright, a fiesta of vibrant tones that both clashed and complemented at the same time, a palette that shouted *good times!* against the quiet whisper of the brick and sandstone buildings that surrounded it. In the fifteen months or so of the margarita club's existence, they'd eaten at other places on their adventures out of town—including the Tulsa State Fair, where she'd upchucked a funnel cake and a fried Snickers bar on the Ferris wheel. Thanks to her, there were people in northeastern Oklahoma who cringed at the mere mention of food and a fair ride.

But Tuesday nights belonged to The Three Amigos. Everyone loved Mexican food, and The Three Amigos' staff loved them.

Bypassing the front door, she circled to the patio entrance on the east side, where the building shaded the seating from the late afternoon sun and tables had been pushed together to seat twelve. They usually numbered eight to ten, though on occasion had twice that many.

She'd barely had time to settle when the restaurant door swung open and their usual waitress, Miriam, set a margarita in front of her. After unloading a tall stack of menus, she smiled at Jessy. "I don't believe you've ever been the first one here."

Jessy eyed the drink. Should she send it back? That seemed rude and wasteful, and she tried never to be wasteful. Maybe she should push it aside for the next person to arrive. But who wanted a half-melted frozen margarita?

Deliberately she forced her gaze back to Miriam. "You know me. I usually like to make an entrance."

Miriam's smile grew, deepening her dimples. "You're so gorgeous, just walking through the door is an entrance." She sighed, lifting her arms in an embrace of nothing. "Isn't it a beautiful day?"

Jessy surreptitiously scooted the glass an inch away under the guise of taking a menu. "Beautiful. I got out and took some pictures today."

"Of what?"

Scrub and weeds. Dalton's dry words quirked the corner of her mouth. "Wildflowers, cows, horses." And one man. She hadn't transferred the photos to her computer yet, hadn't clicked back to view the shot of him on the camera. Later. Tonight when she was alone and tired and tempted.

"A wonderful way to spend a day." Miriam glanced past Jessy, then gestured. "The Tuesday Night Margarita Club will soon be in session. I'd best get plenty of chips and salsa."

The first to arrive was Lucy, her hair hanging in loose waves, her face mostly makeup-free. She wore a print sundress a size too big and an expression that...Hmm. Jessy couldn't quite read it.

She took the chair across from Jessy, hanging her purse over the back of it, settling in with a deep exhalation. "Ah, I've waited all day for this." She hesitated, then gestured toward the margarita. "Do you mind?"

Containing a grateful shudder, Jessy pushed it across the table to her. "Tough time at work?"

"I didn't go in. I've been at Patricia's since you left yesterday."

Jessy didn't ask how the woman was doing. She knew. She'd thought about her a few times during the day, but always she pushed the thoughts away. Too many reminders, too much sorrow.

"Her son showed up early this afternoon."

Jessy raised one brow. "Mr. I-don't-care?"

"Ben cares. He just hasn't let himself admit it. Things were really tough between them for a long time, and it was his mother's fault. It's hard to forget that."

Jessy understood. She'd often thought her life would have been much better if she'd been raised by a pack of wolves. But she ignored the topic in favor of a much more interesting one. "Ben, huh? Let me guess...Tall? Handsome? Wildly successful?" She would add *charming* if it wouldn't make her laugh. There'd been nothing charming about their brief conversation the day before.

Lucy's cheeks turned pink. No, they went beyond that straight to candy apple red. She wouldn't make eye contact, either, but instead fiddled with her napkin and silverware. "You're the same height I am. Everyone's tall from our perspective. And yeah, I guess he's handsome. Dark hair, dark eyes, nice hands. And he's a surgeon. It pretty much goes that he's successful."

"And single?"

Her face turned even redder. "I didn't ask."

"But those nice hands weren't wearing a wedding band, were they?"

"No...and he might have mentioned something about not being married. I wasn't really paying attention." Lucy shifted to scan the parking lot behind her. Relief washed over her. "Look—there's Marti and Ilena, and Carly's just pulling in."

Jessy spared their friends a quick glance. "Doll, you're crushing on Dr. Noble, aren't you?" she whispered. "It's about damn time." She hoped the doctor lived up to his name. She'd have to kick his ass if he so much as thought about breaking Lucy's heart.

"Don't tell anyone," Lucy whispered back.

Jessy raised both hands in a hands-off sign. It wasn't her place to tell, and she respected that.

As the newcomers settled around the table, Miriam brought baskets of chips and bowls of salsa, along with more margaritas and an iced tea for Ilena, who dropped into the chair beside Jessy as if the walk across the lot had exhausted her. She patted her round belly and said, "Aw, man, Hector Junior is hungry. I'm ready for him to be born. It's hard eating for two."

"I've been doing it a long time," Lucy said as she dipped a chip in spicy salsa. "It just takes practice and determination."

Marti leaned across to hug her. "And with that same determination, you can stop it," she said gently. Talk about

Lucy's weight was always done disparagingly by Lucy, gently by the others. No one cared about her weight except in the way it affected her health and happiness. They wanted her around for a long, long time. "We know you, Lucy. You're strong. You're a survivor."

Was determination enough? If Jessy practiced not drinking, if she was determined to stay sober, would the need go away? Would she have the strength to say no to an icy margarita or to the oblivion alcohol brought? She was afraid the answer was no. How many times in recent weeks had she told herself that she wasn't going to overindulge again, only to find herself waking up with no clue of the previous night's events?

Her determination was there, but her weakness was stronger.

And if she gave up the oblivion, how would she survive? How could she stay sober when she didn't like the person she was, when she couldn't bear to *be* the person she was?

The other regulars arrived: Therese, looking serene and beautiful as ever, and Fia Thomas, holding her left arm in an awkward position, the backs of her fingers twisted unnaturally against her chest. Something was going on with her health that was slowly changing her from an athlete and trainer into a woman whose movements were sometimes actually painful to watch. She'd been having problems for a few months, but the doctors she'd seen had diagnosed little stuff like a strained muscle, a pulled ligament.

Jessy worried about her. Of the main margarita group, she and Fia were alike in the family department. They had relatives, just none that gave a damn about them. If something was seriously wrong with Fia, she had no one outside the club to turn to. But they would be there for her.

Jessy would be there for her. She might have disappointed everyone else in her life, but not her girls.

Not yet.

Please, God, not ever.

*   *   *

Shortly after their mutually pointless apologies, Patricia's doorbell began ringing and a steady flow of visitors started, offering condolences, bringing more food, sharing memories. There were men, soldiers all of them, looking the part even in civilian clothes, and plenty of women, some whose own husbands were deployed. There was genuine regret, perfunctory remarks, and with the women awaiting a return, a mix of emotions: sympathy, anxiety, relief.

Wandering into the kitchen to find a cold bottle of water, Ben wondered what it was like to be thousands of miles from your spouse, waking every day knowing that he or she was in danger, knowing how many people who made that trip overseas didn't come back. How had Patricia dealt with the possibility of George not coming home? Had she wondered every time she saw Lucy if she might wind up in the younger woman's position? Had she acknowledged that she might never see her husband again except in her dreams?

The questions made him uncomfortable. Thinking of her loss reminded him of his father. Rick had never gotten over Patricia's betrayal. Her abandonment had taken the pleasure out of his life. He'd done his best to take care of Ben and his sisters, but they'd lost the father they loved— in spirit when she left, in body as soon as Sara graduated from high school.

The sound of an engine outside came as a welcome distraction, drawing him to the large windows next to the dining table. A guy wearing a ripped T-shirt, shorts, and beat-up running shoes was pushing a mower across Patricia's yard, starting at the back edge and moving inward. He was sweaty, as if he'd been at it awhile. With Lucy's freshly cut lawn behind him, as well as the one next to hers, he probably had been.

Ben would give an awful lot to trade places with him. A little physical activity would go a long way toward easing the knots in his muscles.

The voices down the hall rose and fell, moving from the living room to the front door. Tension spread through him as he continued to watch the yard guy. In a minute, Patricia would walk into the kitchen, and until the doorbell rang again, there would be no excuse not to finish the conversation they'd barely started.

What was the point? She was sorry. He was sorry. Together it meant nothing.

Heels tapped as Patricia came into the room. She made herself a cup of coffee, put a chocolate whoopie pie on a plate, and carried both, with a fork, to the table.

"That's your fifth or sixth cup of coffee since lunch," he commented.

"I've always needed coffee to get me through the day. Some days require more than others." Her voice wobbled on the last words, then grew stronger. "Find something over there to eat. You never could make it more than a few hours without sustenance."

That was a long time ago. I've grown up since then. He didn't say that, though, but crossed to the counter to scan the offerings. His choice was also a whoopie pie, this one yellow with banana cream filling. He didn't bother with a fork.

When he sat down across from her, she was gazing out the window. "That's Joe Cadore. He's Lucy's neighbor. I tell you, those two take better care of me than—"

My own children. Ben's jaw tightened, and he squeezed a bit of filling out of the cookie.

"Well," she went on after an embarrassed moment, "their mothers raised them right. And I didn't stick around to finish raising you or the girls." Her sigh was wistful. "I never intended to drop out of your lives, Ben. I thought you'd get over the surprise of the divorce and...everything would be fine."

Ben could believe that. Patricia had never been overly responsible. A free spirit and a dreamer—that was how his father described her. Add in a naïve belief that she could have whatever she wanted, plus a touch of avoiding any reality that she didn't want, and that was his mother.

"I wanted to give you time to adjust, and then I was going to contact you. Then I decided you probably needed a little more time, and a little more, until so much time had passed that I just thought it was better to let things be. There would be lots of chances in the future to resolve things with you three—when we came back from Europe, when George left this command or got that promotion, when he finished his deployment, when he retired..." Another wobble, this one more tearful than before. She cut the cookie into fat chunks with her fork, then began mashing it until nothing but cream-coated crumbs remained.

Lifting her gaze, she smiled faintly. "And here I am with three grown children and three grandchildren who don't know Grandma from a jack-in-the-box."

Whose fault is that? She'd *left* them. She'd missed more of their lives than she'd shared. All their birthdays, holidays, important events, all the times they'd wanted and missed and needed her…And now, when it was convenient, she regretted it. Now she wanted from them what she'd refused to give to them.

The injustice of it made his head throb.

The mower came closer as Joe Cadore continued the back-and-forth swipes. The name sounded Italian, but the hair sticking out underneath an orange-and-white OSU ball cap was blond. Being Osage on his father's side, Ben knew better than to stereotype. Every ethnicity had its diversities.

"How—how *are* the girls?"

"They're fine," he said stiffly, then forced himself to go on. "Brianne does consulting with oil companies and runs marathons. She's dating a guy who plays for the Oilers."

"I know the Drillers are baseball. Is that a basketball team?"

"Hockey. Sara's husband is in the oil business, too, and she stays home with the kids. She's homeschooling Matthew and Lainie—they're eight and six—and Eli's four."

"Wow." The near-whisper was less an exclamation of surprise than a lament. She'd missed out on a lot, and she was right that the little ones wouldn't know her. Sara didn't have a single picture of Patricia in the house. It wasn't that his kid sister held a grudge—that was his job—but Sara excelled at writing off disappointments. She didn't keep unnecessary people in her life.

Sara's kids weren't missing out, either. They knew their grandpa had died a long time ago. Despite the formal titles their paternal grandparents had chosen—Grandmother and

Grandfather—they had a great relationship with them. They adored their aunt Brianne and their uncle Ben and didn't yet equate having a grandpa with also having a grandma.

"George warned me," Patricia continued, her voice softer, distant, as if she were thinking aloud. "It was the only thing we ever really fought about it. I gave up so much—threw away so much—and then I kept putting off trying to fix it. I'll think about it tomorrow, I used to tell him. I'll do something next week. And before I knew it, twenty years had passed and now..."

As Ben looked away from the tears welling in her eyes, the lawn mower out back shut down. A moment later voices reached the patio, one male, the other higher in pitch, rounder in tone. Lucy was back from her widows' thing.

Her timing couldn't have been better.

* * *

Dalton stood at the porch railing, one shoulder leaning against a solid post that had supported the roof since the house was built over a hundred years ago. Oz curled at the top of the steps, so relaxed his body was limp but always ready to leap off at the sight or sound of any critter brave enough to encroach on his territory.

The sky was darkening, and the pole light near the barn buzzed as no-see-ums swarmed around it. The front door stood open behind him, and so did the kitchen door, the screens allowing the evening breeze to drift through the rooms with its cool night scent.

It was quiet—no neighbors, no traffic, no planes overhead, the stock settled in the pastures. It was one of the things he loved about the place, and one that sometimes drove him crazy. Depending on his mood, it was the most peaceful place on earth or the loneliest. Tonight he felt lonely, and it was Jessy's fault for leaving memories of herself everywhere.

No, not Jessy's. His fault for bringing her here. Sandra's fault for leaving him here.

She'd broken every promise she'd ever made him. She'd said they would be together forever. She'd said she would always love him. She'd said she trusted him more than anyone else in her life. She'd said they would have kids and teach them to ride and rodeo and ranch and live, that they would watch them grow up together, watch their grandbabies and great-grandbabies grow up.

She'd sworn they would be happy every day of their lives.

It was easy to be happy when everything was going their way. Even her deployment to Afghanistan was just a bump in the road. She'd been to Iraq, and she'd compared it to playing baseball: long periods of boredom broken up by sudden bursts of adrenaline. Another tour was nothing, just a minor delay in the long, wonderful life they had ahead of them.

Opening the door to two Army officers on his porch had been bad enough. Like anyone else married to someone in the military, he'd known instantly what that meant. All the life had drained out of him in that instant—all the hope, all the good things. His heartbeat had slowed, and filling his lungs with a full breath became impossible. He'd thought he'd been hurt when Dillon took off, but hell, that was nothing—a scratch on a callused finger compared to someone ripping his chest open.

Then it had gotten really bad.

To this day, he remembered only words: *sorry, inform, dead.* He'd been in a curious place, between so numb that nothing made sense and feeling as if his skin was being ripped off, one small strip at a time. Then a word or two began to penetrate his brain. *IED. Alert. Awake. Legs gone. Pleading. Loosened tourniquet.*

He had to ask them to repeat the last part. What they said couldn't possibly be true. Sandra was smart and determined and strong. If things didn't go the way she wanted, then she changed what she wanted to make them fit.

But there had been no mistake. She had unfastened the tourniquet on her right leg and bled to death before anyone realized it. She had chosen to die. Had chosen to stop loving him, to stop trusting him, to give up the babies and her family and their happily ever after. She'd chosen suicide over all the people who loved her.

It had been a terrible choice for her and a terrible burden for him. Once he'd seen firsthand how the knowledge sliced through every nerve, how it burned and stung and filled a man with questions that ate at his soul, he'd sworn their families would never know. Let her parents see her as a hero. Let her sisters adore her. Let them believe she'd died doing what she loved—instead of killing herself because she couldn't accept what she'd become.

Does the pain ever go away? he wanted to ask someone—Jessy, Dane's fiancée, any of the margarita club women.

Another question: If he *wanted* it to go away, didn't that mean she'd been right not to trust him? That he hadn't loved her enough?

The sigh that should have been frustrated was lonesome

instead. It made Oz lift his head and stare at him, his blue-brown eye in shadow, the other reflecting light from the window. He whined and stretched on his side, his signal that he'd accept scratching if it was offered. Dalton sat down on the top step and obliged him. The dog all but groaned with pleasure.

"A full belly, shade for a nap, a good scratch, and a bed to sleep in. That's all it takes to make you forget the tough times. I envy you." He'd spent a lot of years living the tough times, pissed off, pitying himself, pushing away his family and friends.

And then he'd met Jessy.

Maybe the tough times were on their way out, and just like her and her widow friends, he was going to start living again.

She wasn't his type. He liked quieter, more thoughtful women, while Jessy was flashy and brash and overtly sexy. She liked to have a good time and good friends, while his only regular company was Oz and, on weekends, Noah. Partying and shopping were an art for Jessy, while he hardly remembered how to talk to anyone besides Oz and Noah.

But he'd had a good time in her bed. She'd been through the same loss as him, though she was handling hers a hell of a lot better. She liked his dog, his horses, and his cattle. She'd gotten under his skin the first time they met, and she made him want more.

He hadn't wanted anything but numbness for so long.

The wind quickened, ruffling his hair, bringing with it the sweet promise of rain. A rancher succeeded or failed based on the weather. The best skills, management, planning, and breeding in the world were all put to the test by brutal summers, drought, tornadoes, or frigid winters, and nature dealt Oklahoma all four on a pretty regular basis. He never wished rain away, but prayed for it—when he remembered to pray—to refill the stock ponds and nourish the bluestem, Indian, and switch grasses that kept his animals fat and happy.

Then thunder rumbled across the prairie, rattling the floorboards beneath them. Oz heaved a sigh as if to say, *Not again.* Springtime, summertime, storm time.

"Come on, buddy." Dalton pushed to his feet and stretched to work out the kinks in his back. "Let's go in."

The dog did the same, then trotted to the screen door, waiting for Dalton to open it before clicking his nails across the wood floor on his way to the stairs.

Dalton wondered idly as he followed what Jessy thought about sharing her bed with a dog.

*   *   *

Jessy had turned down offers of a ride home from every one of the regulars except Lucy—who'd been quick to leave the restaurant when dinner broke up and to get back to Patricia Sanderson's house...and Patricia's son. In all the time they'd known each other, Lucy hadn't gone out on one date, not even with the good-looking football coach who lived next door. Jessy didn't care for sports, but she would have taken Joe Cadore for a spin in a heartbeat if she'd ever had occasion to meet him away from Lucy.

"If he'd ever shown the least interest in you," she added tartly as she stepped up the curb onto her block. Then she glanced around to see if anyone was close enough to have seen her talking to herself. With the last of the downtown businesses in the process of closing up for the night, the street was pretty much deserted. A foam drink cup, flattened by a passing car, scooted along the pavement ahead of the wind, and she bent to gingerly pick it up, then tossed it into the next trash can she passed.

She'd made it through the entire evening without taking a sip of the margarita, and if any of her girls had noticed, they'd kept it to themselves. She'd done a lot of worrying for nothing.

So that was one meeting down. The questions, the wondering, the whispers, could come next time.

She was only yards from her door, passing Serena's, when Miss Patsy rapped on the plate-glass window, gesturing. Jessy obediently went to the door, where the old lady met her, a large foam box in hand. "What's this?"

Patsy gruffly pushed the box at her. "Got three pieces of pie left over. You might as well take 'em."

When Jessy lifted the lid, the incredible aromas of butter, sugar, and pastry drifted to meet her. One pecan, one coconut cream, and one strawberry with a thin drizzle of bittersweet chocolate over the top. Despite her promise to start eating healthy, the sweets-loving devil rose inside her, licking its lips and anticipating the first calorie-laden bites. "Aw, Miss Patsy, my favorites. Let me pay you—"

"Serena already closed out the register. Besides, if you don't take them, I'd just have to eat them myself." Patsy tapped her solid belly. "You need the calories way more than I do."

"You're a sweetheart."

Predictably the woman got huffy. She was brusque and short with everyone, but Jessy had long suspected she was softer inside than she wanted people to know. Making shooing gestures as if Jessy were holding her up, Patsy closed the door, locked it, then...Was that a wink, or had her eye merely twitched?

Raindrops were falling with heavy plops as Jessy walked the last few feet to her door. She let herself in, then turned to watch as thundering wind chased debris down the street, following it with the heavy kind of rain that ran off before it could soak into the dirt.

A long flight of stairs led to her second-floor apartment. No fan of shadows, she had 300-watt bulbs screwed into the fixtures at the foot and the top of the stairs. After securing the dead bolt, she trotted up the steps, having to catch her breath at the top. "Yeah, like you need a million calories of pie tonight," she grumbled as she walked into the large living room/dining room/kitchen.

The blinds were open on the windows that gave her a good view of the courthouse across the street and the branches of the tall oaks on its grounds whipping back and forth with the storm. She'd once seen high winds blow through—no thunder, no lightning, minimal rain— and leave the flagpole on the courthouse lawn bent in two, like a giant inverted V.

Restlessly she put the pie in the refrigerator, got ready for bed, then wandered through the apartment. One bedroom, one bath, one tiny balcony over the alley, not much to wander. Drawn to the couch, she turned on the television for company, but not a single channel of the way too many offered interested her.

In the weeks after Aaron died, she'd found herself turning to alcohol too often to cope. She had no family to help her; he'd had no family, period; she hadn't met her girls yet. She'd just wanted to take the edge off her sorrow and guilt, just until she was strong enough emotionally to deal with it.

Of course, there were consequences to taking the edge off.

Her usual nighttime routine was simple: something sweet to eat, something distilled to drink. She had the sweet, thanks to Miss Patsy, and the Patrón was in its usual place in the kitchen. How easy it would be to walk in there, feel the cool heft of the bottle in her hand, remove the cap, catch the first whiff of tequila wafting out the narrow neck into the air, watch the overhead light play on the lovely amber as she poured just a drink, a tiny sip, into a glass.

Just a sip. Just enough to savor the flavor, to send a little liquid sunshine into her bloodstream and warm all the chilled places. It was okay to have a sip, wasn't it? After all, when Lucy began each of her diets, no one expected her to give up all her favorite foods cold turkey. No one would expect Jessy to, either.

A shudder rippled through her, turning the craving building inside her upside down and tumbling her stomach with it. No sip. No, no, no. Not at night. Not when she was restless. Not yet.

"Yeah, let's wait until you're desperate." The shaky sound of her own voice sent her roaming again, away from the kitchen and its temptations. She considered a warm bubble bath, downloading a book and actually reading it, standing still as a statue at the window until the storm passed—

Her gaze caught on the camera where she'd left it this afternoon. Grabbing it, she headed to the laptop on the desk in a corner of the living room, made herself comfortable, and transferred the pictures from memory card to hard drive. Back in her teens, she'd gone through a phase with tradition—a 35-millimeter SLR camera and rolls of film—but it had lasted only about as long as it had taken to get the film back from the developer. Digital was just entirely too cool, with all the no-cost, no-waste chances she got to take the perfect picture.

Drawing her feet onto her chair, she scrolled through the shots. She had a routine for this, too: Upload the pictures, scan through them, see if anything caught her eye, then seriously cull them, deleting bad or so-so images before adding captions, dates, and keywords so she could find them later. She was just following her habit, not looking for anything in particular.

Yeah, sure. That was why she stopped scrolling the instant the thumbnail of Dalton appeared.

It wasn't a great shot. She'd taken it so quickly that it was blurred around the edges, but it was good enough to give her a shiver at the strength and the hardness etched into every line of his face. He was a handsome man, though not a happy one. His younger brother, whom she'd literally bumped into a week after she'd met Dalton, gave her a good idea how the older brother would look if he didn't have so many cares. Noah shared the same features but with a lighter, more satisfied air about him.

How much had Dalton loved Sandra? Enough that he'd wished he could climb into the grave with her, Jessy would bet. All of the margarita girls had loved their husbands like that—wildly, passionately, permanently.

Jessy had once loved Aaron like that, but something had happened. Maybe it was his being gone so much. Maybe it was where he had gone, war zones where the chance of him not returning was considerable. Maybe partying and being happy and responsible only for herself had been too appealing, or maybe it was his growing desire to be a father. With his schedule, Jessy would have been the primary caregiver to any child, and what she knew about that would fit in the cap of a liquor bottle and still leave room for a swig.

All she knew was that somewhere along the way, she'd fallen out of love with Aaron and had been merely awaiting his return so she could serve him with divorce papers.

She didn't deserve to be in the same room with Carly, Therese, and the others, much less to call them friends. They had almost drowned in sorrow, while her drowning was mostly guilt.

The rain continued to slash against the windows, with an occasional flash of lightning and the kind of low, grumbling thunder that seemed to go on forever, while she worked with the pictures. She deleted dozens of less-than-stellar shots, noted a few that she would get prints of for Dalton—*another chance to see him,* her inner voice whispered—then filed them in folders. When a yawn split her face, she checked the time—two fifteen—and somberly considered how she felt. She was tired, but was she sleepy?

Another yawn convinced her the answer was yes, so she shut off the computer, put the camera on its closet shelf, and began turning off lights. A little yen deep inside, just a twinge that drew her gaze to the liquor cabinet, persuaded her that the light over the kitchen sink could stay on all night. Better to pay a few cents more on her electric bill than to get too close to her temptation.

But the yen was still there, strong enough to make her mouth water. It made her look over her shoulder before going into the bedroom, where she shut the door for extra protection.

She should throw it out. Wasn't that what the experts said about dieters? To purge their kitchens of any unhealthy or high-calorie food they needed to avoid. She should pour the Patrón down the drain, along with the other assorted liquor in the cabinet. Wouldn't it be easier to abstain if there was nothing in the apartment to abstain from?

But she'd tried that a half-dozen times and found herself at odd hours in convenience stores or at one of the dives that stayed open late enough to practically see the sun rise. These days, a person could buy booze any time, any place.

Anyway, wasn't that the coward's way out? Liquor was everywhere—at every restaurant and bar she frequented, at every friend's house, part of every celebration, everyday life. If she could stay sober only by creating a liquor-free safety zone around herself, it didn't say much for her chances, did it?

And besides, that ugly little voice inside her whispered, *you never know when you'll wake up all fragile and really needing a drink. You're weak that way, Jess, and you know it.*

Scowling, she turned the lock on the bedroom door, stepped out of her flip-flops, and turned back the covers on the bed, a king size that had been too big for her and Aaron together and was damn sure too big for her alone. No wonder she sometimes felt lost in the night. She could share it with Oz and a few of Dalton's Oreo-striped cows and still have room left over for a gorgeous foal or two.

Or forget the animals and invite their owner in instead.

Damn, that put the image of Dalton in her head—big, strong, muscular, naked—and the thought of sex with Dalton, or any man, stone-cold sober, made her need that tiny sip even more.

No, not need. Want. There was a huge distinction.

And she was determined to figure it out.

Chapter 5

Lucy took the rare gift of turning off her alarm and sleeping Wednesday morning until she woke up on her own. The sun was shining, Norton was sprawled across his bed against the wall with his rubber ducky tucked under his chin, and her stomach was grumbling. The clock on the bedside table flipped to 9 a.m. as she rolled over and swung her feet to the floor. The dog opened one eye and looked at her, as if trying to determine whether this was an official rising/feeding/letting him out or merely a bathroom break.

"Yes, I'm actually getting up," she said with a yawn, standing and stretching, then headed for the kitchen. Nails scrabbled on hardwood as he jumped to his feet, then an instant later he passed her in the hall at a hell-bent-for-leather pace. She was used to the flybys—rather, had gotten used to them after he knocked her to the floor one day and happily sat on her back, glad to have her at his level for once—and routinely walked next to the wall to give him room.

By the time she reached the kitchen, Norton was waiting at the door, panting, reaching out a time or two to paw at it. "You really have to go, huh? You're not the only one, buddy, but at least I can hold it long enough to let you go first."

Actually, he could hold it, too. He just refused.

Giving him a gentle shove back, she undid the lock, then opened the door. Norton lunged outside and made a beeline for the iron-and-tile table on the patio, where Joe sat with a cup of coffee and a Krispy Kreme box. He shared a dough-nut with the dog before glancing her way. "Jeez, Luce, I thought you were never gonna get up. I've been awake for three hours."

Doughnuts. Aw, damn it, today was going to be the first day on my diet. How can I start a diet with doughnuts?

It would be rude to say no when he'd gone to the trouble of bringing the treats. The shop was on the other side of town, and he always ran there—as in, on his own two feet—instead of driving. The trade-off, he said, for the in-dulgence. That was why he looked the way he did, and she looked the way she did. She indulged; she just skipped the trade-off.

And she could indulge one more day. Hell, she could even start her diet with lunch.

She raised one finger in signal for him to wait a minute, went to the bathroom, poured herself a cup of coffee from the auto-start pot on the counter, grabbed creamer and sugar—since she was postponing the diet a few hours—then joined him at the table. "I know. And you've run five miles and done a thousand push-ups and updated the play-book and designed new uniforms for the team."

"It was only nine hundred and ninety push-ups," he said

with a smirk, then tilted his head to one side. "Are you try-ing something new with your hair? 'Cause I'm pretty sure it's not working."

She returned his smirk before combing her fingers through her hair. It probably was a sight. Mike once joked that sleeping with her was like snuggling up to a hyper-active sidewinder. Images of wildly coiling snakes had haunted her nights for a week after that.

"I got your favorites." Joe pushed the box toward her.

It was nice that at least one man knew her favorites in something. Not that it was a sign of anything more than friendship with Joe. They were buddies, pals, excel-lent neighbors. Besides, she knew his favorites, too, and with women he was pretty reliable: tall, reed-thin, and buff, more likely to run a marathon than make marshmallow fudge.

"Thanks." She chose a maple-glazed bar, loving the scent released when the slight pressure of her fingertips cracked the frosting. The first bite was pure goodness—deep-fried, airy, overly sweet. She could eat a half dozen.

Hence, the extra pounds she carried.

"Any word on when George's funeral will be?"

She shook her head while swallowing the bite. "LoLo will let Patricia know when he—when his transfer will be made." Dignified transfer—that was what the Army called the shipping of the fallen soldier to his home. "A chartered jet will bring him to Tulsa, where the family will meet him, then he'll be brought here with an escort of law enforce-ment and the Patriot Guards motorcycle group." It was very impressive, very sad, and—

Oh, Lord, would Patricia want her to go along? Would she have to stand on the tarmac a second time and watch as the body of someone she knew and cared for was unloaded in a casket?

She could keep Patricia company. She could help her hold together. She could help with the funeral plans, if needed, and she could stand on Main Street with a flag in her hand, tears in her eyes, and a prayer in her heart.

But she didn't think she could make it through another heartrending transfer at the airport.

"Are you spending the day with her again?"

"Yeah, after I shower and get ready."

Joe tore another glazed doughnut in half and tossed one piece to Norton, who gulped it in one bite. "Is her son going to be there?"

"Ben? I don't know. He spent the night." When she'd gone over after dinner last night, the atmosphere had been a little less tense. She'd wondered how much of that had been from Ben and Patricia talking and how much from Joe and Lucy showing up. Patricia adored Joe and had doted on him, as always, fixing a plate of food for him, brewing his tea fresh, setting aside pieces of his favorite sweets. How had Ben felt, practically a stranger to his own mother by her choice, watching her fuss over another man as if he were her own?

"Ben?" Joe mocked. "You have to ask, or did you just want to say his name? He *is* the only son she's got."

Lucy blinked in surprise. Next to Mike, Joe was the easiest-going person she knew. He liked people, and his openness, modesty, and sincere, what-you-see-is-what-you-get attitude made them like him back. She'd never known him to make a snap judgment about anyone, but after only thirty minutes in Ben's company, he had done just that.

Maybe he was being overprotective on Patricia's behalf. With his own mother living in Alaska, Patricia was like a surrogate mother to him. Maybe—

The middle part of what he'd said registered belatedly. *Did you just want to say his name?* Oh, crap, had he seen that she had a crush on Ben? Her face flushed. It was one thing for Jessy to recognize it. Jessy knew her in a best-friends woman-to-woman sort of way. But Joe...he was clueless half the time, especially if there was food anywhere in the vicinity. He shouldn't have noticed *any*thing.

"Don't be ridiculous," she said, giving him only the quickest of glances. "I wasn't sure you remembered his name." She shoved the rest of the maple bar into her mouth, chewed, then took a big drink of coffee. The taste made her gag.

Joe smirked again. "You might want to put some sugar and cream in that coffee."

Lucy scowled as she added a spoonful of sugar, then relied on a lot of the thick French vanilla–flavored creamer to add a few more layers of sweetness. When the coffee was diluted to a nice *café au lait* hue, she took a sip and sighed gratefully. "Much better."

Deliberately keeping her tone light, she went on. "I love summer. I should have become a teacher so I could have summers off."

After a moment's silence, Joe apparently agreed to follow her lead. "The downside is you have to put up with kids all day the rest of the year."

"I love kids." She and Mike had planned to have three, three years apart. He'd wanted boys he could do manly stuff with, while she'd hoped for at least one girl. She had so loved seeing his little nieces wrap him around their pinkies.

"I guarantee you, there are kids in high school even you would find hard to love. Besides, the worst part is their parents. Whatever goes wrong is never the kids' fault. You don't know how often parents have tried to coerce me into changing their kids' grades or letting them play even though they hadn't shown up a single day since the last game." He grinned the way she liked, abruptly, unexpectedly, the brighten-your-day sort of grin. "If I had ten bucks for every time a parent has threatened to have my job, I'd be sitting on a beach in the Caribbean instead of your patio."

"Which you'll be doing in a few weeks anyway."

"Seven days, six nights, in the U.S. Virgin Islands." His tone turned coaxing. "It's not too late to go with me. You've got the vacation time. You've got the money. Come on, Luce, think how much fun you'd have."

Closing her eyes, she tilted her face up to the sun, imagining tropical heat, ocean breezes, island music, incredible food fresh from the sea…and appearing in shorts or a swimsuit in front of the world. While she was perfectly comfortable sitting on the patio in her pajamas, without makeup, her hair combed, or her teeth brushed, with Joe, there was no way she would subject anyone to the view of her in a swimsuit. She wouldn't subject *herself* to it, and she saw herself naked every day. And what would that leave her to do while everyone else enjoyed Paradise?

Eat. A lot.

Giving her head a shake, she opened her eyes again. "You're going to have a great time anyway. Diving, snorkeling, seducing all the beautiful girls. Besides, it's a family trip."

"Nah, it's just my brother and me."

"That's family, Joe. And isn't he bringing his girl-friend?"

"Yeah, so if you came, that would balance everything out."

Because the swimsuit image wouldn't leave her head—and the girlfriend was probably a perfect size zero—she shook her head again. "Follow Nicky's lead, Joe. Find a woman to go with you."

His gaze narrowed to slits as he leaned closer. "Guess what, Luce? *You're* a woman." Then he moved closer still. "And guess what else? *Ben* just came out of Patricia's house and is headed this way."

She darted a look across the lawn, caught a glimpse of Ben indeed walking toward them, let out a tiny yelp, and rushed inside. "I'm taking a shower!" she hissed through the crack in the door. "I'll be ready soon as possible."

He mumbled something in response before she slammed the door shut. Given his earlier mood, she was pretty glad she didn't understand it.

* * *

Ben's jaw tightened as Lucy disappeared into her house. Great, he'd come looking for sweet-woman-he'd-like-to-get-to-know-better and instead he was stuck with perfect-surrogate-son Joe while he waited for Lucy's return. The guy was kicked back on the patio as if he belonged there, and the way her dog hovered beside him, drawn no doubt by the doughnuts but also by the scratching, looked propri-etary.

Cadore wore another orange-and-white Cowboys ball

cap, and his T-shirt was emblazoned with the name of the local high school football team. Ben had learned last night that Cadore was the head coach of the team, as well as a teacher. Probably physical education, if schools actually offered that anymore.

It wasn't like Ben not to get along with strangers. He was a nice guy, a little too driven to describe himself as overly friendly but still likable. He got along great everywhere—at the coffee shop he frequented, the restaurants and shops, the hospitals and the clinic. He didn't get along with rude, obnoxious people, but Cadore wasn't any of that, and he still set Ben's teeth on edge.

Was it jealousy? Ben dismissed it out of hand. He wasn't a jealous person—hadn't dated any woman regularly enough since graduating medical school to justify it. And what did Cadore have to make him jealous?

A better relationship with Ben's mother than Ben himself.

Nope. Couldn't be. Ben had given up on Patricia so long ago that he couldn't possibly be jealous of any guy she allowed into her life. He didn't have the emotional attachment. It was just that everything was screwed up at the moment. That had to be the reason.

As soon as he set foot on the patio, the dog shifted deep brown eyes his way and let out a rumble, the kind that vibrated so low it was barely distinguishable from the birds in the trees and the car passing out front. Cadore scratched his head again. "Norton says hello."

"Sounded more like, 'You've come far enough.'" Ben didn't dislike dogs. He didn't have much experience with them, other than Sara's squeaky piece of fur that always tried to chew on his shoes. Frankly, he preferred his shoes unchewed, his quiet undisturbed, and his downtown loft dog hair- and saliva-free.

"Give him a doughnut, and he'll love you for life."

The mention of the word *doughnut* was enough to make the dog's gaze jerk quickly to the box, and drool formed at the corners of his mouth.

"Yeah. No, thanks. I use these fingers to do my job. I don't want to lose any."

With a shrug, Cadore tossed half a doughnut to Norton. The dog's jaws snapped shut with surprising force. "Lucy's getting dressed. It won't take her long. Have a seat."

Ben hesitated. Technically, all he had to do was issue Patricia's invitation for breakfast. He didn't have to sit, didn't have to be friendly, didn't have to keep wondering in the back of his mind if Cadore annoyed him for a legitimate reason or if he did somehow resent his place in his mother's life.

But avoiding Cadore meant returning to the house and Patricia, whose best cosmetic efforts couldn't hide the puffy redness of her eyes. She must have cried half the night. It had been awkward to start, him sleeping in George's house, without listening to her sob as if her heart was breaking.

He sat. "Patricia sent me over with an invitation for you and Lucy for a late breakfast, early lunch, whatever."

Cadore continued to scratch the dog. "You call your mom Patricia?"

"Yeah, well, after twenty years, *Mom* seems a little personal." The snideness that crept into his own voice annoyed Ben. He didn't want to discuss his private life with a stranger.

Though Lucy had been a stranger when they'd met. For

maybe ten minutes. But talking with her was totally different. She was warm, understanding, and going to a lot of effort to comfort a friend. She was what Brianne called a Nice Woman. Brianne insisted that Nice Women were hard to come by and should be recognized, cherished, and held on to.

Cadore looked as if he wanted to say something else—maybe ask whose choice that was—but instead he gave the rest of the doughnut to the dog, then chugged back his coffee. "Lucy says you're an orthopedic surgeon in Tulsa. We went through one season where we kept the surgeons in town in business. The worst bad-luck team I've ever seen."

Okay, Ben could make an effort, couldn't he? It was either that or go back to the house and be alone with Patricia. "Yeah. I do ankles, knees, and hips. A lot of my patients are athletes. A lot of them end up broken down before they're thirty."

Cadore's expression tightened, his eyes narrowing. *Great. Criticize the man's profession.*

"A lot of them finish their football career without so much as a sprain and use their talent to get through college. Even medical school." Cadore waited a beat before adding, "George—your stepfather—played at West Point."

Now it was his own face tightening. George Sanderson didn't merit any form of that designation. The only two *fathers* of any kind in his life were his father and his grandfather. "You mean Patricia's husband. He wasn't my—"

The back door opened, and Lucy almost stumbled on her way out. Heat flushed her face, and her hands fluttered a moment before she clenched them tightly together. "Good morning, Ben. Pardon my graceful entrance. Or would that be exit?"

He forced his gaze away from Cadore and automatically smiled. Her brown hair was damp and scraped into a ponytail that made her look ten years younger. She wore a sleeveless shirt in a bright pattern and denim pants that came just below her knee. Her shoes were flip-flops, the straps decorated with vividly colored fish made of sequins.

She made such a pretty, bright, happy picture that Ben couldn't help but feel better about his day just at the sight of her.

"Everyone fumbles at some time," he said as he stood. From the corner of his eye, he saw Cadore stiffen at the comment. "Patricia would like you to come over and eat. She's cooking."

"I was just heading that way. She's a great cook, and I haven't had a chance for breakfast yet."

Cadore unfolded from his chair, too, standing several inches shorter than Ben. "What about that—"

Her smile never wavering, Lucy punched him on the shoulder. "Yeah, that was a long time ago. Norton, time to go inside."

The dog looked at Lucy, then showed a hint of teeth to Ben before squeezing close to Cadore's leg and gazing up at him with a wolfish grin and a question in his eyes. Norton might belong to Lucy, but there was no doubt he was Cadore's dog.

Ben wasn't convinced that dogs were as smart as people claimed. For two years, Sara's little furball had been crazy in lust with a yellow stuffed dragon, and he still thought his reflection in the window was another dog invading his turf.

"Don't encourage him, Joe," Lucy said with a scowl. "Norton, get inside. Your breakfast is in the dish, and I'll be back later."

At the mention of breakfast, Norton abandoned his human and trotted inside, tail banging the door on the way. Cadore frowned. "What did I do?"

"He never obeys around you because you're fine with everything he does." Turning to Ben, she rolled her eyes as if they'd had the conversation a hundred times before. "Kids and dogs. What can you do with either of them?"

Cadore made a face behind her back, looking remarkably like Norton, showing more than a few teeth. Ben definitely wasn't jealous of this guy. He and Patricia were a much better match than she and Ben ever were.

*   *   *

Wednesday, like every other day in Jessy's life, had come too damn soon and couldn't be over fast enough. She'd awakened out of sorts and stayed that way all day. She went to the store and actually came home with groceries this time—fresh stuff, healthy stuff, stuff that promised to aid her digestion, ease bloating, clear her complexion, and protect her from all the nasty illnesses out there. She had even fixed lunch—a fish fillet, steamed green beans, and a salad with low-fat, low-calorie, no-taste dressing—and thought that a future of such meals was no great incentive to actively work at prolonging her days.

What she needed was something to *do*. Maybe she would join the gym where Fia worked as a personal trainer, though the thought of lifting weights and sweating was enough to make her retreat to bed with a box of chocolates.

Maybe she should get a job. Not that she was qualified for anything besides being an account rep at the bank where she'd been fired or waiting tables. She loved servers—had her favorites at every restaurant where she routinely dined and tipped them well—but she'd already proven she wasn't exactly qualified for getting along with difficult customers.

If she could cook like Lucy, she could open her own restaurant and hire someone to be nice. If she had wicked math skills like Marti, or was a great motivator like Fia or people friendly like Ilena, or liked kids like Carly and Therese...

Everyone was good at something. What was Jessy's talent?

Drinking and sleeping around and acting like none of it mattered and feeling guilty and wishing she could change something, anything, everything about herself.

Jeez, the only job she was qualified for was being mistress to a married man.

When the only man who interested her in the slightest was widowed.

The man who would be here before long to take her to dinner. The thought made her hands tremble just a touch.

Was that why she'd been edgy all day? Was she nervous about this dinner date? Ridiculous. She'd started dating when she was fourteen, and she'd been out with enough men to staff a brigade before she'd met Aaron. She'd broken hearts all over Atlanta—had never been at a loss for male interest even when she'd worn her wedding ring and her husband had stood right next to her. How could she possibly be nervous?

Because this was her first, honest-to-God date since Aaron. Her first date where she intended to start sober and stay that way. Her first date where she was no longer a carefree girl who sincerely believed a woman could never have too many beaus.

This was her first date as a woman who knew a little about having too many beaus, too many disappointments, too many sorrows, too little self-respect. This was her first date where she wanted to be *good*.

Too restless to settle down, she went into the bathroom once more to check her reflection in the mirror. She'd gone through her closet twice to figure out what to wear to dinner with a cowboy. He, she knew from living in Tallgrass, would probably wear indigo blue jeans, probably sharply creased, with his good boots, his good hat, and maybe a big flashy rodeo belt buckle if he'd won one when he was younger and more reckless.

Dalton. Reckless. Two words that just didn't belong in a sentence together.

She'd started with jeans and an incredibly cool pair of red Justin boots, but discarded them as party clothes, not date clothes. Next she'd tried a peacock blue dress, simply cut, snugly fit, one that Dalton had seen her in before and, as she recalled, had shown a moment's appreciation. But she didn't want to be reminded of *before* any more than necessary.

So here she was: in a forest green sheath that skimmed over her curves and covered a significant amount of thigh, with gold hoops in her ears, an expanse of bangles on her right wrist, heels that raised her to average-woman height, her makeup expertly done, and a subtle fragrance perfuming the air around her. She was shooting for a little demure, a little elegant, with a faint hint of sexy. She thought she'd achieved all three, along with *hot damn!*

Except for that anxious little wrinkle between her eyes.

"God, I need a drink."

Mouth watering, she checked the clock again. Dalton

was due in five minutes—enough time to take a swig of Patrón, rinse her mouth, and reapply her lipstick. But she didn't move toward the kitchen. Through sheer will, she held herself motionless, swallowing hard, breathing shallowly, staring at her reflection as her nerves wound tighter.

She'd never been so glad to hear the doorbell in her life.

Grabbing her purse and a black sweater, she negotiated the stairs with a fair amount of skill, given the height of her heels, and a mounting sense of...It wasn't fun enough to be excitement, not ugly enough to be dread. Maybe equal parts anticipation and anxiety. This was a big deal for her, going out on an honest-to-God date. It was a huge deal, going out with a man she'd already slept with. Doing both when she was trying to clean herself up and get good and permanently sober...

Oh, God. Jessy wasn't much of a praying woman, but if God didn't mind listening to her, she didn't mind asking.

She didn't bother with the peephole, but unlocked the door and pulled it open, an unsteady smile pasted on her face. It slid away, then she quickly recovered it as her guests gave her the once-over. They knew she went out to dinner a lot and to bars on occasion, or so they thought, but somehow they knew this was more than either.

Ilena gave a wolf whistle while Bennie Ford, one of their semi-regular girls, twirled one finger in the air, drawling, "Oh, my, my, my. Miss Jessy has got plans."

Obeying the silent signal, Jessy turned in a circle, showing the dress's modest front, the matching back, the heels that had cost her half a month's salary, then she placed both hands on her hips. "What are you two doing, wandering the streets?"

"I ran into Bennie after work—"

"Both of us grocery shopping—"

"And we decided we'd much rather go out to eat than cook—"

"Amen, sister—"

"So here we are," Ilena finished expectantly.

Jessy couldn't help but check the street for any sign of Dalton. *Please be late, please let me get rid of them first.* Immediately she felt guilty. She didn't want to *get rid* of them. She loved them. She just didn't want them to know about Dalton until she was ready to tell them.

The block, remarkably, was free of pickup trucks, so she looked back at her friends. "So you're here . . . Do you expect me to cook for you? Because you guys know, I don't cook."

Ilena laughed the lightest, sweetest laugh Jessy had ever heard. With white-blond hair, fair skin, and blue eyes, she looked angelic and sounded it, too. "We know that. We thought maybe you were tired of eating alone, too, and would like to join us. We're going to Serena's or maybe Luca's. We haven't decided yet."

"But," Bennie said, her dark eyes sparkling, "you obviously have plans of your own. Are you keeping secrets from us?"

God, was she ever. Jessy's gut clenched, but she managed a cocky smile. "What kind of secrets?"

"The man kind. The fall-in-love, get-married, wind-up-like-this kind," Ilena replied, patting her belly.

Jessy's expression of horror was sincere. She wasn't sure she was cut out for falling in love and getting married again, but she damn well knew she wasn't cut out for bringing babies into the world. She didn't know what to do with them, how to treat them, how to raise them to not be sorry, screwed-up adults like her. "If any man made me wind up like that, I'd cut his thing off. You can have all the babies, Ilena, and I'll be the best Aunt Jessy ever—from a distance—but my maternal instincts are sadly lacking."

"My mother's older sister used to say, 'If God had intended me to have children, He wouldn't have given me such an incredible body.'" Bennie laughed and patted her own solid curves.

Striking a pose, Jessy repeated Bennie's earlier words. "Amen, sister."

In a singsong voice, Ilena asked, "So if you don't have a date, what are you all dolled up for?"

"Dinner with Julia, from the bank." The lie rolled so easily off Jessy's tongue, so naturally, that she would be disappointed with herself later. When had she become so comfortable with lying that she could do it with her friends without conscious thought?

Maybe back when she'd fallen out of love with Aaron but continued to tell him the words that had become habit, repeated automatically but without the supporting emotion.

"All right, sweetie." Ilena leaned forward to hug her. "If you want to have dessert later on, you know where to find us. We won't be hurrying home tonight."

Yeah, empty houses could be hard to leave but were damn harder to go home to.

"Have fun," Bennie said, adding her own hug.

Jessy watched them walk away, envying the laughter that drifted back to her on the evening air. She didn't deserve good friends, but she had them. They made the lack of a family easier to bear, but...She needed more. Someone she could live with, be contented with. Not another person, not a man or a husband or a sex partner.

She needed herself. She needed to be a Jessy she could be happy with. Proud of.

Rather than climb the stairs again, she locked up, then sat on the cast-iron bench a few yards away. The sun was lowering on the horizon, but the heat of the day lingered, radiating through the metal. She loved hot weather—the sun on her skin, the heat absorbing through her shoes into her feet and up through her body, the moisture evaporating from her pores and making her feel lighter, freer, as if she might blow away with the next prairie breeze.

Sometimes she thought if she sat still long enough in the intense Oklahoma sun, every part of her would dry up and slowly turn to stone, the beautiful tan/rusty/brown shades of the native sandstone, a monument to the meaningless person her parents had always told her she would be.

"Damn," she whispered over the lump in her throat. "Guess I didn't disappoint you, Mom, Dad. I lived down to every expectation you had and then some."

She thought about going back upstairs, stripping, and standing in the shower until the water went cold. She thought about walking down the street to Buddy's and letting every guy in there buy her a drink or three and going home with one of them and to hell with the remorse in the morning. She thought about standing up and walking away—from the apartment, from Tallgrass, from life. She could change her name, dye her hair, make herself into someone she wasn't because any kind of fraud she could create would be a whole lot better than the real one.

The problem was the real Jessy was always there, always remembering.

Then a pickup pulled to the curb right in front of her, engine idling, droplets from a very recent car wash gleaming in the evening sun as they slowly disappeared. She was about to rise and cross the few feet of sidewalk, but the driver's door closed with a thunk and Dalton appeared, walking behind the truck and stepping up.

She'd been right about his clothes. His hat was straw, a shade between white and cream, and his shirt was white, button-down, the sleeves folded back to his elbows. The jeans were deep blue, the color unfaded, the fabric un-ripped, and the hem unfrayed. His boots were polished, his belt stitched brown leather.

Something inside her stilled, caught the breath in her lungs, and held it a moment longer than usual. That something was quiet, calming, and very much needed. It sim-mered through her, settled her nerves, and let her breathe deeply for the first time all day.

As he stopped just in front of her, she deliberately shifted her gaze to his middle. "No rodeo buckle?"

"No rodeoing. I did enough steer wrestling, roping, and bronc riding in my job. Why would I want to do it for fun?"

"Because girls love a rodeo cowboy?"

His gaze narrowed, and he tugged his hat a little lower over his eyes. "When I was young enough to rodeo, I had a girl. I wasn't looking for another. But you're right. She loved a rodeo cowboy."

Not Sandra, then. Someone else who'd broken his heart? Or just one of many that he'd had fun with in the course of growing up?

She stood, a much better view of him, and watched his gaze skim over her, all the way down to her scarlet toenails. Though he didn't comment, she knew approval when she saw it. "Where are we going tonight?"

"Wherever you want." He led the way to the truck, opening the passenger door, watching as she delicately stepped onto the running board, then slid into the seat. Jeez, with half her wardrobe, she wouldn't have been able to make the steps without showing her prettiest thong to Dalton and anyone else within flashing distance. But the longer skirt allowed her to do it gracefully while protecting her modesty.

She waited until he sat opposite, a totally effortless step up for him, to respond. "Not Serena's. Not Luca's. And not Three Amigos." That still left a surprising number of restaurants for a town Tallgrass's size, thanks to the tens of thousands of soldiers stationed there. "You have any preferences I should know?"

He slanted her a look that created a response totally different from her first view of him tonight: shivering, disquiet, a nearly forgotten little trill of pleasure and awareness skipping through her. It felt remarkably like arousal, something she hadn't experienced, not sober anyway, in a very long time. But no. No, no. She didn't do sober arousal. She damn well didn't do sober sex.

"Mom always said my brothers and I would eat dirt if you poured gravy on it and handed us a spoon."

Brothers. Until now, she'd been aware of only the younger Smith boy. Filing the information away, she considered the food options. "How about Walleyed Joe's?" Though their specialty was catfish, the place served a little bit of everything, the food was good, and an extra bonus, it was located a couple of miles out of town on the lake. They weren't likely to run into any of the margarita club there. She definitely didn't want to see any of her besties. For now, Dalton—and anything that might develop between them—was her secret.

The only good one she'd had in a very long time.

Chapter 6

Walleyed Joe's hadn't changed much in the years since Dalton's last visit. Maybe the wood was silvered a little more, and the deck had a few more tables squeezed onto it than before, but the aromas drifting on the air when he and Jessy walked through the door took him back twenty-five years, when he, his parents, and Dillon had come there the first Sunday of every month for dinner. Eating out had been a rarity back then, and for them it had nearly always been here. The tradition had continued until his parents moved away. He'd brought Sandra a few times, but she hadn't liked the smell of fried everything. She preferred a tradition of sleeping in late on Sunday, eating breakfast in bed, then making love.

He waited to feel some sense of sorrow or anger, something to remind him of everything he'd lost, but it didn't come. It was okay to be in this place with all its memories. The past was past, right? At least, he was trying to make it so.

A waitress on the fly hustled them to a table on the deck at Jessy's request, dropped off menus and napkins, took their drink orders, then disappeared back inside. Jessy chose a chair at the table for four that allowed her to face the lake, and he sat to her right, where the water stretched out into the distance.

When the girl had asked what they wanted to drink, he'd been about to ask for beer—nothing went better with fried catfish—but the last time he'd shared a meal and a beer with Jessy, he'd wound up drunk and in bed with her. Not his finest hour. No booze tonight. He was driving. He wanted all his faculties intact. He didn't want to screw up again.

Not that having sex with a woman he knew was the same as having sex with one he'd just met. Besides, this was a new start. Same woman, same man, different situation, for damn sure a different outcome.

So when Jessy ordered iced tea, he ordered Coke.

Neither of them picked up the menus. She unrolled the thick paper napkin from the silverware and spread it primly across her lap, took a deep breath, and sighed. "I had fish for lunch today. Squeezed with fresh lemon juice, seasoned with pepper, steamed to perfection." The sun glinted off her red hair as she shook her head. "People who eat fish any other way besides fried or in soup should be shot."

"So why'd you do it?"

"I had this weak moment where I thought I should eat healthy. You know, if I'm going to live another fifty years, I might as well try to be in shape to enjoy them?"

He couldn't help it. He tried to keep his gaze on hers, but his eyes had developed a will of their own, his attention sliding downward. He'd seen her looking like every guy's kid sister and every man's killer fantasy. The dress she wore tonight was definitely in between. The color was good for her. It didn't hide her assets but didn't scream *look at me!* either. Her in-your-face sex appeal was toned down, but the subtlety didn't hide the fact that it was still there, or that she was beautiful. Red hair, green eyes, golden skin. Lots of curves. Tiny waist. Great legs for someone so short. Hell, she'd look incredible in a feed sack.

"Nothing wrong with your current shape."

A smile flitted across her face. "Genetics. Mostly my parents gave me a bunch of baggage, but they did share their great genes. The most exercise they've ever done is looking for faults, but people mistake them for decades younger than they are." The smile flitted again. "Their life's goal is making everyone around them feel inferior, so of course they'll live to at least a hundred and five."

He couldn't imagine feeling that way about his parents—Dillon, sure, but not David and Ramona—but he also couldn't imagine David and Ramona trying to make anyone feel bad about themselves, especially their kids. God knew, he and Dillon had given them plenty of reason.

"Do you see them often?"

"Not since I left home at eighteen." She fiddled with the napkin in her lap, one pink-tipped finger smoothing out the creases. "My parents were perfect younger versions of their parents, and they were determined to turn us into perfect versions of themselves. We lived in the same house my great-grandfather's great-grandfather lived in. We went to the same schools, belonged to the same social groups, were friends with the same families.

"My life was mapped out before I was even born: what preschool I would go to, what prep school, which sorority I would join when I attended Mother's alma mater. The only thing missing was the man I would marry, but they'd already narrowed down the suitable families to a handful."

She quit toying with the napkin, breathed deeply, and skimmed her gaze across his. "I never really fit in with their plans. The schools kept me because my parents donated a lot of money, and there was ever the hope that some teacher or advisor would save me at the last minute. But at eighteen, instead of heading off to college like a good daughter, I took off, fell in love, and got married."

She fell silent and still for a long time. Dalton didn't mind the wait. After a sigh with a hitch in the middle, she quietly went on. "I invited them to the wedding. Never heard anything from them. When Aaron died, LoLo, the casualty notification officer, contacted them. Never heard anything then, either."

Her cheeks pinked, and her laugh was halfhearted. "They always said I'd be a disappointment, so I proved them right."

Her shrug made the green fabric cling just for a moment to her breasts. He'd seen her naked but knew practically nothing about her.

Except that he'd like to see her naked again. Sober this time.

Both of them.

The thought raised his blood pressure and added an extra layer of heat to his skin that couldn't be blamed on the sun, blocked now by the deck overhang. As he looked at her again, searching for a distraction, the warmth got uncomfortably close to rising into his face.

"What about the rest of your family?" he all but blurted out. "You have aunts, uncles, grandparents?"

"No one I really knew. They chose not to fit in with the family, so we never spent much time together. My grandparents were just like my parents, so no joy there, either."

Where the hell was the waitress with his pop? He could seriously use a wash of something cold to chase the hoarseness from his voice. "In-laws?"

She shook her head. "Aaron grew up in the foster system. When he aged out, he joined the Army. They were his family." Before he could think of another question, she turned that one back on him. "What about Sandra's family? You still in touch?"

"I get birthday and Christmas cards and cards on the anniversary of her death. But pick up the phone and call?" He shook his head. "They live in Seattle. We never had much chance to get to know each other."

And he'd never figured out how to face them knowing the secret he kept. Sandra's family took comfort in the idea that she'd died a hero, doing the job she'd chosen. If they found out that her wounds had been survivable, that she could have come home and had a full life, that she could have chosen to live...

They'd already had their heart broken once. Why let it happen again?

Instead of the bitterness that had eaten away at him for four and a half years, all he felt was resignation. *I lost my wife to an IED,* he'd told Dane Clark weeks ago, but at the time it hadn't been the complete truth. The improvised explosive device had claimed him, too. Like Sandra, he'd been too cowardly to work through the pain and come out the other side. He'd grieved, withdrawn into himself, shoved away everyone who tried to come close, and damn near wallowed in his sorrow and anger.

He'd been pissed at her for not living a full life, and yet he hadn't, either. Though that was changing. It was hard to stay withdrawn into himself when people—like Jessy, like Dane—kept drawing him out.

After a moment's silence while the waitress finally delivered their drinks, then took their orders, Jessy gazed across the water. "I met Aaron at a club in Savannah. I'd settled there, and he was stationed at Fort Stewart. He was funny and sweet and cocky as hell. We got married a couple years later and had a lot of good times."

Dalton was surprised by the attempt at a chuckle that escaped him. "Sandra and I met at the feed store in town. We were married ten days later."

"Wow. I never would have pegged you as impulsive."

"I never was." He'd been the patient one, thinking things through, considering consequences, and Dillon was the reckless one who didn't give a damn about consequences, even though he'd left a trail of them behind him.

Was his brother out there somewhere, still screwing up people's lives? Or had he changed, grown up, settled down, and made things right?

Was he even still alive?

They were identical twins. Everyone thought they had some kind of mystical connection, that they felt each other's happiness and pain, that they shared a deep mysterious bond. If that were true, if Dillon sensed that Dalton was suffering, wouldn't he have stopped being an ass years ago? Would he have inflicted so damn much pain if he felt it himself?

Surely, if Dillon were even half the man their parents had taught him to be, he would have at least let them know where he was, what he was doing, how he was doing.

A fish plopped in the water near the deck, drawing Jessy's gaze. A faint smile tugged at her lips. "My friend's dad took us fishing when we were about ten. I'd never been before, and I thought it was a most excellent way to spend a few hours. I had a pretty good catch, and I took them home and asked Mom if the cook could fix them for dinner that evening. She threw the fish in the trash, lectured me about proper behavior for a young lady and especially for a Wilkes, sent me to scrub away those awful smells— being fish and sweat and sun—and forbade me to ever go again. So naturally every time I could get away for a few hours when my friend's dad was going out, I went, too. I just made sure to throw my catch back. It was my secret rebellion, but not letting her know took some of the power out of it."

"Not letting her know was your way of keeping the peace." Not that it sounded like there had been much of it in their family. "The important thing is you knew. And I'm pretty sure it wasn't your first or your last."

Fine lines appeared at the corners of her eyes as discomfort shadowed them. "First secret? Or rebellion?"

She sounded relatively normal, but he was pretty sure it took some effort. What secrets was she hiding, and from whom? Was he a secret? Was that why she'd suggested a restaurant outside town? So no one would know she had a date, or a date with him?

"Either. Both."

After a moment, the shadows faded, and her shrug looked as careless as she'd intended it to. "People who don't have secrets or rebellions haven't taken enough chances in their lives. Nobody will ever say Jessamine Wilkes Lawrence didn't take chances."

He wondered what those secrets, rebellions, and chances were—wondered what she'd done in the past to cause that uncomfortable look. He could bluntly ask. He'd been so unsociable the past four years that people overlooked his behavior. He didn't, though. Instead, he took a long drink of pop, savored the faint burn on its way down, then in the closest-to-teasing tone he'd managed in a long time, repeated, "Jessamine? Your name is Jessamine? Hell, I'd be rebelling, too."

* * *

By the time dinner was over, darkness had settled like a shadow of protection around Jessy. Whippoorwills and bobwhites sang in the trees nearby, accompanied occasionally by the mournful note of the hoot owl. Distant lights on the water marked where boaters tried their hand at night fishing or lures and catches of an entirely different sort. She felt a very distinct sense of pleasure, all warm and cozy and *nice*. She didn't have a lot of nice moments in her life, but this evening had mostly been one after another.

Though now that the end loomed, some of her coziness was taking on a sharp edge of dread.

This was the point where most people would have their after-dinner drink, but not her. Other than margaritas with the girls, she did most of her drinking solo—or at least, away from her friends. The bartenders at every bar and club in town knew her tastes, and it had long been her motto that there was no finer way to end the day than curling up on the couch with Patrón or, before that made it into her budget, Cuervo. It was her routine.

So far she'd been able to avoid it for two nights in a row.

But she'd done this too many times: gone out to dinner, gone home, had a drink or two or who-the-hell-was-counting before bed. She'd narrowly avoided it the last two nights. She'd missed it the last two nights.

How would it play out tonight? Would she stay strong, or would weak Jessy win?

The waitress brought the check, and Dalton slid two twenties beneath the tab. Jessy stared at the bills, grateful to them for pushing the night ahead to the back of her mind. "I don't think I've seen anyone pay for dinner with cash in ages."

"I have a debit card. I just prefer cash."

"I bet I haven't had money in my purse for at least a year."

"So if our debit cards got lost or stolen, I'd still be able to buy myself a Coke, and you wouldn't." His half smile was smug and dry, one eyebrow quirked in a silent *So there*.

Slowly she rose to her full height, giving a little shimmy to send her dress fluttering into place. "I would still get my Coke, which would actually be Sprite Zero," she said with an innocent smile. "I just wouldn't have to pay for it." Demonstrating the behavior that had gotten her way more than pop over the years, she sashayed to the railing at the far end of the deck.

Dalton told the waitress to keep the change, then followed, stopping a short distance to her right. "So you smile and flirt, and men do what you want?"

"Pretty much. It's a birthright of Southern women. We learn it by the time we leave the nursery."

He leaned against the railing, hands next to his hips on the well-worn wood. "Your accent gets heavier when you talk about home."

"Does it?" People had pointed out before that thoughts of home made her sound like a cross between Scarlett O'Hara and Suzanne Sugarbaker. Good Georgia girls. "I bet you don't fall for smiles and flirting."

"I haven't fallen for anything in a long time."

Not since he'd picked up a girl at the feed store and she'd broken his heart. It must have been as close to love at first sight as possible, for them to have married ten days later and him still mourning four years after her death. If he knew the state of her relationship with Aaron at the time he died, he wouldn't want anything to do with her.

She didn't want anything to do with herself.

After a long, pensive quiet, he looked at her. "You ready?"

She nodded, stopped at the table to get her purse and the sweater she hadn't needed, then they went inside the restaurant. They'd reached the vestibule when a man waiting with two small boys did a double-take, then spoke. "Hey, Dalton. I haven't seen you since—"

He broke off, his gaze darting away, leaving no doubt how he would have finished: *since Sandra's funeral.* Color bleeding into his face, he cleared his throat. "In a long time. How're you doing?"

Jessy waited for Dalton's answer. The man she'd met two months ago would have mumbled something and pushed on past. No, that man wouldn't have been here in the first place.

"I'm okay," he said and sounded as if it were at least half true.

"And your parents?"

"They're good. They came through a few days ago."

"Yeah, I ran into them getting gas on their way out of town."

The guy's gaze shifted to Jessy, accompanied by a polite smile and a nod, but Dalton didn't take the hint and introduce her. She was glad he didn't, she told herself, but somewhere deep inside, a part of her smarted at the slight.

The realist chastised her. *Fair's fair. You hoped he wouldn't pick you up until Ilena and Bennie were gone because you didn't want to introduce him to them.*

Of course, Ilena and Bennie wouldn't have waited for an introduction. They would have overwhelmed him with greetings and sly questions until he began looking for the nearest gopher hole to dive into. The margarita girls had that effect on a lot of people.

"Well." The man gestured toward the bathrooms. "We're just waiting on my wife and little girl. It's good to see you."

Dalton looked at the hand he offered before hesitantly taking it, letting go in the fastest handshake in history. "Yeah, you, too," he said even as he ushered Jessy out the door.

Forcing him to slow his pace with her own deliberate steps, Jessy gazed into the starry sky. "Old friend?"

"Yeah. Lives down the road a couple miles."

A neighbor, too, and he hadn't seen Dalton in four and a half years. He'd taken the hermit thing much more seriously than she'd realized. How had he stood grieving alone, with no one but the animals for comfort? She'd done the first eighteen months alone, with only casual friends, co-workers, and pickups for company, and it had almost killed her. If she hadn't met Carly, Therese, and the others when she did, she might not have survived.

But she had survived. Now it was up to her to make something worthwhile of her life.

Again the gentleman, he opened the door and waited while she climbed into the truck. Balancing on the running board, she faced him instead of sliding onto the seat. Finally she had the height advantage. Grasping the brim of his cowboy hat, she pulled it from his head and settled it on her own. It sank to cover her eyes and ears until she tilted it way back, then she studied him. "Do you get tired of being alone?"

Without the hat, he couldn't hide his eyes in the shadows. The moonlight glinted on his face, on every hard line of his somber expression. He was still so long that she thought he could have turned to stone, the way she imagined herself doing, then slowly his lips parted and he exhaled. "Yeah. Sometimes."

She gazed down at him, and he looked back, until the restaurant door banged, followed by kids' voices. He had to know it was his neighbor's family coming out, that they would be heading for one of the few vehicles left in the parking lot, but he didn't tense, jerk his head around to look, or impatiently hustle her into the truck. For that reason, she stepped inside, sitting on the cloth-covered seat, fastening her seat belt.

She removed the hat when it bumped the headrest, started to set it on the console, then rubbed her fingers across it instead. When she heard *straw hat*, she always thought of the rough-woven hats she saw on beach vacations, not the elegant weave of this cowboy hat. It was soft to touch, nubby, and when she lifted it once more to lay it on the console, she caught a whiff of Dalton on it.

She missed manly smells.

The good ones, at least.

Once he was settled, he put the hat on again, backed out of the space, then asked, "AC or windows down?"

"Windows down, please. I spend way too much of my life in air-conditioned places."

"I'll trade you," he said dryly as he lowered the windows.

Of course he spent most of his days outside. The deep bronze of his skin was testament to that, as far as it went. To the best of her fuzzy memories, that was somewhere just south of his waist. From there down, he was paler than she was. And muscular. Well formed. Long legged, narrow hipped, and—

Don't go there, Jessy.

The breeze coming through the windows fluttered a piece of paper from under her seat, tickling her leg as it swirled upward. She caught it, glanced at the Double D Ranch logo on it, then tucked it under a pair of sunglasses in the cup holder. "Men and breasts," she said, faking a reproving tone. "Tell me you didn't name the ranch after Sandra. Better yet, tell me you didn't name it at all."

He sat easily, all loose and comfortable, with one hand resting on the steering wheel. The look he gave her was tinged with just a little bit of humor. "Okay. I didn't name it. The first Smiths to work the land did—Dooley and Donald. Every generation since then has had two sons whose names begin with D to continue the tradition."

His younger brother's name was Noah, which meant... "So it's you and..."

"Don't ask."

His voice was as level and benign as it had been most of the evening, but she sensed he meant the words seriously.

Mystery Brother was obviously not a subject he wanted to talk about. Okay, she had no problem with that. "You know what my parents named my sisters? I'm named after a damned vine, and my sisters are Anne and Mary. You can't get any more normal than that. When Mary was born, it proved what I had suspected all along—that my mother had it in for me."

He snorted. "And you were how old at the time?"

"Three. But I was a very wise three."

"Did Anne and Mary ever rebel?"

Wishing she had long hair so she could take it down and feel the wind blow through it, she combed her fingers through it anyway. "They showed potential when we were young, but by middle school, they'd decided to follow the path of least resistance." She paused a moment, then slyly added, "Traitors," and earned a chuckle from him.

She didn't blame her sisters for taking the easy way out. Their parents were formidable people. *She* had tried her damnedest to be malleable, but something inside had refused to back down, to conform into a perfect, fragile-smiled, superficial mini-Wilkes. Lord, she had regrets, but that wasn't one of them.

Tilting her head, she gazed out the side window into the dark, hearing occasional snatches of barking, catching occasional whiffs of honeysuckle in bloom. No matter how sorry her life was now, it was preferable to the one her parents had wanted for her. That sense of entitlement, smug superiority, absolute lack of obligation, empathy, understanding . . . It would have smothered her.

She'd never felt as free as the day she moved out of the family home. She would never be welcomed back, and the family bank had dispensed its last dollar, but she hadn't cared. She'd walked out anyway, with the sense that *finally* she could breathe.

The rest of the trip passed in silence, and she was okay with that. Sometimes she talked just to hear the sound of a voice, but being quiet with someone else was a whole different thing than being quiet alone. With Dalton—at least, right now—it was mostly comfortable.

When he pulled to the curb in front of her apartment, she wondered if he would walk her to the door or expect to be invited inside for coffee, a drink, sex. The thought made her stomach cramp. She didn't do sex in her apartment, didn't do it without booze, was trying to avoid—

He shifted into park and shut off the engine, and she swallowed hard. But he made no move to undo his seat belt, made no move at all except to turn his head in her direction. "Isn't it noisy living downtown?"

The question pulled her from the mini-panic tumbling in her gut and allowed her to draw a full breath. "Not as much as you'd think. These old buildings are solid. You hear the trains, the church bells on Sunday, big trucks, but regular traffic, people, business, not much."

"Still a lot compared to where I live. Lots of light, too. But at least you have a good warm overlook for the Christmas parade."

Normal conversation. She could do that. She could appreciate that. "Oh, no, no, no. Christmas parades are meant to be enjoyed up close and personal, in the cold—preferably snow—and near enough to snag an occasional piece of candy thrown to the little ones. After I've ogled the firefighters, waved at Santa Claus, and admired the horses, *then* I go inside and warm up with a mug of hot chocolate." With a splash of dark rum, Kahlua, or Bailey's.

Again she swallowed hard, for a totally different reason. She wished she could blink and it would be morning. She would feel stronger in the morning, with bright sunlight and the promise of a hot day.

"You spend too much time in heated places if you like the cold."

Jessy shrugged carelessly. "Hey, you can always put on more clothes, but once you've stripped down naked, that's all the cooling you're gonna get."

The image of bare skin and lots of it hung in the air between them, turning the air thick, damn near making it sizzle. Between the two of them, they didn't have a complete recollection of being together, but she'd seen enough of his muscles, his long legs, his broad shoulders, and his solid chest, and she had a smokin' hot imagination.

No, no, no. No naked thoughts, she counseled herself frantically, but damn, once they were there, they were hard to push back into their corner.

Dalton cleared his throat, his voice sounding as if he had a decent imagination himself. "Yeah, tell me that when your prize mare has decided to foal in a subzero wind chill and you're wearing so many clothes you look like the Michelin tire man."

And had a smokin' hot cowboy to help her out of them. Peeling off layers was good. They made reaching the last layer that much more rewarding, stirring steam and heat and hunger…

She would have fanned herself if he wasn't watching. Instead, she focused on the first part of the image he'd conjured—her all bundled up in coveralls and thermals and whatever the hell else ranchers wore to brave the winter temperatures—but it refused to form. That was enough to steer her thoughts in the right direction. After all, for one, she didn't do ugly clothes. Two—she didn't do *birthing* of any sort. Three—well, one and two were enough.

"Sorry, cowboy, that's not happening." She opened the door, gathered her purse and sweater, then looked back at him. "Thanks for dinner. I enjoyed the company."

Though he'd commented earlier about downtown's excess of lights, she couldn't make out the expression on his face before he slowly responded with a bit of a smile. "Yeah. I did, too."

She leaned closer to him, voice lowered, breathing shallowly to avoid the intoxicating scent of him. "Good night, Dalton."

As she slid to the ground, he murmured to her back, "See you later."

Vague words, as much a brush-off as a promise, but they sent a tiny spark of pleasure through her as she closed the door, flashed him a smile through the open window, then sashayed to her apartment door.

She didn't hear the truck pull away until she was locked safely inside. But how safe was it, really? she wondered as thirst tugged at her.

She'd made it through two nights. Would she manage a third, or was she going to be one sorry mess in the morning?

* * *

The only funeral services Lucy had ever thought she would help plan were for her parents, when they were in their eighth or ninth decades, but on Thursday afternoon she found herself at one of the local funeral homes. One of the grimmest places on earth, though she'd been in others even grimmer.

To her left sat Patricia and LoLo Baxter. Declining the offer of a seat, Ben stood behind them, clearly uncomfortable in the setting. While Patricia answered the director's questions about George's background for the obituary, he wandered away. After a moment, Lucy followed him into the room next door, filled with caskets and discreet signs listing their features.

"At least Patricia doesn't have to deal with this," she said quietly when she stopped beside him. "The Army provides it."

He nodded, though his look was distant as if he hadn't really heard her words. He touched the gunmetal finish of one sample casket, then laid his fingertips against the pale gray satin lining. "I was twenty-five when I did my father's funeral arrangements."

"I was twenty-eight when I did Mike's. Thank God, his mother and mine were with me." As soon as she said the words, she grimaced. Ben's mother hadn't been with him, having long since married George. Hopefully, he'd had an aunt, an uncle, a friend, to help him get through it.

"How did you stand it? Losing your husband so young?"

She stared at the rich grain of the only wood casket in the room. It was mahogany, elegant and expensive and far too beautiful to lower into the ground and cover with dirt. The body it was meant to hold was no longer anyone's loved one. It was just a symbol for a spirit that had already moved on.

After a time, she sighed softly. "I got through the first year the way most of us do—sheer will. I went to work at a job I didn't like, came home every night to a house that was no longer home, wondered every other day why I didn't move back to California, where I'd have family to get me through the days, and I did a lot of crying on Marti's shoulder. Then on the anniversary of Mike's death, I realized I had two choices: I could give up and disappoint Mike, or I could start living again. I cleaned out his closet, got a new job, stopped avoiding everyone, and started over."

It sounded so simple put that way, but it hadn't been. Every choice had been difficult, every action unbearably tough. Even getting groceries had been traumatic—seeing couples and families in the aisles, automatically reaching for Mike's favorites, scaling down to feed only one. How many times had she gone to the commissary and left without a single purchase because she didn't have a clue how to be *one* instead of part of a couple?

"Everyone recovers on their own schedule," she went on, moving slowly to look at the other caskets, grateful she would never have a need for one. After seeing Mike's body, all decked out in his dress uniform, the left chest decorated with ribbons and medals, after watching his casket lowered into the ground at Fort Rosecrans National Cemetery in San Diego, and getting on a plane to leave California and him behind, she'd decided cremation was for her.

"My friend Marti—we were friends before the margarita club. Mike and Joshua were in the same unit and died in the same battle." Her voice choked. The only thing worse than getting a notification call was your best friend getting one at the same time. "Anyway, Marti finds comfort in physical things. She's still got everything Joshua ever owned. Our friend Ilena gave away Juan's stuff within a month or so. She carries him in her heart. She doesn't need external reminders. Your mom—"

A muscle twitched in his jaw, and she quickly corrected herself. "Patricia's in a different place. Where Ilena and Marti and Carly and the rest of us didn't have enough time with our husbands, Patricia had twenty years with George. He would have retired in a year or so, and they had a lot of plans that didn't include traveling. They'd seen the world already. They had projects around the house, volunteer work they were going to do, charities they were going to work with." She hesitated, then delicately went on. "They were going to *be* together—go to bed every night and wake up every morning in the same bed, share meals, share activities, share their blessings."

Again, that muscle in Ben's jaw twitched. He looked at her, his gaze intense. This place stirred bleak memories for him, too, of the father who'd died too young, of the man Ben had been forced to become too soon. "Funny," he murmured. "Those were pretty much the same plans my dad had."

She stopped in front of a heartbreakingly small casket, pale pink metal with white satin lining. Like most of the margarita club, she and Mike had thought they had plenty of time to start a family. Of them all, only Ilena had had the good luck to get pregnant, and that had been due to a birth control failure. Time had taken the edge off Lucy's longing for kids, but sometimes it swelled up with a raw ache, especially since her last birthday.

Deliberately she turned her back on the casket. "I take it the divorce wasn't his choice."

Ben shoved his hands into his hip pockets and rocked back on his heels. "No one had a choice but Patricia. We sat down to dinner one night without Dad—she'd already surprised the hell out of him—and she announced that she was leaving. She'd already talked to a lawyer, and as soon as the divorce went through, she was marrying George. In the meantime, she was leaving to be with him. Within two hours, she destroyed our family and was on a plane to Germany. I was fifteen, the girls eleven and nine. We didn't see her again for three years."

Sympathy welled through Lucy. Having your family fall apart around you would always be hard, but for the news to come out of nowhere, to find out that your mother had fallen in love with another man and chosen him over her own husband and children...No wonder he was still bitter.

The part of her that wanted to understand both sides spoke up: Did the fact that Patricia had loved George mitigate her guilt? Clearly, they'd been meant for each other, or their marriage wouldn't have lasted and flourished. Absolutely, it was wrong for her to get involved with him while still married to Ben's father, but shouldn't that mistake be forgiven if she truly regretted it?

Hesitantly, Lucy touched Ben's arm, sending heat sizzling through her palm. How wrong was it to be sensually aware of someone in the casket showroom of a funeral home? But it had been six long years since she'd felt this kind of attraction to a man, six years without cuddling or kissing or making love, without feeling a strong pair of arms around her in the night, and the lonely woman inside her missed all that, Lord, more than she could say.

Mentally shaking off the thoughts, she said, "I'm sorry, Ben. That must have been a really tough thing for you and your sisters and especially your father. I don't blame you for feeling wronged." At fifteen, he'd had a good grasp of concepts like fidelity, honor, trustworthiness. Finding out his mother lacked them all, at least with regards to their family, had hurt deeply, no doubt.

"Everyone's sorry, Lucy," he said. The softness of his voice was at odds with the emotion starkly written on his features. "But 'sorry' doesn't make anything okay."

When he left the room, she remained where she was, wishing she had the superpower to make everything okay. So much sorrow, so much anger and hurt and betrayal... *But how would we appreciate the good times, child, if we didn't go through the bad?* her grandmother's voice whispered in her head.

Nana was probably right—she always was—but Lucy would still like to give nothing-but-good a shot.

"You okay?"

She blinked and saw LoLo standing a few feet in front of her. The woman could have posed for a recruiting poster, her body well toned, her posture erect, her face unlined, minimally made up, and not beautiful exactly, but stunning. Everything about her whispered competent, controlled, dignified, compassionate. Lucy envied and adored her.

"Yeah." It was true. She'd be much happier if George hadn't been killed, if she'd spent the past three days going to work and worrying about nothing more than keeping Norton from peeing where he shouldn't. But given that she couldn't control life or death or heartache, she was doing okay.

"The colonel's remains will arrive in Tulsa on Tuesday morning. There will be a visitation at the funeral home that evening, and the service will be Wednesday morning at the post chapel."

Lucy contained the shudder that rippled through her. Such a simple statement: *The colonel's remains will arrive Tuesday morning.* But it meant so much more. Having Mike home had made the whole nightmare even realer. It had put Lucy that much closer to the final end of their life together. All her love, all her prayers, all her dreams, all for nothing. Once he'd arrived home, the only thing left for her to do was say good-bye.

The hardest word she'd ever known.

LoLo touched her arm. "I'm going to the airport with Patricia. You and I both know how difficult the transfer is. You do not have to go through it again."

A shiver ripped through Lucy. "Is Ben going to be there?"

"He has to reschedule a couple surgeries, but he plans to."

Lucy examined her fingernails, thinking she needed a manicure—a pedicure, too, while she was at it—soon. Definitely before Tuesday. Finally, having avoided LoLo long enough, she met her gaze. "I'm a strong woman."

"I know. But this isn't about strength, Lucy. It's about protecting your heart from breaking again. The chaplain and I will be with her. Her pastor and his wife will join us. Ben will likely be there. We will take care of her."

Lucy's exhalation was soft but sounded cowardly in her own ears. "I was just thinking yesterday that I couldn't go through another dignified transfer. Everything else, anything else, but..."

LoLo hugged her. "You're a good friend, Lucy. You've been a lifesaver for Patricia these past few days, and we both know you'll be there for her in the months to come. Leave this one thing to us."

Chapter 7

It appeared Patricia's business with the funeral director was almost finished as they stood near the desk, her hand clasped in his. Ben glanced at Lucy and Major Baxter in the display room, then toward the glass double doors that led into the warm sun. He doubted he could really smell anything inside besides the overly strong air freshener, that any other odors were the product of his imagination. Still, he had spent enough time there.

He crossed the lobby in a few paces, pushed the door open, and stepped into the sun. The heat seemed doubly hot against his cool skin, and it took longer for it to soak in than he'd expected. Maybe because some of the chill inside him had nothing to do with temperature. Automatically he pulled his phone out to switch the ring audio from vibrate to loud and found a text message from Brianne. *Do you have a date and time yet?*

He hadn't discussed the funeral with either of his sisters,

but he'd known if one of them decided to attend, it would be Brianne. The older sister was a businesswoman, compassionate, a Nice Woman. While he and Sara understood the idea of forgiveness, Brianne got the reality of it. No bad karma for her.

Rather than texting the information, he dialed her cell, then walked thirty feet from the doors, turning to face them so no one could surprise him.

"This is Brianne." Her voice was pleasant, but he recognized the distracted tone.

"George's remains will arrive in Tulsa on Tuesday, funeral will be Wednesday."

"Hello to you, too. I'm fine. How are you?" It was easy to imagine her shaking her head in dismay. "Will there be a big deal like you see on the local news—people at the airport, escorts, and everything?"

"Apparently so."

"Will you be there?"

He bent his head side to side until his neck creaked, releasing the tension there. "Apparently so." Major Baxter had taken a private moment to ask him that, to give her opinion that it might be too much for Lucy. She'd already done so much for Patricia, and the last thing he wanted was for her to go through another wrenching reminder of her husband's death.

"Give me the details," Brianne requested, and he told her everything.

"Are you coming to the funeral?" Though he'd known she would be the one most likely to come, he was a little surprised, too.

She didn't sidestep the question. "Yes. Whatever's wrong between us, she is our mother, and he is—was her husband and a decorated United States Army soldier. That in itself deserves respect."

After a moment, in a less certain tone, she added, "Showing respect doesn't mean forgetting the past, Ben. But if Mom and I get to the point where we can put it behind us, I don't want the fact that I skipped her husband's funeral to get in the way."

Mom. They hadn't called her that in years. Ben always used her first name, and Sara's go-to was *she* or *her.* *Mom* felt foreign, too affectionate, a name she hadn't earned.

Quietly he asked, "Do you want her back in your life?"

The silence went on so long that he might have thought the phone had dropped the call if not for the slow, steady breathing coming over the line. Finally came a sigh. "She was a huge part of our lives, Ben. She's our *mother.* If not for her, we wouldn't be here. She made mistakes, no doubt about that. But we never knew why she left, why she fell in love with George or . . . why she fell out of love with Daddy."

How could she have fallen out of love with their dad? That was the one thing Ben had never been able to understand.

The funeral director opened one door, then stepped outside to hold it for the women. Though they were too far away to hear, he lowered his voice even more. "How long have you felt this way, Bree?"

"Twenty years."

Twenty—the entire time Patricia had been gone. "You never said . . ."

She laughed. "You and Sara always had very strong opinions of your own. I didn't want to be the odd one out. Besides, with Daddy so sad . . ." With a breath, her voice strengthened. "Someday I'm going to get married, have babies. They'll never know their grandpa, but maybe they can know Grandma. Maybe they can have one more person to love them and spoil them. You can never have too many of those, can you?"

His gaze settled on the subject of their conversation. She wore light green pants, a flowery shirt that matched, high-heeled sandals, and the full makeup routine. While waiting for the major to meet them, she'd fretted over her hair and nails, asking Lucy to remind her to make appointments for the weekend. As if realizing the issues were insignificant in the bigger picture, she'd smiled ruefully and said, *George always appreciated me making the effort for him.*

His dad had always appreciated her made up, dressed up, dressed down, in anything at all.

"You can't hold that against me, Ben," Brianne said, her stubborn intent clear in her voice. "I won't let you. We're all grown up. You get to choose for yourself. I get to choose for myself."

"Of course I wouldn't hold it against you," he replied, using his free hand to pinch the bridge of his nose. Holding a grudge against Patricia was one thing, but Brianne...she was his little sister. Nothing could make him turn his back on her. "Listen, Bree, I've got to go. I guess I'll see you Wednesday."

"If not before. Take care of yourself."

"Yeah, you, too." Sliding the phone into his pocket, he started across the parking lot to his mother.

* * *

Jessy made it through Wednesday night, and she'd gotten through Thursday morning, too, without pulling one of the bottles out of the liquor cabinet, but by three thirty, she was holding on by her fingernails. She'd been pacing the apartment since lunch, getting one step closer to the kitchen every time, when it occurred to her that maybe pacing outside would help.

When was the last time she'd gone for a walk? Not a quick rush to the bank because she'd overslept or a hike across a parking lot because all the close spots were taken or walking to Three Amigos most Tuesday nights so she could drink and not drive afterward, but an actual walk. A stroll. Purely for pleasure.

She couldn't remember.

A pair of practically new running shoes sat on a shelf in the closet. The girls had laughed when she brought them, cracking jokes about how they would dwarf the sandals and boots and strappy heels that spoke to her soul. They'd said she would never wear them again after the occasion she'd bought them for—one of their outings in March to Turner Falls—and they'd been right. All she'd done since was move them from one place to another to make room for something barely there and sexy.

Before she could talk herself out of it, she put on a pair of cute little socks that, sadly, weren't meant to show, then laced the runners, grabbed her keys and cell, and headed downstairs. When she got outside, she wavered, unsure which way to turn. She never left the apartment without a destination in mind, even if it was only to *get out of town*. With a mental coin flip, she headed east.

She liked Tallgrass with its old brick and sandstone buildings, murals painted on walls, and quaint feel—and she meant quaint in the good way. It wasn't fancy, though there were a bunch of houses that wouldn't look out of place in the neighborhood she'd grown up in. It wasn't just a town that existed to support the fort, either. If the Army closed Fort Murphy next week, Tallgrass would live on, smaller, less busy, with fewer options, but still a nice town.

Wishing she'd brought earbuds to give her a little music to stroll to, she passed a twenty-four-hour gym in a space that had once been a five-and-dime. Could intense exertion deliver enough feel-good endorphins to make any additional self-medication unnecessary? If it would, much as she hated sweating, she would willingly show up sixteen hours a day. Talk about buff then.

She took a left when she reached the last intersection before Buddy Watson's. It was the most respectable of the downtown clubs, a place where businessmen ate lunch and stopped after work. It wasn't her favorite, but it got a few points for its location. With her nerves on edge and her mouth watering, it could *be* her favorite for the next few hours.

No no no no. It had been three and a half days. Surely she could make it four. What kind of sorry-ass loser couldn't make it four days?

Her gaze focused on the sidewalk ahead, she pushed on, one step after another. She didn't let her mind wander to anything beyond those steps, the cracks in the sidewalk, the occasional car she had to let pass before crossing the street. She left businesses behind, passed a church and an elementary school, newly abandoned for the summer, and moved into a residential neighborhood. The trees were tall, established long ago, and the houses, some suffering neglect more than others, were firmly rooted in their yards.

Next time she would bring her camera and document them. The well-maintained ones would shine on their own. The shabbier ones, in stark black-and-white tones, would be poignant, faded memories of better times.

As she walked, the houses thinned, with shrinking footage on shrinking lots, until the final block: no structures at all, but sidewalks and concrete steps showing where they had once been. Alerted by barking, she raised her gaze to the view and saw she'd reached the end of the street, the dividing line between town and country.

The only thing ahead of her was a large building, constructed of tin siding over a sturdy metal frame, and the only thing gazing back was a dog behind a chain-link fence. His dignity should have been reduced to nothing thanks to the round plastic cone that encircled his head, but he didn't cower or try to hide. He simply stood there and stared.

Jessy's clunky shoes crunched on gravel as she crossed the parking lot and went to the fence. Signs posted every five feet warned against sticking fingers inside the fence— if a person needed the warning, wasn't he likely too dumb to heed it?—and another sign, attached to the building, identified it as the Tallgrass Animal Shelter.

"Hey, puppy."

Like her, the dog stood about three feet back from the chain-link. He wasn't very big and lacked the giant paws that suggested he would get that way. In fact, he was very...elegant, even with the ridiculous cone. He deserved a better life than a shelter.

Didn't they all.

"I never knew you guys lived here. I should get out more often."

He cocked his head to one side, looking as if he was

listening intently. He probably was, for the magic words: *cookie, treat, walk, go for a ride*. Though it was pointless, Jessy checked her pockets. Still just keys and cell phone. She hadn't even brought her debit card, thinking it might lead her into temptation, while knowing for a fact what she'd told Dalton last night: She could get a drink. She just wouldn't have to pay.

Slowly more dogs approached, rousing themselves from the shady enclosure next to the building, others coming from around back. They were every color, size, and breed, yippy and silent, curious and wary. They all had one thing in common: Their families hadn't wanted them.

"I can so relate, puppies," she said dryly.

"I'm glad I'm not the only one who carries on conversations with them when no one's around." A woman coming from the direction of the front door offered Jessy one of the two bottles of cold water she carried, then drank down half of her own. Her hair was blond on the ends, dark gold where the roots were soaked with sweat. Her clothes were stained and dirty, and her work boots looked better suited to a roofer on top of a newly built house, but her manicure was damn near perfect, the coral polish popping against the drabness of everything else.

"I figure they have to understand at least as much as most men I know," Jessy replied before taking a drink of water. It was incredibly just-shy-of-frozen cold and made her throat tingle on the way down. Of all the things she'd drunk—and hadn't drunk—the past week, it truly was refreshing. She should buy this brand.

"Isn't that true." The woman offered her right hand. "I'm Angela, the director here. Are you interested in a new pet, or have you come about the ad?"

Jessy blinked. She'd been meaning all week to pick up the local paper for a job search, but it kept slipping her mind. It was as if she had more important things to think about. Like Dalton.

And staying sober.

A job at the animal shelter would probably include duties like poopy-scooping, de-fleaing, de-ticking, and bathing dogs who weren't accustomed to a weekly spa day. She could easily imagine a half-dozen or so disasters awaiting to befall her if she said yes. *But you're facing disasters anyway, Jess, and at least you wouldn't be dealing much with people. Wasn't that what you wanted?*

Mrs. Dauterive would say this was exactly where she belonged, with a lot of mangy unwanted animals. Julia and the rest of the bank staff would give her pitying looks. With the margarita club, if it made her happy, by God they would be happy.

"Yes," she said cheerfully. "I'm here to apply for the job."

She followed Angela inside and filled out an application that was as thorough as the bank's. She didn't mind. She'd be just as leery of some stranger taking care of her animals, if she had any, as she would of someone taking care of her money.

Angela skimmed the form, then gave Jessy a smile. "It'll be tomorrow before I can check your references, then I'll give you a call. I can tell you it looks good, sweetie, 'cause you're the only one who's applied so far."

It hadn't occurred to her that others might be vying for the job. How would it feel, being told she wasn't good enough to shovel dog poop? *Please,* she prayed to whoever might be listening, *don't make me find out for myself.*

Jessy allowed herself a flashy grin. "Some people have a talent for shoveling shit—I mean poop," she hastily corrected, "and some don't. I suspect I do."

"Then you'll fit in perfectly here," Angela replied with a laugh. "I hate to chase you off, but I've got an appointment in town. Can I give you a ride?"

"Thanks, no. Exercise, you know." Like she did it every day. Saying good-bye while Angela locked up, Jessy stopped at the fence, finding the same dog in the same spot, and said good-bye to him, lighthearted enough to give him a grin, too. Leaning forward, she conspiratorially whispered, "Next time I'll bring treats."

* * *

Showered, shaved, and dressed in clean clothes, Dalton made it as far as the front door before Oz leaped from the recliner and trotted over, nosing the door as he waited impatiently.

"Not tonight, Oz. I already told you."

The shepherd head-butted the door and whined.

"I know you had to stay home alone last night—like that was any big deal. When I came home, you were asleep in the same place as when I'd left."

Oz looked up at him, unblinking. The mutt actually succeeded in making Dalton feel a little...Not guilty. Manipulated. "No. Last time. Back off." Then he rolled his eyes. "Crap, I'm explaining myself to a dog. What the hell?"

He nudged the dog aside, ordered him to stay, then went out the door. Oz followed his progress from one window to the next, whining, barking little squeaks of displeasure.

"By the time I back out, he'll be curled up on his chair," Dalton muttered, then rolled his eyes again. "Talking to myself now. Is that one step up from the dog or down?"

Down, he was pretty sure. Maybe more than one step.

He hadn't planned to leave the ranch today, until the phone call around lunchtime. It was Dane Clark, inviting him to dinner to meet his fiancée, Carly. His first impulse had been to make an excuse, but he'd been following bad impulses for a long time and they hadn't made anything better.

No more.

So here he was, headed into Tallgrass early on a Thursday evening. Hell, he'd done it enough times this week that his truck could make the trip on autopilot. He was going to Dane's house, and he was going to do his best to be the polite, sociable person his mother had raised him to be. He was out of practice—not so much now, thanks to Jessy, as he'd been a week ago—but he could do it. He needed to do it. Starting that day back in March, she'd made him want more from life.

When the dirt road bisected the highway, he sat for a moment at the stop sign, recalling the sight of Jessy perched on the board fence or crouched at the edge of the ditch, so intent on what she saw through her camera that she hardly noticed anything else.

He had no talent with a camera. Even with the small digital he owned, things came out blurry, heads cut off, or just plain boring. When he needed photos of his stock, he hired someone to come in and take them.

Though he'd never seen her work, it was a fair bet that it was top-notch. The intensity in her expression, the comfort she felt with the equipment, her fingers moving fast and sure over the various adjustments...It was the way he worked, repeating actions he'd made ten thousand times over the years.

The miles into town passed quickly. His truck bumped over the railroad tracks that were a rough marker of city limits, and then he was passing the flower shop where he bought bouquets for Sandra's grave. A block south of that, a figure on the east side of the street caught his attention. It was hard to miss such fiery red hair anytime, especially when the woman was the only one on the sidewalk for blocks in either direction. Especially when, from the back, she looked just like Jessy.

She wore blue shorts with lots of pockets and a white T-shirt that played up the gold of her skin. Her shoes were gray and pink, walking shoes like most women wore, but they seemed out of place, because Jessy preferred much more delicate shoes.

His hands gripped the steering wheel, his foot automatically shifting from the gas pedal to the brake, before he turned onto the next street. It *was* Jessy, looking girl-next-door, active, walking as if it were a breezy eighty degrees instead of a humid ninety-four. Jessy, her face red, her skin glistening with sweat, lost somewhere inside her head as she tapped an empty water bottle against her palm.

He stopped as soon as he made the turn, and she stopped as soon as she became aware of him. After a moment, she swiped one hand through her hair, slicking it back, then came toward him.

He'd never seen her looking quite so wholesome and sexy and sweet. Any makeup she'd put on had long since sweated away, and the pink tinge to the skin exposed by the rounded neck of her shirt suggested she'd been out longer than she was accustomed to. She wasn't carrying a purse, though she could have hidden all its contents, including her camera, in those shorts pockets, and those shoes . . .

"What are you doing?" he asked when she was close enough.

"It's called walking. It's the oldest method of getting from here to there known to man. It tones your muscles, burns calories, and revs up your metabolism."

"You're *exercising*?" He appreciated her body—had appreciated it one day for a couple hours. Naked. But he just figured she had great genes, like she'd said. He couldn't picture her working out. That was like Scarlett O'Hara in spandex and sweatband training for a 5K.

"Dear God, no. I'm taking a walk. You know, strolling aimlessly taking in the beauty around me?"

"You picked the wrong part of town. There's not much beauty here."

She didn't bother to glance around, as if she was all too aware that these few blocks weren't one of Tallgrass's selling points. "Of course there is. There's the sky. The clouds. The trees." She gestured with both hands, then pointed to the ground. "Look at that flower. It's beautiful."

"It's a dandelion."

"A beautiful dandelion. I bet I could take a picture of it, print it, frame it, and it would be so incredible that even you wouldn't mind hanging it on your wall."

He leaned back against the truck, the heat absorbing through his shirt into his skin. "Let's say I agree so you don't actually have to take the picture."

Her snort reminded him of his most spoiled mare. "You mean, so you don't have to actually hang it on your wall."

His only response to that was a shrug before he gestured

to her water bottle. "You went for a walk in this heat with only one small bottle of water?"

She studied the bottle before dropping it to her side. "Nope. I didn't think to take any. The woman who runs the animal shelter gave it to me. Hey, it's my first walk. Give me a break. Besides..." She ran her hand through her hair again, deep coppery red where it was wet. "I wasn't exactly planning on walking so far. I learned the first lesson of going for a stroll today: However far you walk, that's how far back you've gotta go."

"Unless someone takes pity and offers you a ride."

"Yeah." She squinted at him. "Are you taking pity?"

He replied with a nod of his head toward the passenger door. She may have been hot and tired, but she hustled around the truck and climbed in in less time than it took Dalton to turn, open the door, and do the same.

Jessy turned the passenger's air-conditioning vents directly on her, one on her face, the other on her body, then gave a low groan. "I love heat, I do, but damn, that cold feels good."

He glanced at her, saw the tiny goose bumps rising on her arms, damp red hair fluttering back from her face, her nipples hardening under the thin fabric of her top. With a knot in his throat, he deliberately looked forward again while listening to the sounds of her seat belt fastening, and slowly pulled away from the curb. "So you walked all the way to the animal shelter, where they took pity on you and gave you water."

She kicked off one shoe, then the other, and propped both feet on the dash. "Yeah, the dogs wouldn't share theirs. Damn, do you know how hot these shoes are?"

Her legs were damp, too, and her socks were soaked.

They were white, with black skulls centered in red hearts. They didn't even reach her ankle bone, and from there up it was all smooth tanned skin, right up to where the shorts hugged her thighs.

This was some kind of payback for trying to be sociable—everything about her, sweat and all, looking damn good.

"I wear leather boots all day," he said, his voice huskier than he wanted. "You won't get any sympathy from me on a pair of lightweight nylon walking shoes."

She made that dismissive sound again before saying, "I didn't realize ranchers spent so much time in town."

He wasn't that far out—six, seven miles—but he'd always preferred to keep his town visits to a minimum except for the times he'd been dating someone. Those seemed a lifetime ago. "I usually don't. I'm having dinner with a guy I know." He didn't mention it was Dane Clark or that he was going to meet her good friend Carly for the first time. He wasn't sure why.

He turned at the next street, and within moments, he was parking in front of Jessy's building. Her feet hit the floorboard with a dull thud, then she bent to scoop up her shoes. "Thanks for the ride."

"You're not putting those on?"

She gazed at the shoes, then the expanse of sidewalk separating them from her door. "I may never put them on again. When I torture my feet, I prefer to do it with something not so functional." She slid out onto the running board, giving him a nice view of legs, butt, and lower back, before ducking down to see him. "If you find yourself back this way after dinner and can spare the time..."

Before he could answer either way, she hopped down

and hotfooted it in her socks to the apartment door. The last thing he saw was a flash of honey-colored legs before the door blocked her from sight.

Come over and see her again. The idea held a lot of appeal, given how rocky their start had been. But things changed, and not always for the worse, as he'd come to believe. Once a man reached flat bottom, there was nowhere to go but up. If he needed a helping hand on that climb back up, well, Jessy's delicate little hand was stronger than it looked.

The house Dane shared with his fiancée was easy to find. The house was small, painted white, the grass lush and green and flowers softening all the straight lines. Dalton's house could use a few flowers, and probably a new coat of paint to boot. But the only thing he was interested in growing was livestock, and the next paint job on his list was the barn. It wasn't like there was a woman living there who cared about flowers or paint. His mother had, but Sandra hadn't, and Jessy . . . He squinted into the evening sun, remembering her pleasure with the wildflowers but failing to picture her as a gardener.

Though there was still a hell of a lot about her that he didn't know.

The front door opened as he climbed the steps, and a woman greeted him with a smile. Dalton had seen her a few times at Three Amigos. He'd been there the night Dane had proposed to her, though no one knew. He'd gone with the intent of approaching the margarita club, but then he'd seen Jessy, so he'd drunk alone at the bar instead.

"You must be Dalton."

"I haven't been offered any other options today, so I must be." He took the hand she extended for a quick shake.

She rolled her eyes. "It's kind of a pointless question, isn't it? I'm Carly Lowry. Dane's out back watching the grill. Come on in."

She ushered him inside, where he got a quick glimpse of rooms on the way to the back door: burnt orange living room, gray dining room, light yellow hallway, white-and-blue kitchen. He corrected his earlier thought. His house couldn't just use a coat of paint. Compared to this place, it *needed* it.

"Dalton's here, babe," Carly said from the doorway. "You need anything?"

"No, I've got it. Thanks. Hey, Dalton, have a seat."

Dane *was* watching the grill, from the comfort of a lawn chair, the wood stained dark, the cushion fat and the color of rust. Wearing shorts, he rested his prosthetic leg on a matching footstool, propped his good leg next to it, and cradled a bottle of beer in both hands.

"Dane." Dalton chose another chair, red and white flowers on the same rusty background, and stretched out his legs. A light breeze tinkled the chimes hanging from a catalpa tree and carried the thin aroma of charring food from the grill. Nearby a table was set for three, across the patio from a fountain that sounded like his favorite stretch of creek at home.

"There's drinks in the cooler there." Dane pointed to the small chest between their chairs. "Carly and I made a deal that I'd take care of the grill if she'd do the rest. I'm not sure she realized my part's a lot easier. Drink beer, flip things once in a while, then take 'em off."

"Or she gave you the easy job on purpose." Dalton scanned the contents of the cooler—bottled water, pop, and beer—and pulled a long-necked bottle from the ice.

"That may be. I'm not much good in the kitchen, but I *can* grill. How's the ranch business?"

"Hard as hell and don't pay worth a damn." His dad used to say that, picking it up from his own father. Dalton hadn't thought of it for a long time.

"Sounds like the Army, son."

"Yeah, well, at least the cattle and horses don't try to kill me. They're satisfied with just kicking me into next week from time to time."

Dane laughed. He'd changed in the past couple months. When Dalton had met him back in March, the soldier had been going through a tough time, back from the desert alive but not yet in a place where he truly appreciated it. It had taken time—and Carly—for him to get to that place.

If Sandra had given herself time, could she have learned to be thankful for what she had?

Could Dalton learn to be thankful for what *he* had? For what he *could* have?

"I'm done with being a target," Dane said. "Carly and I finally decided. I'm transitioning out, going back to school, and finishing my degree. I'm probably going to end up teaching school."

"Good for you." Being indoors all day with a bunch of kids...Dalton would rather be a target. But if that was what Dane wanted—and it was pretty damn sure what Carly wanted; she'd already lost her first husband to war—good for both of them.

"It's not jumping out of airplanes," Dane said with a shrug, "but I can be happy."

And that was all that mattered, wasn't it? Being healthy, being happy, and having hope. Dalton had the first one, and it was looking like he could have the second two, as well.

And if the thought of being happy brought a picture of Jessy Lawrence to mind...Good. Good for him.

*   *   *

The clock on the kitchen wall said four minutes to eight when Lucy walked in. She'd been home three times throughout the day to let Norton out, but this time she was back for the night. After Patricia had finished at the funeral home, they'd gone to Pansy's Flowers to choose floral displays, then to the Sandersons' church to meet with the pastor about the service and the music. The last few hours had been spent going through Patricia's clothes to pick suitable outfits for the dignified transfer, the viewing, and the service.

I won't wear black, she'd said, her smile unsteady, her eyes overly bright. *George loved color. He never wanted me to have even one little black dress, and he didn't give a good damn how classic it was. Don't you wear it, either, Lucy. Let's make him smile up there in Heaven with our pretty outfits.*

Lucy was happy to comply, she reflected as she filled Norton's food dish, then his water bowl. No matter how many times she heard it, she didn't look any slimmer when she wore black. She just looked like a fat chick wearing black.

"Norton!" she called. She rarely managed to set the food dish on the floor before the mutt came tearing into the room, colliding with the furniture and walls on his way.

She listened. No scrabbling of claws on wood, no snoring. She was about to head down the hall to the bedroom—the center of her bed was his likeliest location—when a knock at the back door stopped her. Switching directions, she did a cursory look through the glass and saw Joe on the patio.

"Is my dog out there with you?" she asked as she opened the door.

"Yeah. We decided it was a fine night for dining al fresco."

"Norton doesn't even know what al fresco means. Want something to drink?"

"Nah, I've got water."

Barefooted, Joe turned to go back to the patio table while she stopped by the fridge. She nudged her shoes off before stepping out the door, padded across the still-warm concrete, and sat in the chair nearest his, also still warm from the day's sun. Her body seemed to sink and sink into the cushion as the tightness drained from her, head to toe.

They sat silently for a while, whippoorwills and bob-whites singing unseen in the trees. Norton lay beside Joe's chair, his spare food dish empty, the water dish half so. Remains of a pizza from The Hideaway sat in the box on the table, beside three empty water bottles. The fourth was in Joe's hand.

Lucy was raising her can of pop when she felt his chastising look. A little bit of guilt tickled the back of her neck. Despite her intentions, she hadn't yet started her diet—it was hard when she was eating virtually every meal at someone else's house, where she had no say in the menu—but still, she should have chosen water if for no other reason than to avoid a repeat of this conversation.

"Do you know how bad that stuff is for you?"

She glanced at the familiar logo on the can, then took a defiant swallow. "I do."

"It's full of chemicals. One can has a hundred and fifty calories. If you drink one a day for a year, that's 54,750 calories. Each can has twenty-eight grams of simple carbs. Plain old sugar. And it doesn't even quench your thirst."

"But sometimes it's the only thing that'll do. Besides, I'm not one of your students, Joe."

"You're telling me. My students listen."

She punched him, though with all his muscle, it hurt her hand more that it did his arm. "That's rude."

"Drinking that stuff is nasty. And we didn't even get to what it does to your teeth."

"My teeth are fine and none of your business," she retorted. "I can't believe the man who brought Krispy Kreme doughnuts over here on the first day of my diet is now criticizing my one splurge for the day." That little bit of guilt stirred again.

Joe slid lower in his chair to prop his feet on the seat across from him, tilting his head back to gaze into the darkening sky. "You're on a diet?"

Bless his heart—he didn't say *again?* She did diets. She just never managed to do them well enough or long enough. When she'd started a diet to get into the cute summery clothes everyone else was wearing, he'd told her that her motivation was the problem. She had to want it for herself—her health, her well-being, her own personal goals that had nothing to do with fashion or clothing or anything else.

"I just want to lose ten or fifteen pounds," she said, miffed that she sounded defensive. "They say if you lose just ten percent of your total weight, it makes drastic improvements to your health."

Bless his heart again—he didn't do the math to figure

out what ten percent of her total weight actually was. "What about exercise?"

Lucy mimicked his position. "I've been a little preoccupied this week."

"Luce, you're preoccupied *every* week. It's called life. You still have to make time to work out." He swigged more water. "Meet me in the morning at six."

The sedentary loved-her-sleep part of her cringed at the idea. "I'm going to work tomorrow."

"You don't have to be there until eight. We'll just walk around the neighborhood."

She *hmphed*. "I've seen you walk. I have to take three steps for every one of yours."

"I'll slow down." He poked her shoulder, and again she was pretty sure it hurt her more than him. He was so solid, and she was so soft. "Luce, I'm offering to help you lose those ten pounds, and I won't even say anything about the timing of your new diet versus your meeting Dr. Ben."

A blush burned her cheeks, making her grateful the dusk hid it. Was she so gracelessly juvenile that she couldn't hide a crush from anyone? Oh, crap, was Ben aware of it, as well? Was he amused? Embarrassed? Wondering how to let her down gently?

Though he did seem to like her. It wasn't impossible. Joe was good-looking, hot, had a great body, and he liked her. Not romantically, but that had never even been a desire for either of them. They were just best buds. But Ben *could* like her in a boyfriend/girlfriend sort of way. Stranger things had happened.

Joe was smart about this diet/exercise stuff. He coached football, taught nutrition and fitness. Part of his job was to help people get in shape and stay there, and she liked spending time with him. If he was willing to help her, wasn't helping herself the least she could do?

Her forehead wrinkled into a scowl. "Six o'clock, huh? Is the sun even up then?"

His grin was quick, charming, teasing. "You'll find out tomorrow."

She was wondering just how much she might regret it when her cell rang. She glanced at the screen. "This is Marti. I haven't talked to her since Tuesday."

"Go ahead." He got to his feet and gathered his trash. "I'll see you at the butt-crack of dawn."

After giving him a wave, she raised the phone to her ear. "Hey, sweetie, long time."

"Yeah, I know you've been busy."

Marti Levin was another of her besties. She was blessed to have so many. Marti was everything Lucy wasn't— tall, elegant, reed-slender, black-haired and fair-skinned, beamed confidence, and had never met a stranger. She told great stories and had a knack for making people laugh, though she insisted she wasn't funny. *All you need is a mother like mine.*

Marti asked about Patricia, and Lucy filled her in. The margarita club members had all agreed to meet up at Jessy's before lining up on the street for George's dignified transfer and to sit together at the funeral. Though only Marti had met the Sandersons, and then only once, being there was the sort of thing they did for each other.

"So we'll have the Memorial Day parade on Monday morning, the cookout at Carly's that afternoon, the dignified transfer Tuesday, and the funeral Wednesday," Marti listed. "A full start to the week."

"Oh, I forgot about the cookout." Their first Memorial

Day, they'd had a picnic at Tall Grass Lake. This year, with Dane and Therese's fiancé, Keegan, to man the grill, they'd settled on a cookout. Everyone was bringing dishes, and she'd been assigned desserts. Wonderful. More temptation.

She thought of Patricia—her first Memorial Day as a widow and she hadn't even buried her husband yet—but it didn't seem appropriate to invite a grieving widow to a party. Plus, her sister and a couple of nieces were due to arrive sometime that day.

It didn't seem appropriate to invite Ben, either. Though she hated the idea of anyone being alone on a holiday, she was pretty sure he wouldn't be in a party mood.

"You're not canceling, are you?" Marti's voice held a note of warning.

"Oh, no. If I can't be with my family in El Cajon, I want to be with my family in Tallgrass."

"Good, because I'd hate to have to drag you in a head-lock all the way to Carly's house, but I could. My brothers taught me how."

Marti was the last of the margarita girls, along with Ilena, whom Lucy could imagine getting physical. She figured Jessy could do some serious harm, and she *knew* Fia could. Therese had grown up on a ranch, and Carly wrangled third-graders all day, so they had some experience. But anyone who annoyed Ilena would get loved to death, and Marti—well, she wasn't going to risk her manicure or muss her clothing for less than a life-or-death situation.

"You and whose army?" Lucy responded to the threat.

"Don't underestimate me, California girl. I'm an Army wife—"

"And I am strong," they said together.

"Damn straight. Now, what's been keeping you so busy

that you haven't even texted me this week? I know the number one answer is Patricia, of course, but I'm pretty sure she's had some alone time. I heard Jessy say something about her having a son come visit who would probably be, oh, about our age. Is that what you're doing when she's resting? Comforting the son?"

Once more Lucy's face warmed. "The son doesn't need comforting. He didn't know George." Though he did have plenty of old wounds that weren't hers to share.

"He didn't know his mother's husband of twenty years? Hell, I've met every one of my mother's husbands and special friends, and some of those relationships didn't last three months, plus I live halfway across the country from her."

"It's complicated."

Marti laughed. "No one's personal life could be more complicated than Eugenie's."

With an *hmm* of agreement, Lucy deliberately changed subjects. "I'm being responsible and proactive by telling you that I'm starting a diet."

"Good for you." A pause then, guiltily... "Are you still bringing angel food cake with berries and real whipped cream to the cookout?"

"Yes."

"Whew, that's a relief. Good for you, LucyLu," Marti repeated with real enthusiasm. "I will be certain to eat every bite of it so you won't be tempted."

Lucy wasted a moment wishing she had the metabolism to eat the way Marti did, but only a moment. She'd been that way before Mike died, average weight and mindful of what she ate and pretty. Lord, she missed how pretty she'd been. But then she'd become a sorrowful eater, stuffing herself to numb her grief until it became an ugly and annoyingly stubborn habit. If she ever got blissfully happy again, would her eating return to normal, or had she created a lifelong monster to deal with?

The thought was too depressing to consider, so she pushed it away. "Tell me your new Eugenie stories, please. I need a laugh."

Chapter 8

Dinner was long over, the sun had set, and the breeze still jingled the chimes. Dalton had helped Carly clear the table and bring out dessert, a tray of two-bite pastries from CaraCakes, and they'd polished those off an hour ago. It was time to head home.

To his? Or Jessy's?

He deliberately refused to think about it. He would just let instinct guide him.

Dane and Carly were holding hands, their chairs angled close enough to bump shoulders. He fiddled with her engagement ring for a moment before clearing his throat, then looking up. "Listen, Dalton, I—we have a favor to ask."

A lump formed in his own throat, and he swallowed hard over it. Favors had never been a problem for him; he'd done them for everyone until Sandra's death. Sometime after that, Noah had muttered he'd rather ask help of a pissed-off rattlesnake than his brother. The memory embarrassed Dalton.

"Okay," he said because it seemed the thing to say.

"Carly and I are getting married on June first. It's a week from Saturday. Her family's coming in from Utah and Colorado, and my mom from Texas, and her sister-in-law Lisa is going to be her maid of honor, so..."

Dane took a breath, then looked at Carly. She gave him the kind of sweet, gentle smile Dalton would always remember from Sandra. "If it's not too much to ask, would you be my best man?"

Hell. It *was* too much to ask. He hadn't been in a church since Sandra's funeral, before that not since the Las Vegas chapel where they were married. He hadn't worn a suit since then, hadn't stood before God, hadn't done anything flat-out, no-excuses, gotta-be-happy in so long that he didn't know if he could.

But to even be asked... After Dillon left town, Dalton figured the only groom he might ever stand up for would be Noah, if the kid could settle down with just one girl.

Carly laid her free hand over Dalton's, the pressure light, warmth radiating from her skin. "If it brings back too many memories, Dalton, we understand."

"You don't need anything to bring back the memories, do you?" he asked quietly. "They're just always there, and you live with them. I'm learning to live with them." Then he managed a phony smile. "I'd be happy to." Okay, so he lied. *Happy* was over the top. But he owed Dane for listening to his story about Sandra's betrayal, for lightening his burden a little.

"All right!" Carly exclaimed. "When I tell Lisa she'll be escorted down the aisle by an honest-to-God Oklahoma cowboy, she'll be delighted. Cowboys are a rarity in her world."

"What world is that?" They were so common in his world that he forgot they didn't exist everywhere.

"She's a genius rocket scientist," Dane remarked.

Carly gave him a chastising look. "She's not a rocket scientist. My younger brother is." To Dalton, she added, "She *is* a PhD, but a normal one. She can relate to people and use regular language and everything."

Taking part in a wedding, standing up in a house of God, with a woman whose IQ probably wasn't even in view from his own spot on the intelligence scale...He'd better get out of there before he got himself into something even worse, like having to plan a bachelor party or something.

It took him about ten minutes between starting good-byes and actually getting into his truck. He thanked them for the dinner; they invited him to a cookout on Monday; Carly told him about the rehearsal the night before the wedding.

He should've grabbed a beer for the road. He could have beaten himself in the head with the bottle after he'd drunk it.

He drove west along Cimarron toward First Street. Now it was time for instinct to kick in, to tell him whether he was going home or accepting Jessy's invitation. He couldn't say it was instinct exactly, but something prompted him to turn left on Third and, a few blocks later, right on Main. Soon he was parked in front of her apartment.

A few strides took him to the door, painted brown, peeling at the edges, with crooked adhesive numbers: 108½. His index finger hovered over the doorbell but didn't press it. Maybe he should go home. He'd seen enough people for one day. He had books to work on, and Oz would need to go out before long, and—

The door jerked open and Jessy burst out, practically plowing into him. She stopped so suddenly that she had to grab the door frame and she actually lost one flip-flop. Her eyes widened, her breath escaping in a small, "Oh!"

He took a step back, wondering where she was headed at this time of night, whether what he'd taken as an invitation had merely been politeness, how she managed to look so damn good even when startled speechless.

It took her a moment to gather herself—catch her balance, catch her breath, slide her shoe on again. When she did, a sly, teasing smile curved her mouth and her natural sexiness amped up. "Well, well, look what someone left on my doorstep."

"You going somewhere?"

She looked at the purse in her left hand, the keys in her right, before slowly bringing her gaze back to him. "Just to get some coffee. Something possessed me to buy decaf last time, and it just doesn't cut it. I need the hard stuff." Her expression quirked at the last words.

"You looking for a cup or a few potfuls?"

Tilting her head to one side, she considered it for a moment. "I think one mega-sized cup will do for tonight. Java Dave's is still open for"—she checked the time and temp display at the bank—"fifteen minutes. Want to walk over?"

In response he gestured, and she stepped out and locked up, then they crossed the street. Java Dave's was on First, south of the courthouse, so they cut across the lawn, passed the gazebo behind it, and came out on the street. Except for a tiny restaurant a few doors down, everything else on the block was closed.

"How was dinner with your friend?" she asked, slinging her purse so the strap was over her head, the bag riding on her right hip. She wore another little skinny top, and the leather strap crossed right between her breasts, making it clear that she wasn't wearing a bra. It was a tempting sight, one that he let himself get lost in for a moment. It had been so damn long since he'd truly admired a woman's body, the differences, the softness, the roundness, the delicate bones, the satiny skin, the curve of a breast or a hip, the—

"Hey, cowboy. My face is up here." Her voice was a little ragged, its edges a little sharp. Like she was teasing, but not quite.

His gaze jerked to hers, heat warming his cheeks. Noah would have made some smart-ass comment. Dillon would have been a smart-ass and charming at the same time. There was a time Dalton would have had an at least semi-charming comeback, but damned if he could think of one now.

Except for that one afternoon with Jessy, he'd been alone a hell of a long time. If he took a moment, he could calculate it to the exact date: the night before Sandra had shipped out. Five years and a few weeks. For a long time he hadn't missed sex, but since that afternoon with Jessy...

Now he not only missed it, but missed thinking about it without guilt. Guilt for feeling like he'd betrayed Sandra. Guilt for having sex with Jessy knowing nothing about her. Guilt for getting drunk and acting out of character, because sex had never been *that* casual for him. For regretting it and for her pretending not to remember it and for being pissed off by that more than what they'd done.

He didn't want to feel so damn low for wanting what every man in the world wanted.

It was complicated, maybe not for other men in the

same situation but for Dalton, definitely. *You* make *things complicated,* Dillon's voice taunted.

Yeah, well, life was easy when you didn't give a damn about anyone besides yourself.

Dalton realized they'd stopped and were standing in front of the coffee shop, lights casting angles across the sidewalk. Jessy was watching him, an expression he'd never seen on her face. Uncertainty? She opened her mouth, then apparently decided better of what she'd been about to say and gestured instead. "Let's get our coffee to go. We can sit in the gazebo."

Nodding, he opened the door, then followed her inside. Every table in the small space was occupied, and he'd guess not one of the customers was over eighteen. The kids ignored them as they walked to the counter, though the boy behind the register did check out Jessy and her thin little top without looking the least damn bit embarrassed.

She paid for the coffee—*I invited you,* she said when he pulled out a twenty and she swiped her card instead— then they stepped back out into the quiet evening. Neither of them spoke until they settled on a bench in the gazebo.

She pulled the lid off her cup, blew away the steam rising from the coffee, then took a cautious sip before saying, "It's kind of awkward sometimes, isn't it? You, me, two months ago, now."

"Yeah. Sometimes." Though he'd come a long way in two months, from wishing to God they'd never had sex to wondering if they would again. From never wanting to see her to seeking her out. Wanting to get to know her. Wanting sex with her again. Wanting...*something*.

"We could forget it ever happened," she suggested.

He gave her a dry look. "Yeah. I was never very good at forgetting."

"Then you didn't have the right incentive. I've spent my entire life doing it."

He didn't have to ask what she tried to forget: that her parents hadn't loved her enough; that she couldn't turn to her family when she needed them; that her husband had died. It sucked that the Wilkes parents were self-centered and petty and that the Wilkes daughters valued peace more than their sister.

"Or..." He took a deep breath, noticing that despite the warmth of the cup, his fingers were cold. The first taste of coffee had turned sour in his gut, and his nerves had wound tighter than a roll of barbed wire in about two seconds flat. "We could acknowledge that it"—*shouldn't have happened* was what he'd intended to say, but his brain switched words on him—"was too soon, and we can...not screw it up next time. We can...know what we're doing and...why."

Even in the dim light from the streetlamps, he could see her expression: surprise, a little bit of anxiety, maybe even a bit of panic. He felt the same way. Damned if he knew what he was doing.

But he wouldn't take the words back if he could.

*   *   *

Next time. The words kept echoing in Jessy's brain, demanding attention one second, a backbeat to her emotions the next.

Dalton wanted to have sex with her again. Not careless, stinking-drunk, didn't-know-what-they-were-doing sex, but deliberate. On purpose. Sober. He'd seen her at her worst, but he wanted a next time.

No one had ever wanted Jessy after they'd seen her at her worst. Even Aaron, bless his heart, had never known what depths she was capable of. Dalton didn't know all of them, granted, but he still wanted to give her a chance, to give a relationship with her a chance.

The thought scared the pee out of her.

She had watched the clock all evening, wondering how long dinner with friends could take, whether he'd come by again, and why he would bother. She'd waffled a lot, too: If he came back, cool; if he didn't, that was cool, too. No big deal either way. She spent the majority of her evenings alone. She could handle one more.

Then seven thirty passed, eight, eight thirty. He was a rancher. He had to get up before the sun. He probably had nighttime chores to take care of. She'd already kept him out the night before. He had better things to do than deal with her.

By eight forty, she'd wanted a drink more than anything in the world. Wanted it badly enough that she was already savoring the taste, feeling the smooth burn. Needed it so much that her stomach was queasy with anticipation, her hands were trembling, her head was aching, and her chest was hurting.

Using midnight Sunday as her officially gone-sober time, she figured she'd gone 5,560 minutes without any alcohol. Best she'd done in months, but not good enough.

Because she'd been on her way to Buddy's when she'd met Dalton at the door.

All the shakes and aches were gone. She couldn't help thinking how much better her coffee would taste with a splash of rum, but she wasn't hurting for it now. No wonder Alcoholics Anonymous used sponsors. Having someone to distract her helped.

And what a hell of a distraction Dalton offered.

"If you need that long to think about it—" he began stiffly, but she interrupted.

"I have a tendency to act on impulse. That's why we did"—hell, they were both adults, and neither of them could say *had sex* to the other—"why *I* did what we did too soon. So now I'm trying to be grown-up and not blurt out the first answer that comes to mind."

Her words eased some of his tension, but the rest remained evident in the taut lines of his face, the shadows in his eyes, and the stillness that radiated from him.

We can not screw it up next time. "I'm not very good at not screwing things up," she admitted. "It started when I was born ten days past my delivery date and forced my parents to postpone the postpartum vacation they had planned before they'd planned me, and I've never gotten better. I screwed up my relationship with my whole family, I screwed up my job at the bank, I screwed up—"

Her mouth clamped shut. She'd been about to say *my marriage*—one of the secrets she hadn't shared with *anyone*. She was the only soul on earth who knew how badly she'd let Aaron down, and she intended to take it to her grave.

"Everything," she said with a lame shrug.

"Then it sounds like you're due for a break."

It sounded like he was willing to give her one.

Jessy, who pretended she never cried, who told her girls that life was too damn short to waste on tears, had to blink rapidly to clear her eyes, and right then and there she fell just a little bit in love with Dalton Smith.

* * *

The sun was up at 6 a.m. but just barely, still sleepy like Lucy, its rays able to penetrate the cloud layer only here or there with shafts of pale golden light. It was pretty, really it was, but she was praying for rain and an extra forty-five minutes in bed.

She didn't get either. Joe let himself into the kitchen as she quickly swallowed the last of her cereal bar, then inhaled the rest of her coffee. He was too damn cheerful, greeting Norton, filling his food and water bowls, giving him the chance to gobble down both while retrieving his leash from a hook near the front door.

"Good morning," he said at last.

She grunted.

"I thought we'd take Norton with us. He could use some exercise, too."

"He wouldn't need it if you didn't feed him from your plate all the time." She pulled her hair into a ponytail, then looked down at herself. Cropped pants and a T-shirt that both fit more snugly than she'd like, moisture-wicking socks, her comfy walking shoes, keys, cell phone, and lip balm in her pockets. "Let the punishment begin."

Joe frowned at her as he hooked the leash onto Norton's collar, then followed her outside. "Adjust your attitude, or we're gonna have to change your name. You know Luce means light in most languages, don't you?"

"My light only shines at a decent hour." She picked up one of the bottled waters he'd left on the patio table, then at the corner of the house made a left turn to get to the street. "If the Lord had wanted me up at the break of dawn, He'd have made me a chicken." Large breasts, large thighs, preferring to hide rather than face her weight problems head-on—oh, wait, maybe He had.

Joe ignored her crabbiness. That was one of the things she loved about him. "This is my favorite time of day. The sunrise is awesome—well, when it's not all clouded over. It's not hot yet, there's not a lot of traffic, not many people. It's a good time to think."

Another time, she would have given him a verbal poke—*You actually think?*—but she wasn't in the mood today. Joe was a jock, but there was a lot more to him than just sports. He loved his family, his friends, his kids at school. If he ever settled down, he'd make a great, if sometimes immature, husband and a wonderful father.

And what man around wasn't sometimes immature?

Ben, her crush whispered. She'd seen nothing the least bit immature about him. Gorgeous, sexy, intelligent, caring, even if he did have problems with his mother.

Not that Joe isn't adorably cute, the friend in her felt obliged to say on his behalf. His workout clothes were disreputable, he owned more OSU baseball caps than he did shirts, and he didn't think twice about dropping a bundle on running shoes every few months. Still, every single woman in town flirted with him. His smile was killer, he really was interested in people, and he was so darn nice that people couldn't help but adore him.

"You're being awful quiet."

She slanted a gaze at him before turning her attention back to the sidewalk. He'd promised to shorten his stride, and he'd done so, setting a reasonable pace that was no problem for her...yet. "I'm thinking about finding you a girlfriend."

As soon as she said it, she recognized it for the great

idea it was. Wasn't that a fair trade? He would help her lose weight so she could be thin and sexy and pretty, and she would help him find the love of his own life. Then he and Ben would lose the animosity, and the four of them would live happily ever after as best friends.

A scowl knitted his brows beneath the brim of the black-and-orange cap. "I can find my own girlfriends."

"I know, but you're in between right now, and I know a lot of women. Let's see, there's Fia. She's twenty-three, a personal trainer, your type."

"What's my type?"

She ticked the list off on her fingers. "Tall, thin, muscles on muscles, athletic, beautiful."

"You think that's all I'm looking for in a woman?" He sounded injured and managed the expression to go with it, but she knew him. It was all put on.

"I've seen every girl you've gone out with since you moved to Oklahoma. Of course that's all you're looking for. That's all most men are looking for."

He reined in Norton as a mom with a stroller approached. He and Lucy automatically stepped into the grass on opposite sides, giving Mom the sidewalk. The little girl in the stroller grinned at Norton, then reached both hands to Joe as they passed.

Even toddlers couldn't resist him.

When they were side by side again, Joe gave a mournful shake of his head. "If that's all the men you know are looking for, Luce, then you know the wrong men."

Wrong. She didn't really know *any* men who weren't already off the market. Just Joe and Ben, who probably liked tall and thin, too. She couldn't do anything about her height, but she would work hard on the other. *Today is the first day of the rest of my life,* and not as a fat chick.

Today, even though her breath was getting a little tougher to come by. Even though her legs were starting to tire and she was pretty sure her moisture-wicking socks were rubbing blisters on her little toes. Even though she couldn't help but notice, mouth watering, how close they were to Serena's—*breakfast, yumm*—when Joe took a turn in the opposite direction.

Today, just like the first day of every other diet she'd started, she was hopeful and determined. Unlike every other diet she'd failed, she was going to claw her way to pre-widowhood weight on that hope and determination.

Joe was going to help her, and along the way, she was going to find him the perfect girl.

*   *   *

Every time her cell phone rang, Jessy checked the screen, even though the only guarantee that she would answer was if it was one of the margarita girls. She had lied to, withheld things from, and misled them, but other than that, she'd never disappointed them. There wasn't anyone else in her life she could say that about, not even herself.

The call coming through Friday morning showed the animal shelter on the screen. A welcome-to-the-poop-crew call? Or sorry-we-can't-trust-you-with-our-animals?

With a deep breath—as if something really serious and life-changing was about to happen—she answered with her phony, fooled-everyone cheery voice.

"Hi, Jessy, this is Angela. You have a pair of work boots or old sneakers?"

She swallowed back her snort. Seriously? The closest she'd come to work boots was sharing her closet with Aaron's combat boots. And old sneakers? She didn't even like brand-new ones.

"I have some that can get old real fast," she replied. Did this mean she got the job? Suddenly her heart was pounding double its normal rate. A job would make a difference. She'd convinced herself of that last night in the few minutes she hadn't been thinking about Dalton or a drink. It would give her a place to go, people to see, a chance to do good.

It would give her purpose, and she'd been missing that, damn, for a long time.

"Good," Angela said. "If you can come after lunch, I'll show you around, we'll figure out your schedule, and get you started. Does that work for you?"

Her heart slammed on the brakes, returning to its normal rate so quickly that she sank into the nearest chair. "Yeah. Sure. No problem," she said breezily while her brain was chanting, *I got the job. I'm good enough to pull ticks off abandoned dogs and walk them and clean up after them. I may not be fit to work at the damned bank, but dogs and ticks and fleas are so much better anyway.*

"Be prepared to get dirty, okay?" Angela advised.

"I can do dirty." She *hadn't* in years, but she *could.* There was no shame in getting dirty on the job. Aaron had done it; Dalton did it every day.

"Then I'll see you about twelve thirty?"

"Sounds good. Great. Thanks, Angela." Jessy hung up, then went to the bedroom closet. She was surprised by the need to tell someone, and naturally the girls came to mind first. But telling them would necessitate admitting that she'd left the bank—been *fired* from the bank—over a month ago, and that was best done in person. To say nothing of the fact that in person would save her five repetitions.

Kneeling, she dragged the running shoes from the back corner where she'd thrown them yesterday. She hated those shoes. They deserved to get filthy. Then she sat back on her heels, gazing at the long row of skimpy, sexy dresses hanging above her and thinking that the person she wanted most to tell was Dalton. He would *get it*. He wouldn't be surprised, like the girls, or think she was crazy or finally where she belonged, like everyone else.

Of course, there was the small problem that she didn't have his phone number.

But she knew her way to his house.

Pushing herself off the floor as she shoved the idea aside for this evening, when she could actually do it—or not—she dressed in cropped pants, a T-shirt, cute socks, and the awful shoes again. She rummaged through the kitchen, throwing together a sandwich of chicken from last night's takeout with lettuce, tomato, and onion bought for the salads she hadn't made after the first time.

After scarfing down the food and a bottle of water, she grabbed her purse, paused to stuff a small camera inside, then headed to her car. Though the temperature had passed warm fifteen degrees ago, she rolled the windows down for the drive, letting the breeze chase out the heat and the cobwebs that had taken hold after her month of aimlessness.

The same dog was standing in the same place when she got out of her car at the shelter. Her entire face scrunched into a frown. "Oh, man, I promised I'd bring treats next

time. I was just so"—dare she say it?—"excited that I forgot. But I promise on my margarita girls, next time."

She would have sworn the dog gave her a you've-gotta-
prove-yourself sort of look.

Purse bumping her hip, she went inside the shelter. Except for the bell over the door, it was quieter than she'd
expected, given that there were twenty-two dogs and sixteen cats on the premises.

"I'll be right out," a woman called from somewhere in
back.

"No hurry," Jessy replied as she wandered around the
room. The ceiling was high, two fans slowly stirring the air.
The furniture—desk and chair, two wooden chairs, a couple sofas—was hand-me-down, and the floor was concrete,
painted at one time and worn bare in the heavy travel areas. Tattered magazines sat on a dented end table, and three
cats stretched out on the west-facing windowsills. Only
one deigned to acknowledge Jessy's presence.

The no-kill shelter was Angela's baby, along with her
partner. They got some money from the city, more from animal aid groups, and relied on a couple of fund-raisers a
year, plus small salaries and few benefits—*beyond the satisfaction in our souls*—to keep the place running. Salary
was always nice, but Jessy had some money to fall back on;
she had great medical benefits, courtesy of the Army; and
she really needed some satisfaction in her soul.

Footsteps slapped in the hall, then a woman came into
the room. "Can I help—are you Jessy?" She walked right
up to her, hand extended, a ready smile. "Angela said you'd
be in today. Welcome to the Tallgrass Animal Shelter. I'm
Meredith."

Like Angela, Meredith was blond, tanned, and tall

enough to make Jessy aware of the height she lacked. Though she didn't like words like short or petite, she didn't mind being the least tall person in a room. There was something about a short woman that appealed to an awful lot of men, and a woman could never have too many beaus.

Though she could damn well have too many men.

"I'm glad to meet you."

They shook hands, then Meredith went to the desk, searching through piles of papers until she found her objective. "We just need you to sign some forms to make it official. Bureaucracy, you know."

Jessy signed the X-ed places, then Meredith stuck the forms in a desk drawer. Pocketing the key to the drawer, she gestured toward the hall. "Want to see what you've gotten yourself into?"

In the next five hours, Jessy saw everything and met every animal, including the handsome guy out in the yard, a mix named Oliver. His protective cone was to keep him from licking the healing wounds where some bastard had shot him with a BB gun. His standoffishness wasn't directed to her personally, Meredith had explained. He didn't care for any of the humans he'd met yet.

She'd taken four dogs for walks, played with others for a while—they called it socializing—and yeah, she'd done some shoveling. Her shoes were officially relegated to the bottom of the stairs or the trunk of her car from now on.

It was the best day's work she'd ever done.

By the time she got home at six, she couldn't wait to take a shower, put on clean clothes, and jump right back in the car. She picked up barbecue from her favorite rib joint, then headed north out of town.

As town gave way to country, she wondered about her

decision. What if Dalton was busy? If he'd seen enough of her for one week? If he wanted a quiet evening at home, just him and Oz and the animals?

She was a big girl. She'd been raised on rejection. It would roll off her shoulders like rain off the outer coat of his Oreo cows. She wouldn't even be disappointed. Hell, warmed-up barbecue was just as good as fresh out of the pit. And she had pictures to organize, taken during her afternoon break outside with the dogs. That could keep her busy for a few hours.

She'd talked herself halfway out of her anticipation by the time she turned off the paved road. It was a good thing, too, she saw a few minutes later. Dalton's pickup was parked near the house, and behind it were two more, a shiny black one and a rusty, dusty silver one.

He had company. Not a good time for her to drop in, even if she was bearing food.

Despite her best plans, a lump of disappointment started in her throat and slid slowly to her stomach. It was okay, she told herself. He had his life, she had hers, and until—unless—they were ever officially together, she was all right with that. She wasn't a clingy woman. She didn't need to spend every single moment with a guy, or her marriage to Aaron, with all his deployments, never would have survived the first year.

But it didn't survive the last one, Realist Jessy pointed out.

There was a reason they weren't best friends, like her and the margarita girls. Realist Jessy was a bitch.

She kept driving east, past the neat fence, the long driveway that ran between pastures, on down the dirt-and-gravel road. Eventually, she knew from previous rambling,

it wound back into town, running along the west edge of
the fort. She would come out on Main about half a mile
from the gym where Fia worked until seven most nights,
and in that instant, she decided she would check on her
friend.

With a flick of her fingers, she turned on the stereo,
tuned to a rock station, and turned the music up loud. She
sang along with the songs she knew and kept her mind
blank for the songs she didn't. She didn't think about life
or Dalton or guilt or regret or anticipation. She didn't think
at all until she was back in town, skirting the post's prairie
and windbreaks on the left, blocks of cookie-cutter houses
on the right.

Fia's gym was on the south side of the highway, in a
strip center with a Starbucks and a storage facility. Jessy
parked in a spot underneath an old oak and hiked the distance to the gym. One rule that had transferred well from
Georgia to Oklahoma: The best parking space in summer
wasn't the closest; it was the one with the most shade.

The place was filled with exactly the kind of people she
expected: mostly young, well toned, tanned, long and lean
or bulging with hard-packed muscle. They were sweaty
with exertion, most of them listening to their own music
via earbuds. These weren't people who *strolled*.

Jessy didn't like them.

The woman behind the counter scanned her head to toe,
then asked, "Can I help you?" in a tone that suggested she
was doubtful. Like Jessy wasn't their kind.

Realist bitch Jessy might be.

"I'm looking for Fia Thomas."

"Back there."

Following the jerk of her head, Jessy located Fia at the

back of the gym, head bent, fingers flying on a computer. "Hey, Fee."

"Jess!" Fia's eyes widened. "Wow. This is the first time you've set foot in this place."

"Probably the last one, too. Listen, doll, I have barbecue—the works—from Bad Hank's, and I was hoping we could kick back and share it at your place or mine. Do you have the time?"

A puzzled look flitted across Fia's face. This wasn't the first time they'd gotten together without the other girls. It wasn't even the first time Jessy had brought food to her. But the puzzlement was replaced by a smile that reminded Jessy how young—and how old—twenty-three could be. "I've got the time and the appetite. I can be out of here in five minutes. Do you mind if we go to your apartment? Mine's a mess."

"My place is fine." Jessy had done a lot of cleaning in the past month—much of it late at night when sleep eluded her, but cleaning was cleaning. "Do you want to ride with me?"

"Nah, I can drive. I just need a quick shower."

A little bit of pink crept into Fia's cheeks as she answered. Twice in the past month and a half, Jessy had picked her up after work, when the kid had a headache too intense to drive. Fia had hated asking, but Jessy had been honored, even if she figured she *was* Fia's last choice. She'd worried more about Fia since then, but she was ashamed to admit she hadn't followed up on it. She had let herself get overwhelmed with her own problems instead.

She would do better, she promised. *Be* better.

"Okay. I'll head home and stick the Q in the oven to stay warm. I'll leave the downstairs door unlocked for you."

She started to walk away, then stepped back, bent, and hugged Fia. The woman was five inches taller than Jessy and had no body fat, every muscle sleekly defined, and yet she felt frail in Jessy's arms. The injuries and illnesses that had been plaguing her the past few months had really taken their toll.

One of their girls, Bennie, was an LPN, going to school to finish her bachelor's degree in nursing, and there was Lucy's doctor crush. Maybe between them, they could get some advice to cure whatever ailed Fia. They would do *something*, because the margarita girls *never* let each other down.

Chapter 9

After dinner, Ben rinsed the dishes, then put away the leftovers while Patricia loaded the dishwasher. He'd done that, too, a couple of times before he'd noticed her coming along behind and quietly rearranging things. It made him roll his eyes. At home, their dad had just been happy to get the dishes done. He hadn't cared if the bowls faced this way or the silverware was upside down.

Then Ben's mouth tightened. It was her dishes, her dishwasher. Who cared? He was known in the clinic for liking things a certain way, and an irritated nurse at the hospital had once called him fussy. *Like a cranky old woman,* she'd added.

Not the comparison a hotshot surgeon was looking for, but the patients were his and the choices were his. The nurse had gotten over it after a while. So had he.

He fixed a cup of coffee for Patricia, then green tea for himself. As he picked up the two mugs, she started the dishwasher, dried her hands, and smiled wearily. "Let's take it in the study. Do you mind?"

It was one of only two rooms he hadn't gone inside yet. The other was the master bedroom. While there were places a lot more inviting—outside with a view of Lucy's house came to mind—he nodded and followed Patricia.

The study was directly across from the living room, and it had obviously been George's space. The furniture was darker, heavier, and the only art on the wall was military-themed prints. There were plenty of framed citations and letters of commendation, along with his degree from West Point, and a lot of photographs taken in exotic places.

Patricia settled on a leather couch, feet tucked beneath her, and held her coffee close enough to inhale its aroma. "I wish you kids had had the chance to know George."

Ben chose a chair with its back to the wall that gave him a good view of everything and nothing in particular. "Do you think it would have mattered? That we ever would have seen him as anything other than the man who destroyed our family?"

"I think so. Maybe. Though, Lord, you and Sara always were hardheaded." She set her coffee on the end table, then clasped her hands in her lap. "He didn't destroy our family, Ben. If I'd loved your father enough, nothing but death could have taken me away. Even if George hadn't come along, your father and I would have divorced, maybe in five months, maybe five years, but it would have happened."

His jaw clenched, and following her lead, he set his cup down before he squeezed it tightly enough to break it. "So you weren't in love with Dad."

"Not the way I needed to be." Her expression was filled

with pain. A distant memory popped into his mind: the widow of the only patient he'd ever lost in the OR. A horrific accident, massive trauma to his legs, pelvis, rib cage. His wife had looked totally lost.

Then an older, more painful memory: His father in the weeks after Patricia left. Also lost. Stunned. Unable to process the information that his wife was gone. He'd stayed lost for the next nine years, when he'd given up trying.

How could she have fallen out of love with him? How could he not have known? Were there signs? Had her behavior changed those last weeks? Had Dad's?

Ben couldn't remember. He'd been fifteen. His parents hadn't come high on his list of priorities.

"I met George at the Gilcrease Museum," Patricia said, a distant look in her eyes, a bittersweet smile on her mouth. "I loved going to museums, but the only time you kids or your dad was willing to go was for the Christmas tree display at the Philbrook. So I went alone. George was visiting old friends and entertaining himself while they worked. We toured Gilcrease together and had lunch afterward—just two strangers with common interests.

"Then we did Philbrook and the Fenster and the Will Rogers Museum in Claremore, and we took a day trip to Woolaroc and another to Tahlequah to the Cherokee Heritage Center...He told me about all his travels to exotic places I'd always wanted to see, but your father..."

His father hadn't liked to wander far. Rick's idea of a vacation was puttering around the house or going camping at Keystone Lake, only thirty minutes from home. He'd said Oklahoma was God's best work, so why waste time looking at the rest of the world?

It had become a game for Ben and his sisters to try every summer to persuade their dad to take them to Dallas to visit Six Flags Over Texas. He'd held out every time. *There's rides and games and food at Bell's,* he'd said, referring to Tulsa's now-defunct amusement park.

Bell's had been fun, but it wasn't Six Flags.

And Tulsa was great, but it wasn't Paris, Rome, or London.

"I wasn't looking to fall in love. It was just so refreshing to talk to a man who paid attention to me, who truly wanted to know my opinions. Your dad, bless his heart, knew the girl he'd married, but he didn't know the woman I'd become. He thought nothing would ever change, that we would always stay the same, that we would always want the same thing, and that it would always be *his* thing. *His* interests. *His* choices."

She'd hated camping. Ben had known it. Brianne and Sara had known it. Had their dad somehow missed that, or had he just not cared?

A throb began in Ben's left temple, spreading tension through his body with every beat of his heart. He didn't want to hear this conversation, didn't want to sit in another man's house and hear these criticisms about the father who had given up so much for his family, who had invested every bit of himself into his wife and kids.

He surged to his feet, anxiety to get out practically vibrating through him. "I'm—I'm gonna take a walk, clear my head. I'll be back..."

Patricia started to speak, then pressed her lips together and nodded with a weak smile. When he closed the front door behind him, he caught a glimpse of her, sipping her coffee, with what looked like a tear rolling down her cheek.

*   *   *

Jessy considered herself the master of quick changes—
oversleeping so many mornings when she was working had
forced her to develop the talent—but Fia gave her a run for
the title. Less than fifteen minutes after Jessy got home, Fia
had finished work, showered, changed, and driven halfway
across town to Jessy's door. Her hair was loosely secured
with a wide clip that kept the damp strands off her neck,
and instead of the second-skin workout clothes, she wore
denim shorts and a T-shirt that looked a size too big.

But she was moving well. No limps, no cautious steps,
no hand painfully twisted. Tonight she looked like a thinner, more fragile but recovering version of her old self.

Jessy set out the barbecue and plates, and they helped
themselves to their favorites before moving to the couch.
She'd made a pitcher of Southern sweet mint tea, the
glucose-shock kind that could turn even Mrs. Dauterive,
the old hag at the bank, into something resembling human,
and she carried two tall glasses of it to the coffee table before sitting at the opposite end of the sofa.

They ate like teenagers, washing down sweet-spicy
sauce with heavily sweetened tea, and talked about Carly's
upcoming wedding, Ilena's soon-to-pop kid, and other bits
of gossip, until all they had to show for the meal were
empty plates and full bellies.

They were both sitting sideways, sofa arms at their
backs—though *sprawled after glorious gorging* might be
a better description—when Jessy asked the question in the
back of her mind. Too lazy and sated to try for subtlety,
she blurted it out, the way she usually did. "What's up with
you, doll?"

Normally Fia brushed off questions about her health. *I've seen a doctor, it's just a sprain, just fatigue, just a headache.* This evening, though, she tilted her head back to stare at the plaster medallion in the center of the ceiling and, after a moment, gave a long sigh. "I don't know. I've seen three doctors, and none of them have anything to say besides, 'Take it easy. Ice your muscles. Take an aspirin.'"

"You've seen three idiots. How much weight have you lost?"

"Only eight or ten pounds."

"Only?" That would be like Jessy losing thirty pounds. Fia didn't have even five to spare. "The symptoms come and go, right?"

Fia nodded. "They're worse when I'm tired. I have muscle spasms, headaches, tremors, trouble walking. My vision gets blurry. I can't remember things. I talked to the manager at the apartment complex today about getting a first-floor apartment because sometimes I barely make it up or down the stairs." She was silent for a long time, then she met Jessy's gaze. "Sometimes I'm scared."

The vulnerability in her eyes and the plaintiveness in her voice made Jessy's stomach hurt. Giving comfort and reassurance wasn't among her talents, but there was no one else to do it. Besides, *she'd* started the conversation.

She slid to the middle cushion and took Fia's hands in hers. "You're gonna be okay. We're gonna find out what's going on and get it fixed." She spoke with absolute certainty, as much to convince herself as Fia. "We've all been worried about you, but no one's wanted to pry. Well, doll, now we're going to pry. We're gonna help you find answers and get well again."

Her eyes damp with tears, Fia held tightly to her hands. "Promise?"

Jessy's promises were few and far between. She didn't want to be held to any particular action or behavior, didn't want to disappoint people if she couldn't live up to her offer. But this evening she didn't hesitate. "Absolutely. I may not know anything about medicine, but I know a lot about kicking ass and raising hell. We'll figure this out."

Freeing one hand, Fia swiped at her eyes. "That makes me feel better. I'm used to taking care of myself. I've been doing it forever. But it can make you feel so damn alone, you know? You've got to do everything yourself, you've got to be strong for yourself, you don't want to show weakness or become that needy person that makes everyone groan when they see you coming."

Yes, they were alike, the sweetest, youngest, and most innocent of the margarita girls and the brashest, the boldest, the phoniest. "There's nothing wrong with needing strength from your friends. You don't have to be alone, Fee, not through this or anything else. We're here."

Relief lightened Fia's expression. She twisted her hand so she was now the one holding Jessy's, and she quietly said, "You know that, too, don't you? You don't have to go through anything alone. We're strong, and we're here for you when you need us."

A chill rushed through Jessy, settling in her gut. She'd thought she was such a damn good actress—a damn good liar—that no one could see through the image she chose to portray. She'd had such unshakable faith in her ability to hide who and what she was, in keeping everyone from even guessing at her secrets. And the baby margarita sister knew at least one of them. It was clear in the empathy in Fia's eyes, in the tender yet firm way she held Jessy's hand.

What to do? Lie? Play ignorant? Or try honesty for once?

Jessy opted for honesty.

Just not too much honesty yet.

"You're talking about…" If the girls had reached a wrong opinion of her, no need to correct it by spilling the real secret.

After squeezing her hand, Fia let go, then drew her knees to her chest. "Before I met Scott, my girlfriends and I did a lot of partying. Just about every night we hit the clubs, danced, drank, had a good time. Scott and I had been dating about two weeks when he set me down and said there's more to life than that. He wanted to do other things—enjoy a nice dinner and talk, go for a walk and have an ice cream cone, take a hike or a bike ride, have a picnic. He thought the clubbing and the drinking were just a waste of time and money and potential. He wasn't inter- ested in getting involved with someone who didn't agree with him about that, and he told me I had to choose."

Her shrug was eloquent. "I chose him. I quit drinking, quit partying, and began doing something with my life. I lost my friends because of it, but I got Scott, and that was more than worth it. I found out I had ambitions and dreams. I became a more real person. I lived life better."

Jessy focused on the words that carried the sting of truth. "You think I'm not a real person? Because, honey, I can tell you—"

Fia stopped her. "I'm saying that someone who's wasted part of her life drinking can recognize someone else who's doing the same."

Leaning back against the cushions, Jessy stared at the silent TV. Hadn't she thought before that if Fia's ailments were caused by self-medicating, she would know? She would be able to tell, one drunk to another.

It had never occurred to her that went both ways.

Heat flooded through her body, and shame crawled across her skin, like tiny bugs ripping off flesh with each step. It had been bad enough when it was her own ugly little secret, but to find out that at least one other knew . . .

Her voice small, her Georgia accent thicker, she asked, "Does everyone know?"

"I think Carly's concerned. Maybe Therese. I don't know about the others. Like I said, I've been there. I drank because my friends did, it was expected, I was trying to fill the emptiness inside me. You drink because you've got a huge emptiness inside, too, and booze takes the edge off. Lucy feeds her sorrow. You drown yours."

Unable to sit still a moment longer, Jessy jumped to her feet, gathered the dishes, and carried them into the kitchen. She brought the tea pitcher back, refilling both glasses, then walked over to stare down on the street. "Little sister has insight," she said, shooting for humor, not caring if she fell short. "I didn't expect that."

The couch creaked as Fia stood. A moment later her reflection appeared in the window glass. "People think I'm just a fabulous body. They forget I've got a functioning brain." Her humor fell a little short, too.

They stood there a long time, gazing out, quiet, until Fia murmured, "Look at that sunset."

It was beautiful, shades of blue, purple, violet, red, delicate gold. Jessy had gone up on the roof and taken a hundred pictures of sunsets, and no matter how gorgeous the photos were, they couldn't match the real thing for taking her breath away.

"Every time Scott went away, even if it was just a few weeks' training, we would watch the sun set the night before, and he'd say, 'Distance doesn't matter. Wherever you are, wherever I am, that same sun is going down on both of us, and it'll remind you that I'm thinking of you.'" Fia laid one hand flat against the window. "Every night when the sun sets, I think of him and how much he loved me. He was the first person who ever really did. The first person who thought I was worthy. Who made *me* think I was worthy."

"He was lucky to have you," Jessy murmured.

The smile that touched Fia's mouth was shaky. "Yeah. We were both incredibly lucky."

Jessy was sad enough to cry, except that life was too short to waste on...Oh, hell. Surreptitiously she wiped away a tear...then noticed that Fia's hand against the window was trembling. Not emotional-shaky, but uncontrollable-shaky. Fia realized it, too, and withdrew it, wrapping her fingers tightly around the glass in her left hand. The result was tea splashing on the wood floor.

"I'm sorry. I'll get..." The words came out slurred. *Ah'm suhrry. Ah'll ge...*

After taking the glass from her, Jessy slid her arm around her waist. "I'll do it. Right now let's get you back to the couch."

Fia leaned heavily against her, and Jessy glanced down, surprised to see that the girl's left foot was turned up so that she walked on the outside edge of it. Two questions took turns pounding in her brain. What was wrong with Fia? And what the hell qualified Jessy to guarantee help?

Once she was settled on the couch, Fia smiled

crookedly. "Ah jus' need rest. Ah'll be okay." With effort, she touched her involuntarily curled fingers to Jessy's arm. "You're gon' be okay, too."

*   *   *

Dalton woke to a quiet house Monday morning. Noah, home for the weekend, had stumbled in sometime around 3 a.m., and Dalton had hauled his ass upstairs to his room. *Did you drive?* he'd demanded, and Noah, swaying unsteadily, had grinned. *'Course not.* Those were the last words he'd said before getting dumped on his bed.

Oz gave Dalton a look when he rolled over, then stood and stretched from the tips of his whiskers to the end of his tail. After a good shake, he jumped to the floor and trotted out the door.

It was Memorial Day, and it ranked right up there with Veterans Day as Dalton's least favorite holiday. When he was younger, Memorial Day had always seemed more about family and fun than remembering the dead. His mom had dragged them to the cemetery to place wreaths on various long-gone relatives' graves, but then they'd watched the parade before going to the lake for a picnic with their still-living relatives. Hell, he'd been out of high school before he'd really gotten the meaning of the day, and by then he'd long since managed to avoid those trips to the cemetery.

Now he was back to doing them. He put yellow flowers on Sandra's grave year-round, so she would forgive him for skipping this week, but her mother and his wouldn't. Besides, the idea of her grave being one of the few flowerless ones on this particular day was just sad.

All of the graves surrounding Sandra's were from the

war on terror, all fairly recent. Few would go unmarked, including that of Corporal Aaron Lawrence. Leaving flowers in honor of memories that would never be lost was how Dalton and Jessy had met.

He hadn't seen her since Thursday night. He had intended to drive into town—and finally ask for her phone number—Friday after work, but Noah had shown up with a couple of friends majoring in agriculture who'd been full of questions about the ranch. Saturday and Sunday, it seemed everything that could go wrong had. A couple of cows had gotten out and decided life on the other side of the fence was too interesting to easily surrender. While he and Noah were rounding them up, Noah's horse had bolted at the sound of an oncoming vehicle and unseated him on the road, giving him a nasty knot on the back of his head. The colt who'd injured his leg had opened it up again, requiring a visit from the vet.

Sunday morning, Dalton had gone downstairs to the sight of water rippling through the hall. The hot water tank had burst in the utility room, flooding the first floor. They'd used the wet vac, mopped, and swept water out the back door, making a nice muddy puddle for Oz to wander through every time he came in.

Through all the work, Dalton had anticipated seeing Jessy today. It was a strange feeling, one he hadn't experienced in a long time, one he'd never expected to experience again. But damned if it didn't feel good.

After getting dressed, he followed Oz downstairs to the kitchen, where, major surprise, Noah was dressed, bright-eyed, and cooking bacon and eggs. "I figured you'd be down soon after the mutt. Coffee's ready. Biscuits will be done in five."

Dalton glowered at him as he filled his mug with strong coffee. "You're not even hungover."

"Would you feel better if I was puking my guts out instead of cooking your breakfast? Not that I was anywhere near that shit-faced." Noah set a tub of margarine on the kitchen table next to a hot pad made from one of their grandmother's old quilts.

"You going back to Stillwater today?"

"Yeah. In a couple hours. You have any plans besides taking flowers..."

Dalton sat down at the table and studied the hot pad. Cut from a crazy quilt his grandmother had made, it was roughly eight inches square, wools and cottons and small strips of velvet stitched this way and that, well used, often washed, faded but holding together. He liked to think the same could be said of him fifty years from now.

"Yeah," he answered at last. "This guy I know and his fiancée are having a cookout this afternoon."

Noah turned from the stove, his eyes wide open and his mouth gaping. "Who?"

"No one you know."

"I know *everyone* you know."

That had been true until recently, Dalton acknowledged. He'd cut himself off from everyone except the people he was forced to deal with—family, buyers, suppliers—and Noah did know every one of them. "Not Dane. He's a soldier at the fort, he likes palominos, and..." Deep breath. "I'm going to be the best man at his wedding next weekend."

Leaving Noah speechless was a rare occurrence, and Dalton was appreciating it now. It only lasted until the kid caught a whiff of overcooked bacon, when he turned back to the stove and words came flooding out. "How could you get to know someone well enough to be his best man without me knowing it? Where did you meet him? A soldier? For real? And you're going to a *party*?"

He chose to answer the easiest question and ignore the rest. "Yeah, a party. With people and food and everything."

"And a wedding. Man, you haven't even been to a wedding since—" Noah shot a glance over his shoulder as he began dishing eggs and bacon onto plates.

"Since Sandra and I got married," Dalton said evenly. "I haven't known many people who got married since then."

Noah delivered the plates, then returned for the hot tin of biscuits, setting it on the crazy quilt pad. "Is the maid of honor good-looking? Any chance you'll get laid?"

His little brother always had getting laid on his mind. Granted, the kid was nineteen. And to be fair, it had been on Dalton's mind a lot more than it should have been since Thursday night. *Next time…*

He cleared his throat. "I haven't met her. She's some kind of genius scientist from Utah, and she's married."

Noah slid into the chair across from him and dug into his breakfast. "There are bound to be other women there. Single women at weddings are always easy pickin's." He shook his head disbelievingly. "Damn. You meeting people, going to parties, being in weddings…Next thing I know, I'll come home and find a woman here."

Heat spread through Dalton, and he shifted uncomfortably in his chair. He had no obligation to tell Noah anything about Jessy. He didn't even know where they were headed yet. It could just be a thing. A few dates, sex, it's-been-nice-good-bye. Though in his gut he didn't want that to be the case. There was just something about Jessy…

Lucky for him, Noah was too interested in eating to notice his response. Dalton followed his lead, so for a while, the only sounds in the kitchen were them scarfing down food and Oz's occasional lip licking as he waited for the scraps he knew were coming.

Dalton was spreading butter on his last biscuit when Noah finally spoke again. "Does anybody ever put flowers on Grandma and Grandpa's graves?"

"I don't know. Never thought about it." They hadn't had a lot of relatives in town to start with—the Smith and Reynolds families were spread wide over Oklahoma—and of the ones who'd lived in Tallgrass, the older folks had died off and the younger ones had moved away.

After another silence, Noah pushed his chair back and propped one ankle over the opposite knee. "You think...Do you think Dillon's buried out there somewhere, with nobody to put flowers on his grave?"

Dalton slowly chewed the biscuit in his mouth, then washed it down with a gulp of coffee. He hated talking, even thinking, about his twin, but that didn't keep him out of his mind. Noah had been so young when Dillon took off. In the beginning, he'd asked about him every day— *Where'd he go, when's he coming home?*—but now he rarely mentioned his name. Part of it was just time passing, and part was a desire not to stir Dalton's bitterness. Obviously, Dillon wasn't far from Noah's thoughts, either.

"I don't know," Dalton said at last. "Odds are just as good he's alive."

"Don't you *feel* something? You're his twin. You're supposed to have some kind of connection."

Dalton's first response was derision, his second surprise they'd never had this conversation before. No, no surprise.

He'd never given Noah the chance to ask. "Maybe it works that way for some twins, but not us. I never knew what was going on with him, even when we were kids and shared a room."

"Why'd he leave like that? Why didn't he ever let anyone know he was okay?"

"I imagine part of the reason he sneaked off in the middle of the night was because he took my girlfriend with him. Her daddy would have met him with a shotgun if he'd had any clue what was happening. As for not calling…that's just Dillon. He never thought about anyone but himself."

Noah's eyes went big at the girlfriend part. Had their parents never told him the whole story? Had he been too concerned about bringing up painful memories to ask them? Unlike Dillon, Noah did think about other people's feelings. He might get pissed and pop off something smart on impulse, but as a general rule, he respected people's emotions.

"Sometimes I'm not even sure I remember him," he confessed. "I remember a lot of stuff, but sometimes I'm not sure whether I'm remembering him or you. I mean, you looked alike, acted alike. Like, I don't remember if it was him that threw me in the lake in my church clothes or you."

"Him. It was him who shaved your head while you were asleep. And him who hung you up by your overalls strap on a hook in the barn. And him who told you Santa Claus liked to steal little boys and take them back to his workshop to make toys." Abruptly Dalton grinned. "In fact, if the memory is of someone doing something *to* you, it was him. I was the good twin."

Noah snorted, then leaned down to set his plate on the floor for Oz. "Were you in love with her?"

It took Dalton a moment to realize which *her* he meant. "I thought I was. Turned out, it was just that I was nineteen." Exhaling, he brought the image from the long-past-relevant section of his mind: blond hair, blue eyes, a fondness for fire engine red lipstick, dancing, country music, and fun times. "Her name was Alice, she chewed gum all the time, and every sentence she said, 'you know?' We wouldn't have lasted another month before she got bored or I strangled her for saying 'you know?' one time too many."

"But it's the principle," Noah argued. "She was *your* girlfriend. You don't mess with your brother's girlfriend."

Dalton remembered warning Jessy away from Noah last month. Now he knew there'd been no need. She might have flirted with him, had a beer with him, even danced with him, but Dalton knew his little brother wasn't her type.

He knew, because *he* was.

* * *

Jessy had a blast at the Memorial Day parade with the margarita group staking out a good-sized chunk of sidewalk in front of Jessy's building for themselves and their families. Dane and Keegan, Therese's sweetie, talked a lot of Army stuff, and her kids, Abby and Jacob, entertained Keegan's little girl, Mariah, while visiting with their own friends. Bennie brought her grandmother, a sharp old lady whose cocoa brown eyes seemed to see everything. After that first soul-deep look when they'd been introduced, Jessy had avoided making eye contact with her again. Lucy and Marti were their usual selves. Fia was having a good day, though Jessy had provided her with a chair just in case, right between Bennie's grandmother and so-very-pregnant Ilena.

It seemed all the girls were celebrating this day of remembering with only good memories, or at least they were putting on a damn good show. Jessy's own were bittersweet, as always. A lot of love and good times, sorrow and regret. One surprising thing: She wasn't feeling so much the fraud. Maybe she'd finally hit bottom in her well of guilt. Maybe her psyche was starting to realize that she might be worthy of forgiveness. Of doing enough rights to offset those major wrongs.

After the parade ended, the ones who lived close enough to walk home did so, while the others waited to let traffic thin out. That was how Jessy found herself seated next to Bennie's grandmother. *Call me Mama Maudene,* the old lady had said, clasping Jessy's hands in hers, but Jessy had too much of the old-fashioned Southern girl in her and found the name *Mama* darn near impossible to use.

"What is your name again, dear?" the old lady asked.

"Jessy. Short for Jessamine."

"The state wildflower of South Carolina. Is that where you're from?"

"No, Miss Maudene, I grew up in Georgia." She was a work in progress.

"My people are from South Carolina, down by Beaufort. They're good people."

"Mine are from Atlanta, and they're everything you'd expect of the Old South: old money, old beliefs, old attitudes." There were more than a few plantations in the Wilkes-Hamilton family histories, more than a few slaves and ugly secrets.

"When did you leave?"

"When I was eighteen. When did you?"

"When I was thirty-one, divorced, and looking for a new life in a new place. Haven't decided if I like it yet," Miss Maudene said, then let out a great laugh. "I liked it good enough to pick out my own resting spot in the cemetery. You come to my funeral, Jessamine, and make sure my girl laughs and sings and doesn't shed a tear."

A knot formed in Jessy's throat. Laughing, singing, maybe. Not shedding a tear? When you loved someone, tears were a nonnegotiable part of the whole funeral/burial thing. "I'll laugh and sing with her."

Mama Maudene shook a crooked finger at her. "You didn't say anything about not crying."

"I can't promise that, and you know it."

The old lady laughed again, one that rippled through her entire body. "Oh, well, I got a lot of years left before we have to worry about it. I'm only seventy-eight years young."

When Bennie came to help Mama Maudene out of her chair, Jessy took Maudene's arm, marveling at the fragility of the skin beneath her hands and the strength it covered. The woman had had some tough times in life, but Jessy would bet she'd handled them all with grace, because Miss Maudene was just surrounded by it.

And Jessy, who'd always thought people cluttered up her pictures, wanted to capture some of it in a photograph.

Lucy and Marti were last to leave, and they invited Jessy to join them for lunch. They weren't due at Carly's until two, and the feasting wouldn't start until sometime around five. Lucy, on day four of her diet, couldn't possibly wait that long.

Jessy turned them down. She had one more thing to do before the cookout, and it was the sort of thing, for her, best done alone. She picked up a few bits of trash, folded her camping chairs, and left them inside the door, then ran upstairs. The wreath was in the backseat of her car, and her camera was with her purse. Her clothes were respectable for a graveside visit—a blue sleeveless dress and sandals—and neither her hair nor her makeup required a touch-up.

Fort Murphy National Cemetery was busy, of course. A ceremony was taking place near the war memorials, and the various sections were dotted with people. An American flag fluttered on every grave, the image bringing a lump to her throat. Aaron had been so proud of that flag. He'd worn it on his uniform, hung it outside every day, had decals on his car. To him it stood for everything in the world worth standing for. Worth fighting and dying for. He'd loved that flag.

While she had remembered it for too long as merely the cover draping his casket.

She was patriotic, too, though not as wear-it-on-her-sleeve as Aaron had been. She believed there were principles worth fighting for. She believed there were definitely people worth dying for. She didn't think she'd ever had what it would take to sign up, to carry a gun, to run toward danger instead of away from it. Not everyone *was* cut out to be a hero.

But she'd signed on for her soldier. She'd married him, lived alone a good part of the time, supported, and encouraged him. She'd appreciated the benefits and hadn't minded the low pay, the moves, or the strength the Army forced her to develop.

And she'd always been waiting for him when he came home.

Just as she would have been waiting the last time. She hadn't talked to a lawyer yet. She hadn't filed any papers. If he'd survived the last two weeks on his rotation, he would have come home, like always, to her best welcome. Even though she wanted a divorce, she'd still loved him, just not with the intensity she should have. She would have been thankful for his safe return. She never would have diminished his homecoming in any way.

And who knew? Maybe she would have changed her mind about the divorce.

The part of her so well versed in blaming herself was skeptical. Part of her was intrigued by the idea.

She eased her car past others on the narrow road, pulling to the shoulder when she reached Aaron's section. Circling to the other side of the car, she hung her camera by its strap over her shoulder, lifted out the arrangement, and carried it the few yards to his grave. Pansy, her favorite florist, had made it for her, a woven basket filled with fine silk falls of wisteria, greenery, and a few flowers in matching shades. Jessy set it next to the stone, pulled a few tendrils up and around the dowel that held the miniature flag, and let a few dangle over the top of the stone.

Wisteria had bloomed in the live oaks outside their Savannah apartment when they were first married. How many mornings had she lain there, gazing out the window at the delicate petals, thinking she was the luckiest woman in the world?

She knelt to pull an errant piece of grass that had escaped the trimmer, then laid her hand on the marble, warm, solid. "You deserved to come home, Aaron," she whispered. "You'd fought your battles. You'd done yourself proud. It shouldn't have been your time."

But it had been. God, luck, fate, fortune, misfortune had taken him. They'd cheated the world out of a man it needed.

And they'd left her. For what?

She kneeled there until her feet began to tingle. She kissed her fingertips, then pressed them to the carving of his name, and for an instant, she felt…peaceful. It was a foreign sensation. Her life had always been chaotic—anger, rebellion, loneliness, emptiness, fear, hurt, happiness and uncertainty and no self-esteem and unbearable sadness. The moments of peace—of calm, serenity, the absence of fear and self-loathing and ugly thoughts—had been few and far between. She wished she could grab the feeling and hold on to it forever, but she couldn't.

She just had to learn to find it again.

Getting to her feet, she brushed bits of grass from her legs, then glanced to the south, to Sandra Smith's grave. Its flag wavered over a beautiful sunshine yellow bouquet. Dalton had brought her yellow flowers the day he and Jessy had met. Probably her favorite color. Jessy loved every color, just as long as it screamed, *Look at me! I'm gorgeous!*

She walked between stones to Sandra's marker. "You were a braver woman than me," she murmured. "I would have been way too afraid to do the things you did."

"What's the saying? Bravery is being afraid and doing it anyway?"

The sound of Dalton's voice startled her. She looked over one shoulder, then the other, before spotting him leaning in the shade of a nearby tree. Her emotions were all good: surprise, pleasure, and simple happiness. Had she forgotten that simple could be wonderful?

He pushed away from the tree and came a few steps closer. "You would have done fine. And you would have come home."

"She did her best to come home."

He opened his mouth, then closed it again. After a moment, he gestured to her camera. "You take a lot of pictures in graveyards?"

"I used to, back home. Two-hundred-year-old gravestones always interested me." She removed the lens cap, turned on the camera, and swept her free hand across the area. "I want to get shots of the flags."

The symmetry of the marble markers and flapping colors drew her photographer's eye, and she began snapping, shifting, snapping again. "Did you know that at a lot of the old country cemeteries in the South, when people celebrated Decoration Day, they would put flowers on the graves, then spread a sheet or a tablecloth on the ground, have a picnic, and visit with their families and neighbors while the kids played?"

"I didn't know that. I prefer my picnics someplace a little less somber."

She turned the camera to look at him but didn't take the shot. "I can't imagine you picnicking."

"I haven't done it in a long time."

She wasn't surprised. Neither had she. "What are your plans for today?" Kneeling once again, she lined up rows of markers in the viewfinder, waited for the breeze to still, then pressed the button. She took a couple more for good measure.

"I was planning to surprise you."

Even the comment surprised her. She lowered the camera, then got to her feet. Had he intended to stop by her apartment with an invitation of some sorts? The surprise would have been on him, since she wouldn't be home until dark. "How?"

"You're going to a cookout this afternoon."

"Yeah." She'd probably mentioned it. She did tend to talk a lot.

"So am I."

"At Carly and Dane's?" When he nodded, she thoughtfully turned her camera in another direction, focusing on flowers, trees, shadows, rippling flags. She knew Dalton and Dane were friends, but it still would have surprised her to walk into Carly's backyard and find him there. All the margarita girls would have been wondering who the handsome cowboy was, and she wouldn't have known how to act around him, and someone would have gotten suspicious and guessed...

Or she would have acted perfectly normal with him. Everyone would have realized they knew each other. Maybe she even would have said, *This is Dalton, my*— Friend? Boyfriend? The man she'd slept with first and was getting acquainted with now? The man who occupied an awful lot of her time and made her want more?

"I can skip it if it would make you uncomfortable."

She looked at him again through the lens. His dark gaze was steady, searching, and this time she captured it. When had his face become so familiar that she could trace the lines etching it from memory? When had the yearning to do just that taken control of her fingers?

Deliberately she gripped the camera tighter. "Of course

not. If you don't mind tagging along for a bit, we can go together and surprise everyone there."

"I don't mind."

He did literally tag along, walking with her to the next section, an older one with fewer flowers, lonelier graves. These troops' families didn't live locally, she guessed, or they'd passed on themselves, or they celebrated Memorial Day simply as a day off work, a time to go to the lake or hang out by the pool and socialize. It should have made her feel blue, but it didn't. The troops weren't in those plots, and distance couldn't diminish love. Eventually, everyone's grave went unvisited. It was the way of things.

"You have any other surprises?" she asked as she turned away to allow an elderly woman privacy at her loved one's grave.

"I'll be at the wedding Saturday."

Dalton, Dane, friends. Of course he was invited to the wedding. Then the thought occurred to her: Would he ask her to go with him? Wouldn't that be a fabulous date, watching one of the people she loved best make her new love official before God and everybody? That was practically enough to make a woman swoon.

As if he'd read her mind, he said, "I have to be there early because I'm the best man, but I thought maybe afterward, we could go out to dinner. Since I'll be dressed up in a suit and tie for the first time in years, maybe someplace nice."

She'd had cuter, funnier, smoother invitations but couldn't think of one she'd been more eager to accept. "Sure. I'll dress up extra nice, too."

"Just your usual glamour will be enough. You don't want to steal attention from the bride."

A smile curving her lips at the suggestion that she could outshine Carly on her wedding day, she began snapping pictures again and thinking of the addition she would make to her calendar when she got home tonight. Saturday was already marked in red as An Important Date.

Tonight she would write beneath that: A *Very* Important Date.

Chapter 10

If she hadn't had desserts to carry, Lucy so could have walked to Carly's house for the celebration. After four morning walks with Joe—and three in the evening that she hadn't expected—she'd noticed at least a smidge more strength and endurance. It wasn't a race, he'd told her. The point was to eat better, live healthier, and exercise regularly. She wouldn't see huge results like a ten-pound loss in the first week—*you're breaking my heart,* she'd told him snidely—but she would get there.

She kept to herself that she had to get there quickly enough to get Ben's attention. They were definitely friends, but she wanted him to see her as so much more, and his time in Tallgrass was limited. He'd put his life on hold to come here, and once Patricia's immediate need had passed, he would return home. Would it be another twenty years before they saw each other again?

Could Lucy interest him enough during this short visit to bring him back?

Fingers and toes crossed, and all girlish crushes prayed, *Yes!*

Carly and Dane had rented two big canvas canopies and set up one on each side of the yard to provide shade. Tables, stadium chairs, and lawn chairs were gathered underneath, while on the patio, two grills were in use, smoking briskets and chicken and pork.

"These men take their barbecuing seriously," Leah Black, one of the semi-regulars in the club, remarked as she selected a bottle of pop from the galvanized tub filled with ice at one end of the patio. "Marco couldn't boil an egg, but give him tongs and charcoal, and he could turn out a five-star dinner from appetizer to dessert."

"It must be in their chromosomes. Mike's steaks and burgers were the best, but if I gave him the same ingredients and stood him in front of a stove, he'd stare awhile, poke a few things, then look at me and go"—Lucy switched to a caveman imitation—"*Where fire? Smoke go away?*"

Lucy reached into the tub for a bottle of water and got pop instead. Setting her jaw, she put it back and found the water, telling herself it tasted every bit as good as her favorite pop. Yep, she was great at lying to herself on these issues of taste. Steamed was better than fried. Fish was better than a burger. She *loved* broccoli. The untruths went on.

She and Leah headed to the shaded area where the other club girls had gathered. Marti looked cool and beautiful as always. Bennie had dropped her grandmother off for a potluck with her church prayer group—*in air-conditioning*, Mama Maudene had said with a satisfied nod—and Ilena was radiant even if she couldn't get out of her chair without help. She'd accepted a boost after the parade from Carly and Lucy, but had warned the men to be prepared. After an evening of eating for two, she would need serious muscle to get her on her feet again.

Scanning the rest of the group, Lucy noticed the only one missing was Jessy, and at that moment, the side gate into the yard opened, and in she walked...followed by a tall, broad-shouldered, muscular, well-tanned, Stetson-boots-and-all cowboy. Fia gave a low whistle, and the rest of the women turned to look.

"Oh, my," Ilena said, her simple words and delicate voice saying it all. *Oh, my, indeed.*

"Do you think they're together or they just happened to arrive at the same time?" Therese asked.

The cowboy chose that time to adjust the camera hanging over Jessy's shoulder, and his hand lingered long enough to make several of them chime in, "They're together."

"Who is he?"

"It's Dane's best man, Dalton," Carly said. "I didn't know he knew..."

"Hey, Dalton," Bennie called. "Why didn't Carly know you knew Jessy?" Under different circumstances, it would have been Jessy asking the question, but Bennie was a good stand-in, with the same attitude.

If he was uncomfortable having the group's attention focused on him, it didn't show. Jessy's cheeks were red, but not his. That could be due to his tan and the brim of his hat. "Sorry, Carly. I'll get you a list of my distant relatives, neighbors, friends, and acquaintances."

Carly flushed and poked Bennie in the ribs, but it didn't slow Bennie. "See that you do."

The two continued to the tables where the food was

laid out. Considering herself a nonperformer in the kitchen, Jessy always brought platters of beautiful fresh fruits and vegetables. That was probably all Lucy'd be able to eat, though Joe had reminded her of the magic word: *moderation.*

After a few minutes, Dalton joined the guys at the grill—Dane, Keegan, and some of Dane's wounded warrior buddies—and Jessy had no choice but to join them. Every woman under the tent was watching her with an *uh-huh, let's get this discussion started* look.

Bennie took the plunge. "Anything you want to share with us, missy?"

Lucy watched Jessy clasp the camera, her security blanket, before gazing around the group. She almost pulled off the careless air she was trying for. "You know how I always complained about how much I hated my job? I got a new one. I'm the latest flea-comber, tick-puller, fur-bathing, poo-raking employee at the Tallgrass Animal Shelter."

And, of course, everyone let her announcement distract them from the sexy cowboy, Lucy included. They all looked at her crisp linen dress, her leather sandals, her perfect manicure and pedicure and carefully tousled hair and exquisite makeup job, then exchanged glances before Marti asked the question on everyone's mind. "Do you even like dogs?"

"Of course I do. Why wouldn't I?"

"Because they shed and lick and get stinky and pee wherever they want," Lucy replied. "They jump on you and your furniture and leave scratch marks on your wood floors and want to sleep in the middle of your bed, preferably breathing their brimstone breath in your face."

"I didn't take one to raise," Jessy said. "I'm just taking

care of them. They're very sweet, and if any of you are looking for a pet, we have plenty to choose from. Adoption fees are seventy-five bucks, and the pet is neutered or spayed and up to date on his or her shots."

"How about the cowboy?" Fia asked. "Is he up to date on his shots? Because...hot damn."

Settling back in a chair, Lucy agreed. Dalton was worthy of a *hot damn* or two. Ben, on the other hand, was worthy of a whole chorus of them. She wished she could have invited him, wished she could have walked in with him, had all the girls stare wide-eyed at them and wonder where the hell she'd found him.

Someday.

After all, a woman had to dream, didn't she?

* * *

Clouds hung low in the sky Tuesday morning, dark and heavy, waiting to spill their rain. Ben stared at them all the way to Tulsa from the backseat of the family car the funeral home had provided for George's dignified transfer. Patricia sat a mile away from him, at the other passenger window, lost in thought, and Major Baxter, along with Lieutenant Graham, the chaplain, occupied one of the side seats.

It had rained the day of his father's funeral, making everything that much drearier, though Brianne hadn't minded. *It should rain on all funerals,* she'd commented. *The heavens weeping to share our sorrow.*

It would be a damned gray world they lived in if it did.

Their first stop as they reached the Inner Dispersal Loop, which arced around downtown Tulsa, would be

Ben's loft. He'd already showered and shaved, but he needed something more appropriate than jeans and a button-down. If she was able, Brianne was going to meet them there; if not, she'd assured him she would be at the funeral the next morning. He hadn't said anything yet to Patricia, in case Bree's plans didn't work out.

The driver stopped across the street from Ben's building in the Brady District. For the first time, Patricia seemed to notice she wasn't alone, looking at the building, then him. "You live here?"

"Yeah."

"How unexpected."

He didn't ask why. Hell, it still surprised him sometimes. But he liked the high ceilings, the recycled wood floors, and the ten-by-twelve-foot windows that made up most of the outside walls. He liked living on the third floor, a little above the city but not too much, and the restaurants within walking distance. Even the drive to his clinic or the hospital was minimal.

He crossed the street, entered the lobby, and took the stairs to his floor. It took him only a few minutes to change into a pale gray suit, knot a tie, and pack a few clothes to take back to Tallgrass. Depending on how things went, he figured he could return home on Thursday, maybe Friday, and then . . .

Would he go back? He would have to see Patricia again, at least from time to time to see how she was doing. He didn't know that he would ever forgive her, but he would see her.

And as a bonus, there was Lucy. If they'd met under different circumstances, they would have already had their first date, maybe the second. She was exactly what he liked in a woman: sweet, intelligent, generous, and kindhearted. He wanted to see what might develop between them.

When he reached the lobby again, suit bag thrown over his shoulder, he stopped short. Brianne had shown up, after all. She'd come from the office, wearing a navy skirt a few inches longer than she preferred, crisp white shirt, and loose, flowy navy print jacket with sleeves that barely reached her elbows. Her black hair was pulled back from her face in one of those braids he could never figure out, and the look in her eyes was a mix of excitement and nerves.

Then she stepped aside, and he saw Sara behind her. Her dress had flowers all over it, the colors subdued, short and tight but not inappropriately so. Her dark hair, highlighted golden, was short and could survive anything, she bragged, including Hurricanes Matthew, Lainie, and Eli.

"Don't you look somberly handsome?" Sara said, her mouth quirking, one brow lifting. "Is that the car?"

All three of them turned to look at the same time. "That's it."

"Who's in there with her?"

"The casualty notification officer and the chaplain."

"What about their family?" That came from Sara with another quirk.

"We're family, too," Brianne was quick to point out.

"The others will be getting in later today—Aunt Joan, Uncle Ralph, some of their kids."

They stood there a moment, looking at each other and outside, then Brianne, with a quiver in her voice, said, "We shouldn't keep her waiting."

"Yeah. It's not like we've been waiting for twenty years," Sara muttered.

Ben scowled at her behind Brianne's back, a silent threat that Sara accepted with a roll of her eyes.

Through the heavily tinted windows, they couldn't see Patricia's reaction when the three of them walked out together. They circled to the passenger side of the vehicle, and Ben opened the door, forcing his sisters to get in before him.

"Oh! Oh, my Lord!" Hands pressed to her mouth, Patricia was blinking rapidly as Brianne and Sara claimed the side seat opposite the two officers. She made a few squeaky sounds before finally lowering her hands. "Oh, you are more beautiful than I ever imagined."

A flush colored Brianne's face, but Ben thought most of the heat probably came from the huge smile she was beaming. It troubled him that he hadn't given her a chance to have her own opinion about their mother. No kid should ever have had to hide the fact that she missed her mother, especially for twenty years.

"This is a wonderful surprise," Patricia said, using one fingertip to wipe tears from her eyes. "Bree. Sara."

Sara's voice matched the stiffness of her posture. "We're sorry about your loss."

If the lack of warmth stung Patricia, Bree more than made up for it. She launched into the seat beside Patricia, enveloping her in a hug and murmuring, "I'm so sorry about George, Mama. I know how much you loved him."

Sara gave Ben a *what-the-hell* look, and he just shrugged. At least he hadn't been the only one Brianne fooled.

The major leaned forward, offering her hand. "I'm Major Baxter, and this is Lieutenant Graham. We'll be assisting Patricia."

Sara provided her name and Brianne's, who took barely a moment from Patricia to shake hands.

There was little conversation from there to Tulsa International Airport, though Sara's frequent glares left no doubt she had plenty to say. Ben stared out the window at people going about their everyday lives, preoccupied with work and family, not thinking that other people's lives had abruptly ended. Of course, they couldn't focus on death all the time; then what would be the point of living?

At the main gate into the Tulsa Air National Guard Base, the Patriot Guard were staged, most wearing denim and leather, motorcycles gleaming, flags on full display. Ahead were military personnel, presumably from Fort Murphy and the national guard, and a lot of law enforcement vehicles: Tulsa and Tallgrass Police, Tulsa County Sheriff, Oklahoma Highway Patrol.

Sara leaned closer to the major and grimly asked, "Are those protestors going to be here today?"

The possibility of a bunch of ultraconservative bigots disrupting the transfer hadn't occurred to Ben. Even before he'd gotten this personal connection, he'd wondered how the hell anyone could look in the mirror after intruding so hatefully on a family's grief and not be disgusted with himself. He bent forward, too, to hear the answer.

"They said they would, but there's been no sign of them," Major Baxter said quietly. "If they are around, you probably won't see them. The Patriot Guard are very good at keeping them at a distance from the family."

"Good, because I'd hate to kick someone's ass today—I didn't dress for it—but I could." Sara's jaw jutted forward, reminding Ben of all the times she'd played the protector as a kid. She'd rarely gotten into an actual fight, but she'd held her own those few times. Ben would put his money on her today, especially with those deadly heels she wore.

Patricia smiled faintly. "Still the defender," she murmured, making Sara's jaw clench.

Then the car stopped. They were there. After getting out of the car, Ben took note of all the people: the funeral director; Patricia's pastor, Reverend Vernon, and his wife; several couples from their church. A short distance away, the officers belonging to the police vehicles stood with the military personnel. Most of them had never heard of Colonel George Sanderson. Some of them had known and loved him. All of them were somber and respectful.

After a few moments, the major touched Patricia's arm and gestured. Flags snapped in the breeze, traffic sounded on the nearby highway, and a bird chittered nearby, but everyone's attention was locked on the plane on the ground in the distance.

It glinted in the sun as it steadily approached, taxiing beneath a water cannon, the spray glistening in the air. Everyone saluted until, after a final turn, the Kalitta Charters plane eased to a stop some yards away.

The silence after the engines shut down was palpable. The pilot was first off the plane, followed by the copilot. They put ramps in place to unload the casket lift, then one climbed inside again. It was a moment before the flag-draped wood casket appeared in the plane's doorway, drawing a gasp from Patricia, and another moment before she managed to breathe again. Sorrow etched deep lines in her face.

"They used to send the casualties home on commercial airlines," she murmured. "In the baggage section. Then one father said, 'My son is not baggage,' and that started the charters." Her voice broke on the last words, and a shudder rippled through her. She clung to Brianne with one hand, to Mrs. Vernon with the other, and for a moment Ben thought even their support couldn't hold her.

Seven solemn soldiers marched to the plane, taking up position on either side of the lift. *The casket team,* Lieutenant Graham whispered. Once the casket was loaded onto the lift, the team stood at attention while those in uniform around them saluted. Swallowing over the lump in his throat, Ben followed the pilot's lead and laid his hand over his heart. Its next few beats were painful, and his vision was growing blurry.

He didn't know this man, his rational mind argued, but it didn't matter. George Sanderson had devoted his life to military service. While other men were working nine to five, going home to their wife and kids every night, he'd been training to protect his country. He'd gone to war multiple times. His life was the last of the sacrifices he'd made.

His passing deserved respect, regret, and sorrow.

Once the lift stopped, the casket team marched away again. "Now that they've received the casket," the chaplain murmured to Ben and his sisters, "your mother will have some time alone, then the team will return and transfer the casket to the hearse."

The funeral director took position on Patricia's left side, Reverend and Mrs. Vernon on the right, and Major Baxter led them across the tarmac to the casket. Ten feet from the plane, Patricia straightened her shoulders, held her head up, and walked alone to the casket. She stood straight as any soldier, one steady hand resting on a slash of red and white stripes. Then like an inflatable toy with a leak, she slowly folded in on herself, ducking her chin, tears flowing, sobs shuddering through her.

Ben squeezed his eyes shut. He still held a lot of anger for Patricia, but everything else aside, she had loved this man. She'd given up everything, even her family, for him. She'd stayed in love with him, loyal, supportive, happy, for every one of the twenty years they'd had together, and now she'd lost him. It was no mistake, no terrible case of misidentification, no nightmare. That wooden casket contained her husband's body, all that was left of him in this world besides the memories. He was gone, and she was still here, and even though Ben had believed his heart was rock-solid safe where Patricia was concerned, this sight—his mother weeping, the flag-draped casket, the dreary skies, the solemn onlookers here to honor George's memory...

This broke his heart.

* * *

Though it had been raining most of the day, the margarita club occupied its usual summertime seats on the patio of The Three Amigos. The temperature was warm enough that getting an occasional splatter wasn't a problem, the rain cool enough to offset the heat. Jessy sat facing away from the building, where a shift of her gaze replaced besties with sheets of water, fat drops that plopped into puddles, tiny rivers seeking the low spots in the parking lot. The sight and the sound and the smell made her want to kick off her shoes, curl up in a comfy chair, and contemplate the benefits of washing away in a good torrent.

Her usual margarita sat in front of her, melted into

a puddle with an occasional chunk of frozen stuff. It tempted her, but she hadn't touched it yet. She was marking time somewhere around 12,720 minutes without a taste. The end of the ninth day. Pretty damn good for someone who'd screwed up practically everything in her life.

Oh, but there were times she wanted it. Wanted it so bad that she would claw her way through a crowd to get to it. Times when she felt so damn alone, when she was absolutely certain that a drink would cure everything that ailed her. Just one drink. No getting hammered, no blacking out, no misbehaving. One single drink. Moderation.

She was thinking maybe that was the problem. She and Moderation weren't on a first-name basis.

The door opened behind Jessy, conversation and music spilling out, as Ilena and Therese returned from the bathroom. Ilena sank into her chair, blowing out her breath as if the trip had exhausted her. Grinning broadly, she looked around the table before her gaze settled on Jessy. "There's a cowboy on the premises," she said with delight.

"This is Tallgrass," Marti replied, a chip with salsa halfway to her mouth. "There's always cowboys— Oh!"

Jessy couldn't help it. She automatically twisted around to look through the windows.

"In the bar," Therese said helpfully. "With Dane and his friend, watching a soccer game."

"I thought about joining them," Ilena said. "Hector Junior's going to play soccer—his daddy was a great soccer player—and I'm going to coach."

Unable to locate Dalton from where she sat, Jessy turned her attention back to her friends, trying to minimize the whiplash she'd gotten from looking for him. "You're planning to coach everything. Have you actually ever played any of those sports?"

Ilena made a dismissive gesture. "I'm not the fragile flower I appear to be."

"You're just a regular steel dandelion," Carly said. "And you'd better quit calling our godson Hector before he gets here, or we'll be calling him that forever. Say it with me now."

Everyone around the table dutifully joined in. "John." Then Ilena's little voice: "Hector Junior."

After a moment's laughter, Lucy said, "So...Jessy. You went off and got a new job and started dating a hot-damn cowboy without sharing with us. What other secrets have you been keeping?"

Every woman at the table turned Jessy's way, until she actually squirmed a bit in her chair. She hadn't squirmed away from attention in a hell of a long time. Still minimizing: "The job wasn't a secret. I just started Friday, and I told you all the next time I saw you."

"And the cowboy?"

"It's...complicated."

Fia and Bennie had the audacity to snort. "He's a good-looking man," Bennie pointed out, "and you're a damn hot woman. The air sizzles when you two get together. Nothing complicated about that."

"Have you two...you know?" Lucy finished with her eyebrows reaching for her hairline.

"Yeah, please tell us Carly and Therese aren't the only ones getting sex on a regular basis," Marti added. "Give the rest of us something to hope for."

Jessy's entire body flushed. "Oh, my God, I can't believe you guys, asking about my sex life! Would I ever poke and pry about what's going on in your beds?"

More snorts. "You're the first one to ask," Carly reminded her.

"Oh. Yeah. Well." Jessy huffed out a breath. "Jeez, I need a drink."

"You've got one."

Marti nudged the full glass a little closer, and in that instant the atmosphere changed. Carly and Therese exchanged glances. Fia's gaze remained steadily locked on Jessy. The other women silently looked from those three to Jessy.

The silence inside Jessy grew and grew until she thought it might burst, scattering bits of her everywhere to be swept up or washed away by the rain. Her nerves stretched thinner, tauter, and a thousand little voices waited expectantly for something to break—for *her* to break—so they could end their silence and whisper, whimper, shriek, wail, or maybe just breathe a profound sigh of relief.

"I—" She picked up the margarita, smelled the lime, and swallowed back the need for just a sip. After a moment, she did something she'd never before done: she poured good liquor onto the pavement, where the water dripping from the roof rinsed it away.

When she set the glass down again, she risked a glance around the table. No one's expression had changed, but something inside her had. Something felt...freer. Stronger. It gave her the courage to commit to her goal by saying the words out loud to her best friends.

They came haltingly, her voice shaky but strong. "I am doing my damnedest to give up drinking. Today is my ninth day."

Silence dropped over the table, each woman registering a reaction for one frozen moment. It took all of Jessy's courage to look at them: the worry, the relief, the awkwardness, a little surprise, a lot of pleasure. In her nightmares, she'd imagined horror, shock, or repulsion, but bless their hearts, she didn't see any of that.

When the moment unfroze and their voices mingled into the lovely, treasured cacophony that was Margarita Girls, Usual Style, finally Jessy allowed herself to breathe. They congratulated her. They assured her she could do it, promised they were there for her. Underneath the table, Fia gave her hand a tight squeeze. They accepted her. They embraced her with their words and their arms and their hearts. Through all the conversation, the laughter, the funny tales, and the somber planning for the next day's funeral, their words kept echoing in her head.

You can do this.

For the first time, she honestly, no fingers-crossed-behind-her-back thought she could.

Lucy broke up the evening first so she could stop by the funeral home for the colonel's visitation. The others followed soon after, Fia pausing to hug Jessy. "I'm so proud of you," she whispered.

Jessy went still and warm at the same time. Simple words that she couldn't recall anyone ever saying to her before. Certainly not her parents, not her sisters, not even Aaron. He'd told her how much he loved her, missed her, wanted her, but never how proud he was of her.

I'm so proud of you. She would never forget the words, would always keep them tucked away to pull out when she needed encouragement in those alone times.

She said her good-byes, picked up her purse and umbrella—never let it be said that a little rain could keep Jessy Lawrence from her girls—then hesitated, wavering between the gate leading to the parking lot and the door going into the restaurant.

"Oh, no. You're not gonna slip off while Dalton's in there with Dane." Carly slipped her arm through Jessy's and pulled her inside. "You know he didn't drive all the way into town just to watch the game with the guys."

"He knows where I live."

Carly grinned. "You suck at acting like the too-cool girl who doesn't want to let on how excited she is."

"Hey, doll, I'm not acting. I *am* too cool. Now, if you want to talk about all the things I suck at, better pull up a chair 'cause this will take a while."

"You know what? My cousin—she's a neuroscientist—does research on the power of words, specifically the impact of repeated words. Basically, that if you say or hear something often enough, good or bad, eventually you begin to believe it. Life is hard enough on us, Jessy. Don't give it a hand by beating yourself up. Look at you. You're healthy. You've got a new job and a new relationship with a gorgeous guy. You're surrounded by people who love you, and you're nine days sober. You're blessed, sweetie. We all are."

Blessed. Damn. That was a word Jessy never associated with herself. It seemed too...good. She was so used to focusing on the bad: the drinking, the regrets about Aaron, what should have been with her family. But she *was* surrounded by people who loved her. She loved her job—yep, even after only a day and a half, she knew that. She was going to be a godmother in another couple weeks. And there was Dalton.

Literally, sitting at a round table in the bar, the heels of his boots hooked over the lower rung of the stool, his hat hanging on a wall hook beside them. His jeans were faded, well worn, and his T-shirt looked new in comparison. Both hugged him like a seductive woman, smoothing over muscles and hard planes.

To quote Lucy, he was one hot-damn cowboy.

Carly lightly squeezed her shoulder. "Yes, ma'am, you are certainly blessed." Then she let go and passed Dalton to sidle up to Dane and kiss his temple. He automatically slid his arm around her waist and pulled her near, giving her a look, just a look, that could have melted the polar ice cap. He loved her and considered himself lucky to have her. All that was in his expression, in the way he touched her, the way he...treasured her.

A big message for a nonromantic like Jessy to translate from a little simple body language.

After they'd exchanged greetings, Carly asked, "You need a ride home, Jessy?"

"Thank you, but I'm going the way I came—walking."

"What if we get lightning?"

"Then I'll sprint."

"I know your sentiments toward exercise," Carly said dryly. "I happen to share them. Maybe you should accept a ride. Dalton will be going right by your place."

Jessy looked at Dalton, who was unfazed by her volunteering him. "Let me take a look out and see. You guys have fun." She fluttered her fingers in a wave, then turned toward the exit. A moment later, the stool scraped across the concrete, then boot falls thudded behind her.

As they stepped outside the restaurant, she let a slow smile spread through her. Carly was right. Dalton hadn't come to town just to watch the game. It had been a long time since Jessy had felt this excited about a little time with a man, but tonight it was there, pushing past all the negatives, all shiny and blinky to catch her attention.

She was one lucky girl.

* * *

Dalton stood near Jessy under the bright-striped canopy, watching the rain fall as steadily as when it had started. It was a good rain. All over the ranch, the grass, the trees, and the creeks were drinking it up, always ready for a soaker, never knowing when the next one might come.

"You know, if I walk you home, I'm just gonna have to come back by myself to get the truck."

She tilted her head to gaze up at him. "It's just rain. You won't melt."

"Neither will you. That umbrella's almost bigger than you are. You could use it for a weapon."

Smiling, she took a stance and wielded it like a clumsy sword covered in yellow daisies and hot pink. "I never use the umbrella on the way home. The idea is to arrive to dinner looking fabulous. If I come back looking like a drenched cat, there's no one to see."

"So why don't you ride home with me, put the umbrella up, then we can walk over to Java Dave's for coffee."

"It's a deal," she said with an expression that made him think she'd planned to agree all along. True to her word, she didn't unfurl the umbrella, hustle to the truck, or try to shield herself using her purse. The air could have been dry as the most boring Sunday sermon for all the care she paid.

Inside the truck, it smelled like wet leather, clean rain, and delicately scented shampoo. Underneath those aromas was the staleness of dust and grit, plus just a whiff of a per-

fume that, like outstanding food, could damn near make his
mouth water.

After he turned onto Main, he remarked, "Dane told me
about the dignified transfer today." Most of the margarita
club had gathered outside her apartment, holding flags or
their hands over their hearts as the processional passed. He
had only dim memories of Sandra's transfer. He'd been in
shock, heartbroken, and angry. His parents and hers, her
sisters and their families, and Noah had accompanied them
to the airport. He didn't remember saying a word to anyone, not even casket-side. There'd been no point when the
only thing he'd wanted to know was *why*, and it was far too
late for her to tell him that.

"How many of those have you seen make their way
through town?" he went on, his voice a little thick.

"The first one was too many, and it wasn't even
Aaron's." She looked at him. "I remember them all. I always will. But sometimes I need to keep them in the back
of my mind."

He nodded. He'd witnessed one dignified transfer, one
military funeral, and sometimes keeping them in the back
of his mind was the only way he'd kept his sanity.

Within moments, he was parking in front of her building. "It's convenient that you always have parking available."

"It's harder during the day when the businesses are
open. But I have a private space in the alley out back." She
dipped one small hand into her oversized bag and came out
with a key ring before opening the door. "Give me a minute
to set the umbrella inside, then I'll race you to the coffee
shop."

He shook his head, remembering Carly's comment

about Jessy and exercise. He shut off the engine, pocketed his own keys, and was opening the door when she streaked across the street in front of the truck, jumping puddles, splashing her way to the other side. "Damn," he muttered, slamming the door, darting a look left and right, then running after her. For someone who boasted sedentary preferences, she was light and quick on her feet. She made it halfway to Java Dave's before he got close enough to grab her hand and stop her.

"You forgot your hat," she said, huffing out the words as she swiped her sodden hair from her face.

"You cheated. A race means we start at the same time."

"You're taller, in a lot better shape, and have longer legs. How would I win if I didn't cheat?"

"I like your shape." Her hair stood on end, her purple shirt looked as if it had shrunk two sizes, and her shorts had gone baggy, making her waist look narrower, her hips look curvier, in contrast. "It couldn't get any better."

Still holding hands, they started toward the shop. "Thank you," she said airily, as if the compliment was nothing less than she expected. Dalton had seen that reaction enough to know it was a cover.

"When I was a kid, I prayed to the tooth fairies, the Christmas fairies, the ninja fairies, everyone, to please let me top five and a half feet. Everyone in my family was small, including the men. My friends used to call us the toy family. Sadly, the fairies and genetics let me down. I'd still like another six inches of height, but..." She stepped aside to let him open the door, then smiled breezily. "That's what they make outrageous heels for."

The air-conditioning inside hit like an arctic blast. Like before, they got their coffees to go, then walked back through the rain to the gazebo. Jessy settled on a bench, railing at her back, and drew her feet onto the seat before taking a tentative sip of whipped-cream-topped caffeine. "I love this place. I came here sometimes on my afternoon breaks from the bank. You know, hardly anyone ever takes the time to sit here and relax."

"You don't strike me as the take-time-and-relax kind."

"Mostly with the bank, this was my release-steam-or-explode place. Whatever fool came up with the idea that the customer is always right was out of his freaking mind." She shuddered, then took a long, appreciative sip of coffee. "I hated that job. Getting fired—" Breaking off, she darted her gaze his way, off to the street, then back again. Her slender shoulders rounded in a shrug as if she was acknowledging that the words couldn't be recalled.

After a moment, she sighed. "One day, this girl came in—beautiful, dumber than dirt, bratty and snotty and smug. Her father was on the bank's board, and after my patience wore thin from repeating the same information over and over, she threatened to have my job and I told her—"

"That she was too stupid to do it?" Dalton pressed his lips together to control the grin trying to break free.

"Pretty much. Sundrae—can you believe that name?—went to the boss, and I . . . got fired." She stared at her coffee while doing another of those shoulder lifts-and-rolls that looked almost sensual. Granted, most everything she did was sensual.

Finally his grin escaped. "First time?"

"Yeah." She looked at him again, her gaze narrowing, forehead wrinkling, before slowly her own smile started to edge out the frown. "I *hated* that job. Despised everything about it. Had to force myself out of bed every morning to go to it. But getting fired mortified me. It was just one more way I screwed up. I curled up in bed for a week, wanting it back at least long enough so I could quit on my own terms. How dumb is that?"

He'd never lost a job—not much of an accomplishment considering that he'd worked his whole life for his dad, then himself. But he could imagine the impact. With some people, being shown the door just rolled off their backs; Dillon automatically came to mind. Others, like Jessy, took it personally. Dalton figured he would have, too.

He figured she hadn't told anyone, either, wanting to keep what she saw as her failure from her friends.

It meant something that she'd told him, even if it'd been by accident.

"How's the new job?" There had been some surprise among her friends at the cookout, as if none of them had ever imagined her working with animals. After watching her with Oz and his stock, Dalton thought it seemed logical, even natural. When you'd been hurt enough, sometimes the best thing to do was surround yourself with animals. As a general rule, they were smarter, more loyal, and more compassionate than most people, and they couldn't talk you to death with advice.

The last bit of embarrassment disappeared from her expression. "Aw, it's great. Most of the dogs are sweethearts. Most of the cats think they're royalty and I'm there to await their bidding. There are a few babies, though, who have some serious trust issues to work through." Her face wrinkled into a frown as if thinking about those animals in particular troubled her, then she went on. "I'm taking pictures of them for the website and Facebook to see if it helps stir interest in them. Whatever else I've messed up—"

She broke off, and her gaze went distant. After a moment, she said, "I'm a good photographer. I take great pictures."

"You never showed me any pictures of my stock," he reminded her.

"That's right, I didn't." She took another long drink of coffee, leaving a bit of whipped cream in the corner of her mouth. "When I invite you to my apartment, I'll do that."

The two of them alone in her apartment... There was an image to make a man want. He didn't have a clue what the place looked like or how her tastes in furniture and colors ran, but he didn't need one to picture the two of them in her bed or on her couch, the floor, any reasonably stable surface. The thought—the possibility—spread heat through him so quickly he was pretty sure he could hear the hissing of steam from his wet clothes.

His hand was unsteady as he reached out to her, using the tip of his index finger to wipe away the cream. She was amazingly soft and warm and delicate, but the look in her green eyes as she stared at him was as shaky as his fingers. They'd agreed to take it slow, not to repeat the mistake of sex too soon. Was this too soon?

If he had to ask, it probably was.

Damned if the part of him that had been celibate too long didn't care. The part that thought one afternoon of sex was nowhere near enough to make up for five years without was willing to take the risk.

But the part that wanted not just sex but Jessy herself had a little more patience, a little more determination.

Slowly he drew his hand away, missing the contact immediately. There weren't enough soft things in his life, but he could wait.

Awhile.

Chapter 11

On Wednesday the margarita sisters filled an entire row at the post chapel, their dresses bright splashes of color per Patricia's request. Dane sat at one end in his dress uniform, Joe at the other in a dark suit. Lucy sat between him and Marti, her thoughts flowing from the eulogy to bittersweet memories and back again.

There was much more to say about George and his accomplishments than her family pastor had managed with Mike. Mike had lived only half the years George had. Her husband never would have attended college or become an officer; he would have done his twenty, then gone home to California to work in his father's carpentry business.

Still, he would have done great things. He would have helped her raise wonderful children; he would have cared for his parents as they aged; he would have been the one all the neighbors called on when they needed help.

He wouldn't have been the kind of guy who made a place for himself in the history books, but he would have been—*had* been—the guy everyone loved and respected and missed.

Damn, she missed him.

Warm, strong fingers closed over her hands, and she realized they'd begun to tremble. She glanced at Joe, staring straight ahead, gaze locked on the carved cross on the wall behind the reverend. The sight of Joe at her door this morning in a suit and tie had startled her even more than the fact that he'd gotten his hair cut. For a man who lived in sweats, shorts, and T-shirts, he wore the suit amazingly well. He was, the sisters had all pointed out, amazingly handsome.

Bennie, her ebony skin glowing in contrast to the fiery purple of her dress, had given her a skeptical look. *I don't get this just-friends stuff, Lucy.*

You don't think men and women can be friends?

Of course I do. But a guy who looks like Joe? He's way too fine, chica, to waste on just friendship.

But Lucy's heart already belonged to Mike.

And she was looking to give a piece of it to Ben.

Ben sat in the second row between his sisters, flanked by distant relatives. He wore a suit, too, pale gray with an even lighter gray shirt. He'd been in a mood when she'd seen him the night before and again this morning—contemplative, she thought. Even Sara and Brianne hadn't been able to draw him out.

Patricia was composed in the front row. Though she looked unbearably weary, she sat erect, and her eyes were dry. Lucy had always wondered, on seeing photos and videos of military widows at their husbands' funerals, how they held themselves together. Was it some special quality she lacked, maybe some secret they learned that had been denied her?

Then Mike had died, and she'd found out, in her own case, at least, that it wasn't composure. She'd sat erect through his service, eyes dry, because she was too tired to do anything else, because she had already cried so many tears that she just didn't have the energy to produce one more. She'd been numbed by grief and shock, coping only one minute at a time, not yet thinking ahead to the huge scope of her loss: the rest of her life without Mike.

Her hands trembled again, and Joe held them a little tighter.

The minister quoted Marine Corps General Paul X. Kelley: *Lord, where do we get such men?* And General George S. Patton: *We came here to thank God that men like these have lived.* And Mike's favorite: *The only thing necessary for the triumph of evil is for good men to do nothing.*

Mike and George, Marti's husband and Bennie's and Ilena's, all of them, had been such men, good men, and they'd given their lives in the fight against evil, and she was so very thankful they had lived.

But so very heartbroken they had died.

* * *

Patricia's house began clearing out around seven. Ben couldn't even guess at how many people had been in and out, how much food had been brought, how much eaten. The funeral home had delivered enough flowers and plants to fill the house with competing fragrances, to occupy most surfaces and spread across the front porch in a rainbow of color. He'd met so many strangers that he'd given up trying to remember names and connections to Patricia and George.

He was exhausted. Mentally. Physically. He wanted—needed—the busyness of his practice and the comfort of his own bed. He needed to go home.

Then images from the day passed through his mind—Patricia accepting condolences from dozens of people, sitting under the funeral home canopy at the cemetery like a windup doll that was finally running down, murmuring a prayer, flinching at the firing of the salute, accepting the casket flag from the post's commanding general, saying good-bye at the grave site, leaving a handful of red roses on George's casket, getting lost inside herself on the way home.

Ben couldn't go just yet. The staff had rearranged his schedule; his partners were taking over the cases that couldn't be put off. He wasn't needed there.

He'd shed the coat and tie and rolled his sleeves up, but hadn't changed clothes yet. Tired of voices, of people, of the little bit of guilt crawling along his spine periodically, he went outside to stand on the patio. Thanks to the tall trees next door, the bricked area was shaded from the evening sun, the chairs with their thick padding inviting, the subtler smells of tree, earth, and flowers more pleasing to breathe.

"How long have you known about Bree?"

He didn't glance at Sara as she joined him. Instead, he gazed at the back of Lucy's house. She'd left a while ago to feed the dog and walk him—probably to decompress, too. Today hadn't been easy for her. He'd seen it in the lines that framed her mouth, that edged out from the corners of her eyes. Too many memories, and few of them happy.

"She told me a couple days ago."

"I can't believe all these years she's been missing Mom."

"Haven't you? At least a little?"

"No," Sara replied bluntly.

"You were nine."

"And smart enough to see that she chose him over us." She sipped a glass of wine from the supply one of Patricia's friends had brought. "Have you missed her?"

He shrugged. "I never really thought about it. About her." It was true. She'd left them to make their way the best they could, and for him, that had been by shutting her out. He'd gotten very good at it, but the past week and a half had changed that.

"She wants to meet my family," Sara said. "Bree mentioned it. She thinks it's a great idea."

"What do you think?"

"I don't know. She chose to skip out on two thirds of my life—important times. Why should she get to come back now?" With a deep exhalation, she sat on the edge of a chair. "Bree says the past is past. It can't be undone."

That was true. Their perfect family had been shattered. Their father had been broken. They'd lost their balance and happiness and illusions, and none of that could be changed. So should they forget it? Set it aside as if she hadn't been responsible for the shattering and give her a chance? Trust her, forgive her, welcome her, and maybe even start to love her again?

And what if she abandoned them again?

"You don't have to decide anything this minute," he said at last. A lame answer, but sometimes *lame* was the best he could offer.

"I know. In fact, Bree and I have to head back to Tulsa.

If we make good time, I'll get to tuck the kids in and read them a story." She stood and swallowed the last of the wine. "When are you going home?"

"Soon. Tomorrow. Friday."

Her expression suggested the answer didn't quite please her, but she didn't comment on it. "Help me pry Bree away, will you?"

They returned to the house, where they did, in fact, have to pry Brianne from Patricia's side. She wanted to delay going home, but three words from Sara—*Matt, Lainie, Eli*—stopped her protest. Patricia hugged her tightly and said a more subdued good-bye to Sara, then Ben walked them outside to Sara's car.

He hugged them both, ruffling Sara's hair just to make her grimace, then shoved his hands into his pants pockets and watched as they drove away. Part of him wished he could follow behind them in his own car. But another part knew that leaving Tallgrass just now would be a mistake. He didn't know why he felt the need to stay another few days. He just did.

After gazing at the crowded house for a moment, he circled around the side to the backyard, then ignored the patio and headed for Lucy's. He was tired, his head ached, and his nerves were wound tight. If anything could make him feel better, it was Lucy with her soft voice, reasonable mind, and even softer hands.

As he reached the patio, the back door opened and the mutt burst out, dragging his owner behind him with his leash. A quiet growl vibrated from the animal.

"Oh! Hey, Ben." Lucy reeled the dog in, her expression all pleasant surprise. Already Ben was feeling evidence of improvement. "Norton, sit. Behave."

The dog ignored the first and studied Ben, tongue hanging out, a calculating look in his doggy eyes.

"Hey." Ben backed a step away from Norton. "I was wondering if you'd like to go somewhere. Dinner. Dessert. A drive." Even as he said it, he realized it was exactly what he needed: a quiet time, not judging or being judged, no bitterness, no history separating them, just friendship drawing them together and the possibility of a future.

"Oh. Wow. Um…" She tucked a strand of hair worked free of her ponytail behind her ear, then her gaze moved past him. Ben didn't need to hear footsteps to know someone was approaching or to hear a voice to know it was Joe Cadore. The mutt was having a fit of glee.

"Joe, hey," Lucy said. "Uh, listen, would you mind walking Norton for me tonight? Ben asked me to—to go somewhere. Dinner. A drive. Out."

Cadore was wearing a ball cap backward, along with gym shorts and a T-shirt with the sleeves ripped out. He reminded Ben of a kid, with no responsibilities, no interest except in good times, and not a serious thought in his head—plus a good dose of suspicion. His gaze went from Lucy to Ben to Lucy again, his eyes narrowed, and a muscle twitched in his jaw. "What about—"

A look from Lucy stopped his question, and he grudgingly said, "Yeah, sure, I guess."

She thrust the leash at him. "Let me change real quick, Ben, and I'll be ready."

Before he could say she looked fine, the door closed behind her and he was left alone with Cadore and the dog. He didn't say anything—talking would only encourage them to stay—but Cadore didn't take the hint. Norton sat at his feet, leaned against his leg, and watched them.

Ben shoved his hands into his pockets again and studied the house. It was well maintained, painted within the last year or two, the color somewhere between white and light yellow. The shutters and door were green, and the same shade striped the cushions on the patio chairs. With tubs of flowers grouped in corners, the place would have been comfortable without the two nuisances eight feet away.

Before manners or sheer discomfort forced Ben to say *something*, the door opened again and Lucy stepped out. She'd changed into a dress, sleeveless, vivid blue, with flip-flops. Her hair was down again, soft waves reaching to her shoulders, and she'd touched up her lipstick. She was about the prettiest and sweetest companion he could ever want for enjoying a warm summer evening and a setting sun.

"Thanks, Joe," she said, oblivious to the tension in the air. "Just put him back inside when you're done. See you later."

Ben followed her across the patio and into the grass. He couldn't resist looking back just once. Cadore scowled back before muttering something to the dog, then taking off at a slow jog around the house and toward the street.

*   *   *

By noon Friday, Jessy was stinky, damp, and tired, but she had five sweet-smelling dogs ready to meet prospective owners to show for her efforts. None of them had enjoyed their baths—*What's wrong with you?* she'd asked. *Don't you know a long soak in a tub is one of the great pleasures in life?*—but they had endured in exchange for the serious combing and treats she and Angela had given each of them.

Now she sat in an inexpensive webbed lawn chair in a

back room, a bottle of cold water on the table in front of her. Angela had gone to get lunch—sprouts or something from a little health food place Jessy had never noticed—and Meredith was at her other job, so Jessy was alone in the place. She liked it—the smells, the stealth of the cats, the play and barking and snores of the dogs. Who knew she would feel so at home at an animal shelter?

"I'm back," Angela called a moment before she appeared in the hallway. Cats swished around her feet. Somehow, with her, the action appeared sweet and affectionate. Jessy was pretty sure that when they did the same to her, they were just trying to trip her.

The blonde began unpacking the plastic bag she carried before snagging a folding chair on the other side of the table. A large plate in hand, she hesitated. "I forgot to ask if you have any dietary restrictions. Are you vegetarian? Vegan? Gluten-free? Diabetic? Paleo, Atkins, South Beach?"

Jessy blinked. "I eat everything."

"Good." With a grin, Angela continued unpacking. "So do we, but when Meredith and I lived in L.A., our friends were following so many different diet paths that we couldn't even have a dinner party."

Jessy began peeling foil from the containers, each containing two portions of food: grilled chicken strips; tomato, onion, and feta salad; black beans with cilantro in a spicy dressing; blackened pepper strips, grilled rings of red onion, sticky sweet slices of mushroom; and soft corn tortillas to wrap it all up. If this was health food, she needed to sign up.

"What brought you to Oklahoma?" she asked after they'd each made a taco/wrap hybrid and taken the first few bites.

"Meredith went to vet med school at OSU. I didn't want to be apart that long, and she didn't want to practice in California, so I came with her. We'd both been involved with animal rescue groups, so when she came to work in Tallgrass, I got a job here, and now we run the place."

She made it sound so simple, as if uprooting her life and moving from Los Angeles to small-town Oklahoma was no more difficult a decision than what to have for dinner.

But it really wasn't, Jessy reminded herself. Not when you were going with someone you loved. She'd done it. So had all her friends, numerous times, and they would all do it again if necessary. She hoped it never became necessary...though she wouldn't mind a move of six or eight miles.

If things progressed to that point with Dalton. He hadn't even kissed her yet. She hadn't even kissed *him* yet. She knew he wanted to, and damn well she wanted to, but there was that nagging worry. What if they did it too soon again? What if they screwed up what was turning into a very good thing?

But what if they waited too long and he met someone else? She knew too well how loneliness and dissatisfaction turned a rational person into an easy pickup who felt like crap in the morning.

"You look awfully somber," Angela said, drawing Jessy's gaze. "If you need to talk about something, I'm a very good listener."

"Thanks." *But I'm a very good secret keeper.* But keeping secrets took its toll on her. It made her antsy and embarrassed and filled her with dread. Look at how hard she'd tried to keep her drinking and attempts to stop it to herself, convinced the margarita sisters would be so disappointed in her that they'd dump her, but they hadn't. They'd supported her. Encouraged her. Fia said she was proud of her.

And keeping getting fired to herself…Dalton hadn't gone running the other way. He'd seen the humor in it. He'd smiled about it. He'd made *her* smile about it.

She swallowed the last bite of her wrap, then slowly put another together. "There's this guy," she said with a calculatedly careless shrug.

"Oh, honey." Angela laughed. "Do you know how many stories start with 'There's this guy'? That's why I prefer women."

Jessy laughed, too. "No, this guy…he's a good one."

"Is he the first one since your husband?"

Not the first, though she wished he were. But the first serious one? "Yeah. His wife died in the war, too. We're kind of…feeling our way, I guess." Feeling emotionally, but not physically. Wednesday night, when Dalton had held her hand, it had made her almost light-headed. Like she was young and innocent and starting all over again, luxuriating in that small intimacy and anticipating more.

But when they got back to her apartment, he hadn't done anything more. He'd seemed reluctant to let go of her, but he hadn't moved closer, hadn't nuzzled her neck, hadn't wrapped his arms around her. He hadn't even looked her longingly in the eyes, though he'd asked if he could take her to dinner after the wedding rehearsal. Since this was the second time for both of them, Carly and Dane had decided against the formal rehearsal dinner, along with most of the other trappings of a wedding. They were committing to each other, not to a ceremony.

"Wow. You don't look for the path of least resistance, do you?" Angela said. "Was he happy with his wife?"

Jessy's muscles went stiff, her jaw clenching, as she lifted her gaze to her boss's face. Angela's blond hair was pulled up on her head with a big clip, her blue eyes were clear, her expression showing nothing but curiosity. "Why do you ask that?" Jessy asked, wondering if her voice sounded hollow because of the fifteen-foot metal walls and ceiling or because she'd suddenly gone empty inside.

"A lot of married people aren't happy." Angela shrugged. "And sometimes fate interferes before they have to do anything about it. I had a friend in L.A. who'd wanted a divorce practically from the beginning. The day she planned to tell her husband, he was in a wreck on the way home. Died at the scene. I had another friend in the same situation—trying to find the courage to get out of a marriage with a guy who absolutely adored her. She worked out what she was going to tell him and practiced in front of us, like auditioning for a part on TV, and when she was finally ready to tell *him*, she went home, found his stuff gone, their bank accounts cleaned out, everything she had of value disappeared, and a note from her adoring husband who'd run off with his pregnant girlfriend. Fate," she repeated with a shrug.

Jessy had wanted out of her marriage, but a few weeks before she'd planned to tell Aaron, he'd died. Fate? Was that all it was? Some universal force taking things into His/its own hands? Or had Angela's friends set off some sort of bad karma in the universe that caused the results they got? Had Jessy's bad karma made Aaron the target of that sniper's bullet?

She shook her head, trying to clear it. "No, Dalton and

Sandra were very happy." All of her friends had been bliss-
ful in their marriages; they'd all had tough times, but they
had survived them. Only Jessy had given up. Only she had
planned an escape.

For two years and nearly nine months, that knowledge
had made her feel so much *less* than them.

"So if you're feeling your way, I'm guessing you're the
first woman Dalton's been serious about since his wife. I
can see where that would be tough...but worth it. Sometimes that's how you get through, by keeping your eye on
the prize. You may make some missteps, but look at the reward. Forever with a good man. How cool is that?"

Everything inside Jessy wanted that—believed she
could have it. But she summoned a careless grin to hide
that aching need. "Cooler for me than it would be for you."

"True. I'm perfectly happy with Meredith, thank you."

"How long have you two been together?"

"Twenty-one years. Since we were fifteen. We always
figured we'd get married someday, but then we chose to
live in Oklahoma, so not for a good long while."

Probably not. Oklahoma was a great place, but the state
as a whole bled conservative red.

Outside a bark sounded, followed by more both inside
and out. Two cats scurried for dark corners while two
others, tails held high, regally walked down the hall pre-
paring to be worshiped. "That should be our prospective
parents," Angela said, starting to gather leftovers. "Right
on time."

"Go on. I'll clean up here." Down the hall, Jessy saw
a mother, well dressed, with matching children, clean
and neat and waiting politely. A doctor's wife, according
to Angela, who homeschooled her ten-year-old daughter

and twelve-year-old son, had a large fenced yard, was active in her church, fervently believed in pet adoption, and was a major donor to the shelter. Jessy wished the family could take all of the animals. Hell, she wished *she* could take all of them, but her apartment was too small, and more puppies and cats in need would come along. They always did.

After straightening the break/storage room, she went outside, put clean water in the bowls, and refilled the plastic wading pools in the backyard. After she'd scratched every furry bundle of quivering joy there, she went to the front yard and took a seat on another cheap lawn chair.

Oliver stood about six feet away. He tolerated people getting closer but didn't like it. His cone showed little battering from miscalculating doorways or play, maybe because he spent most of his day in the same spot. Was he waiting for his owner to find him? Did he like the way the sparse grass smelled there? Did he simply like doing something that made humans wonder?

"You're a pretty boy, Oliver."

His brown eyes didn't blink.

"I wonder what happened to you." When the economy started to tank, Meredith had told her, a lot of people couldn't afford to feed their pets so they surrendered them or, worse, dumped them somewhere. Sometimes people moved to a place that didn't allow pets, or they didn't want the hassle of taking their animals with them, so they just left them behind.

"You know you've got people out there somewhere. They might not know they're yours yet, but they'll figure it out."

He gazed at the front door for a moment, then turned in

a circle and settled to the ground, chin resting on his cone, front paws flat on the grass as if he might need to leap to his feet unexpectedly.

"In the meantime, this isn't a bad place to be. You get to lie in the sun when you want, go inside where it's air-conditioned when you get hot. Your belly's full, Meredith's taking care of all your owies, and you've got me." She laughed softly, first at the idea that she was having an actual conversation with a dog, and second at the proposition that she was any great prize, even for a homeless puppy who'd just had pellets picked out of his flea- and tick-riddled hide.

She raised one finger to the dog. "Don't go thinking like me, that I'm no big deal. I've been good, and I've been bad, and a lot of places in between, but I'm getting better. I haven't had a drink in…hell, a lot of minutes. At least a year in doggie time. I'm a work in progress, just like you."

Oliver stretched out his front legs, then scooted forward on his belly. He repeated it until he'd closed half the distance between them, where he settled again.

"Aw, see? You do like me. A lot of people do." A faint smile curved her lips at the truth of her comment. "Some people, in fact, adore me. And some don't. But you know, life is too short to care about people who don't care about you. So if you sit out here alone all the time because you like it, that's fine, but if you're watching for your old humans, don't bother, sweetie. Your new ones will be so much better."

And everyone deserved better humans, just as she deserved to be a better one.

* * *

"You having any second thoughts, son?"

Standing in a corridor that opened off the sanctuary of Carly and Dane's church, Dalton looked up as the pastor joined them, offering his hand to Dane. It was a rhetorical question. A blind man could see that hesitation was the last thing on Dane's mind.

"No, sir. I'm ready to make it official."

"You'll never meet anyone more ready than him." Keegan Logan, the other groomsman, was leaning against the wall with his little girl holding his hands, her feet planted between his, swinging her chubby little self left to right like a pendulum.

Though Keegan himself might be more ready. According to Jessy, the guy was crazy mad in love with their friend Therese and counting the days until his current enlistment was up so he and Mariah could move to Tallgrass to make a family with the Mathesons.

Family. Dalton had resigned himself to not having one of his own. He'd figured he'd be the odd uncle that Noah's kids didn't quite know what to think of, nothing more. But for the first time in a long time, he could see himself getting married again. Maybe having kids, maybe not, but definitely not spending the rest of his life alone.

He could see himself with Jessy.

Somebody signaled to the pastor that the rest of the wedding party was ready, and he walked into the sanctuary. The setup was pretty much like every wedding Dalton had ever seen. He, Dane, and Keegan followed the minister in; Carly's niece and nephew came down the aisle with flowers and the ringbearer's pillow; Therese and Carly's sister-in-law Lisa followed; then the father of the bride escorted her to the altar.

After a quick run-through, Dalton met Lisa at the center aisle and they headed to the back behind Carly and Dane. "So you're the cowboy," she said. "Yippee-kai-yai-yay."

"And you're the rocket scientist."

"Anthropologist, actually. These days I'm mostly mom to Isaac and Eleanor." She gestured to the kids at the back tussling over the embroidered pillow. "At the moment, I'm pretending I don't see them misbehaving. Our entire family is thrilled to see Carly happy and in love again, though you might miss the obvious signs."

She gestured again, and he looked at the large group filling the two back pews: mother, father, three brothers, two wives, a passel of kids. The kids mostly appeared bored while the adults looked, alternately, uncomfortable or lost in thought. They were absentminded professors, Dane said, every last one of them a bona fide genius. *Lacking at least one social skill for every ten points of IQ over 140,* Carly had added with obvious affection.

Across the aisle from them, Dane's mother and a couple he'd pointed out as Carly's former in-laws seemed over-the-top engaged-in-the-moment in comparison.

"Do you have a wife hanging out here?" Lisa asked with a glance at the others in the back, more relatives, he assumed, but strangers to him.

"No. She died on her second tour."

Lisa's fingers tightened around his arm. "Oh, sweetie, I'm so sorry." They reached the end of the aisle, and she released her hold only to wrap her arms around him in a quick hug. "Now that Carly's found Dane, I'll worry about you in her place. I'm so sorry."

A lump formed in his throat, heat flooding his face. He wasn't embarrassed exactly. Just taken aback that a woman he'd met minutes ago could be so bone-deep sincere and make him feel that she really cared.

As Lisa's hug loosened, he cleared his throat and gazed past her to make sure his eyes weren't damp. "Thanks. I appreciate it. But right now Eleanor's hitting Isaac with his pillow. He's got age and height on her, but she's got a pretty wicked swing going for her."

Lisa rolled her eyes, then gasped as she turned in time to see Isaac hit the floor and roll under the nearest pew. "Eleanor! Isaac! Roger!"

One of the Andersen brothers turned, brows lifted, and automatically said, "I didn't do anything."

"Your children are wrestling right underneath you! In church!"

Roger looked over his shoulder, twisted, and hauled Eleanor over the back of the pew into his lap while Lisa pulled Isaac to his feet. Both kids were sticking their tongues out at each other from the protection of their parents' embraces.

Dane and Carly, arms around each other, stopped beside Dalton. "Isaac's going to be a scientist and make clones of his sister that can't talk and have to do everything he says," Carly said.

"And Eleanor's going to be a superhero or a supervillain. She hasn't decided yet," Dane added. "Whichever gives her the most chances to smack her brother."

"Our family. We're so proud." Carly copied his grin. "We're all going to Zeke's out on Main. You're welcome to join us."

Dalton thanked them politely, made it out the door without distraction, and climbed into his truck for the drive to Jessy's. She occupied the entire bench outside her apartment, back against the curved arm, legs stretched out to the other end. Her shorts were white, her top black, her shoes a black, pink, and green print with delicate heels. The usual overnight-bag-sized purse rested on the bench beneath her propped-up feet, and she was fanning herself with a couple of white paper rectangles.

He parked in front of her, rolled down the passenger window, and called, "Hey, you waiting on Prince Charming?"

Slowly she pushed the dark glasses up to rest on top of her head. "Princes are too stuffy. I'd prefer a cowboy on a fiery steed."

"Huh. Palominos aren't very fiery."

"I don't know. A good photographer, sunset, that golden coat reflecting the light..." Moving lazily—sensually— she swung her feet to the ground, stood to her full height, bent to slide the purse strap over her shoulder, and strolled toward the truck. Everything about her looked so good and touchable and kissable, and he'd almost decided to forget dinner and turn this truck toward home when she settled and directed a purely innocent smile at him. "Take me somewhere that serves beef, cowboy. I've got a craving for red meat."

Home qualified for that. He had a side of beef in the freezer from the last butchering, and he was sure they could find things to occupy them while the steaks thawed. It would only take five, maybe seven, twenty-four hours.

After pulling away from the curb, he turned south on First, putting the setting sun on her side, her golden skin reflecting all that light.

"How was rehearsal?"

"Uneventful, unless you count the flower girl beating up the ring bearer."

She laughed. "I went to a wedding years ago where the bride and groom each had a five-year-old daughter so they were both flower girls. They got into a fight during the ceremony, kicking, screaming, pulling hair, and the bridesmaids had to pull them apart, then drag them down the aisle afterward."

"That must have been a fun new family," he said dryly.

"Like having twins who despise each other."

Bingo. "What have you got in your hands?"

She looked at the papers, then smiled. "Photographs."

"Of my animals?"

"He could be." She waved the pictures for emphasis, and he caught a glimpse of a solemn-faced dog.

He swallowed back a groan. "Did I tell you Oz was a stray? Covered with fleas and ticks and half-starved?"

"See? They have so much in common already. Oliver was dumped with fleas and ticks and half-starved, plus someone used him for target practice with a pellet gun."

A knot tightened in Dalton's gut. He'd spent his entire life taking care of animals. He'd just as soon shoot someone who abused them. But he hadn't wanted a dog when Oz adopted him, and he didn't want another dog now.

You already have two small herds. What could one more animal hurt?

His father's voice echoed in his head: *That damn "what could one more hurt?"* David's parents, his wife, his neighbors, and his kids had used that question to guilt him into taking every stray dog and cat, injured horses, cattle that were nothing more than pets, even a herd of goats when their owner went into a nursing home.

He delayed his answer by turning into the parking lot of an old cinder block building. A crooked neon sign that hadn't lit up since he was a teenager welcomed them to Holy Cow, where a short line was forming at the door.

"I've seen this place, but I've never been here," Jessy said, sliding to the ground.

"Your loss. Those beeves you were taking pictures of—"

Meeting him at the front of the truck, she frowned up. "Cows. Pretty bovine animals."

"Beeves," he repeated. "Damn good dinner on hooves. Anyway, those folks sell their beef to this restaurant. The place isn't fancy, but the food is the best."

They joined the line, the tin roof blocking them from the sun slanting in from the west. She tapped the pictures together, then offered them to him. He took hold of one corner, but before pulling them free, he warned, "I'm just looking, all right?"

She nodded.

The dog was Dalton's favorite breed: a little bit of this, a little bit of that. He looked full grown, no more than thirty pounds, and his big brown eyes...God, those eyes alone were enough to win him a home. Thoughtful, sad, confused, a good show of bravado underscored with traces of fear.

Jessy didn't gush, coo, or point out all of Oliver's good points. She just watched Dalton as he thumbed through the pictures. When he handed them back, she put them in her purse, then laced her fingers together.

"There's no rush, is there?" he asked after a while. "The shelter's a no-kill shelter, right?"

Another nod.

"Is there any reason you aren't adopting him?"

Her face wrinkled delicately. "Can you imagine a living, breathing being depending on me for everything?"

"I have a whole lot of living, breathing beings depending on me. You could handle one dog. You could even take him to work so he wouldn't have to be alone during the day."

"Yeah, but you're responsible. I'm—"

When she broke off, he quietly said, "You put a lot of energy into criticizing yourself, Jess. Why?"

Her face flushed. "I'm trying to stop. Old habits, you know. They're hard to break."

He understood that. He'd buried himself in bad habits and dark places for too long.

Gently, he pulled her hands apart, then twined his fingers with hers. "I'll offer this. I'll be Oliver's last resort. If you don't find the perfect people for him, we'll take him. Okay?"

The smile that lit up her face was sweet enough, honest enough, that he would have agreed to take all the shelter's dogs just to see it again.

Maybe even their cats.

Chapter 12

Jessy dressed carefully Saturday afternoon, giving herself more than two hours for a task she could often pull off more than adequately in under ten minutes, but she still wasn't ready when Ilena and Lucy came to pick her up. Normally, she would have just walked to the church, especially since she was leaving with Dalton, but when the sisters had offered, she'd accepted. Accepting little things like rides was something friends did, right?

Hands bracing her lower back, Ilena trailed Lucy into the apartment and to the bedroom. "Jessy, my girl, this is my last visit until my boy is born. Those stairs are a killer."

"I'm sorry, *Mamacita*. I didn't think of that or I would have been waiting on the street."

Lucy waved a dismissive hand. "I offered to leave the car running and the AC blasting while I came up to get you, but she said—"

Ilena chimed in with her. "'Aw, exercise is good for Hector Junior.'"

Jessy kicked off a shoe and wiggled her foot into another, the same shade of red but two inches taller with a sexy little bow off-center on the ankle strap. "I thought we were under orders to call him John," she said, twisting her foot this way and that in front of the full-length mirror in the closet.

"Carly is not the boss of me," Ilena said with a huge grin. "Gorgeous shoes. Loan them to me when I can see my feet again, will you?"

"You bet." Jessy struck a pose. "Okay, bows or no bows?"

"Bows," they answered together.

"Dress okay?"

Lucy elbowed Ilena. "I think Jessy's dressing for more than a wedding."

"Yeah, I bet she's got something set up with the best man afterward."

"*I'd* set something up with the best man if he ever gave me a second look," Lucy said enviously.

"I can only *dream* of setting something up at the moment," Ilena said on a sigh as she patted her belly. "I bet she's wearing her sexiest underwear."

Jessy gave them an arch look in the mirror while fastening one ankle strap, then the other. "You're assuming I'm *wearing* underwear. Besides, *all* my undies are sexy."

This time it was Lucy who sighed. "I miss sexy underwear."

"Me, too," Ilena agreed.

Jessy took a long last look in the mirror. Her dress was a respectable length, form-fitting, a bright red, green, and sapphire print, and she'd laid out a green shawl to take. The odds of getting cold in the church were slim—she swore sometimes she felt the fires of hell inside sacred walls—but she wanted to be prepared for whichever restaurant Dalton had chosen for dinner.

"Okay, girls. I guess I'm ready. Unless—" She reached for another dress, the only shade of pink her red hair would tolerate, but Lucy pulled it from her hands.

"You look perfect, honey. Besides, no matter which dress you wear, Dalton won't be thinking about anything besides getting you out of it."

Oh, Jessy sincerely hoped she wasn't the only one thinking about it. Even if they didn't do it tonight. As long as he *wanted* to, she'd be happy. For a while, at least.

When they got to the church ten minutes later, the Andersen clan filled the first four rows on the left side, looking less like a scientific convention and more like a wedding party. "Can you believe Carly's whole family came out from Utah?" she murmured as they walked down the aisle to join the other sisters.

Both Lucy and Ilena gave her questioning looks. "Your family would come from Georgia if you got married again, wouldn't they?"

It was obvious in their expressions that their families would. There was a reason, Jessy reminded herself, why she rarely discussed the Wilkses with her friends.

Though she had no problem telling Dalton all about them.

With a shrug, she said, "My family wasn't at my first wedding. They didn't come for Aaron's funeral, either. In fact, they never met him."

"Oh, Jessy." Lucy hugged her and Ilena squeezed her hand before they sat down.

As everyone exchanged greetings and compliments on

outfits, Jessy gazed at the stained-glass windows and examined her feelings about the exchange. Most notable was
the absence of embarrassment. Her cheeks weren't flushed,
and her gut wasn't knotted. She didn't feel like the object
of pity or like she was some huge failure whose own family
didn't give a damn about her. Just sympathy. Her friends
felt bad for her, not bad about her.

The knowledge created a small well of pleasure deep inside her.

The wedding began exactly on time—in a military
world, punctuality counted—and Jessy pulled her small
camera from her purse. Carly had hired a photographer, but
there were a couple shots Jessy specifically wanted.

The men entered from a side hall. Dane and Keegan
wore their dress uniforms, drawing sighs from practically
every woman in the church, while the minister and Dalton
wore suits. She saved her own sighs for Dalton: tall, broad-
shouldered, handsome, so damn solemn he just about
broke her heart.

What was he thinking about? Remembering his own
wedding to Sandra? Hoping Carly and Dane found a happier ending than he had? Was he blue? Wishing he'd been
one of the lucky ones? Lost in bittersweet memories?

As if drawn by her attention, he turned his head, met her
gaze, and smiled. It was small, private, just for her, and it
promised *more*.

Her breath caught in her chest as her heart quietly, delicately broke, but in a good way. Jessy Lawrence, who'd
sworn never to love a man again, never to risk disappointing another man, was in love with *this* man.

And she had just enough faith to believe he might love
her back, at least a bit.

The knowledge made her feel as if she'd just gotten a little bit happier, a little bit shinier, and a whole lot more normal.

The organist launched into the "Bridal Chorus," and everyone automatically turned toward the back of the church except Jessy. She focused the camera on Dane, waiting for that instant when Carly entered the sanctuary on her father's arm. She didn't need to look for herself or to hear her friends' sighs. The moment was obvious in the emotions that crossed Dane's face. Love, of course. Devotion. Commitment. Peace. Not just happiness but pure joy. And best of all: awe at this new blessing in his life.

Swallowing the lump in her throat, Jessy snapped rapid-fire, sure that one of the dozen or more shots would be perfect.

Therese and Lisa were radiant in off-the-shoulder dresses the orange-reddish hue of late-fall maple leaves. Carly, of course, was simply beautiful. Her dress bared her shoulders, as well, a creamy-tannish-bronzish taupe that hugged her curves and ended a few inches above her knees, lovely, elegant, and oh, so happy.

The music was fitting; there was no rumbling between the flower girl and the ring bearer, no stumbling over the vows. It was romantic and perfect and so well deserved by both bride and groom that all the margarita girls were sniffling by the time the minister made his pronouncement that Dane and Carly were now husband and wife. The sisters' side of the house punctuated the kiss with envious, happy sighs.

As the recessional started, Jessy swiped at her eyes, then lifted the camera again. She began snapping shots the moment Carly and Dane started toward the back and didn't stop until Therese and Keegan had passed their row. The picture she'd really wanted had come in the middle: Dalton escorting Lisa, his steps slowing slightly as they approached, his gaze shifting to look straight at Jessy.

This time he didn't smile. He simply looked, and even through the protection of the camera, it was a look that reached somewhere way deep inside her and made her feel breathless. Nervous. A little bit scared. A month ago, a look like that would have sent her running to the nearest bar. A look like that promised a hell of a lot more than she'd wanted or deserved or could handle.

Now her mouth was watering. Her insides were quivering. She was damn near shaking from need, but not for liquor. It took her a moment to fumble the camera back into its case, then her purse. Another moment to assess whether her legs were steady enough to support her. Another to find the breath to actually push to her feet and balance on her heels.

The celebration moved to the reception hall, where the cake held the place of honor. It came from CaraCakes, made to Carly's specifications: the round bottom layer with both cake and frosting caramel-flavored, the square center layer carrot cake with cream cheese frosting, and the round top layer caramel again. Amid the frosting swirls, curlicues, and flowers nestled handmade sea salt caramels, Carly's only vice before Dane. *I knew I loved him when I shared my Mags' Mojos with him,* she'd said.

"Aw, man. And here I've been so good on my diet." Lucy was looking at the cake with the same greediness Jessy would have felt if confronted by a champagne fountain.

Jessy slid her arm around her waist. "I don't know what it's like for you," she said softly, "if a little piece is okay or if that'll only lead to you wiping out the entire bakery case at CaraCake's on the way home. If it were alcohol, one sip and I would wake up tomorrow morning with a hangover and no clue about what I'd done."

"Is it rationalizing to say it's a wedding, a special day, made for celebrating?"

"I don't know. I think—for me, at least—I have to redefine 'celebrating' so it doesn't involve drinking."

"Or eating." Lucy's voice was soft, thoughtful. "They say to be successful at losing weight, you have to find out why you eat. I've been on enough diets to tell you that. I eat when I'm happy, nervous, excited, celebrating, sad, tired, angry, lonely, bored, heartbroken...It's my response to everything."

Jessy had it easier in that regard. She only tried to drink away the dark emotions, to compensate for the fact that she was a fraud and all-around disappointment. Lately, though, she hadn't felt so much a loser. She still found herself fighting cravings, still held on by her fingertips sometimes, and savored the thought of a margarita, a beer, or Patrón the way she imagined Lucy savored the temptation of chocolate. But she hadn't given in yet.

Then she rephrased that. She hadn't given in, period. Not *yet*, as in likely to happen. She was strong. She believed in herself. More important, other people believed in her. How could she fail with her sisters behind her...and Dalton ahead of her?

*   *   *

Celebrations didn't have to be about food. Lucy kept reminding herself of that throughout the reception, along with the fact that she was going out to dinner with Ben again tonight. He was returning to Tulsa the next day—said he'd been away from the office too long—and his sisters were coming tomorrow morning to spend the day with Patricia, just the four of them.

Lord, how she hated to see him go. It wasn't far in terms of miles, but in terms of their lives...He had an everyday ordinary life that she wasn't a part of. Though she knew from experience that absence made the heart fonder, she'd also seen plenty of instances where absence had made the heart look closer to home for someone who could share every part of your life, not just weekends and holidays.

But Ben had said he would come back. He'd mentioned a restaurant in Tulsa that he wanted to take her to. Asked if she liked the Drillers, talked about the great farmers' market on Cherry Street, the new art gallery near his loft, his favorite jazz club that she would enjoy.

He wanted to see her again, and that fact eased the fluttering in her stomach and strengthened her will to avoid the cake. Sure, it would only be one little piece—and, of course, a couple of decadent caramels. Ten, twelve bites max, and probably a week's worth of two-a-day walks to burn off the calories versus finding the thin, pretty Lucy still living inside her. Oh, yeah, no contest...even though she couldn't watch her friends eat their own cake and caramels without drooling inside.

Sitting with her back to the food table, she let a mantra run through her head: *Remember how much better you'll feel, how much better you'll look, how much prettier you'll be.* Sometimes in weak moments, she got on the Internet and browsed websites that didn't even carry her size, looking over all the cool, skimpy, fitted, adorable clothes that she would be able to wear again. No more shapeless dresses, elastic waists, or ill-fitting garments to try to hide her body. No more mortification at even the idea of being seen naked by a man.

And sexy undies, she thought with a glance at Jessy. She really did miss those.

Low music played over the sound system, jazz, Wayman Tisdale, she thought. Mike had been a fan of his basketball playing at OU, then the pros; she'd loved his music. Like Mike, Wayman had died far too young, but he'd left an incredible legacy of music.

Though the room wasn't officially set up for dancing, Therese and Keegan had claimed a space for themselves. They didn't need much, since they were barely moving. All that mattered to them was being in each other's arms.

"I miss dancing," Fia said with a sigh.

"J'Myel wouldn't slow dance. His moves were too cool and energetic to contain with a slow beat." Bennie smiled wistfully. "Truth was, he looked like a spastic jackrabbit on the dance floor. Mama Maudene told me don't let the fool dance at our wedding, but I couldn't have stopped him for nothing." She laughed. "It was a sight."

"Joshua and I only danced together once," Marti said. "On our wedding night, in our hotel room. I couldn't wear any of the pretty shoes I'd taken on our honeymoon because my bruised toes could only stand flip-flops. I never asked him to dance again."

A few moments later, Mr. and Mrs. Lowry cleared out their own space, followed by Lisa Andersen and her husband. Lucy kept waiting for Dalton to come claim Jessy— he hadn't taken his gaze from her since they'd entered the reception hall—but he kept his distance, though they were exchanging looks, furtive, intimate, private. Yep, Lucy and Ilena had been right. The handsome cowboy was definitely getting lucky tonight.

Picking up her bottle of water, its label commemorating the day, Lucy raised it to her girls. "Here's to Carly and Dane and to the happiest day in the last six years of my life. Let's keep the celebrations coming, okay?"

With laughter and responses ranging from *hear, hear* to *you bet!*, they tapped bottles, then drank. In that moment, not one of them looked as if she had a care in the world. The grief and the sorrow were gone—not forgotten, but not so near the surface, either—and they were just dear friends being friends.

She was so lucky to be a part of them.

* * *

Dalton thought he was just about free to go when the photographer called the wedding party back for pictures, first in the sanctuary, then outside in the warm sun. He hadn't had to hold a smile for such a long time that his face muscles were starting to protest when the guy decided ten thousand shots were enough.

Finally he could slip out of his jacket. His cattle's black-and-white coats might keep them warm in winter and cool in summer, but he was about to dissolve into a giant drop of sweat. As the rest of the guests came out of the church to say good-bye to the happy couple, he loosened his tie, then saw Jessy, standing in the shade of an oak, arms folded over her middle, watching him.

God, she'd been watching him all through the reception, and him her. He couldn't say why he hadn't approached her, asked her to share a piece of cake, talk with him, dance with him. Then his gut clenched hard, his chest tightening, and he remembered: because he would have spontaneously combusted, and wouldn't that have been an ugly page in Dane and Carly's wedding album? From the moment he'd walked into the church and seen her sitting there all beautiful and sexy and focused on him, all he could think was, *Is it time? Please, can it be time?*

He was surprised God hadn't struck him down where he stood.

It was stupid, he thought as he walked to her. He was thirty-two years old. He'd been married. He'd had sex with his share of women. Hell, he'd had sex with *this* woman. But he hadn't known then what he knew now. Then it had been horniness and loneliness, and any woman who persisted until he was drunk would have satisfied. Now it was...

Well, he didn't know what it was, exactly. Important. They had something special, a second chance for both of them to make things right, to make each other right. Something to not screw up.

Good job of giving yourself a case of performance anxiety, buddy.

Then he got close enough to catch a whiff of her perfume, and his entire body reacted with a jerk. The only anxiety there was what if it was too soon for her and then how long would he have to wait.

"Didn't I tell you not to steal attention from the bride?" he murmured when he reached her.

"Nobody noticed."

"Yeah, the four scientists from Utah were struck dumb through the entire reception."

"It was probably just the shoes. They were trying to figure out the whole height of the shoes, shape of the feet, impossible to balance thing."

"Yeah, honey, they weren't looking at your shoes." One hand lightly touching her back, he nudged her forward. "Go join your friends. I don't know about Carly, but Dane's anxious to get going." *And so am I.*

Her eyes, the exact perfect shade of green for her red hair and delicate skin, locked with his. "Frankly, I prefer to have flowers handed to me, preferably already in a container with water. Not lobbed in my direction like a live grenade."

"I'll make a note of that." He nudged her again. "Go so you can get in on the group hug."

"How do you know there'll be a group hug?"

He rolled his gaze to the clear blue sky. "You women hug. A lot."

With a wry look, she handed him her purse, then wound through the guests to join the margarita girls. Keegan, holding his daughter and trailed by a teenage girl and a boy a few years younger, moved over to share the shade. "You understand the point of throwing perfectly good flowers?"

"Nope."

"Me, either," Keegan replied. Taking a cue from him, the little girl shook her head vigorously. "Me, neither," she added. "We *plant* flowers."

While the women got set up, joking and calling, Keegan shifted the girl to his other arm. "These are Therese's and my kids, Mariah, Abby, and Jacob. This is Dalton Smith. You can call him Mr. Dalton or Mr. Smith."

Dalton vaguely remembered kids calling his grandfather

Mr. Doug. It felt old-fashioned, but he liked the connection.

"Where's your uniform, Mr. Dalton?" Mariah asked, playing with the ribbons attached to her father's jacket.

"I don't wear a uniform. I'm a rancher."

Abby shifted her gaze his way. "You have horses?"

"Palominos. Their coat's about the color of your hair."

Her features narrowed as if she were plotting a way to wrangle an invitation to see them. Kids and horses...some things never went out of style. If it was okay with her mother, sometime he'd have Jessy invite them out.

Raised voices from the gathering on the lawn drew their attention to the women. Carly stood a few yards from them, arm drawn back, then she threw the flowers directly at Jessy. Instead of ducking—or catching—them, Jessy bounced them into a high arc straight at Dalton.

Keegan and the kids backed away, leaving him no choice but to catch them. When he did so, Jessy smiled smugly before diving into the group hug. After crying, laughing, and whispering, they freed Carly to join Dane in his pickup, then Jessy strolled toward him. "Did I mention I used to play volleyball? I may have been short, but my spikes were deadly."

He passed her purse over, claimed her hand, and started toward his own truck. She waved good-bye to her friends as they passed, grinning when one of them called, "Ooh, a man in a hurry. She'd better be smiling real big when we see her again, cowboy."

Face heating, he asked, "Is there anything your friends won't say?"

She pretended to think about it as he helped her into the seat. "Some of them are quite proper. Some of us, if it crosses our minds, it crosses our lips. Where are we going for dinner?"

He closed her door, then went around to the driver's side, tossing his jacket in the backseat and laying the bouquet on top of it before climbing in. "We've got three options. We can drive to Tulsa, or we can go to Luca's."

"Or?"

Though his tie was already loose, he tugged at it, then ran his fingers through his hair. His throat suddenly swelled like a bad case of mumps, and his palms were as damp as if he'd dunked them in a tub of water. "We could, uh, get takeout or—or see what's in my freezer and, uh, just have dinner, uh, alone."

After a long still moment, her gaze intense, managing both sensual and innocent in one look, she asked, "Are you thinking about getting me out of this dress?"

Her voice was husky, her accent pronounced, her question enough to raise his temperature to wildfire level. His fingers tightened and loosened on the steering wheel before he swallowed hard and gave voice to his own husky words. "Yeah. From the first moment I saw you in it."

Her smile came slowly, teasing and satisfied. "Good. Let's explore your freezer."

With another hard swallow, he pulled out of the parking lot and took the backstreets to First, where he turned north out of town. Beside him in her pretty dress, Jessy rested one arm on the door and softly hummed a melody. Dalton didn't recognize it, though he didn't know whether it was because he didn't know the song or her rendition was pretty awful. A gorgeous, incredibly hot woman who couldn't hit a note solidly even with a hammer. Damned if he knew how that was endearing, but it was.

When he turned off the paved road at the pasture where she'd mistaken a bull for a cow, her sigh echoed. "Poor cows. They look so content. They don't have a clue that they're going to end up on a dinner plate at Holy Cow."

"They're born, they graze, they breed, they give birth, they die. They're not that much different from us."

Her eyebrows arched when she looked at him. "No one grills us up and charges fifteen bucks a cut."

"If they could get fifteen bucks a cut, someone would try." Wanting contact, no matter how little, he reached for her hand, rubbing his thumb over her pink nails. The day they'd met, her polish had been bright, screaming-in-your-face purple. He'd never known a woman who considered that an appropriate color past second grade. "I saw how you inhaled that ribeye. However much you don't like looking your food in the eye, the beef industry's in no danger of losing you as a customer."

"No," she agreed. "It's just that cows are *cute*. I mean, a chicken or a pig—bless their hearts, pigs are just fat and ugly and rooting around in the mud. Cows could be pets." Her hair gleamed as she shook her head. "That sounds shallow, doesn't it? 'Save the pretty animals. Eat pork.'"

"If your livelihood depended on pigs, trust me, you'd think they're the most beautiful animals in the world."

"Did you always want to be a rancher?"

"Pretty much. It's what I knew. My dad always expected us to take over, and I always figured I would." Though David had had the same expectations of Dillon, and look how that had turned out.

"The night we went to Walleyed Joe's, you mentioned your brothers and the family tradition of naming the sons."

Damn, she'd caught his use of *us*. He released her hand to turn into the driveway but didn't say anything. That night, she'd asked, *So it's you and...*, and he'd replied, *Don't ask.* She hadn't. Now she would. They knew each other better. Hell, they were about to get intimate. Any woman would feel entitled to know little things like the existence of a worthless charmer of a brother.

But she didn't ask. She gazed ahead as he drove the narrow lane, parking under a big oak for shade. Soon the sap would start to drip, and he'd have to park elsewhere or risk getting stuck to the door handle every time he touched it.

They were home. Time to go inside, let Oz out, make small talk, eventually wander up the stairs to his room, or fix dinner and maybe make out a bit before moving upstairs, or... Or tell her what she wanted to know.

Talk about Dillon or get naked with Jessy. Damn, that was no contest.

"Someday I'll tell you about him," he said after shutting off the engine. "But today's been way too good a day to ruin with talk about Dillon."

She held his gaze for a moment, then nodded before getting out of the truck and strolling toward the front porch. Oz was barking at the living room window, probably delighted that Dalton had brought Jessy home for him. The horses were grazing in the pasture, paying the dog no attention, and fat bees buzzed around the white-flowered bushes growing along the west side of the house.

Definitely too good a day to ruin and promising to get better.

* * *

After giving Oz an enthusiastic greeting and a scratching that made his left back leg twitch, Jessy slowly straightened, a bad case of nerves practically making *her* twitch. How long had it been since she'd gone home with a man? Not counting the guys she'd hooked up with when she was drinking because, in the present, they *didn't* count. A long time. Aaron had been the last one. There had been guys before him, of course, but that was when she was young and single, looking to have a good time.

She was definitely single now, though *young* was a matter of perspective, and she wasn't looking for just a good time. She wanted so much more. A scary thought, hence the unsteady hands and the somersaulting stomach.

Then she looked at Dalton. He'd closed the door, tossed his jacket over the back of a chair just inside the living room, then taken the bouquet to the kitchen. After rattling through the cabinets, he came up with a quart canning jar, filled it with water, and stuffed the flowers inside. He carried it to her, offering it solemnly. His dark eyes were shadowed with the same uncertainty she felt, the same need, the same bone-deep desire. *I prefer to have flowers handed to me,* she'd told him at the church, *preferably already in a container with water.*

She accepted the blooms, her nerves settling, her anxiety changing to anticipation. She'd made a lot of mistakes in her life, done things she wasn't proud of, things she dearly regretted, but this wasn't one of them. In fact, this man—having drunken sex with him, getting to know him, trusting him, loving him—just might be the best choice she'd ever made.

Blindly she set the flowers on the step and found the

staircase newel post to hold on to. She lifted one foot, unfastened the delicate ankle strap, then let the shoe slide off.
After removing the other, she left them lying on the wood
floor, one standing upright, the other tilted against the first
stair, their little bows cute and sexy, reclaimed the flowers,
and slowly started up. She trailed her fingers along the rail
that generations of Smiths had touched, felt the smooth-
ness they'd worn into each step, noticed the temperature
rising slightly as she climbed.

She could live in this house—coming down the stairs at
dawn each morning, learning to cook in the big kitchen,
helping with the livestock, going up the stairs every night
to sleep in Dalton's arms. She could listen to its old creaks
and groans, open the windows depending on which way
the wind was blowing, leave her mark on it. She could belong in it. Belong *to* it.

At the top, the hallway ran west to east, two doors to the
left, three to the right. The doors on the left were closed,
so she turned right, where one open door revealed a bathroom, easily twice the size of hers, with white wainscoting
beneath pale green paint, a mirror framed in barn wood that
still showed traces of its original dark red color, a stand-
alone shower, and a claw-foot tub.

"I always swore the first thing I'd do when I bought the
place was yank out that tub and put in a whirlpool." Dalton's voice came from right behind her, breath fanning her
neck. How had such a big man moved so quietly?

She glanced over her shoulder and smiled her sultriest
smile. "If you don't love that tub, sweetheart, you haven't
been using it right."

"Maybe you can show me."

Images of the two of them in the tub made her shiver.

Shower/bath sex didn't rate high on her favorites, but warm, wet, and soapy was a great way to start.

Of the remaining two doors, only one was open. She turned into it: a large rectangular room, two sets of double windows looking over the backyard, two more facing the cows' pasture. The bed was queen-sized, the covers on one side tossed back, a stack of jeans and shirts that smelled faintly of fabric softener taking up the entire rocker in the corner.

"If I'd known we'd end up here, I would have made the bed this morning."

She picked up a ball cap from the dresser, bearing the logo of a local feed store, before slanting him a look. "So you weren't planning on seducing me?"

"It was the shoes that did it."

"Ah. If I'd known that, I would have left them on and taken the dress off. Let me run downstairs and get them." Of course she didn't move toward the door. Of course he knew she wouldn't. "However, it's good to know. I'll remember next time I debate wearing them."

He took the hat from her hands, tossing it back onto the dresser, then slid his arms around her waist and drew her close. "Maybe I'll just keep them here."

"You don't like to share?"

A muscle twitched in his jaw, and his gaze narrowed before he blew out a breath. "Hell, no."

That hit a nerve, she acknowledged, filing the information away as she wound her arms around his neck. "Neither do I." With those words—that promise—she kissed him, stretching onto her toes, pulling his head to meet hers.

It was the first time they'd kissed since... well, the first time. She'd always been grateful that she remembered very little of those encounters once she sobered up, and now was no different. In a way, not remembering allowed *this* to be their first time. Though she did wonder if she'd had the faintest clue that he was different from the other men. That he was going to change her life, that he was going to *be* a large part of her life.

If she'd known that back then, she probably would have run far away.

His tongue stroked hers, and his muscles clenched beneath her hands. Hard muscles built by hard work, tempting her to slide her hands beneath his shirt and stroke them on bare skin. She was about to do a hell of a lot more than touch him, so it was okay to tug at his tie, the silk cool and sliding easily between her fingers, to toss it aside and move to the buttons of his shirt. They opened easily, too, the backs of her fingers brushing the soft, heated skin of his chest as each button gave way. About halfway down, she lost interest in actually removing his shirt, and instead her fingers explored that skin, dark, though not as dark as his face and arms, darker than his flat stomach and long muscular legs.

So she did remember something from the first time.

Heavy breathing sounded nearby, and she realized it was coming from her. Her chest was tight, and what little air her lungs could get was superheated, making her blood pump hot and her skin turn slick. In need of air, she ended the kiss, took another quick taste, then sucked in oxygen as she tilted her head to look at him.

"You're damn gorgeous, you know." Her voice was out-of-breath raspy...or was that turned-on-all-the-way-to-her-toes husky?

Slowly the intensity of his gaze lightened, and an incredible smile spread across his face. "Aw, you're just saying that because you want to get lucky."

She raised her hand to his face, fingers trembling against his jaw. "I got lucky the day I met you."

Dalton's smile didn't dim at the reference to that day. Had they both made peace with the embarrassing start of this relationship?

She undid a couple more buttons on his shirt before he caught her hand, lifted it to his mouth, and pressed a kiss to the palm, his tongue touching it delicately. Half surprised that steam didn't rise from the contact, Jessy jerked his shirt from his pants and finished the unbuttoning one-handed, twisted her fingers around to catch his, and pulled him toward the bed. "Do you have condoms?"

"Yes, ma'am. A new box just for you."

"Only one box?" She arched her brow as she raised her arms to the zipper running down the back of her dress. She'd always had a talent for getting stripped down fast, not generally useful, though it served her well now. Within seconds, she was pulling the dress over her head, dropping it in the direction of the rocker, neither noticing nor caring where it landed.

For a long moment he just looked at her, his gaze searching as if he might be asked later to give an intimate description. Contrary to her earlier teasing, she *was* wearing underwear, and it was her sexiest: tiny bits of crimson silk decorated with tiny bits of matching lace, ridiculously expensive but ridiculously flattering. A line from a favorite song drifted through her head as Dalton finally drew a long breath. *Man, I feel like a woman.*

He wasn't smiling anymore. His eyes were dark, his features stark, the skin of his face somehow tighter, more strained. It had been a long time since she'd seen that look—so hungry, so tautly controlled, so fiercely possessive. In fact, she wasn't sure she'd ever seen that look before.

She would never forget it.

"My turn for a thrill." Not even trying to strengthen her breathy voice, she looked at him, head to toe, then gestured. Giddily, she anticipated seeing more, like the erection that impressively tented his trousers.

A low growl escaped his throat. His movements economical, he shucked his shirt, unfastened his belt, and shoved his trousers over his hips, kicked off his shoes, yanked away trousers, boxers, and socks all in a jumble, and lifted her around the middle, taking her down onto the bed with him, and kissing her.

Oh, yeah, she loved his kisses. It was a good thing they hadn't agreed to make out while they were waiting for the right time. She could have spent forever just kissing him.

Okay, not *forever*. She did have that flair for exaggeration.

Dalton balanced her on top of him with one hand splayed across her ass, stretched to the right, and found the box of condoms in the top nightstand drawer. Turning his gaze from her, catching a breath, he squinted at the box. "Contains twenty-four. You're right. Not enough."

With a laugh, she grabbed the box, ripped open the top, and pulled out a condom. He didn't protest, didn't insist they had more to explore, didn't suggest she was rushing it. No, he helped her out of her sexy lingerie, and he touched her with impossibly talented fingers as she maneuvered the condom into place, and he claimed her mouth again as she slid along the length of his erection.

As they began moving, matching each other's rhythms, Jessy was absolutely certain of one fact: It hadn't been too soon or too late.

Their being together at this time, in this way, on this special day, made everything damn perfect.

Chapter 13

Luca's was everyone's favorite date restaurant in Tallgrass, according to Patricia, so Ben had made reservations—*ask for a table on the porch*—at her direction. After changing into trousers and a deep green button-down, he went onto the patio, where his mother was sharing a glass of wine with Brianne while something flavorful cooked on the grill.

"Don't you look handsome," Patricia said, saluting him with her glass. "You should roll your sleeves up, though, so you don't look too hot."

"Hot's a good thing," Brianne said. "At least when it comes to dating." She hadn't been scheduled to arrive until the next morning, but she'd been too impatient to wait. Sara was still coming Sunday, too stubborn to change her plans because of Bree's impulses.

Taking Patricia's advice, Ben started rolling his sleeves. He'd just finished one when a bark came from across the yard. When he looked that way, he saw Lucy standing on her patio, handing Norton's leash to Cadore, then the three of them started across the yard.

Brianne fluffed her hair. "Joe is awfully cute. Is he available?"

"For what?" Patricia asked absently, then made an exaggerated face. "Pretend I didn't ask that. As far as I know, the only things Joe's seriously involved with are his football team and...Hm. I guess it's just the team."

"What about your hockey player?" Ben asked. Jeez, the last man he wanted to see his sister with was Joe Cadore. The guy was a Neanderthal...with blond hair, way-too-blue eyes, and a lot of muscles. Just like the hockey player and every other guy Brianne had dated in the past five years.

"Nigel's around." Brianne smiled wickedly. "But he's not here."

Ben shifted his attention to Lucy. She wore a dress, light pink flowers on a background of curacao blue with sandals that gave her a couple inches' height, and her hair was pulled back. She looked fresh and pretty and sweet, and it hit him in the gut that he really was going to miss seeing her every day. He liked her, and she'd made what could have been an impossible visit a hell of a lot more bearable, and there could be an awful lot more if luck was with them.

Cadore hugged Patricia—habit or for Ben's benefit?—then dropped into the chair closest to Brianne's. "Hey, Bree, you gonna do the Green Corn Run in Bixby?"

Nobody called Brianne by her nickname except family, but judging by her ear-to-ear grin, she didn't mind. Ben tuned out her answer, said good-bye to Patricia, then he and Lucy walked around the house to his car.

"Your sister is single, isn't she?" Lucy asked as he opened the door for her.

He groaned. "Please don't try to set her up with him." Though a rational voice inside him pointed out that Lucy wanting to find her neighbor a girlfriend was a good thing. It meant she wasn't interested in him herself.

"I don't know that I need to try. She seems to like him. They have a lot in common."

He admired her legs as she settled in the seat. He was definitely a leg man, and Lucy's had nice curves. After closing her door, he went around and slid into the driver's seat. "What? They both like to jog?"

"Relationships have been built on less." She gave him a sly look. "You're such a big brother."

"I don't care if my sister dates. I don't even care if she has sex."

Lucy snorted. "That's awfully generous of you."

"It is, isn't it?" He couldn't help but laugh with her. "I'd just rather see her with someone more suitable. She's already got Nigel for the jock stuff—"

"And the sex," Lucy helpfully added.

Ben grimaced. He really didn't want to think about his sisters' sex lives. He knew they had them—after all, he did have a niece and two nephews—but he didn't need details.

"Nigel. I'm guessing he took up hockey so the other kids wouldn't have the nerve to laugh at his name." Then she reached across the console, patted his knee. It was a natural gesture, comforting, familiar. "If Brianne is destined to be with Joe—"

"Doomed."

"All you can do is accept it."

Yeah. Here lately Ben was learning a lot about accepting things he couldn't change. So far, he wasn't very good at it, and he couldn't imagine his slender tolerance extending to Joe Cadore.

He found Luca's with no problem, though parking close by on a Saturday night was another matter. Lucy assured him she didn't mind walking, so he took the next space he found, and they strolled the couple blocks back to the restaurant. Halfway there, he took her hand, small and soft, in his, and something inside him loosened, relaxed.

Luca's occupied an old house with a wraparound porch. Tables filled the back side of the porch, along with a few in the garden. "Oh, these are new," Lucy said delightedly, and the hostess immediately offered them one near the central fountain.

He liked a woman who appreciated the simple pleasures in life. Who helped him appreciate them.

After they ordered, Lucy sipped her tea. "I bet your patients will be happy to see you again."

He was surprised he'd lasted this long in Tallgrass, but at the same time, he felt a little ambivalent about leaving. The break had been good for him; so had seeing Patricia and meeting Lucy. But returning to Tulsa didn't mean he wouldn't be back.

"I'd like to think so," he said, "but we're a group practice, literally. We share physician's assistants, nurses, techs, and, more or less, patients. I may do the surgery on a patient while a PA or another doctor does the post-op follow-ups. It just depends on how busy I am or if I'm in the clinic that day. My surgery days have overtaken my clinic days." He watched the water splash in the fountain, drops catching the rays of the setting sun, glistening silver for an instant before they fell again.

"Is that good or bad?"

"It's not quite the way I imagined things back when I was in medical school," he said after a moment. "I always wanted to be a doctor and decided to go into surgery in school, but I don't think I grasped that I'd be doing so many procedures, I wouldn't have much time left for actual patient care. I never see a post-op patient in the hospital unless there's a complication, and in the clinic, time is limited. I try to take the time *I* think I need with each one, but that puts us way behind schedule."

"Time is money," Lucy said, sympathy softening her voice.

Ben nodded, wondering where those complaints had come from, because he *wasn't* dissatisfied with his job. He did a lot of good, and if he was sometimes—usually—busier than he'd like, that was a good thing, too. Better to have too many patients than not enough.

He shook his head to clear it. "If you'd asked me a couple weeks ago, I would have said that I love my job and wouldn't change a thing. I think all this time off has gotten to me." Pausing while the waiter delivered bread and salads, he unrolled his silverware from the napkin, then when they were alone again, he said the words that guaranteed a subject change. "Tell me about your friend's wedding."

* * *

Dalton rolled onto his back, drenched with sweat, short of breath, and his limbs so tired he wasn't sure he could move them. His heart pounding in his ears, he figured this was a hell of a way to end all those years of celibacy...if Jessy didn't kill him.

She snuggled close to his side, and his arm automatically pulled her closer, disproving that he was too tired to move. Her skin was damp, too, her face flushed a shade of red that just looked wrong with her, but while he felt like he'd been rode hard—*and damned good*—and put away wet, she just looked gorgeous. Satisfied.

"Now *this* is the kind of exercise I like," she murmured, tilting her head back to grin at him.

He glanced at the bedside clock. "Three hours of this every day might be the death of me."

"But what a way to go."

Amen to that. Stroking the soft skin on her side, right where the swell of her breast started, he gazed at the ceiling and the fan that lazily swirled there. He'd never brought any woman but Sandra into this room, this bed. For years, he'd thought he would never quit hurting enough to trust another woman.

He was trusting Jessy with more than his life. With his heart.

Outside the room, Oz stirred, then ran downstairs to give a low bark. About the same time, the creak he'd been meaning to fix announced the opening of the front door.

"Shit," he muttered. "Noah said he wasn't coming home this weekend."

"Is that the brother you warned me to stay away from?"

Though his body had finally started to cool, heat collected in his face again, a healthy dose of guilt and shame. "I was out of line...but I told you I don't share." Wasn't it damn well enough that he shared his birthday—hell, even his face—with Dillon?

"You didn't have to worry. I don't do brothers. That's just icky. Besides, he's a boy."

"Yeah, you tell him—"

"Dalton?" The voice came from downstairs, making all his muscles go tight again.

"Holy shit." Letting go of Jessy, he rolled to his feet.

She pulled the sheet over her, crossed arms holding it in close over her breasts. "That doesn't sound like Noah."

"It's my parents. Damn it, that's it. I'm taking away everyone's keys. This is *my* house now." He yanked on his boxers, then grabbed a pair of jeans from the clean laundry pile and struggled into them before jerking up a shirt, too. "I'll be down in a minute," he called.

"Should I hide in the closet?"

The quick look he'd intended to give her caught and held. She was sitting now, knees drawn up, and she looked vulnerable, taking cover behind the sheet. He fastened his jeans, pulled on the T-shirt, then sat beside her, combing his fingers through her hair. "I knew the chances of ever meeting your parents were somewhere between slim and none, but I figured you'd meet Mom and Dad on their next visit. With advance notice. And clothes on. And not looking all wanton and sexual and shameless."

The words made her smile, the way he'd wanted, then she immediately turned serious again. "What do you want me to do?"

It was a simple decision. "Get dressed. Come down."

Her expression took on a sickly tinge. "They'll know what we were doing."

He looked at her—she was damn near glowing—and grinned. "They have three sons. They'll figure it out." Pushing to his feet, he kissed the top of her head. "Come on down. Make my folks delirious with relief."

As he left the room and headed down the stairs, he heard noises—pans rattling, cabinet doors opening. His parents were in the kitchen, of course, his dad probably settling at the table, his mother starting to cook. She always thought Dalton was going to starve if she didn't feed him well when she was here.

Instead of hanging around the kitchen the way he usually did when there was food around, Oz hunkered in the recliner, with one eye on the guests. "Mom try to throw you out again?" Dalton asked when he reached the broad hallway.

He turned left and saw his parents standing in the middle of the kitchen. David had his glasses in hand, along with a towel to clean them, and Ramona was holding a skillet and a bottle of olive oil, but they were both motionless, staring his way. Stopping short, he looked at them, glanced at Oz, and wondered what the hell...

"Is there something you want to tell us, sweetie?" Ramona asked. Her eyes seemed brighter than usual, like she was about to cry, and suddenly his dad was grinning like a Halloween pumpkin.

"I, uh..." He couldn't think of a damn thing.

His father gestured with the towel, and Dalton looked down. Jessy's sexy-as-hell shoes were where she'd left them at the foot of the stairs, a few inches from his bare feet, as obvious as a trail of cast-off clothes through the house.

Ramona came a few steps closer and whispered, "Is she going to come downstairs so we can meet her, or is she feeling a little awkward? It *is* a little awkward. We should have called to let you know we were coming."

"We didn't know ourselves until we hit Tulsa, and I doubt he would have answered the phone an hour ago," David said dryly.

Ramona elbowed him. "Of course, we won't stay. We don't want to overwhelm her. We would like to meet her, but if she's not comfortable..."

Jessy was nervous, but she had to meet them sooner or later. Besides, his parents were nothing like hers. The fact that he loved her was enough to make them welcome her like the daughter they'd never had.

Nudging the shoes closer to the hall table, he called, "Jessy?"

After a long silence, she appeared at the top of the stairs, dressed again, hair combed with her fingers. Where she'd looked sophisticated at the wedding, now, bare-footed and mostly bare-faced, she looked...perfect. Except her green eyes were big enough to pop, and considering the last few hours' exertion, she was awfully pale. As she began a slow, hesitant descent, he realized her question about hiding in the closet hadn't been a joke. She really would have preferred to hide, to meet his parents under better circumstances.

"Jessy Lawrence," he said when she finally stopped beside him, "my parents, Ramona and David Smith."

Her gaze darting his way, she stepped forward to accept the hand David offered. "Mr. Smith."

"Oh, call me David. Everyone does. Ramona—"

Ramona hadn't met Jessy halfway, like David. He caught her wrist and pulled her to his side, then eased the cast-iron skillet and oil bottle from her hands.

"Mrs. Smith." Jessy held out her hand, and for a long moment, Mom just looked at it. Looked at her. Her gaze swept over Jessy all the way from the top of her head to her dark red painted toenails, then back up again. She gave a little start—a poke from Dad on his way back from putting the skillet and oil on the counter—and abruptly took Jessy's hand.

"Jessy. It's nice to meet you." It wasn't the warmest welcome Dalton had ever heard her give, and it didn't include the automatic, *Call me Ramona*. Those were the first words she'd said to Sandra, in a sincere, *yay-I've-got-me-a-daughter!* tone.

Dalton was puzzled. A few minutes ago, his mom had been cheerful as hell, wanting to meet the woman in his bed, shaking with excitement, and now she was...Disappointed? Sad?

Jessy saw it, too, of course, and that vulnerability was back in her eyes, though she tried to subdue it. When he sidled close enough to reach for her hand, she pulled away, folding both hands behind her back. Nails clacking, Oz trotted in from the living room, looked from side to side, then sat down in front of Jessy. Appointing himself her guard for the moment?

"Well, uh, Jessy." David shoved his glasses back into place. "You live in Tallgrass?"

"Yes."

End of that conversation.

Dalton didn't know what to say or do. He'd never experienced this kind of discomfort with his parents. His mom had always liked everyone...except maybe Alice, even before she'd run off with Dillon. He'd honestly thought she would love Jessy for saving him, if nothing else.

In a sudden flurry of activity, Ramona put away all the stuff she'd gotten out to cook with, then grabbed her purse from the back of a dining chair. "Well, if we're going to get to Stillwater in time to catch Noah before he goes out clubbing, we'd better get going. Nice to meet you, Jessy.

Dalton, I'll talk to you later." With that, she walked stiffly through the house and out onto the porch.

David hesitated. "Jessy, it *is* nice meeting you, though I'm sorry to surprise you this way. Dalton..." At a loss for words, he shrugged, shook his head, and followed Ramona.

After the screen door closed behind him, the house vibrated with silence. Dalton's breathing seemed excessively loud, while Jessy didn't seem to be breathing at all. She had this pale, stark, insecure thing going on that made his gut knot.

Long after the RV motor had faded into the distance, she finally breathed. "So *that* was delirious with relief. I'm glad you told me. I never would have recognized it if you hadn't."

He combed his fingers through his hair. "I don't know *what* that was. I don't understand. She *wanted* to meet you—even said she didn't want to overwhelm you."

"As first meetings go, I think it was pretty underwhelming." As if her legs would finally move again, Jessy crossed to the refrigerator and took out a bottle of water.

Wedding cake notwithstanding, it had been a long time since lunch, and though his stomach was still unsettled, he was hungry. Surely she was, too. "Listen, you want to head back into town—"

Jessy looked sharply at him. "You want me to go home?"

"No," he said slowly. "I want you to spend the night. I was just thinking about food. Unless you're a better cook than me, our best chance for a good dinner this late is in Tallgrass."

It took her a long time to break his gaze, then turn back to the refrigerator. "I can't cook much. I can steam fish—"

"Though why would you want to."

"And I can make egg and grilled cheese sandwiches." She set a carton of eggs on the counter, found a package of sliced cheese and the butter, then closed the door with her hip and asked, "Bread?"

He was out of his mom's homemade bread, so he got a store-bought loaf from the pantry, then set the griddle pan on the stove. He leaned against the counter, watching her, getting things for her as she needed them, and thought this was something he could get used to. Having her in his bed. Feeling her beside him when he slept. Knowing she would be there when he woke. Sharing that big old bathtub. Living the rest of their lives together...

Damn it, why had his mom reacted that way?

Jessy slathered butter over the hot griddle, then began assembling three sandwiches: slices of bread, butter side down; slices of cheese; hard fried eggs; more cheese; bread, butter side up.

As he watched her watch the cooking, he said, "Jess, I'm sorry about Mom. I don't know—"

A muscle twitched in her jaw, but her pretty, phony smile almost hid it. "Hey, I have a lifetime's experience at disappointing mothers. It's one of my talents."

"She wasn't disappointed." But that was exactly how it had seemed.

"Sure she was. Maybe because I'm so obviously not Sandra. Maybe she expected someone more like her. Maybe she knows who I am. She must still have friends in town. She doesn't seem the type who wouldn't keep in touch just because she moved."

"And what could her friends possibly tell her about you?"

She lifted the first sandwich to check the browning, then carefully flipped it before looking at him. "You are not the only man I've hooked up with since Aaron died."

Dalton widened his eyes and raised his voice half an octave. "Oh, my God, you mean you've had sex with other men? You've gone out, shared meals, shared drinks, maybe even danced with other men?" After a pause for effect, he kissed the top of her head. "Welcome to the world of being single, sweetheart."

He couldn't dig up even a hint of jealousy over it. What happened when they weren't together didn't matter. From now on...that was the important stuff.

"You know what? You and me—we're the ones who count here. Mom will come around, or she won't." Cradling her face in his palms, he brushed his mouth across hers. "Either way"—his tongue stroked between her full lips—"we'll be fine."

*   *   *

It was the middle of the night, and Jessy couldn't sleep. She'd eased out of bed, pulling on Dalton's discarded dress shirt, and wandered barefoot out of the room. Oz, curled on the floor, lifted his head as she passed, did a stretch that would make any yoga master proud, then got up and trailed along behind her.

Moonlight through the windows lit the way, guiding her down the stairs, down the broad hall, and into the living room, where she did a slow circle around the perimeter. It was a comfortable room, square, big windows and a sandstone fireplace on one inside wall. She could easily imagine the mantel holding family pictures of Dalton, Noah, and the mysterious Dillon, David and Ramona and Sandra, the oh, so much more acceptable daughter-in-law in Ramona's eyes.

But it didn't hold any pictures. Except for a stack of magazines, the mantel was bare. In fact, Jessy hadn't seen any reminders of Sandra anywhere. No tacky but fun Vegas wedding photo, no shots of her in uniform or with the animals, no flag from her coffin, no medals, nothing.

Not that she could blame Dalton for that. All her reminders of Aaron, except for the pictures on her computer, were put away. She couldn't bear to live with them but couldn't bear to get rid of them, so she'd carefully packed them in heavy-duty tubs and moved them to her basement storage room.

Not yet ready to settle, she continued her self-guided tour. Dalton's office was across the hall, every flat surface covered with papers, folders, catalogs, and magazines. Even in the pale light, she could see a layer of dust settled unevenly over the room, as if he came in only to work, then got out again as quickly as he could. She imagined a ranch, like any business, required a lot of paperwork, and she *couldn't* imagine Dalton having nearly as much interest in that as he did in the outside part.

She was very good with paperwork. Organized to perfection. She could find any one of her ten-thousand-some pictures in seconds.

Sandra had probably been incredibly organized, too. And his parents had adored her.

If the fact that Jessy wasn't Sandra was all his mother had against her, Jessy would be relieved. It was the other possibility, that Ramona knew through gossip from old friends what kind of person Jessy was, that made her feel ragged inside. Dalton said it didn't matter, and he'd made love to her again after dinner as if it really didn't, but still...She already had one train wreck of a family. She didn't need another.

She did a quick walk-through of the dining room, as formal as anything in this homey place got, then the laundry room next to the kitchen. There was one door she hadn't opened, across from the bath, so she did and saw a handful of stairs disappearing into the absolute blackness of a basement.

Still restless, she closed the door, padded down the hall, and let herself out. Oz, who'd taken a seat in the recliner, leaped after her before the screen door closed and ran into the yard.

The night was quiet, the air sweet with the scent of flowers, the moonlight gleaming off a lone curious palomino, turning its coat silver, ethereal. The scene should have been peaceful, should have soothed every last raw nerve in her body. How could anyone have a problem that mattered when surrounded by this beauty, by this sense of *all is right with the world*?

Once again, Jessy was the exception to the rule, and not in a good way.

She settled on the porch swing, knees drawn to her chest, catching occasional glimpses of Oz as he wandered the yard sniffing, then peeing. Life was good for the dog. Could it ever be that good for her?

The screen door didn't squeak exactly—more like the hinges rubbed as it swung open—and Dalton stepped out, hair standing on end, jeans hugging his hips, feet and chest bare. Was it odd that she found the first as appealing as the last?

Not odd. She just loved her a cowboy. Would God or karma or destiny let her have a happily ever after this time? Or was she doomed to another broken heart?

He sat on the swing and set it in motion. The swaying tried to lull her into a serene state, but she had too many insecurities to give in easily. He wasn't feeling too complacent, either. The air around him was practically simmering.

She didn't have anything to say, so she didn't. After a while, he broke the silence. "I told you, it's family tradition to give the first two sons names beginning with a D. Mom was okay with that, as long as she got to choose the names. She'd originally picked something normal like Daniel and Douglas, but when we were born, she changed her mind and went with Dillon—like Marshal Dillon on the TV show *Gunsmoke*—and Dalton, from the outlaw gang that operated in Oklahoma when it was still Indian Territory."

When we were born. Jessy's breath caught. Dalton was a twin. The brother he never talked about was his *twin*. Identical? Was there another man walking around out there with the same black hair, brown eyes, awesome smile, smoldering good looks, incredible body? *Holy crap.*

"Of course, she got it wrong. We each lived up to the other's name. I was the respectable marshal, Dillon the reckless outlaw. We looked exactly alike, but it would have been hard to find two brothers as different as we were." He glanced at her. "Though I suspect you and your sisters qualify."

Identical twins who were smokin' hot. They must have left a trail of fluttering teenage hearts everywhere they went.

"We weren't inseparable. We never had that bond people talk about, but still, he was my *twin*. That was supposed to mean something...but apparently not to him. When we were nineteen, he ran off in the middle of the night. Took his clothes, his beat-up old truck, and my girlfriend and just *left*. Turned out, he'd been seeing her behind my back. They'd been planning their great escape from small-town life and family expectations for weeks. The whole thing broke my parents' heart, and..."

He cleared his throat, but it didn't erase the huskiness in his voice. "It kind of...broke mine, too. I mean, it pissed me off that, with all the girls he dated, he couldn't keep his damn hands off the only one I was with. But the fact that he didn't care any more about the family than to just blow us all off...Disappear. Never come back. Never call. Never let us know if he's even still alive. Hell, Noah doesn't even really remember him. Mom and Dad have never gotten over it, and...I guess I haven't, either."

He and his brother had more of a bond that he was admitting to, Jessy ventured. If they didn't, the hurt and anger would have faded over the years. Dalton would have realized one day that it was a done deal—selfish for Dillon, sad for the family, but the broken hearts would be in the past with their memories, where they belonged.

No, this was Dalton subconsciously trying to keep as much of the hurt as possible deeply buried. With all he'd gone through with Sandra, he didn't need the unanswered questions of Dillon haunting him.

He gave a heavy sigh, the tension leaving his body. "So that's all there is to know about Dillon."

"Wow." Jessy hadn't seen or talked to her sisters in longer than she could remember—a lie she told herself; of course, she knew to the month how long it had been—but she hadn't tried in all that time. She knew where they were, she had their e-mail addresses and phone numbers, and they had hers, and she knew they were okay. How would it feel not to know? To have no clue whether they were happy and well? Whether they were alive or dead?

And twins... She could—and did—put her sisters out of her mind, but every time Dalton looked at himself, he saw Dillon, and he must wonder and feel bitter.

"I wonder if my sisters ever felt that I'd betrayed them by leaving. I don't think so. By then, I was such an embarrassment to the family and their great name."

"Your situation was different. They were trying to force you to be someone you're not. Dillon was just being Dillon."

Giving him a flirtatious smile, she scooted closer to him. "Lucky for us that I ran. You never would have looked twice at the Jessamine they wanted me to be, and I would never have known what it was like to be happy."

He lifted her onto his lap, just as she'd hoped he would, and she rested her head against his heated broad shoulder. As his fingers skimmed lightly across her skin, he asked, "Are you happy, Jessy?" Before she could take a breath, he touched his index finger gently to her mouth. "Be grown up. Don't blurt out the first answer that comes to mind."

I have a tendency to act on impulse, she'd told him that night in the gazebo behind the courthouse. It was natural that at times he wanted from her a thoughtful answer, just as there would be times when she would be pleased with a totally impulsive response from him.

After a moment, she pulled his hand away. "For as

long as I can remember, I've had issues. When your own parents don't love you, you get some warped ideas. And Aaron's death...Feeling like I didn't deserve to live and—and things. I think I have all the family stuff way behind me, then out of nowhere, I get this yearning for the relationship we never had. Carly says I beat myself up too much, so I'm focusing on not focusing on all the messes I've made, but—"

Chuckling, Dalton interrupted, "Impulsive answers have their place sometimes."

She fixed her gaze on his face, and automatically her mouth turned up in a smile. "Seeing you makes me happy. Spending time with you, hanging out with my girls, working at the animal shelter, taking care of Oliver and the other animals, knowing that I can make someone's day better just by being in it, even if it is a stray dog..."

Her chest tightened as she realized she'd told the gospel truth. All those things did make her happy—not just content, not just helped her through the day, but filled her with happiness. Like Carly had told her, she was blessed.

Laying her palm against his cheek, she murmured, "Yes, I'm happy. Let me tell you what else would make me happy right now."

Wiggling her butt against his lap, she whispered the words into his ear, going into enough detail to steal the breath from his lungs and to make his heart stutter as the swelling of his erection commandeered blood flow that should have gone to his brain.

He pushed to his feet, his hands cradling her butt, and he reached the door in a couple long strides. Jessy opened the screen, then called for Oz. The dog streaked through the shadows, leapt onto the porch and inside the house, panting and heading for his water dish. His master was also panting but headed straight up the stairs to the bedroom. They slipped out of their clothes, shoved aside the mussed covers, and with a string of unused condoms trailing across the sheet, they proceeded to make each other very happy, indeed.

Chapter 14

After work Tuesday, Jessy opted to drive her car to The Three Amigos for dinner. Sure, the girls would tease, but it had been a long couple days...and a busy couple nights. She smiled at the memories as she climbed out of her car in the parking lot outside the restaurant and sighed contentedly.

It was hard to believe she'd been afraid of sober sex. Hell, it was the best thing ever invented. Of course, the man she was sober with made a huge freaking difference.

As she approached the patio, Marti gave her a brows-raised stare. "You drove. I can't remember you ever driving. Can you, Lucy?"

"Nope," Lucy agreed, and Fia added, "Me, either."

"I walked to work this morning, I walked seven dogs—long walks—and then I walked home. Even my toenails are tired. Hey, *Mamacita*." She sank into the chair next to Ilena, then bent toward her belly. "John, aren't you ready to make an appearance in this world? Your mama needs to be able to see her feet so she knows when her shoes don't match, but right now, you're kinda in the way."

"My shoes don't match?" Ilena wailed. She twisted to the left, then the right. "Oh, my gosh, my shoes don't match! I wore these to work!"

"Relax, doll. One's navy blue, and the other's red-and-white stripes." Bennie popped a chip in her mouth. "You're being patriotic. Besides, you know how the kids wear mismatched socks. Maybe you'll start a trend of mismatched shoes."

"I'll tell you, I'm ready to get this little guy born. My house is a mess. If I drop something, it just stays where it landed because I can't bend that far. I haven't made my bed in a month, and I shave my legs blind because I'm not going into the delivery room with hairy legs. It's a wonder I haven't bled to death yet."

"Poor baby," Lucy said, and Therese and Fia joined in. "Poor, poor baby."

After the laughter faded, Jessy said, "I'll come over tomorrow after work and pick up everything you've dropped. I'll even change your sheets and make your bed and make sure all your shoes are lined up together in matching pairs." When everyone's gaze turned her way, she scowled. "Hey, I clean house."

"We know," Therese said. "But only because you hate clutter more than you hate housework."

Jessy gestured to Ilena's belly. "Special circumstances."

"Do you clean the cowboy's house?" A sly grin lit Bennie's face.

"I help with the dishes and make the—" As their expressions turned to smug delight, she narrowed her gaze again.

"You guys were talking about me before I got here, weren't you?"

"We were just placing bets on how big you'd be smiling."

She'd better be smiling real big when we see her again, cowboy, Bennie had called out when they'd left the church Saturday.

She could ignore them, if they were in a being-ignored sort of mood, which they never were. She could inform them that her sex life was private, but that would make them laugh too hard. *Nothing* in their world was totally private. It was one of the things she loved about them.

Instead, she smiled. Bigger. Wider. When her mouth stretched as far as it could, she used her fingers to force it farther.

The dolls sighed, some of them melodramatically. "Was it wonderful?" Marti asked wistfully.

She opened her mouth to respond with equal melodrama, but the words that came out were quiet, simple truth. "It was incredible."

Fia fanned herself with a menu. "That does it, girls. We have got to get ourselves some boyfriends. We're too young to be giving up sex."

"You work around hard bodies at the gym all day," Marti pointed out. "Haven't you seen at least one you're attracted to?"

Fia shook her head. "A gorgeous body isn't everything."

"No, but it's a start." Bennie punctuated the words with her own menu fan.

"I—" Lucy glanced around the group and flushed. "I've met someone. You guys have met him, too. Ben Noble, Patricia's son."

Self-consciously she ran her finger along the rim of her glass—iced tea, Jessy realized. There wasn't a margarita on the table. The fact that her girls had given up their trademark drinks in support of her efforts at sobriety made her choke up, and her vision went blurry.

Must be pollen in the air.

All the little voices in her head snorted.

"We went to dinner at Luca's on Saturday night," Lucy went on, "and this Saturday we're going to the Drillers game."

There were *oohs* and *ahs*, then Ilena asked, "Do you like baseball?"

"No...but...I like Ben." The last came out in a soft voice loaded with insecurities.

Jessy knew Lucy well enough to know the taunts the little voices in *her* head were throwing at her: *He's gorgeous. You're plain. He's a doctor. You're a secretary to a doctor. He makes a boatload of money. You get by. He's got a great body. You're fat. Guys like him don't fall for women like you.* She wanted to wrap her arms around Lucy and assure her that guys like Ben *did* fall for women like her. What else would explain why Dalton had fallen for Jessy?

Though she didn't know what would come of it, if it was a short-term thing or if he had something more in mind. She was afraid to admit even to herself that she wanted *more*. It made Realist Jessy snipe even louder than usual. *You were a horrible wife to Aaron. What makes you think you deserve another chance? Sandra never would have planned to divorce Dalton when she finally got home. Only a selfish bitch would.*

"You okay?"

Startled, Jessy glanced around and saw that their food had been delivered. Therese's hand was resting lightly on her arm, her expression solemn. "Yeah. I was just…"

Something surged through her, made her stomach tumble, sent quivers along her nerves. She wanted to silence Realist Jessy—to strangle her, truthfully—but she needed help from her sisters. Quickly, before she could come to her senses, before the trembling inside her spread to the outside, she blurted out, "Can I tell you guys something?"

Everyone exchanged looks, then Ilena said, as if it was obvious, "Honey, you can tell us *any*thing."

"Will you still love me?" Jessy managed a weak smile, hoping it covered the fear bubbling through her. Without her margarita sisters, how would she survive?

"Of course we will." The answer came in a chorus from around the table before an expectant silence fell over them.

Her palms were sweaty, and her heart rate was pounding somewhere in the range between orgasm and imminent death. She wished she could say *Never mind*, or better yet, take back the questions. Wasn't it better to simply wonder if she was an awful person than to have it confirmed by the people who knew her best?

No, it wasn't. She had issues. While she didn't put them out there for all the world to see, like Lucy, she did keep them front and center in her mind. The opinions of people she loved and respected might help her put them to rest once and for all.

She forced a breath into her tight lungs and fixed her gaze on the flip menu on the table, showing a tall frozen margarita. One of those would help this go easier. Five would make it a breeze.

Swallowing hard to settle that sudden craving, she began haltingly, "I know every one of you loved your husbands dearly and you were devastated when they died. I loved Aaron, and I was heartbroken, too, but...I wasn't...I didn't..." She took another breath to ease the raspiness in her voice, to blurt out the words in a rush she couldn't stop. "I wasn't as happy in my marriage as you guys were. In fact, I—I intended to file for divorce after Aaron came home."

There. She'd said it. The churning gut calmed. The tremors stopped. Good or bad, she'd done it. Now she would find out if she deserved these friends, Dalton, love, marriage—anything at all—or if she truly was the huge self-centered disappointment her parents had believed.

After a moment of stunned stillness, Leah Black rose from her chair at the far end of the table, circled around one side, and bent to hug Jessy. "Thank you," she said, her voice heavy with relief.

"For what?" Jessy asked.

"Making me feel not so alone." Leah hugged her again before returning to her chair. "When I first started coming here, you guys gave me so much strength and encouragement. But the more I got to know you, the more I realized that you all *adored* your husbands. You had been so happy."

She pressed her lips together, her eyes shadowed with sadness and shame. Jessy could recognize shame from a hundred yards away and blindfolded. "Marco and I—our marriage was so far from perfect. It barely even qualified as good on occasions. We fought a lot, and there were times, especially after the war started, that I thought about divorcing him. I didn't want to argue. I didn't want to live alone month after month. I wanted to have kids and have a husband here to help raise them every single day. Don't get me wrong. I loved him. I'll always love him. But..."

She shrugged as if she couldn't find the right words, and Jessy filled them in. "It wasn't the way he wanted and needed and deserved to be loved."

Leah nodded. "I just feel so...unworthy of you guys. Of everything. Marco expected to come back to life as usual, and I wanted to shake up that life until he couldn't even recognize it."

This time it was Jessy nodding. She so understood.

Therese, the only founding member of the club present—damn, Jessy missed Carly—stretched hands out to each of them, her fingers warm, her grip comforting. "Do any of you remember filling out a form when you joined the club that asked you to rate how happy your marriage was, how much you loved your husband, or where you saw yourself and him in five years?"

Everyone shook their heads, of course. There'd been no such form.

"Because none of that mattered. We'd all gone through the same experiences. We'd all lost someone who was a huge part of our lives. We all needed the same support." Therese paused. "Don't ever feel embarrassed because your marriage wasn't perfect. No marriage is. Look at mine—finding out years after he died that Paul had been unfaithful, that he'd had a daughter with a stranger while we'd put off having our own kids...But if not for Mariah, I never would have met Keegan, and that would be a much greater loss than my illusion of my perfect marriage. Good things come out of bad times, ladies. We're proof of it."

Her vision a little blurry—damn that pollen—Jessy looked around the table, letting her gaze settle for an instant on each woman. She searched for but found no disapproval or disappointment, no judgmental looks. All she saw were the same things welling inside her. Acceptance. Affection. Love.

Her smile wobbled. "So you're not going to banish Leah and me to a table for two in the corner?"

"Of course not," several voices chimed together. Then Ilena said, "Well, someday we probably will, but it will be for your outrageous behavior at that moment, not anything that happened before that day." With an angelic grin, she added, "Hell, someday we'll probably be bailing you out of jail, Jess, and Fia and Marti will be right beside you shouting, *'Hot damn, let's do it again!'*"

The tension easing from her body with an ear-to-ear grin, Jessy relaxed in her chair and drained half of her iced tea in one gulp. She very well might need bailing out of jail sometime—she'd partied a little too over-the-top a few times before and slept it off behind bars—but without booze, she rarely got that lively.

But in the event she managed, it was comforting all the way down into her soul that she would have friends with her and friends to rescue her.

Good things come out of bad times.
Amen to that.

* * *

For the second time in four days, the dusty RV rumbled along Dalton's driveway. He sat on the porch, Oz stretched out at his feet, and watched its progress and the clouds of dust trailing behind it. They needed a good rain. It was no wonder everything in his house except his bed and the kitchen table had a layer of dust on it. No point in cleaning it up inside until it settled some outside. At least, that was his excuse.

On Saturday night, when his mother had said she would talk to him later, he had assumed she would call once they got home. The conversation was one he would rather have on the phone. Her reaction had confused him and hurt Jessy, and he was liable to be more emotional about it in person than on the phone. But when her call had come a few hours ago, it had only been to let him know that they were stopping by again tonight. She wanted to talk face to face.

Great.

His dad drove past Dalton's pickup and parked near the barn, where trees cast a shadow over the RV. David was first out, offering Ramona a hand down. Both looking grim, they came to the porch and traded cautious greetings. Soon as that was over, David said, "I'm gonna go check out the Belties. One of our friends at home is interested in acquiring a couple."

He disappeared too quickly to hear Ramona mutter, "Coward."

She took a seat on the porch swing but kept both feet flat on the floor. Her hair was pulled back in a ponytail, a mix of browns, silvers, and grays, and there were more lines on her face than he remembered. But then, how long had it been since he'd taken a really good look at anything?

"Noah was happy to see us," she said after a moment. "Actually, happier to see the food I left in his freezer. You'd think one of my boys would have learned to cook *something*. Nita, next door, her grandson is a chef at some fancy hotel, and her husband would much rather fix dinner than wash dishes."

"Neither of us has starved yet." Dalton's tone was dry but not stiff, not ticked off.

"Of course not. It's just part of being independent. Men today cook."

"Not even all women today cook."

Her nose wrinkled. "Aw, Jessy can't cook?"

"She makes a great fried-egg grilled-cheese sandwich."

"I guess you could live on that if you're not worried about your cholesterol going through the roof. Of course, you're both young and not packing an extra forty pounds." She patted her midsection, then laced her fingers together. "She's a beautiful girl."

He nodded.

"I know you're wondering what happened Saturday night."

Another nod. Anything he said would likely contain a four-letter word or two and earn him a chastising look or a swat. He'd gotten his share of both over the years.

She gazed off at the view she'd seen every day of her life for nearly forty years: pasture, cows, fences, trees. Had it been hard for her to leave this place? Had warmer weather and the freedom to travel been worth giving up the ranch?

For her, probably. Him, never. He'd lived his entire life here, and he intended to die here—if he was lucky, with Jessy at his side.

Good thing he'd begun believing in luck again.

Still gazing out, Ramona said, "When you called from Las Vegas to tell me you and Sandra had gotten married, I was shocked. I expected stuff like that from Dillon, but you...you were my responsible son. I hadn't even met her yet and you were married after only ten days. But it was obvious she was good for you, and by your first anniversary, I couldn't have loved her more if I'd given birth to her myself."

For four and a half years, Dalton had focused on *his* grief, *his* loss. He'd rarely considered the grief and the loss of other people who'd loved Sandra: her parents and sisters, his parents and Noah, her friends.

"You know I've worried about what a tough time you were having. I've prayed every day and every night for God to help you find joy in life again—and yes, my version of *joy* included another woman to love. I know in my head people can be satisfied without a partner to share their lives. I just can't really grasp it in my heart. I can't imagine my life without you boys and your father."

Oz opened one eye and looked around, then focused on Ramona. He stretched, crossed to the swing, and hopped up and sniffed before sitting to face her from a few feet away. She gave him a reproving look before going on.

"When your dad and I walked in and saw those shoes...I never thought I'd say this, but I was thrilled that you had a woman in your bed. It had been so long. You had been so lost. And to bring her *here*...We know you, and we knew she must be special to you." She looked at him and repeated the words as if making sure he believed her. "I really was thrilled."

He didn't doubt that. All she'd ever wanted was for her sons to survive each other and live to see eighteen, stay off bucking broncs and bulls, remember their manners, love someone, and be loved back. Giving her grandchildren to spoil was optional, but just barely. "At least until you met her."

"I was so happy one moment, and then I saw her, and...she wasn't Sandra." Even though she tried to hide it, there was a bit of heartbreak in her voice. "Logically, of course, I knew that, but to see her standing beside you, to imagine her filling all the places in your life where Sandra used to be...It just knocked me off balance. It was kind of like losing her all over again." Bending her head, she swiped at one eye, then tried to cover it by scowling at Oz, who'd sneakily closed half the distance between them. "Don't you come any closer. I've lived my whole life without getting attached to a dog, and a scruffy thing like you isn't going to become the first."

Oz smiled his dog smile and continued to watch her.

Dalton cleared the emotion from his throat. "Jessy's a good person, Mom. Her husband was killed in the war, so she knows...She's smart and funny and loyal to her friends, and she loves animals, and she..." Everything he said was true, but none of it came close to explaining why he loved her. He didn't know if it could be explained, but borrowing his mother's words, he tried once more. "She's my joy."

This time Ramona didn't try to hide the tears welling in her eyes. "I know. I'm sorry I wasn't prepared for seeing you with a woman other than Sandra, and I'm sorry I made such a bad impression on her, but I want to make it up. We were halfway home when I made your dad turn around and come back so I could apologize not only to you but to Jessy, too. Do you think she'd be willing to talk to me to-morrow?"

"I'm sure she will." For him, if no other reason.

Because even if she hadn't put it into words yet, he knew he was Jessy's joy, too.

* * *

Wednesday was shaping up to be the first truly hot day of the summer, and Jessy was loving every minute of it. Having realized that everything that got on her at work washed off just as easily, she'd dressed for real comfort that morning in shorts, a tank, and heavy-duty sandals that responded well to a hose. After her first three walks, she went inside the shelter long enough to get another bottle of water and to slather on sunscreen. Settling her ball cap on her head, she headed into the play yard again, leash dangling over her shoulder, and asked, "Who wants to go next?"

The dogs danced around her, including the ones she'd just walked, all yipping and yelping, but it was silent movement off to the right that caught her attention. Oliver stopped just at the edge of the shade, sans cone, and looked at her a moment before he came closer. She hadn't taken him out before; he'd shown no interest, though Meredith and Angela insisted that would change.

It appeared today was the day.

"Oliver, wanna go?" She hooked the leash onto his collar and led him back inside. There was a gate from the play yard, but no way was she opening it and trying to get him out without letting everyone else escape. Once outside, she headed west with the dog, her shoes thunking on the pavement a hundred times louder than his paws.

"I told the girls about Aaron last night," she said. She gave lots of verbal approval to the other dogs, but she'd fallen in the habit of actually carrying on conversations with Oliver. He was what she imagined a psychologist would be like, only less responsive, less a know-it-all, and way the hell cheaper. "You know what? They didn't care at all. Leah was even in the same place as me, kinda. I mean, she was just thinking about divorcing Marco. She didn't actually do anything. Though, you know, I didn't actually do anything, either."

Unlike a lot of their dogs, Oliver showed some manners on the leash. He walked just a few steps ahead of her, didn't lunge or pull or try to go in his own direction. When they passed a dog barking behind a fence, he didn't growl and his fur didn't prickle.

"Anyway, they know all my secrets now, and they still love me. Isn't that amazing?" She took a swig of water. "I wish I knew your secrets, sweetie. Where did you come from? What was your life like? Are you missing your people or happy to be away from them? God knows, all families aren't created equal. But we'll find you the best one ever. I don't know if Oz would like a younger brother, but I think he'd adapt, and Dalton said we could take you if necessary."

We. The simple word sent a shiver of well-being through her. She'd missed being part of a *we.*

Though she loved her time with the margarita club, she had missed being with Dalton—just looking at him, touching him, sharing little moments like washing dishes with him. She'd damn well missed making love with him. She intended to see him tonight, since Ilena had turned down her offer to help around the house. *Juan's mother is coming to stay tomorrow,* she'd said along with her thanks. *She wants to be here when her new* nieto *is born.*

Juan's mother loved Ilena. His whole family adored her and treated her like a princess.

Dalton's mother hadn't even wanted to shake Jessy's hand.

"You know, years ago, I dreamed about marrying into a huge, friendly, warm, loving family where I would finally have parents and siblings who cared, even if there wasn't any blood between us. Then I fell in love with Aaron, who'd lost any real family he might have had when he entered the foster system, and now Ramona Smith..."

It hurt, holding her hand out to someone who just looked at it like she had mad cow disease or something. Nearly eighty-four hours later, her fingers cramped a little on Oliver's leash. It wasn't the first time she'd been rejected. In a haze of emotion, she'd tried to hug her mother the day she moved out of the Wilkes house, but Nathalie had stopped her with an outstretched arm, physically blocking the embrace. It had confirmed that leaving was the right thing, but it had still hurt like hell.

They reached First Street, and Oliver politely stopped beside her on the curb. The passing vehicles didn't make him uneasy, not even the semi that blew through over the speed limit, its empty trailer rattling and bouncing. When it was clear, she started across and Oliver trotted beside her.

With the sun inching past the midpoint, the buildings on the other side of the street offered some shade, at least until they reached the parking lot for the Starlite Motel. It had been built in the nineties as a tribute to motels of the 1950s, with neon signs, a lot of tall, peaked angles, vintage stools and booths inside its small restaurant, and some eye-catching paint colors. She and Aaron had stayed there while house hunting in Tallgrass. They both had appreciated quirky and odd.

She picked up her pace, the next bit of shade her goal, but Oliver stopped short. She tugged, but he didn't give. "What's up?" she asked. "You see people inside there eating lots of good, fattening food you don't get?"

His nose was quivering, and the ripples went all the way

down his body to his tail. His ears flattened against his head, but he didn't seem hostile, just excited. Jessy tightened her grip on the leash, just in case, before searching for what held him so captivated.

The vehicle nearest them was an old pickup, decades older than her, a Chevy with its original blue-and-white paint and a heaping splattering of rust. Both doors were open, though she didn't see any sign of life. Then boots thumped the ground on the other side, and a man straightened from the passenger seat, settling a straw cowboy hat on his head.

Oliver took that as his cue to move. He started across the parking lot despite Jessy's attempts to stop him, pulling her along, raising whitish-gray gravel dust in his wake. The closer they got to the truck, the faster he moved, until Jessy was trotting to keep up.

The man closed the pickup door, turned, his hat tugged low over his face, and found Oliver smiling, wagging his tail, shaking all over. Could this be his owner? Had he lost Oliver while passing through and come back looking for him?

"Hey, buddy," the cowboy said, bending to offer the dog his hand. There was none of that tentative sniff-sniff stuff. Oliver licked the hand, then wriggled closer for a scratch. The man crouched, head ducked, and devoted both hands to giving the dog attention, along with some soft words.

"Is this your dog?" Jessy asked at last. "He's been staying the last few weeks at the shelter, but we haven't found his owner. Is he yours? Are you his?"

"No, sorry. Never seen him before."

Disappointed—how cool would it have been for Oliver to find his owner and for his owner to love him?—Jessy took a step back, stumbled on a chunk of gravel, and almost fell off her thick-soled sandal. The cowboy looked up as she caught herself, and the air rushed from her lungs like someone had removed a plate-sized plug.

Identical at birth didn't necessarily mean identical today. People aged differently—put on weight, took it off, went gray or some totally unrelated color, built muscles or wasted away, lived happily or carried a lot of burdens. But differences aside, she saw enough of the identical to recognize the man in front of her.

Dillon Smith had come home.

Thirteen years after running away in the middle of the night and breaking his family's hearts.

"You okay?" he asked, rising to his feet. "Maybe it's too hot for you and this little guy to be out walking."

"When did you get to town?" she asked hoarsely.

His familiar dark eyes narrowed, bleaker than she'd ever seen Dalton's, and he took a quick look to make sure no one else was around. "Do I know you?"

"Would you forget someone this short with hair this red?"

"Maybe." His gaze slid down to her feet and back. "But I wouldn't forget that body."

She snorted. "I'm Jessy Lawrence. I'm dating your brother, Dalton." *Dating.* Saying it out loud gave her a bit of a shiver.

Something passed across his face—a shadow, fear—and his manner immediately changed. He grew nervous, as shaky as Oliver, his movements jerky instead of fluid, his eyes blank instead of friendly. "Good for Dalton," he muttered. "I've got to get going."

He started to step around her, but Jessy blocked his way. "Where?"

"None of your business, Jessy Lawrence."

"Dalton's at the ranch."

"Of course he is. Where else could he possibly be?"

He moved again; she blocked again. "Did you come here to see him?"

He heaved a sigh, then smacked one hand against the tailgate. Oliver moved closer to him, pressing against his leg, and without hesitation, Dillon scratched him again. "I thought about it," he admitted sullenly.

"But?"

"I thought about it the last five times I came here, but I always changed my mind."

"I imagine it's hard to show up after thirteen years and say, 'Hey, guess what? Twin brother's alive and come home.' Though your parents would be excited as hell to hear it." Jessy didn't feel guilty for criticizing him, even though she'd done much the same. But there was one huge difference: Dillon's family loved him.

More emotion in his eyes. "Are they still here? Still…"

"Alive? Yes. Here, no. They live in South Texas. Noah's in school at OSU. Dalton owns the ranch and works it. And you—what have you been doing?"

He shook his head slowly. "Nothing that matters." Then regret pinched his face. She would bet a month's worth of doggy treats that there had been someone in those thirteen years who did matter, who mattered a lot.

Time hadn't been kind to him. She'd imagined a reckless, charmingly disreputable version of Dalton, not this weary, burdened man.

"You know I have to call him."

"No, you don't. No offense, Jessy Lawrence, but it's none of your business."

She smiled stubbornly. "Being with Dalton makes it my business."

"What exactly does that mean—being with? Just dating? Engaged? Friends with benefits? Knocking boots?"

"There's no way I can *not* tell him I saw you. It would be wrong."

He lowered the tailgate with a protesting shriek of metal, sat down, and patted the gate. Oliver leaped up and lay down next to him. "More wrong than if you tell him I was in town but I didn't go to see him? 'Cause I told you, this isn't the first time I got this far before taking off again."

"How about I call him right now? He could be here in fifteen minutes. I can wait with you to make sure you don't go anywhere."

He gave her another all-over look. "You're not much of a deterrent, li'l bit. Hell, you can't even climb up on this tailgate by yourself. Even this guy could do that."

Jessy didn't dignify that with a response or a try. She'd been short all her life. She knew her limits. Instead, she leaned one shoulder against the heated metal. "Why come here if you didn't want to carry through?"

His smile was cynical. "I've learned a lot about myself since I left this place. I'm irresponsible, careless, and selfish, and I'm not interested in changing that. I don't want the responsibilities that come with being like Dalton. I don't want a steady job. I don't want to stay in one place too long. I don't want to get bored or boring. I like having fun. And—" The smile faded, and his face turned deep red. "I'm your basic coward. I'd rather come back here, wonder, and leave again than face bad news."

He had no idea how much she could relate to that. She'd been wondering about things forever, but just last night she'd taken the chance, and it had been worth it. Not just good news but incredible news—sympathy and understanding all the way.

"What if you go to see him and he says, 'Welcome home, Dillon'?"

His laughter was rusty. "You *do* know Dalton, don't you? He holds a grudge better than anyone I know. Hell, he'd probably shoot first and ask questions later."

Yeah, she'd been one of his grudges for a while. And it wasn't easy telling the guy, *Go home, see your brother*, when it was a sure bet that Dalton wasn't ready to see him. Finding out Dillon was alive—sure, Dalton could handle that. Actually looking into his face... he'd probably want to punch it.

"I have to tell—" Her cell phone interrupted her, and she pulled it from her pocket. Though she didn't recognize the number, she answered anyway.

"Jessy, this is Ramona Smith."

A chill passed over her, accompanied by the helpless feeling from Saturday night that she'd disappointed Dalton's mother by merely existing. She wished she hadn't answered, wished she wasn't above pretending to have a bad connection and ending the call. Then she would throw her phone in front of the next big rig to come flying into town.

Of course she had answered, and disconnecting now would only delay the inevitable, and she wasn't about to toss her phone beneath eighty thousand pounds of steel since reprogramming all those numbers and ringtones would be a bitch.

Besides, she was Dalton's mother. Jessy had to make nice with her. *Wanted* to make nice with her.

"Um, hey. Hello."

"David and I are in town—well, we're at the ranch. I talked to Dalton last night, and I'd like to talk to you today. He tells me you work at the animal shelter, and I was wondering if I could come by there in a little bit and get a few minutes of your time."

Jessy swallowed hard. She wasn't crazy about meeting Dalton's mom on her own, but if he trusted letting that happen, he must be sure Ramona would be on her best behavior.

Then she looked at Dillon, scratching and rubbing Oliver as if he'd done it a million times, and a voice in her head began whispering, *If you present Ramona with her long-lost son, she'll have to accept you, right? Out of sheer gratitude?*

"Okay, sure. I'm walking one of the dogs, but we'll be back in fifteen minutes."

"That would be great."

After saying their good-byes, Jessy put the phone away, then rested her hands on her hips. "I have to get Oliver back to the shelter. You should come by and talk to our director about adoption. She's tall, blond, and gorgeous— just your type." She left out the fact that Angela was in a committed relationship with another woman.

"How do you know my type?"

"Tall, blond, and gorgeous is every man's type."

Dillon seemed reluctant to move away from Oliver. He eased one foot to the ground but kept scratching the puppy's ear. Put the other foot on the ground and kept scratching. "Nah, I don't need a dog."

"Everyone needs a dog," Jessy pointed out. And if she was going to face Ramona Smith in fifteen minutes, she wasn't doing it alone. "Besides, the point is, this dog needs you. You're the first person he's approached, the first one he's shown any interest in. The way he dragged me over here, I'm pretty sure he's picked you out as his human. You don't want to break his heart, now do you?"

Dillon studied her a long time, then smiled ruefully. "I've been blackmailed before, but never with a dog."

She waited, knowing to keep her mouth shut when he was looking a whole lot like he was talking himself into it.

After a moment, he said, "Okay. No promises, but I'll talk to her. You want a ride?"

Jessy smiled. She'd been truly surprised to discover that she liked walking, but with the temperature hovering in the high nineties, sweat soaking from every pore of her body, her hair plastered to her head underneath the cap, and the prospect of meeting Ramona again, cutting one walk in half wouldn't matter.

"You bet we would."

Besides, this way she could make sure Dillon didn't flee the county.

Chapter 15

With his dad there to help out with the chores, Dalton decided at the last minute to go into town with his mom. It wasn't that he thought she might get overemotional and make things worse with Jessy, though that was her suspicion. Truth was, he wanted to see Jessy. Tuesday morning seemed a long time ago, tonight too far off.

They were halfway into town when she asked, "Are you going to marry this girl?"

In the bitterness over Sandra's suicide, he'd thought he would never get married again. How could he trust a woman that much again? How could he risk that kind of pure hell again?

But as Ramona had pointed out, Jessy wasn't Sandra. Jessy was a survivor. She might not understand just how important she was to the people around her, but she wouldn't take the easy way out. She never took the easy way out of anything.

"We haven't discussed it."

"But you want to."

Yeah, he wanted to. There were things to figure out—number one being whether *she* was willing to get married again. Would she mind giving up her apartment and moving to the country? Would she get along with his folks or have a problem with Noah living at the ranch when he wasn't in school? Did she want kids?

"It's something we'll have to talk about." He gave her a teasing grin. "*We* being me and Jessy."

"That's fine. Just don't leave us out of the wedding this time, if possible. I've already bought a mother-of-the-groom dress—hope springs eternal, you know—and I'd like a chance to wear it while it still fits."

"I'll do my best." Slowing, he made the first left turn inside the town limits onto the first street that ran through the north side of Tallgrass. It was less than a mile to the shelter. Dogs occupied the yards on both sides, a couple of them wrestling, a few more baking in the sun, the rest seeking out shade.

The only vehicle in the parking lot was parked to one side, an old Chevy truck, the kind he'd learned to drive in. That one had belonged to his grandfather, who'd sold it to Dillon when he graduated from high school.

"Where's her car?" Mom asked. "Surely that little girl doesn't drive that truck. I can't imagine her having the strength to wrestle that old gearshift out of neutral."

"She usually walks to work."

"I walk every day, too, but it still doesn't make up for all those hours sitting in the RV and snacking while your father drives." With a sigh, she patted her stomach. "Oh, well, your dad loves me just like I am, and Nita's grandkids—she's our neighbor—think I'm all soft and squishy just like a grandmother should be."

"You'll get grandkids someday, Mom. Definitely from Noah."

She laughed. "Noah's just a big ol' kid himself. I have trouble imagining him growing up and settling down enough to be a father."

Dalton parked in front of the fence on the right side and shut off the engine. "You ready?"

With a deep breath, Ramona opened the door. "I hate making apologies. Of course, I don't get much practice because I'm so rarely wrong. Are you coming in?"

"Nah. I'm going to look at the dogs. They might have some frou-frou little yipper who'd like nothing more than to sit in your lap in the RV all day."

She frowned at him. "I don't want a dog."

"Yeah, that's what we all say, but in the end, it doesn't seem to matter."

She *hmph*ed as she crossed the parking lot and went inside the shelter. Chuckling, Dalton walked over to the fence, crouched, and looked over the dogs in that yard, but Oliver wasn't among them. If the mutt had been adopted, Jessy would have told him, so maybe he was inside cooling off or being tended to.

There were plenty of others wanting attention. They crowded each other at the fence, shouldering one another aside for a chance at the pitiful scratch that was all he could manage through the chain link. Their eagerness for attention made his gut clench. So many animals abandoned or tossed away by their irresponsible owners. It was no surprise Jessy wanted him to adopt her favorite. In fact, the only surprise was that she hadn't asked him to take a dozen others for good measure.

Voices floated on the still air from the back of the enclosure, one of them husky, Southern, the voice that mattered most in his life. Seeing a gate nearby, its padlock and chain dangling unfastened, Dalton let himself into the yard, then headed for the back, the dogs following him like a pack with their alpha.

When he circled the corner, the first thing he saw was Oliver with a leash hooked to his collar. The second stopped him in his tracks: Jessy, her back to him, standing on her tiptoes, her arms wrapped around a man's neck.

I don't share, he'd told her, and for a moment, that thought flared hot and sharp. It was just a hug, and there had to be a valid explanation for it. Maybe the guy was an old friend of Aaron's, though he wasn't a soldier, judging by the shaggy hair.

Hair the same dark shade as Dalton's. Height was a match for Dalton, too, and the width of the shoulders. In fact, except for the thinner frame, a person could mistake the guy for Dalton from behind, with the worn, washed-out jeans, work shirt, and scuffed, beaten work boots.

She ended the embrace, and Dalton found himself staring at an all too damn familiar face.

Oh, God, Dillon was home, and Jessy was hugging him like a long-lost lover.

Cold sweat broke out on his forehead and spread down his spine. That damned pickup truck. He should have recognized it the instant he'd seen it. He'd parked beside it, behind it, and in front of it a million times in the year and a half before Dillon took off. But old blue-and-white Chevy trucks weren't an unusual sight in Oklahoma, and most of them looked pretty much the same.

For a moment, crazy thoughts ran through Dalton's head: that Jessy had picked up Dillon somehow, some-

where, the same way she had Dalton nearly three months
ago. That she'd been with his brother. That she'd said the
same things, done the same things, with him that she did
with Dalton.

The *cold* part of the sweat was gone. Heat pumped
through his veins, his head throbbing with it, his vision
hazy. He took a step forward, intending to jerk Jessy away
from his brother, to beat the shit out of him, to pound him
until every bit of anger and betrayal was finally gone. But
something stopped him.

Jessy stopped him.

She wasn't Sandra, and she wasn't Alice, either. Jessy
wasn't involved with the bastard. She hadn't hooked
up with him, didn't have any kind of relationship with
him or any other man. She wouldn't do that to Dalton,
wouldn't do it to herself. Hell, this was the woman who
was ashamed to admit she'd gotten fired from the bank,
who'd been merciless with herself for the failure of losing a job.

This was the woman who'd spent three of the last four
nights in his bed. The woman who loved him. The woman
he wanted to spend the rest of his life with.

Dillon glanced up, and over her shoulder, his gaze connected with Dalton's. The color drained from his face, and
his body went stiff. He'd always been able to sense when
Dalton was about to punch him and get ready for it, while
he'd never had any tell of his own. He'd sucker-punched
Dalton too many times to count.

Slowly Jessy turned. Heat flushed her face, and alarm
flashed in her eyes as she put space between herself and
Dillon. Her mouth moved a few times before she managed
his name. "D-Dalton. I—I—I wasn't expecting you. I, um,

I didn't think...I was just, um, finishing up..." She sucked in a quick breath, then blurted out, "We just finished Oliver's adoption papers. He has a new home."

The dog moved behind Dillon, his head thrust forward between his owner's knees. The way he stood, it was hard to tell if he was taking cover or making a stand. He didn't trust anyone yet, Jessy had told Dalton, so of course the first person he responded to was Dillon. The bastard had always had a way with women and animals.

Dalton shifted his attention back to his brother. "You're taking responsibility for a dog?" The words came out dry, the tone disbelieving.

Dillon swallowed a couple times. "I didn't really want a dog—"

Damn.

"But he made his choice."

Jessy's smile quavered. "Kind of like you and Oz." Her green eyes were huge, the way they'd been Saturday night when she'd started downstairs to meet his parents, but instead of simple anxiety, now there was pleading and fear, too. She expected him to be angry with her, to think the worst of her because thinking the worst of herself was one of the things she was really good at.

Before he could reassure her, offer his hand, or anything else, the rear door into the shelter swung out. It hid the newcomer, but the sudden tightening in his chest warned him who it was an instant before she spoke.

"Jessy? Your boss said I could interrupt you—" Ramona saw them and stopped abruptly. Her grip on the door went slack, it slowly swung shut, and like Dillon, she went pale and stiff. "Oh, dear Lord," she whispered. "Dillon. You've come home."

* * *

Ramona swayed as if she might fall, then immediately straightened her spine. "Come over here," she said, her voice sounding of impending tears. "Give your mother a hug, and be quick about it."

As Dillon obeyed, Jessy turned back to Dalton. The acid in her stomach was enough to make her a little unsteady, too, so she stayed close to the building in case her legs gave way. "I was going to call you." She managed little more than a whisper.

His expression was impossible to read.

"I—I took Oliver for a walk, and he saw Dillon in this motel parking lot, and it was like he'd seen his daddy. He was so excited, and Dillon responded to him, too, and they were really good together, so I suggested…" She had to stop to fill her lungs, to clear the lump from her throat. "I was going to call you."

Dalton just stared at her a long time, and pain pierced her chest. When her heart broke the first time, it had been an explosion of grief, set off by the five worst words in the world: *We regret to inform you.* This time it was just one single ache, but she was pretty sure it was going to spread, getting sharper and rawer, until it destroyed her. She'd known getting involved with Dalton was a risk. She'd known the odds were great that she would screw it up just like she'd screwed up everything else in her life, but idiot that she was, she'd done it anyway, and—

Wait just a damned minute.

She took a deep breath that smelled of heat and sweat and dog waste, then another. Folding her arms across her chest, she scowled hard at Dalton, the way he used to look at her every time they met. "You know what? I didn't do anything wrong. I was walking Oliver, I ran into your brother, and you showed up before I had a chance to tell you. That's all. I would have told you, even though he said it was none of my business, but he doesn't get to decide what I do because my loyalty is to you. I don't even know him, and I certainly don't owe anything to anyone who calls me 'li'l bit,' but *you* owe me the courtesy of having faith—"

"Will you marry me?"

"In me after all…we've…done…" Jessy broke off, pulled off her cap, and ran her fingers through her hair before reseating it and narrowing her gaze. "What did you say?"

Slowly Dalton grinned, and the tiny cracks still spreading in her heart suddenly stopped. "I asked you to marry me."

Marry me. Oh, dear God. Grateful for the solid support of the building, she leaned against it. Her heart pounded in her chest, its thud so loud that it overwhelmed all the other noises—Ramona's weeping, Dillon's consoling words, the dogs snuffling and playing, the twelve forty-five train passing a half mile away.

Slowly she slid to the ground, taking off her hat again to bat away the ever-present flies. Dalton crouched in front of her, his dark eyes dancing with amusement, one brow raised in question.

"I look a mess." Stupid, but yeah, that was the first thought that came to her mind after a marriage proposal. *Way to go, Jess.*

"But you clean up good."

She'd thought she would never marry again—thought

that was the kindest thing to do for anyone foolish enough to ask. Hell, she was such a disaster that she'd never intended to let anyone get close enough even to think of asking her.

Marriage. A pastor, her friends, his family, vows. A husband. In-laws, a family of her own. A place to belong forever.

She deserved that, didn't she? She wasn't a disaster anymore. She wasn't perfect, but she wasn't a total failure, either. So her marriage to Aaron probably would have ended if he'd lived to come home. Divorce happened. It didn't make her unlovable, unworthy, or unfit to try again.

"If you need that long to think about it..."

Instead of stiff, the way it had been that night over coffee in the gazebo, his voice was warm, teasing. The man she'd met three months ago who'd had little to say, no softness, no happiness, nothing but hard sorrow, had learned to smile and laugh and tease again, in part because of her. Was that incredible or what?

She blew out her breath. "I was so concerned about you finding out Dillon was back, I never considered...never expected..."

"We'll worry about Dillon later." He didn't even spare a glance for his brother. "Right now, it's just you and me." He took her hand, his fingers warm, strong, callused, and so gentle with her. "Should I do this again tonight? Someplace more appropriate? Dinner at Luca's, with candles and flowers and wine?"

"I don't drink anymore. I can't handle it," she said, still full of wonder inside. Then she realized what she'd blurted out, and her gaze jerked up to his. He didn't seem shocked or surprised or disgusted or anything else bad. He'd started this conversation looking at her as if she were the most important person in his world, and he was still looking at her that way.

You're surrounded by people who love you, Carly had told her. *You're blessed, sweetie.*

Damn straight.

"We haven't talked about a lot of stuff," she said. "Of course we'd live at the ranch. And if your mom has a problem with me, she's just gonna have to deal with it, okay? Because if you put a ring on my finger, I'm not going away. And I don't know about kids, if I want them or not, but I do want dogs. Oz needs a brother or two. And—and—" Damn, she was babbling. She'd never babbled.

Drawing a deep breath, she squeezed her eyes shut to clear the dampness that had suddenly formed. *Must be dog spores in the air.*

All the little voices in her head sniffled with her.

"One more thing," she whispered. "I tend to get a little insecure, so you have to tell me you love me every day."

His smile slowly faded, and he studied her intently, with such emotion on his face. Solemnity. Promise. Hope. Soul-deep sincerity. Along with something she could only describe as great satisfaction. No, more than that. Pleasure, pure and complete. Maybe even joy.

"I want you living in my house, Jessy, because you already haunt me when you're not there," he said in a low, husky voice that made her shiver. "Mom's here to make up with you, and you're damn right you're not going away. Dogs are fine, and if we have kids, great. If we don't, that's okay, too. And as for the other..."

She'd already half forgotten what the other was until he stood, lifted her to her feet, and bent his head to hers. "I love you, Jessy. After Sandra died, well-meaning people told me that when God closed a door, He opened a window. You're my window. You've brought light and warmth and sunshine and fresh air and hope to my life. I know I could live without you, but I don't want to. Say you'll marry me, please."

Still trying to hold back the tears, she squinted at him. "I'm not as perfect as you think I am."

He laughed, the freest, happiest sound she'd ever heard. "You're perfect for me, Jess. That's all that matters. You and me."

"What about Dillon?"

His hands tightened just the slightest where he held her, and annoyance flickered through his eyes, but it was mixed with relief. Anger aside, he was grateful to know his brother was alive and well, as she'd known he would be. "He'll have to find his own girl. Like I told you, I don't share."

For a moment, images ran through her mind: her parents, her sisters, their children who'd never met their aunt Jessy. Aaron, sweet, full of life, always smiling, saving adult behavior for his job, acting like a happy kid the rest of the time. Herself the day of the notification visit, sinking deeper and deeper into trouble in the months that followed. Who could have guessed that a cowboy who'd been part of her trouble would be the one, along with her girls and an abandoned mutt, to help her save herself?

She raised her hand to his face, gently tracing along his jaw, then twining both hands behind his neck. "Yes."

His mouth nuzzled hers. "Yes?"

"Yes, I'll marry you. Yes, I love you. Yes, I could spend the rest of my life without you, but I don't want to."

He gave her one of those kisses then, nibbling at her lips, her tongue, sending tremors through her all the way to her toes, making her languid and lazy and tense and aroused and dazed about everything in the world except Dalton, this kiss, and the promise they were making to be together.

Forever.

* * *

Little in life was perfect, but at nine thirty that night, Jessy's world was as damn close as it could get.

She and Oliver had reunited Dillon with his family. It hadn't been all smiles and hugs, though no one, Dillon least of all, had expected that. Letting go of his resentment wasn't easy for Dalton, but she believed it would happen. He just needed time. Notified of Dillon's return, Noah had coolly said he'd see him the next time he was home . . . if his brother hung around that long. He just needed time, too.

Ramona had made a lovely apology, and Jessy thought she'd been pretty gracious in accepting it. She might have escaped the South first chance she'd gotten, but she hadn't escaped her Southern manners.

Oliver had a new home with Dillon. He and Oz hadn't exactly hit it off on his first visit. In fact, they'd stood nose to nose, fur bristling and growling until their owners separated them. David had leaned close to Jessy and murmured, "Remind you of anyone?"

And the biggest, best, most perfect thing of all: Dalton loved her and wanted to marry her. She'd been so humbled and, at the same time, had wanted to shout her good fortune from the rooftop of her building.

Warm water sloshed as Dalton shifted position an inch or two, the bubbles still covering her breasts but barely. Her head was tilted back, resting on his shoulder, her eyes closed, and she gave a big, lazy, satisfied, happy sigh.

"What are you thinking?" His mouth brushed her ear, sending shivers through her that, she swore, heated the water a degree or two.

"I was just wondering what I did to deserve you."

He nipped her earlobe, then laved the tender skin with his tongue. "I'm the reward for all the good you've done."

Normally, Realist Jessy would have protested that she hadn't done any good. She was a loser who couldn't hold on to a job, had betrayed her husband, had trouble staying sober, and couldn't even earn her family's love.

But tonight Realist Jessy kept her mouth shut. She *was* a good person, not perfect, still struggling, but she still showed up every day. She made the effort. And that counted for a lot.

Her skin wet and sudsy, she slipped and slid until she was facing Dalton, kneeling, his muscular thighs flanking her. Had she mentioned how much she loved this old claw-foot tub? "Am I your reward?"

His grin shot another burst of heat straight through her. "You're my incentive to appreciate life and the people in it." Ruefully, he added, "It's too short to be pissed off all the time."

So he was going to forgive Dillon. She'd known he would. Maybe, before long, the Double D Ranch would have both D's on the place again. Or remembering Dillon's words in the motel lot, maybe not. But she'd still be getting *two* brothers-in-law. How cool was that?

The air conditioner kicked on, and goose bumps appeared on Jessy's exposed flesh—and in this position, that was a lot of flesh. She was about to stretch out in the tub again and snuggle up to Dalton when her cell phone rang. She knew from the ringtone it was one of her girls, so she gave him a *one quick minute* look, stretched across to the small table where the cell rested, and picked it up.

Before she got out more than the *huh* of *hello*, Lucy shrieked. "Jessy, Jessy, Jessy, guess what?" She blurted out her news in one breath before shrieking again, this time with dismay. "*Norton!* Crap, I've got to go."

Grinning, Jessy put the phone back, lowered herself into the water and onto Dalton's long, naked, impressive body, nuzzling his neck. "Eleven minutes ago, Hector Juan Lewis Gomez made his appearance in this world. He's fat, happy, and healthy, and *Mamacita* is ecstatic. Cowboy, we've got us a baby boy to spoil. How about we celebrate?"

Since losing her husband in Afghanistan, Carly Lowry has rebuilt her life. She's comfortable and content... until she meets handsome Dane Clark, who rekindles desires Carly isn't quite sure she's ready to feel. But when Carly discovers the real reason he's come to town, can Dane convince her he's the hero she needs?

Please see the next page for an excerpt from

A Hero to Come Home To.

A Hero to Come Home To

Prologue

Thirteen months, two weeks, and three days.

That was the first conscious thought in Carly Lowry's head when she opened her eyes Tuesday morning. It was like an automatic tote board, adding each day to the total whether she wanted it to or not.

Thirteen months, two weeks, and three days. The way she marked her life now. There weren't events or occasions, no workdays or weekends, holidays or seasons. This was the only important passage of her time.

Thirteen months, two weeks, and three days since the helicopter transporting Jeff had been shot down in Afghanistan. Since her own life had ended. Her stubborn body just didn't recognize it.

Closing her eyes again, she groped for the remote on the nightstand and hit the power button. The morning news was on, though she paid it little mind. She didn't care about the latest bank robbery in Tulsa, or the sleazy lawyer's newest excuse to keep his high-profile client out of court on homicide charges, or which part of the city had construction woes adding to their morning commute.

Here in Tallgrass, Oklahoma, none of those things had happened in a long time. It was a great place to raise kids, Jeff had told her when they'd transferred here. Low crime rate, affordable cost of living if they discounted the air-conditioning bill in the dog months of summer, and all the amenities of Fort Murphy right next door. He'd loved downtown, with its stately buildings of sandstone and brick, none taller than three stories, as solid as if they'd grown right up out of the soil. He'd liked the old-fashioned awnings over the shop windows and the murals of cowboys, buffalo, and oil rigs painted on the sides of some of those buildings, along with restored eighty-year-old ads, back when phone numbers had only three digits. He'd loved the junk stores, where detritus of past lives showed up, their value and sometimes even their purpose forgotten. Rusty faded pieces of the town's history.

He'd loved *her*. Promised their time in Tallgrass would be good. Promised that when he retired from the Army, they would settle in just such a little town to finish raising their kids and turn gray and creaky together.

He'd broken his promise.

A sob escaped her, though she pretended it was a yawn and threw back the covers as if sleep might entice her if she remained in bed one minute longer. Truth was, crying every night wasn't conducive to a good night's sleep.

She avoided looking in the mirror as she got into the shower. She knew she had bed head, her pajamas made no attempt whatsoever at style, and her eyes were red and puffy. When she got out ten minutes later, she concentrated on the tasks of getting dried, dressed, and made up instead of the signs of tears, the fourteen pounds she'd gained, and the simple platinum band on her left hand.

She was ready for work early. She always was. While a cup of coffee brewed in the sleek machine she had bought as a surprise after Jeff had coveted it at the PX, she opened the refrigerator, then the pantry, looking for something to eat. She settled, as she did every morning, on oatmeal labeled as a "weight-control formula." She ate it for the protein, she told herself, because she needed the energy at work, and not because those fourteen pounds were huddled stubbornly on her hips and plotting to become twenty. To help them along, she added creamer and real sugar to her coffee, then topped off the meal with two pieces of rich, chocolate-covered caramel.

It was still too early for work, but too late to stay in the house any longer. After making sure the papers she'd graded the night before were inside her soft-sided messenger bag—of course they were—she stuffed her purse in, too, before grabbing her keys and heading outside to the car.

It was a chilly morning, but she didn't dash back in for a jacket. A utilitarian navy blue one was tossed across the passenger seat. Since college, she'd kept one in the car for cold restaurants—not that she ate out much anymore. Eating alone was bad enough; doing it in public exceeded her capabilities.

Two miles stretched out between her neighborhood and the Fort Murphy gate, then less than another to the post's school complex, where she taught. Most soldiers reported for duty an hour or more before school started, so she could wait that much longer at home and make the trip in less time, but moping was as well done in the car as at home.

She moved into the long double-lane line turning off Main Street and into the post. The only traffic jams Tallgrass ever saw were outside the fort's two main gates in the morning and afternoon. Jeff had liked to go to work early and stay late because life was too damn fun to sit idle in traffic.

He'd never sat idle.

Finally it was her turn to show her license and proof of insurance to the guard at the gate, who waved her through with a courteous, "Have a good day, ma'am."

Oh, yeah. Her days were so good, she wasn't sure how many more of them she could handle.

"You need to talk to someone," her sister-in-law had advised her in last week's phone call.

"To who? I've talked to the grief counselors and the chaplain, I've talked to you, I've even tried to talk to Mom." Carly's voice had broken on that.

Lisa's voice had turned sympathetic. *"You know your mom doesn't 'get' emotional."*

A thin smile curled her lips as she turned into the parking lot for the schools. None of her family "got" emotional. Mom, Dad, and three brothers: scientists, every last one of them. Logical, detached, driven by curiosity and rationale and great mysteries to solve. Unfortunately she, with her overload of emotion, wasn't the right sort of mystery for them. They were sympathetic—to a point. Understanding—to a point. Beyond that, though, she was more alien to them than the slide samples under their microscopes.

Easing into a parking space, she cut off the engine. Large oaks, with last fall's brown leaves waiting to be pushed aside by this spring's new ones, shaded the U-shaped complex. She worked in the one ahead of her, the elementary school; the middle school was, appropriately, in the middle; and the high school stood across the vast lot behind her.

Only two other employees had beaten her: one of the janitors and the elementary principal. He was a nice guy who always came early—problems of his own to escape at home, or so the gossips said—and brought pastries and started the coffee in the teachers' lounge. He was about her father's age, but much more human. He understood emotion.

Still, she didn't open her car door, even when the chill crept over her as the heater's warmth dissipated. The comment about her mother hadn't been the end of her conversation with Lisa. Her sister-in-law had returned to the subject without missing a beat. *"You need to talk to someone who's been there, Carly. Someone who really, truly* knows *what it's like. Another wife."*

Lisa couldn't bring herself to use the word *widow*, not in reference to Carly. Carly couldn't, either.

"I don't know…" She could have finished it several ways. *I don't know if I want to talk to anyone. I'm all talked out.* Or, *I don't know if talking could possibly help. It hasn't yet.* Or, *I don't know any other wives whose husbands have died.*

But that wasn't true. Wives—widows—didn't tend to stay in the town where their husbands had last been assigned. They usually had homes or families to return to. But she knew one who hadn't left: Therese Matheson. Well, she didn't actually *know* her, other than to say hello. Therese's kindergartners were on recess and at lunch at different times than Carly's third-graders, and their free periods didn't coincide, either.

But Therese had been there, done that, and had the flag and posthumous medals to show for it. Therese really, truly knew. Would it hurt to ask if they could meet for dinner one evening? One dinner wasn't much of a commitment. If it didn't pan out, so what? At least she would have eaten something besides a frozen entrée or pizza.

Therese would be at school before the eight fifteen bell. Carly would find out then.

* * *

"Tuh-*reese*, where's my pink shirt?"

Thirteen-year-old Abby's voice had always had a shrill edge, from the first time Therese Matheson had met her, but it had grown even worse over the past months. It was designed to get on her nerves quicker than a classful of kindergartners who'd had too much sugar, too much whine, and not enough rest.

"Tuh-*race*," she murmured for the thousandth time before raising her voice enough to be heard upstairs. "If it's not in your closet, Abby, then it's in the laundry."

Footsteps reminiscent of a *Jurassic Park* T. rex resounded overhead, then Abby appeared at the top of the stairs. She was barely a hundred and ten pounds. How could she make such noise? "You mean you didn't wash it?"

Therese bit back the response that wanted to pop out: *How many times have I told you?* Instead, keeping her tone as normal as possible, she said, "You know the policy. If it's not in the hamper, it's not going to make it to the washer."

The girl's entire body vibrated with her frustration. "Oh

God, the one day a week we don't have to wear our uniforms and we *all* decided to wear pink today, and now I can't because *you* can't be bothered to do your job! My mom *always*..." The words faded as she whirled, her pale blond and scarlet hair flouncing, and stomped back to her room.

Your job. Therese leaned against the door frame. Being a mother was work, sure, tumultuous and chaotic, absolutely, but it wasn't supposed to be a *job*. It was supposed to be balanced by love and affection, common courtesy and respect. While their little family had an overabundance of tumult and chaos and resentment and hostility, there was precious little of the good things that made the rest worthwhile.

"Oh, Paul," she whispered, her gaze shifting to the framed photo above the fireplace. "You were the glue that held us together. Now that you're gone, we're falling apart. I'm trying, I really am, but..." Her voice broke, and tears filled her eyes. "I don't think I can do this without you."

For as long as she could remember, she'd wanted a husband and children, and for the last six years, she'd wanted Paul's children—sweet babies with his ready smile, his good nature and sense of humor, his endless capacity to love.

She'd gotten his children, all right. Just not in the way she'd expected.

A distant rumble penetrated her sorrow, and her gaze flickered to the wall clock. She blinked away the moisture, cleared the lump from her throat, and called, "Jacob! The bus is coming."

Again heavy steps pounded overhead, then her tall, broad-shouldered stepson took the stairs three at a time.

Only eleven, he was built like his father and shared the same coloring—dark blond hair, fair skin, eyes like dark chocolate—but that was where the similarities ended. Where Paul had been warm and funny and considerate, Jacob was moody and distant. Paul had been easy to get along with; Jacob was prickly.

Not that he wasn't entitled—rejected by his mother and abandoned, however unwillingly, by his father. Therese tried to be there for him, to talk to him, to comfort him, and God knew how often she prayed for him. But the last time he'd let her hug him had been right after Paul's funeral fifteen months ago. It seemed the harder she tried, the harder he pushed her away.

He paused only long enough to grab the backpack in the living room, then the door slammed behind him. He didn't say good-bye, didn't even glance her way.

Therese tried to take a calming breath, but her chest was tight, her lungs so compressed that only a fraction of the air she needed could squeeze through. In the beginning, right after she'd gotten the news of Paul's death, the difficulty breathing, the clamminess, the fluttering just beneath her breastbone, had been an occasional thing, but over the months it had come more often.

People asked her how she was doing, and she gave them phony smiles and phony answers, and everyone believed her, even her parents. She was afraid to tell the truth: that every day was getting worse, that she was losing ground with the kids, that her stomach hurt and her chest hurt and her head was about to explode. She did her best to maintain control, but she was only pretending. Whatever control she had was fragile and, worse, sometimes she *wanted* to lose it. To shatter into nothingness. After all, *nothing* couldn't be hurt, couldn't suffer, couldn't grieve. *Nothing* existed in a state of oblivion, and some days—most days lately—she needed the sweet comfort of oblivion.

Another rumble cut through the rushing in her ears, and she forced her mouth open, forced Abby's name to form. Unlike Jacob, Abby didn't ignore her but glared at her all the way down the stairs. Contrary to her earlier shriek, she was wearing pink: a silk blouse from Therese's closet. It was too big for her, so she'd layered it over a torso-hugging tank top and tied the delicate fabric into knots at her waist.

Abby's defiant stare dared Therese to comment. Just as defiant, she ground her teeth and didn't say a word. She had splurged on the blouse for a date night with Paul, but no way she would wear it again now. If it was even salvageable after a day with the princess of I-hate-you.

The door slammed, the sudden quiet vibrating around Therese, so sharp for a moment that it hurt. The house was empty. *She* was empty.

Dear God, she needed help.

She just didn't know where to get it.

* * *

As the warning bell rang, Carly left her class in the capable hands of her aide and made her way to the kindergarten wing, which stood at a right angle to her own wing. Therese Matheson's classroom was at the end of the hallway, next to a door that led to the playground. It was large and heavy, especially compared to the five-year-olds that populated the hall, but since five-year-olds were proven escape artists, it was wired with an alarm to foil any attempts.

Therese stood in the hallway, greeting her students, ushering the stragglers into the room. Pretty, dark haired, she looked serene. Competent. So much more in control of herself than Carly. For a moment, Carly hesitated, unsure about her plan. What could she possibly have to offer Therese?

Then she squared her shoulders, fixed a smile on her face, and approached her. "Hi, Therese, I'm Carly Lowry. Third grade?" One hand raised, thumb pointing back the way she'd come. "I, uh…My husband was…"

Sympathy softened Therese's features even more. "I know. Mine, too."

A pigtailed girl darted between them, pausing long enough to beam up, revealing a missing tooth. "Hi, Miss Trace."

"Good morning, Courtney." Therese touched her lightly on the shoulder before the girl rushed inside.

Kindergartners were unbearably cute, but Carly couldn't have taught them. That young and sweet and cuddly, they would have been a constant reminder of the kids she and Jeff had planned to have. Would never have.

"I was, uh, wondering…well, if you would mind getting together for dinner one night to—to talk. About…our husbands and, uh, things. If…well, if you're interested."

Therese considered it, raising one hand to brush her hair back. Like Carly, she still wore her wedding ring. "I'd like that. Does tonight work for you?"

Carly hadn't expected such a quick response, but it wasn't as if she had any other demands on her time. And if she had too much time to think about this idea, she very well might back out. "Sure. Is Mexican all right?"

Therese smiled. "I haven't had a margarita in months. The Three Amigos?"

It was Tallgrass's best Mexican restaurant, one of Jeff's favorites. Because of that, the only Mexican food Carly had since he died had been takeout from Bueno. "That would be great. Does six work for you?"

Therese's smile widened. "I'll be there."

The bell rang, the last few kids in the hall scurrying toward their classes. Carly summoned her own smile. "Good. Great. Uh, I'll see you tonight."

An unfamiliar emotion settled over her as she walked back to her own classroom. Hope, she realized. For the first time in thirteen months, two weeks, and three days, she felt hopeful. Maybe she could learn how to live without Jeff, after all.

Chapter One

One year later

It had taken only three months of living in Oklahoma for Carly to learn that March could be the most wonderful place on earth or the worst. This particular weekend was definitely in the wonderful category. The temperature was in the midseventies, warm enough for short sleeves and shorts, though occasionally a breeze off the water brought just enough coolness to chill her skin. The sun was bright, shining hard on the stone and concrete surfaces that surrounded them, sharply delineating the new green buds on the trees and the shoots peeking out from the rocky ground.

It was a beautiful clear day, the kind that Jeff had loved, the kind they would have spent on a long walk or maybe just lounging in the backyard with ribs smoking on the grill. There was definitely a game on TV—wasn't it about time for March Madness?—but he'd preferred to spend his time off with her. He could always read about the games in the paper.

Voices competed with the splash of the waterfall as she touched her hand to her hip pocket, feeling the crackle of paper there. The photograph went everywhere with her, especially on each new adventure she took with her friends. And this trip to Turner Falls, just outside Davis, Oklahoma, while tame enough, was an adventure for her. Every time she left their house in Tallgrass, two hours away, was an adventure of sorts. Every night she went to sleep without crying, every morning she found the strength to get up.

"There's the cave." Jessy, petite and red haired, gestured to the opening above and to the right of the waterfall. "Who wants to be first?"

The women looked around at each other, but before anyone else could speak up, Carly did. "I'll go." These adventures were about a lot of things: companionship, support, grieving, crying, laughing, and facing fears.

There was only one fear Carly needed to face today: her fear of heights. She estimated the cave at about eighty feet above the ground, based on the fact that it was above the falls, which were seventy-two feet high, according to the T-shirts they'd all picked up at the gift shop. Not a huge height, so not a huge fear, right? And it wasn't as if they'd be actually climbing. The trail was steep in places, but anyone could do it. She could do it.

"I'll wait here," Ilena said. Being twenty-eight weeks pregnant with a child who would never know his father limited her participation in cave climbing. "Anything you don't want to carry, leave with me. And be sure you secure your cameras. I don't want anything crashing down on me from above."

"Yeah, everyone try not to crash down on Ilena," Jessy said drily as the women began unloading jackets and water bottles on their friend.

"Though if you do fall, aim for me," Ilena added. "I'm

pretty cushiony these days." Smiling, she patted the roundness of her belly with jacket-draped arms. With pale skin and white-blond hair, she resembled a rather anemic snowman whose builders had emptied an entire coat closet on it.

Carly faced the beginning of the trail, her gaze rising to the shadow of the cave mouth. Every journey started with one step—the mantra Jeff had used during his try-jogging-you'll-love-it phase. She hadn't loved it at all, but she'd loved him so she'd given it a shot and spent a week recovering from shocks such as her joints had never known.

One step, then another. The voices faded into the rush of the falls again as she pulled herself up a steep incline. She focused on not noticing that the land around her was more vertical than not. She paid close attention to spindly trees and an occasional bit of fresh green working its way up through piles of last fall's leaves. She listened to the water and thought a fountain would be a nice addition to her backyard this summer, one in the corner where she could hear it from her bedroom with the window open.

And before she realized it, she was squeezing past a boulder and the cave entrance was only a few feet away. A triumphant shout rose inside her and she turned to give it voice, only to catch sight of the water thundering over the cliff, the pool below that collected it, and Ilena, divested of her burden now and calling encouragement.

"Oh, holy crap," she whispered, instinctively backing against the rough rock that formed the floor of the cave entrance.

Heart pounding, she turned away from the view below, grabbed a handful of rock, and hauled herself into the cave. She collapsed on the floor, unmindful of the dirt or any crawly things she might find inside, scooted on her butt until the nearest wall was at her back, then let out the breath squeezing her chest.

Her relieved sigh ended in a squeak as her gaze connected with another no more than six feet away. "Oh, my God!" Jeff's encouragement the first time she'd come eye to eye with a mouse echoed in her head: *"He's probably as scared of you as you are of him."*

The thought almost loosed a giggle, but she was afraid it would have turned hysterical. The man sitting across the cave didn't look as if he was scared of anything, though that might well change when her friends arrived. His eyes were dark, his gaze narrowed, as if he didn't like his solitude interrupted. It was impossible to see what color his hair was, thanks to a very short cut and the baseball cap he wore with the insignia of the 173rd Airborne Brigade Combat Team. He hadn't shaved in a day or two, and he was lean, long, solid, dressed in a T-shirt and faded jeans with brand-new running shoes.

He shifted awkwardly, sliding a few feet farther into the cave, onto the next level of rock, then ran his hands down his legs, smoothing his jeans.

Carly forced a smile. "I apologize for my graceless entrance. Logically, I knew how high I was, but as long as I didn't look, I didn't have to *really* know. I have this thing about heights, but nobody knows"—she tilted her head toward the entrance, where the others' voices were coming closer—"so I'd appreciate it if you didn't say anything."

Stopping for breath, she grimaced. Apparently, she'd learned to babble again, as if she hadn't spoken to a stranger—a male stranger, at least—in far too long. She'd babbled with every man she'd met until Jeff. Though he'd been exactly the type to intimidate her into idiocy, he never had. Talking to him had been easy from the first moment.

"I'm Carly, and I hope you don't mind company because I think the trail is pretty crowded with my friends right now." She gestured toward the ball cap. "Are you with the Hundred Seventy-Third?"

There was a flicker of surprise in his eyes that she'd recognized the embroidered insignia. "I was. It's been a while." His voice was exactly what she expected: dark, raspy, as if he hadn't talked much in a long time.

"Are you at Fort Sill now?" The artillery post at Lawton was about an hour and a half from the falls. It was Oklahoma's only other Army post besides Fort Murphy, two hours northeast at Tallgrass.

"No." His gaze shifted to the entrance when Jessy appeared, and he moved up another level of the ragged stone that led to the back of the shallow cave.

"Whoo!" Jessy's shout echoed off the walls, then her attention locked on the man. The tilt of her green eyes gave her smile a decided feline look. "Hey, guys, we turn our back on her for one minute, and Carly's off making new friends." She heaved herself into the cave and, though there was plenty of room, nudged Carly toward the man before dropping to the stone beside her. She leaned past, offering her hand. "Hi, I'm Jessy. Who are you?"

Carly hadn't thought of offering her hand or even asking his name, but direct was Jessy's style, and it usually brought results. This time was no different, though he hesitated before extending his hand. "I'm Dane."

"Dane," Therese echoed as she climbed up. "Nice name. I'm Therese. And what are you doing up here in Wagon Wheel Cave?"

"Wishing he'd escaped before we got here," Carly murmured, and she wasn't sure but thought she heard an agreeing grunt from him.

The others crowded in, offering their names—Fia, Lucy, and Marti—and he acknowledged each of them with a nod. Somewhere along the way, he'd slipped off the ball cap and pushed it out of sight, as though he didn't want to advertise the fact that he'd been Airborne. As if they wouldn't recognize a high-and-tight haircut, but then, he didn't know he'd been cornered by a squad of Army wives.

Widows, Carly corrected herself. They might consider the loose-knit group of fifteen to twenty women back in Tallgrass just friends. They might jokingly refer to themselves as the Tuesday Night Margarita Club, but everyone around Tallgrass knew who they really were, even if people rarely said the words to them.

The Fort Murphy Widows' Club.

Marti, closest to the entrance, leaned over the edge far enough to make Carly's heart catch in her chest. "Hey, Ilena, say hi to Dane!"

"Hello, Dane!" came a distant shout.

"We left her down below. She's preggers." At Dane's somewhat puzzled gesture, Marti yelled out again, "Dane says hi!"

"Bet you've never been alone in a small cave with six women," someone commented.

"Hope you're not claustrophobic," someone else added.

He did look a bit green, Carly thought, but not from claustrophobia. He'd found the isolation he was seeking, only to have a horde of chatty females descend on him. But who went looking for isolation in a public park on a beautiful warm Saturday?

Probably lots of people, she admitted, given how many millions of acres of public wilderness there were. But Turner Falls wasn't isolated wilderness. Anyone could drive in. And the cave certainly wasn't isolated. Even she could reach it.

Deep inside, elation surged, a quiet celebration. Who knew? Maybe this fall she would strap into the bungee ride at the Tulsa State Fair and let it launch her into the stratosphere. But first she had to get down from here.

Her stomach shuddered at the thought.

After a few minutes' conversation and picture taking, her friends began leaving again in the order in which they'd come. With each departure, Carly put a few inches' space between her and Dane until finally it was her turn. She took a deep breath…and stayed exactly where she was. She could see the ground from here if she leaned forward except no way was she leaning forward with her eyes open. With her luck, she'd get dizzy and pitch out headfirst.

"It's not so bad if you back out." Despite his brief conversation with the others, Dane's voice still sounded rusty. "Keep your attention on your hands and feet, and don't forget to breathe."

"Easy for you to say." Her own voice sounded reedy, unsteady. "You used to jump out of airplanes for a living."

"Yeah, well, it's not the jumping that's hard. It's the landing that can get you in a world of trouble."

On hands and knees, she flashed him a smile as she scooted in reverse until there was nothing but air beneath her feet. Ready to lunge back inside any instant, she felt for the ledge with her toes and found it, solid and wide and really not very different from a sidewalk, if she discounted the fact that it was eighty feet above the ground. "You never did say where you're stationed," she commented.

"Fort Murphy. It's a couple hours away—"

"At Tallgrass." Her smile broadened. "That's where we're all from. Maybe we'll see you around." She eased away from the entrance, silently chanting to keep her gaze from straying. *Hands, feet, breathe. Hands, feet, breathe.*

* * *

Dane Clark stiffly moved to the front of the cave. A nicer guy would've offered to make the descent with Carly, but these days he found that being civil was sometimes the best he could offer. Besides, he wasn't always steady on his feet himself. If she'd slipped and he'd tried to catch her, she likely would have had to catch him instead. Not an experience his ego wanted.

His therapists wouldn't like it if they knew he was sitting in this cave. He'd been in Tallgrass only a few days. The first day, he'd bought a truck. The second, he'd come here. The drive had been too long, the climb too much. But he'd wanted this to be the first thing he'd done here because it was the last thing he'd done with his dad before he died. It was a tribute to him.

The women's voices were still audible, though all he could really make out was laughter. What were the odds he would drive two hours for a little privacy and wind up sharing the cave with six women—seven if he counted the pregnant one, now handing out jackets—from the town where he was stationed?

It really was a small world. He'd traveled a hell of a lot of it. He should know.

Sliding forward a few inches, he let his feet dangle over the edge. God, how many times had doctors and nurses and therapists told him to do that? Too many to think about, so instead he watched Carly's progress, her orange shirt easy to pick out against the drab shades of rock and dirt. Why had she volunteered to lead the climb if she was afraid of heights? To prove she could?

Finally, she jumped the last few feet to the ground and spun in a little circle that he doubted any of her friends noticed. She joined them, and what appeared to be a spontaneous group hug broke out, congratulating each other on their success.

He'd had buddies like that—well, maybe not so touchy-feely. Still did, even if they were scattered all over the world. But after years filled with one tour after another in Iraq or Afghanistan, a lot of them were gone. Sometimes he thought he couldn't possibly remember all their faces and names. Other times, he knew he would never forget.

After posing for more pictures, the women headed away from the falls. With the trail empty as far as he could see, he stood up, both hands touching the rock just in case. Time to see if his right leg and the miracle of modern medicine that served as his left could get him to the bottom without falling on his ass.

He succeeded. Uneven ground made for uncomfortable walking, the prosthetic rubbing the stump of his leg despite its protective sleeve. It was odd, standing, moving, climbing, without more than half of his leg. He could feel it, and yet he couldn't, sensed it was there but knew it wasn't. It was the damnedest thing—sometimes the hardest of all to accept.

He stood for a moment watching the water churn where the falls hit, giving the ache in his leg a chance to subside. Another month or two, and the pool would be filled with swimmers on weekends. He'd always liked to swim, and his various medical people had insisted he would again. He wasn't so sure about that. He'd never considered himself vain, but putting on trunks and removing his prosthesis in public...He wasn't ready for that. He was beginning to think he never would be.

Determinedly he turned away from the water and started for the parking lot. It wasn't far, maybe a quarter mile, sidewalk all the way, but by the time he reached his pickup, his leg and hip were throbbing, and the pain was spreading to his lower back. The two-hour drive home, plus a stop for lunch, would leave him in need of both a hot bath and a pain pill, but he didn't regret the trip.

Dane drove slowly through the park and onto the highway. Once he reached the interstate, he turned north, then took the first exit into Davis. A quick pass through town showed the fast-food options, and he settled on a burger and fries from Sonic. He was headed back to the interstate when traffic stopped him in front of a Mexican restaurant. Inside were the seven women from the cave, toasting each other, margarita glasses held high.

He'd noticed without realizing that most of them wore wedding rings. Were they just friends from Tallgrass, Army wives whose husbands were stationed there or maybe soldiers themselves? Carly, at least, had some military experience, with the way she'd pulled the name of his old unit out of thin air. And neither she nor Jessy nor any of the others had sounded as if they were native to Oklahoma, though he knew how easily accents could be picked up and lost. Best bet, they'd been brought to Tallgrass by the Army, and when their husbands deployed, so did they.

But he knew from firsthand experience there were worse ways for a wife to entertain herself when her husband was gone than hiking with her girlfriends.

He reached Fort Murphy in good time, turning at the end of Main Street into the post's main entrance. A sandstone arch on either side of the four-lane held engraved concrete: WELCOME TO FORT MURPHY on the left, a list of the tenant commands on the right, including the Warrior Transition Unit. That was the unit that currently laid claim to him. In the future...

Once he'd had his life all laid out: Twenty years or more in the Army, retirement, a family, a second career that left him time to travel. He'd thought he might teach history and coach, open a dive shop, or get into some type of wilderness-adventure trek business. Now he didn't have the vaguest idea what the future held. For a man who'd always known where he was going, it was kind of scary, not knowing where he was going or how—or even if—he could get there.

After clearing the guard shack, he drove onto the post, past a bronze statue of the base's namesake—cowboy, actor, and war hero Audie Murphy. The four-lane passed a manicured golf course, a community center with an Olympic-size pool, and the first of many housing areas before he turned onto a secondary street. His quarters were in a barracks, opened only months ago, small apartments to help their occupants adjust to life outside the hospitals where most of them had spent too many months. Dane's own stay had lasted eleven months. Long enough to bring a new life into the world. *Not* long enough to adjust to a totally new life.

He was limping painfully by the time he let himself into his apartment. Tossing the keys on a table near the door, he grabbed a beer from the refrigerator and washed down a couple pills, fumbled his way out of his jeans, then dropped onto the couch before removing the prosthesis. He had two—one that looked pretty real from a distance and this one, which seemed more of a superhero bionic thing. He was grateful to have them—he'd seen nonmilitary people forced by the cost to get by on much less efficient models—but neither was close to the real thing.

Absently rubbing his leg, he used the remote to turn on the television, then surfed the channels. There were lots of sports on today that he didn't want to watch. They reminded him too much of his own years playing football and baseball and running for the pure pleasure of it. No chick flicks, no talking animals, no gung-ho kick-ass action movies. He settled on a documentary on narrow-gauge railroads, a show that let his mind wander.

How had he filled his Saturday afternoons before the amputation? Running for his life sometimes. Taking other people's lives sometimes. Jumping out of helicopters, patrolling barren desert, interfacing with locals. Before Iraq and Afghanistan, it had been riding his motorcycle through the Italian Alps, taking the train to Venice with his buddies, sightseeing and drinking too much. Hanging out, using too many women badly trying to get over his failed marriage.

He replayed weekends all the way back to his teens. Chores, running errands, homework, extra practices if the coach deemed them necessary, dates on Saturday night with Sheryl. Before she'd married him. Before she'd fallen out of love with him. Before she'd run around on him—adding insult to injury, with guys from his own unit.

He was over her. By the time she'd actually filed for divorce, he'd been so disillusioned by her affairs that he hadn't cared. But there was still this knot of resentment. They'd been together since they were fourteen, for God's sake, and she hadn't even had the grace to say, *"It's over."* She'd lied to him. Betrayed him. She'd let him down, then blamed him for it.

And her life was great. She'd gone back home to Texas, married a rich guy who only got richer, and lived in a beautiful mansion with three beautiful kids.

Dane's mother gave him regular updates, despite the fact that he'd never once asked. *"You let her get away,"* Anna Mae always ended with a regretful sigh.

Yeah, sure. *He'd* screwed up. It was all his fault. To Sheryl and Anna Mae, everything that had gone wrong was his fault, even the IED that had cost him his leg. *If you'd listened to Sheryl and me and gotten out of the Army...*

A dim image of the women he'd met that day—Carly, Jessy, and the others—formed in his mind. Did they lie to their husbands, betray them, let them down? It would be easy to think yes. The unfaithful-always-ready-to-party military wife was a stereotype, but stereotypes became that for a reason.

But today, after driving to the park, hiking to the falls, and climbing up to the cave, he'd rather give them the benefit of the doubt. That was something normal people did, and today, he was feeling pretty normal.

* * *

"Do you ever feel guilty for looking at a guy and thinking, 'Wow, he's hot; I'd like to get to know him'?"

The quiet question came from Therese, sitting on the far side of the third-row seat of Marti's Suburban. Carly looked at her over Jessy's head, slumped on her shoulder. The redhead's snores were soft, barely noticeable, and due more to the third margarita she'd had with lunch than anything else, Carly suspected. Jessy was full of life until she got a few drinks in her, then she crashed hard.

"You mean, do I feel like I'm being unfaithful to Jeff, his memory, our marriage, his family, myself? Yeah. We had such plans." Regret robbed her voice of its strength. "Life wasn't supposed to turn out this way."

"But are we meant to spend the rest of our lives honoring our husbands' memories and...alone?"

Alone. That was a scary word even for women as independent as the Army had forced them to become. Even before their husbands had deployed to Iraq and Afghanistan, they'd been gone a lot, training at various bases around the country. They'd worked long hours to get themselves and their troops combat-ready, and most home-life responsibilities had fallen on their wives.

But then, *alone* had been okay. There had been an end to every training mission, to every deployment. The men had come home, and they'd made up for all the time missed.

For the seven of them, though, and the rest of the margarita club, the last return home had been final. There would be no more kisses, no more hugs, no more great sex, no more making up for missed time. There were only flags, medals, grave sites, and memories.

Yes, and some guilt.

"Paul wouldn't want you to spend the rest of your life alone."

The words sounded lame even to Carly. Lord knows, she'd heard them often enough—from friends, from her in-laws, from therapists. The first time, from a grief counselor, she'd wanted to shriek, *How could you possibly know that? You never met him!*

But it was true. Jeff had loved her. He'd always encouraged her to live life. He would be appalled if she grieved it away over him instead. Her head knew that.

Her heart was just having trouble with it.

Therese's laugh broke halfway. "I don't know. Paul was the jealous type. He didn't want me even looking at another guy."

"But that was because *he* was there. Now..." It took a little extra breath to finish the sentence. "He's not."

A few miles passed in silence before Therese spoke again. "What about you guys? What if one of us..."

After her voice trailed off, Fia finished the question from her middle-row seat. "Falls in love and gets another chance at happily ever after?"

Therese swallowed, then nodded. "Would it affect *us*? We became friends because we'd all lost our husbands. Would a new man in one of our lives change that? Would we want to share you with him?"

"Would he want to share you with us?" Ilena asked. "What guy would want his new girlfriend spending time with a group that's tied at its very heart to her husband's death?"

Shifting uncomfortably, Carly stared out the window. She had other friends—a few from college, teachers she worked with, a neighbor or two—but the margarita club, especially these six, were her best friends.

She wanted to say a relationship could never negatively affect their friendship, but truth was, she wasn't sure. She'd had other best friends before Jeff died—they all had—other Army wives, and they'd grown apart after. They'd shown her love and sorrow and sympathy, but they'd also felt a tiny bit of relief that it was *her* door the dress-uniformed officers had knocked at to make the casualty notification, that it was *her* husband who'd died and not theirs. And they'd felt guilty for feeling relieved.

She knew, because she'd been through it herself.

She forced a smile as her gaze slid from woman to woman. "I'll love you guys no matter what. If one of you falls in love, gets married, and lives the perfect life with Prince Charming, I'll envy you. I'll probably hate you at least once a week. But I'll always be there for you."

The others smiled, too, sadly, then silence fell again. The conversation hadn't really answered any questions. It was easy to say it was okay to fall in love, even easier to promise their friendship would never end. But ultimately, it was actions that counted.

The closer they got to Tallgrass, the more regret built in Carly. Though their times together were frequent—dinner every Tuesday, excursions every couple months, impromptu gatherings for shopping or a movie or no reason at all—she couldn't ignore the fact that she was going home to an empty house. All of them were except Therese, who would pick up her resentful stepchildren from the neighbor who was watching them. They would eat their dinners alone, watch TV or read or clean house alone, and they would go to bed alone.

Were they meant to spend the rest of their lives that way? Dear God, she hoped not.

By the time the Suburban pulled into her driveway, Carly was pretty much in a funk. She squeezed out from the third seat, exchanged good-byes with the others, promising to share any good pictures she'd gotten, and headed toward the house as if she didn't dread going inside.

It was a great starter house, the real estate agent had told them when they'd come to Tallgrass. *"That means 'fixer-upper,'"* Carly had whispered to Jeff, and he'd grinned. *"You know me. I love my tools."*

"But you never actually use them."

But the house was close to the fort, and the mortgage payments allowed plenty of money left over for all those repairs. Jeff had actually done some of them himself. Not many, but enough to crow over.

She climbed the steps he'd leveled and inserted the key in the dead bolt he'd installed. A lamp burned in the living room, a habit she'd gained their first night apart, shining on comfortable furniture, good tables, a collection of souvenirs and knickknacks, and of course, photographs. The outrageously sized television had been his choice, to balance the burnished wicker chair she'd chosen for her reading corner. Likewise, he'd picked the leather recliner to hide at least part of the froufrou rug she'd put down.

Their life had been full of little trade-offs like that. He would load the dishwasher if she would unload it. He would take his uniforms to the dry cleaner for knife-sharp creases, and she wouldn't complain if he wore sweats at home. She mowed the lawn, and he cleaned the gutters.

She'd stayed home, and he'd gone to war and died.

And she missed him, God, more than she'd thought possible.

To stave off the melancholy, she went to the kitchen for a bottle of water and a hundred-calorie pack of cookies. Before she reached the living room again, her cell phone rang.

It was Lucy. "I sent you some pictures. Check 'em out." She sounded way too cheerful before her voice cracked. "Norton, don't you dare! Aw, man! I swear to you, that mutt holds his pee all day just so he can see my face when he soaks the kitchen floor. Gotta go."

"Hello and good-bye to you, too." Carly slid the phone back into her pocket and made a turn into the dining room, where her computer occupied a very messy table. She opened her e-mail, and pictures began popping onto the screen—group shots, individuals, posed, candid, all of them happy and smiling.

No, not all. She hovered the cursor over one photo, clicking to enlarge it. Their cave-mate Dane. He was looking directly at the camera, a hint of surprise in his eyes as he realized he was being photographed, as if he wanted to jerk his gaze or his head away and didn't quite manage.

It was a stark photo of a good face: not overly handsome, with a strong jaw and straight nose, intense eyes, and a mouth that was almost too sensitive for the rest of his features. He looked capable, a command-and-control kind of guy, except for his eyes. They were tough to read, even when she magnified the photo until the upper half of his face filled the screen, but there was definitely something haunted—or haunting?—about them.

He had a story to tell, and probably a sad one. It wasn't likely she would see him again to hear it. Tallgrass wasn't a large town, but it was easy enough for people to live their lives without ever running into a specific individual. Unless Dane had a child at the elementary school or happened to crave Mexican food on a Tuesday night, they would probably never see each other again.

Whatever his story, she wished him well with it.

THE DISH

Where Authors Give You the Inside Scoop

♥ ♥ ♥ ♥ ♥ ♥ ♥ ♥ ♥ ♥ ♥ ♥ ♥ ♥ ♥

From the desk of Marilyn Pappano

Dear Reader,

The first time Jessy Lawrence, the heroine of my newest novel, A LOVE TO CALL HER OWN, opened her mouth, I knew she was going to be one of my favorite Tallgrass characters. She's mouthy, brassy, and bold, but underneath the sass, she's keeping a secret or two that threatens her tenuous hold on herself. She loves her friends fiercely with the kind of loyalty I value. Oh, and she's a redhead, too. I can always relate to another "ginger," lol.

I love characters with faults—like me. Characters who do stupid things, good things, bad things, unforgivable things. Characters whose lives haven't been the easiest, but they still show up; they still do their best. They know too well it might not be good enough, but they try, and that's what matters, right?

Jessy is one of those characters in spades—estranged from her family, alone in the world except for the margarita girls, dealing with widowhood, guilt, low self-esteem, and addiction—but she meets her match in Dalton Smith.

I was plotting the first book in the series, *A Hero to Come Home To*, when it occurred to me that there's a lot of talk about the men who die in war and the wives they leave behind, but people seem not to notice that some of our casualties are women, who also leave behind spouses, fiancés, family whose lives are drastically altered. Seconds behind that thought, an image popped into my head of the margarita club gathered around their table at The Three Amigos, talking their girl talk, when a broad-shouldered, six-foot-plus, smokin' handsome cowboy walked up, Stetson in hand, and quietly announced that his wife had died in the war.

Now, when I started writing the first scene from Dalton's point of view, I knew immediately that scene was never going to happen. Dalton has more grief than just the loss of a wife. He's angry, bitter, has isolated himself, and damn sure isn't going to ask anyone for help. He's not just wounded but broken—my favorite kind of hero.

It's easy to write love stories for perfect characters, or for one who's tortured when the other's not. I tend to gravitate to the challenge of finding the happily-ever-after for two seriously broken people. They deserve love and happiness, but they have to work so hard for it. There are no simple solutions for these people. Jessy finds it hard to get out of bed in the morning; Dalton has reached rock bottom with no one in his life but his horses and cattle. It says a lot about them that they're willing to work, to risk their hearts, to take those scary steps out of their grief and sorrow and guilt and back into their lives.

Oh yeah, and I can't forget to mention my other two favorite characters in A LOVE TO CALL HER OWN: Oz, the handsome Australian shepherd on the cover; and Oliver, a mistreated, distrusting dog of unknown breed.

I love my puppers, both real and fictional, and hope you like them, too.

Happy reading!

Marilyn Pappano

MarilynPappano.net
Twitter @MarilynPappano
Facebook.com/MarilynPappanoFanPage

♥ ♥ ♥ ♥ ♥ ♥ ♥ ♥ ♥ ♥ ♥ ♥ ♥ ♥ ♥

From the desk of Kristen Ashley

Dear Reader,

In starting to write *Lady Luck*, the book where Chace Keaton was introduced, I was certain Chace was a bad guy. A dirty cop who was complicit in sending a man to jail for a crime he didn't commit.

Color me stunned when Chace showed up at Ty and Lexie's in *Lady Luck* and a totally different character introduced himself to me.

Now, I am often not the white hat–wearing guy type of girl. My boys have to have at least a bit of an edge (and usually way more than a bit).

That's not to say that I don't get drawn in by the boy next door (quite literally, for instance, with Mitch Lawson of *Law Man*). It just always surprises me when I do.

Therefore, it surprised me when Chace drew me in while he was in Lexie and Ty's closet in *Lady Luck*. I knew in that instant that he had to have his own happily-ever-after. And when Faye Goodknight was introduced later in that book, I knew the path to that was going to be a doozy!

Mentally rubbing my hands together with excitement, when I got down to writing BREATHE, I was certain that it was Chace who would sweep me away.

And he did.

But I *adored* writing Faye.

I love writing about complex, flawed characters, watching them build strength from adversity. Or lean on the strength from adversity they've already built in their lives so they can get through dealing with falling in love with a badass, bossy alpha. The exploration of that is always a thing of beauty for me to be involved in.

Faye, however, knew who she was and what she wanted from life. She had a good family. She lived where she wanted to be. She was shy, but that was her nature. She was no pushover. She had a backbone. But that didn't mean she wasn't thoughtful, sensitive, and loving. She had no issues, no hang-ups, or at least nothing major.

And she was a geek girl.

The inspiration for her came from my nieces, both incredibly intelligent, funny, caring and, beautiful—and both total geek girls. I loved the idea of diving into that (being a bit of a geek girl myself), this concept that is considered stereotypically "on the fringe" but is actually an enormous sect of society that is quite proud of their geekdom. And when I published BREATHE, the geek girls came out of the woodwork, loving seeing one of their own land her hot guy.

But also, it was a pleasure seeing Chace, the one who had major issues and hang-ups, find himself sorted out by his geek girl. I loved watching Faye surprise him, hold up the mirror so he could truly see himself, and take the lead into guiding them both into the happily-ever-after they deserved.

This was one of those books of mine where I could have kept writing forever. Just the antics of the kitties Chace gives to his Faye would be worth a chapter!

But alas, I had to let them go.

Luckily, I get to revisit them whenever I want and let fly the warm thoughts I have of the simple, yet extraordinary lives led by a small-town cop and the librarian wife he adores.

Kristen Ashley

♥ ♥ ♥ ♥ ♥ ♥ ♥ ♥ ♥ ♥ ♥ ♥ ♥ ♥ ♥

From the desk of Sandra Hill

Dear Reader,

Many of you have been begging for a new Tante Lulu story.

When I first started writing my Cajun contemporary books back in 2003, I never expected Tante Lulu would touch so many people's hearts and funny bones. Over the years, readers have fallen in love with the wacky old lady (I like to say, Grandma Moses with cleavage). So many of you have said you have a family member just like her; still more have said they wish they did.

Family…that's what my Cajun/Tante Lulu books are all about. And community…the generosity and unconditional love of friends and neighbors. In these turbulent times, isn't that just what we all want?

You should know that SNOW ON THE BAYOU is the ninth book in my Cajun series, which includes: *The Love Potion*; *Tall, Dark, and Cajun*; *The Cajun Cowboy*; *The Red Hot Cajun*; *Pink Jinx*; *Pearl Jinx*; *Wild Jinx*; and *So Into You*. And there are still more Cajun tales to come, I think. Daniel and Aaron LeDeux, and the newly introduced Simone LeDeux. What do you think?

For more information on these and others of my books, visit my website at www.sandrahill.net or my Facebook page at Sandra Hill Author.

As always, I wish you smiles in your reading.

Sandra Hill

♥ ♥ ♥ ♥ ♥ ♥ ♥ ♥ ♥ ♥ ♥ ♥ ♥ ♥ ♥

From the desk of Mimi Jean Pamfiloff

Dearest Humans,

It's the end of the world. You're an invisible, seventy-thousand-year-old virgin. The Universe wants to snub out the one person you'd like to hook up with. Discuss.

And while you do so, I'd like to take a moment to thank each of you for taking this Accidental journey with me and my insane deities. We've been to Mayan cenotes, pirate ships, jungle battles, cursed pyramids, vampire showdowns, a snappy leather-daddy bar in San Antonio, New York City, Santa Cruz, Giza, Sedona, and we've even been to a beautiful Spanish vineyard with an incubus. Ah. So many fun places with so many fascinating, misunderstood, wacky gods and other immortals. And let's not forget Minky the unicorn, too!

It has truly been a pleasure putting you through the twisty curves, and I hope you enjoy this final piece of the puzzle as Máax, our invisible, bad-boy deity extraordinaire, is taught one final lesson by one very resilient woman who refuses to allow the Universe to dictate her fate.

Because ultimately we make our own way in this world, Hungry Hungry Hippos playoffs included.

Happy reading!

Mimi

P.S.: Hope you like the surprise ending.

♥ ♥ ♥ ♥ ♥ ♥ ♥ ♥ ♥ ♥ ♥ ♥ ♥ ♥ ♥ ♥

From the desk of Karina Halle

Dear Reader,

Morally ambiguous. Duplicitous. Dangerous.

Those words describe not only the cast of characters in my romantic suspense novel SINS & NEEDLES, book one in the Artists Trilogy, but especially the heroine, Ms. Ellie Watt. Though sinfully sexy and utterly suspenseful, it is Ellie's devious nature and con artist profession that makes SINS & NEEDLES one unique and wild ride.

When I first came up with the idea for SINS & NEEDLES, I wanted to write a book that not only touched on some personal issues of mine (physical scarring, bullying, justification), but dealt with a character little seen in modern literature—the antiheroine. Everywhere you look in books these days you see the bad boy, the criminal, the tattooed heartbreaker and ruthless killer. There are always men in these arguably more interesting roles. Where were all the bad girls? Sure, you could read about women in dubious professions, femme fatales, and cold-hearted killers. But when were they ever the main character? When were they ever a heroine you could also sympathize with?

Ellie Watt is definitely one of the most complex and interesting characters I have ever written, particularly as a heroine. On one hand she has all these terrible qualities; on the other she's just a vulnerable, damaged person trying to survive the only way she knows how. You despise Ellie and yet you can't help but root for her at the same time.

Her love interest, hot tattoo artist and ex-friend Camden McQueen, says it perfectly when he tells her this: "That is what I thought of you, Ellie. Heartless, reckless, selfish, and cruel . . . Beautiful, sad, wounded, and lost. A freak, a work of art, a liar, and a lover."

Ellie is all those things, making her a walking contradiction but oh, so human. I think Ellie's humanity is what makes her relatable and brings a sense of realism to a novel that's got plenty of hot sex, car chases, gunplay, murder, and cons. No matter what's going on in the story, through all the many twists and turns, you understand her motives and her actions, no matter how skewed they may be.

Of course, it wouldn't be a romance novel without a love interest. What makes SINS & NEEDLES different is that the love interest isn't her foil—Camden McQueen isn't necessarily a "good" man making a clean living. In fact, he may be as damaged as she is—but he does believe that Ellie can change, let go of her past, and find redemption.

That's easier said than done, of course, for a criminal who has never known any better. And it's hard to escape your past when it's literally chasing you, as is the case with Javier Bernal, Ellie's ex-lover whom she conned six years prior. Now a dangerous drug lord, Javier has been hunting Ellie down, wanting to exact revenge for her misdoings. But sometimes revenge comes in a vice and Javier's appearance in the novel reminds Ellie that she can never escape who she really is, that she may not be redeemable.

For a book that's set in the dry, brown desert of southern California, SINS & NEEDLES is painted in shades of gray. There is no real right and wrong in the novel, and the characters, including Ellie, aren't just good or bad. They're just human, just real, just trying to come to terms with their true selves while living in a world that just wants to screw them over.

I hope you enjoy the ride!

♥ ♥ ♥ ♥ ♥ ♥ ♥ ♥ ♥ ♥ ♥ ♥ ♥ ♥ ♥ ♥ ♥

From the desk of Kristen Callihan

Dear Reader,

The first novels I read belonged to my parents. I was a latchkey kid, so while they were at work, I'd poach their paperbacks. Robert Ludlum, Danielle Steel, Jean M. Auel. I read these authors because my parents did. And it was quite the varied education. I developed a taste for action, adventure, sexy love stories, and historical settings.

But it wasn't until I spent a summer at the beach during high school that I began to pick out books for myself. Of course, being completely ignorant of what I might actually want to read on my own, I helped myself to the beach house's library. The first two books I chose were Mario Puzo's *The Godfather* (yes, I actually read the book before seeing the movie) and Anne Rice's *Interview with the Vampire*.

Those two books taught me about the antihero, that a character could do bad things, make the wrong decisions, and still be compelling. We might still want them to succeed. But why? Maybe because we share in their pain. Or maybe it's because they care, passionately, whether it's the desire for discovering the deeper meaning of life or saving the family business.

In EVERNIGHT, Will Thorne is a bit of an antihero. We meet him attempting to murder the heroine. And he makes no apologies for it, at least not at first. He is also a blood drinker, sensual, wicked, and in love with life and beauty.

Thinking on it now, I realize that the books I've read have, in some shape or form, made me into the author

I am today. So perhaps, instead of the old adage "You are what you eat," it really ought to be: "You are what you read."

[signature]

♥ ♥ ♥ ♥ ♥ ♥ ♥ ♥ ♥ ♥ ♥ ♥ ♥ ♥

From the desk of Laura Drake

Dear Reader,

Hard to believe that SWEET ON YOU is the third book in my Sweet on a Cowboy series set in the world of professional bull riding. The first two, *The Sweet Spot* and *Nothing Sweeter*, involved the life and loves of stock contractors—the ranchers who supply bucking bulls to the circuit. But I couldn't go without writing the story of a bull rider, one of the crazy men who pit themselves against an animal many times stronger and with a much worse attitude.

To introduce you to Katya Smith, the heroine of SWEET ON YOU, I thought I'd share with you her list of life lessons:

1. Remember what your Gypsy grandmother said: Gifts sometimes come in strange wrappings.
2. The good-looking ones aren't *always* assholes.
3. Cowboys aren't the only ones who need a massage. Sometimes bulls do, too.

4. Don't ever forget: You're a soldier. And no one messes with the U.S. military.
5. A goat rodeo has nothing to do with men riding goats.
6. "Courage is being scared to death—and saddling up anyway." —John Wayne
7. Cowgirl hats fit more than just cowgirls.
8. The decision of living in the present or going back to the past is easy once you decide which one you're willing to die for.

I hope you enjoy Katya and Cam's story as much as I enjoyed writing it. And watch for the cameos by JB Denny and Bree and Max Jameson from the first two books!

♥ ♥ ♥ ♥ ♥ ♥ ♥ ♥ ♥ ♥ ♥ ♥ ♥

From the desk of Anna Campbell

Dear Reader,

I love books about Mr. Cool, Calm, and Collected finding himself all at sea once he falls in love. Which means I've been champing at the bit to write Camden Rothermere's story in WHAT A DUKE DARES.

The Duke of Sedgemoor is a man who is always in control. He never lets messy emotion get in the way of a rational decision. He's the voice of wisdom. He's the one who sorts things out. He's the one with his finger on the pulse.

And that's just the way he likes it.

Sadly for Cam, once his own pulse starts racing under wayward Penelope Thorne's influence, all traces of composure and detachment evaporate under a blast of sensual heat. Which *isn't* just the way he likes it!

Pen Thorne was such fun to write, too. She's loved Cam since she was a girl, but she's smart enough to know it's hopeless. So what happens when scandal forces them to marry? It's the classic immovable object and irresistible force scenario. Pen is such a vibrant, passionate, headstrong presence that Cam hasn't got a chance. Although he puts up a pretty good fight!

Another part of WHAT A DUKE DARES that I really enjoyed writing was the secondary romance involving Pen's rakish brother Harry and innocent Sophie Fairbrother. There's a real touch of Romeo and Juliet about this couple. I hadn't written two love stories in one book before and the contrasting trajectories throw each relationship into high relief. As a reader, I always like to get two romances for the price of one.

If you'd like to know more about WHAT A DUKE DARES and the other books in the Sons of Sin series— *Seven Nights in a Rogue's Bed*, *Days of Rakes and Roses*, and *A Rake's Midnight Kiss*—please check out my website: http://annacampbell.info/books.html.

Happy reading—and may all your dukes be daring!

Best wishes,

Anna Campbell

Find out more about Forever Romance!

Visit us at
www.hachettebookgroup.com/publishing_forever.aspx

Find us on Facebook
http://www.facebook.com/ForeverRomance

Follow us on Twitter
http://twitter.com/ForeverRomance

NEW AND UPCOMING TITLES

Each month we feature our new titles
and reader favorites.

CONTESTS AND GIVEAWAYS

We give away galleys, autographed copies,
and all kinds of exclusive items.

AUTHOR INFO

You'll find bios, articles, and links to personal websites
for all your favorite authors—and so much more.

GET SOCIAL

Connect with your favorite authors, editors, and
other Forever fans, and share what's important to you.

THE BUZZ

Sign up for our monthly romance newsletter,
and be the first to read all about it.

VISIT US ONLINE AT

WWW.HACHETTEBOOKGROUP.COM

FEATURES:

**OPENBOOK BROWSE AND
SEARCH EXCERPTS**

•

AUDIOBOOK EXCERPTS AND PODCASTS

•

AUTHOR ARTICLES AND INTERVIEWS

•

**BESTSELLER AND PUBLISHING
GROUP NEWS**

•

SIGN UP FOR E-NEWSLETTERS

•

**AUTHOR APPEARANCES AND TOUR
INFORMATION**

•

SOCIAL MEDIA FEEDS AND WIDGETS

•

DOWNLOAD FREE APPS

BOOKMARK HACHETTE BOOK GROUP
@ WWW.HACHETTEBOOKGROUP.COM